WHEN DREAMS COME TRUE

For a second, Pace wondered what had happened to Mercy. Then he spotted her standing at the far side of the bed. His heart leaped into his throat. In a long white gown, she looked too beautiful to be real. Her dark hair was loose, and a long strand draped over her shoulder and curled around her breast.

She moved across the floor toward him. The candlelight danced on her hair and her skin glowed like the wings of a dove.

"Pace?" Her voice was a breathless whisper in the silent room.

"Mercy, do you know what you're doing?"

"Yes, Pace, I know what I want. I want to be your wife." Her touch burned his skin like a branding iron. "Come to bed with me."

"You don't know what you're asking."

"Yes, I do. I want you as my husband. In every sense of the word." Though soft, her words had the strength of her convictions.

She slipped the wrapper from her shoulders, letting the ivory silk pool at her feet in a puddle of molten silver. The nightgown was little more than two scraps of silk tied together at the shoulders and sides with ribbons.

"You can't possibly want me."

She carried his hand to her face and kissed the palm. Fire raced up his arm and settled right in the center of his chest. His body was aflame with desire.

"Pace, I've never lain with a man, and I want you to be my first—my only."

BOOK YOUR PLACE ON OUR WEBSITE AND MAKE THE READING CONNECTION!

We've created a customized website just for our very special readers, where you can get the inside scoop on everything that's going on with Zebra, Pinnacle and Kensington books.

When you come online, you'll have the exciting opportunity to:

- View covers of upcoming books
- Read sample chapters
- Learn about our future publishing schedule (listed by publication month *and author*)
- Find out when your favorite authors will be visiting a city near you
- Search for and order backlist books from our online catalog
- Check out author bios and background information
- Send e-mail to your favorite authors
- Meet the Kensington staff online
- Join us in weekly chats with authors, readers and other guests
- Get writing guidelines
- AND MUCH MORE!

Visit our website at
http://www.zebrabooks.com

Sweet Dreams

Jean Wilson

Zebra Books
Kensington Publishing Corp.
http://www.zebrabooks.com

ROT

To my husband, Don . . .
For making my sweet dreams come true.

ZEBRA BOOKS are published by

Kensington Publishing Corp.
850 Third Avenue
New York, NY 10022

Zebra and the Z logo Reg. U.S. Pat. & TM Off.

First Printing: April, 1998
10 9 8 7 6 5 4 3 2 1

Printed in the United States of America

One

The jingle of the bell above the mercantile entrance drew Mercy Goodacre's attention from the dress goods spread on the counter. Heavy, muddy footsteps stomped across her newly swept floor.

"Pace Lansing's back in town."

At the sound of the frightened voice, many things happened at once. The old men at the checkerboard propped atop a barrel leaped to their feet. Red and black checkers clattered to the floor.

Customers and clerk alike swung their gazes to the window. The bell echoed throughout the store. Mercy's sister, Charity, gasped and clutched her chest. Charity's shopkeeper husband, Tim Fullenwider, rushed to the doorway.

And Mercy's stomach leaped like a bucking bronco. Pace was back. She dropped the scissors to the bolt of muslin she'd selected for a new apron. Like everybody else's in the store, her gaze shifted to the window. People on the street stopped to stare.

There was no mistaking the dark figure on the ebony stallion. He'd always been an excellent horseman, and even five years in prison hadn't changed the arrogant way Pace Lansing sat his horse.

"What's he doing here?" her brother-in-law, Tim, whispered.

"Pleasant Valley is still his home," Mercy answered. She wiped her clammy palms on her apron. Curiosity overrode good judgment and she moved to the window for a better look.

Tim shot an angry glance at Mercy. "He should know he isn't welcome here."

Speak for yourself, Tim, she thought. Out of all the citizens in Pleasant Valley, only Mercy and her minister father believed Pace had gotten a raw deal by being sent to prison. Although Pace and Billy Blakely had been feuding for years, their quarrel climaxed when Pace had saved Mercy from Billy's unwanted advances. Mercy felt more than a little responsible for Pace's plight. She'd testified in his behalf, not that it did much good. Pace was sentenced to jail. Of course, they'd been outnumbered, and few people even dared mention Pace's name. Guilt had nagged at Mercy for five long years.

Otis Kennedy, a farmer who'd testified against Pace at his trial, cowered behind a stack of men's overalls. "Hear tell he was released nigh onto six months ago. Hoped he'd gone somewhere else to cause trouble."

Mercy opened her mouth to protest the unwarranted censure, when her sister grabbed her arm. "Oh, my Lord, he's coming in here."

Mercy watched as Pace tied his horse to the hitching post and stared at the mercantile. In two long strides he was at the door.

"Get out of here," Tim ordered. He picked up his son and thrust the three-year-old into Mercy's arms. Grabbing his wife's arm, and shoving boldly against Mercy's back, he ushered the women into the rear storeroom.

Glancing over her shoulder, Mercy met Pace's sober gaze as he stepped across the threshold. Under a battered brown hat, his eyes were as cold and dark as a moonless winter night. Apprehension surged through her. She'd never seen an angrier or more savage look on a man's face.

Is that what prison did to a man? she wondered. Cut the very soul out of him?

Once the women were in the rear room, Tim closed the curtain and blocked the doorway with his slender body. On each side of the curtain, Mercy and Charity sneaked a peek. From her vantage point, Mercy had a clear view of the entire store. One by one, the half dozen or so customers eased toward the door, their purchases forgotten and discarded on the counter.

Timmy squealed and tightened his pudgy fingers in the braid coiled above Mercy's ear. "Hush, Timmy," she whispered. Charity held a finger to her lips and continued to study the activity in the store.

Mercy's heart skipped a beat. This was the first time she'd seen Pace since the authorities had carted him off to the penitentiary five years before. The stranger leaning insolently against the counter bore little resemblance to the handsome, cocky young man who'd been unjustly snatched away from his home.

His face pale, Tim took a tentative step toward Pace. He ran a finger under the high neck of his shirt. "What do you want, Lansing?" he asked in a high-pitched squeak.

Pace studied the storekeeper for a long moment before he spoke. He and Tim Fullenwider were the same age, twenty-five, but Pace was a good six inches taller than the other man. They'd been schoolmates until at fifteen, Pace was forced to quit school. His father had been killed and it was left to Pace to scratch out a living for himself and his mother on their run-down ranch. After his mother's death from consumption, he'd struggled alone to achieve his dream of being a successful rancher, something his father had never been. Abner Lansing had been too lazy to profit from his five thousand acres of prime grazing land. Five years in prison hadn't killed Pace's dream, it had only postponed it.

Few men were as lucky as Tim Fullenwider. Following his schooldays, Tim had gone to work in the store. His father was the mayor and owned half the businesses in town. Disgusted at the unfair way life had treated him, Pace slapped a piece of paper on the counter.

"Supplies." If it wasn't too far to the next town, he'd never step foot in Pleasant Valley. But he was known here, which was probably more a curse than a blessing.

Tim studied the list for a moment. "Flour, sugar, coffee, beans? You planning to hang around for a while?"

"Yeah."

"For how long?"

"Forever." This was his home, and it was high time the people learned he'd come back to stay.

While Tim filled the order, Pace took the opportunity to glance around the store. He hadn't missed seeing the merchant hustle the two women and child into the back room. Even now, they were staring at him around the curtain. He'd recognized them instantly as two of Preacher Goodacre's daughters—Mercy and Charity. Clearly one of them was married to Tim. Probably the older girl, Mercy. Charity had been one of the prettiest girls in town five years ago, and surely she could do better than the puny grocer who was already losing his hair.

Mercy, on the other hand, had been plain as white bread. But smart. During his dismal school days, she'd been the only girl willing to teach him to read and cipher. And he'd rewarded her with a quick kiss on her lips.

He remembered her reaction. With a loud squeal, she'd punched him square in the stomach. She'd packed quite a wallop for a twelve-year-old girl. The memory brought an unwarranted smile. But it had been so long since he'd had something to smile about, Pace wasn't sure he knew how.

He pulled his thoughts from the past and tried to consider his present dilemma. A dozen different odors assailed him, causing his stomach to growl. Rows of spices, a barrel of red apples, glass jars of colored candy—licorice, peppermint—tastes he'd missed for five long years. His gaze shifted to the street outside the window. Several faces were pressed to the glass to get a glimpse of the notorious criminal. A lifetime of prejudice had taught Pace to harden himself against hatred and discrimination. If he could survive the brutality of the penitentiary, he could survive the curious citizens of his hometown.

Pleasant Valley had grown. The town now boasted a new three-story hotel, two cafés, a hardware store, and other merchants that crowded into Main Street. He'd noticed a number of white clapboard houses on the outlying streets, and a boardwalk stretched the entire five-block length of Main.

Yet, some things remained the same. Miss Lily LaRose still ran the best establishment west of the Missouri, and Reverend Goodacre was still trying to save lost souls.

"That'll be five dollars and twenty-five cents." Tim's voice brought Pace back to the problem at hand.

Pace didn't have five dollars and twenty-five cents. In fact, he didn't have one thin dime to his name. What little he'd earned from the army had gone for the horse, his gun, and enough to get them both back to Kansas.

"Put it on my account," he said, reaching for the ten-pound sack of flour.

Tim's hand covered Pace's. The merchant hastily snatched his fingers back as if he'd been struck with a hot branding iron. "You don't have an account with us."

"You extend credit to all the farmers and ranchers, don't you? I just need credit until I can sell my stock this fall." Pace hated to beg. He'd gone hungry many a night in prison because he'd refused to grovel at a guard's feet.

The pitifully small pile of commodities was the least he could survive on.

"I need cash on the barrelhead."

Panic threatened to choke Pace. He struggled to control his temper. It wouldn't do him any good to get angry with the storekeeper. "I don't have cash. I'll pay you back as soon as I can."

"Not good enough. You could pull up stakes any day, and I'd be stuck with the bill."

The bell over the door jingled and Pace spied the relief that passed over Tim's face. His color returned to normal. Pace spun around and his gaze fell on the silver star pinned to a big man's shirt. The sheriff had one hand on the gun at his hip.

"You causing trouble already, Lansing?"

Eyes narrowed, Pace studied the lawman for a moment. He took a deep breath. Five years of incarceration had taught him to think before he spoke. "You still sheriff here, Jennings? Thought you'd be grazing in greener pastures by now."

"Nope." Walter Jennings shoved back his wide-brimmed gray hat from his eyes. His cold, hard gaze locked on Pace. Although he stood nose to nose with Jennings, the sheriff outweighed Pace by a good forty pounds. "What's going on here?"

"Nothing," Pace said. "I was just leaving."

Shoulders square, and head held high, Pace sauntered to the door. He wasn't going to beg, he wasn't about to grovel. Somehow he'd find the money. He'd survived worst than anything these people could throw out at him. And he'd survive the two-bit town of Pleasant Valley, Kansas.

Mercy let the curtain fall. Of all the hateful things she'd ever seen, what Tim had done rated right up there near the top. Everybody in the county knew that the merchant extended credit to anybody who asked. Rarely did the farmers and ranchers fail to pay their bills when they harvested their crops or sold their cattle. How else could the farmers survive during the long winter? How did he expect Pace to manage without proper food and supplies?

Plain and simple, he didn't. Tim, like the rest of the townspeople, wished Pace would move on and never come back. She supposed it was partially their guilty consciences. They'd convicted Pace because he'd defended himself against Billy Blakely, the bully of the town. She was certain Pace hadn't meant to kill anyone.

Guilty over her part in the injustices, Mercy set Timmy on the floor. "Go play with your toys," she told her nephew. "I have something to do."

"Where are you going?" Charity asked.

"I'll be back in a few minutes," she shouted over her shoulder. She caught a glimpse of herself in the mirror Charity kept over the desk in the back room. Her brown hair was askew, thanks to Timmy's insistent grip. The little boy was constantly attracted to both her spectacles and her braids. Taking only a moment, she smoothed the wayward tresses behind her ears, then she darted out the rear door.

Mercy hurried along the alley between the mercantile and the bank next door. Funny, she thought, both her sisters had married men whose businesses were so close together, they could stick their arms out the windows and touch fingers.

Four years ago, Charity had chosen a prosperous merchant for a husband. Not to be outdone by her sister, Prudence chose the even wealthier banker, Clifford Blakely. Her beautiful sisters had been courted by every eligible bachelor in the county, and had their choice of husbands. Both were blessed with golden curls, blue eyes, and slim figures like their mother. Mercy had gotten her father's brown hair and eyes. She believed that Charity truly loved Tim, however she'd always wondered if Clifford or his money held the greater attraction for young and spoiled Prudy.

As she emerged onto the boardwalk, Mercy ran smack into a man's wide chest. Her eyes were level with the faded red bandanna that circled the thick column of his neck. "I beg your . . ." she began. The rest of her apology stuck in her throat. She blinked against the glare of the harsh late afternoon sunshine.

Pace Lansing caught her shoulders to keep her from tumbling into the dusty street. Only his strength prevented her from melting right down to the ground like a burned-out candle.

Quickly, he set her away from him. "Are you all right, ma'am?" he asked, his voice husky and raw.

"Yes, yes, I'm fine." She shoved her spectacles back on her nose to get a better view of the man. His once straight nose was slightly off center, and his skin was tanned to a rich bronze. Thick black hair hung far below his frayed collar. Now that she'd caught up with him, she couldn't think of a thing to say.

He folded his arms across a chest as wide as a door. "Well, if it ain't Miss Mercy Goodacre. Or is it Mrs. Fullenwider?"

Heat raced to Mercy's cheeks. Her beautiful younger sisters had married well, while Mercy was still at home taking care of her father. Just as before Pace left. It hurt to admit she was a spinster.

"It's still Miss. My sister Charity is married to Tim."

Pace touched a finger to the brim of his hat, and turned to leave. She caught his shirtsleeve between her fingers. The blue cotton was soft with wear, the flesh beneath as solid as a tree trunk. "Wait," she said, surprised at how shrill her voice sounded.

He lifted a quizzical dark brow. "Did you want something, Miss Goodacre?"

Her hand trembling, she released her grip and jammed

her hands into the pockets of her apron. "Yes." She swallowed the apple-sized lump that threatened to choke her. "I want to help you."

Shock glittered in his eyes, but was quickly blinked away. "What can you do for me?"

She wished they were alone, and that half the town wasn't watching covertly from behind doorways and curtains. Across the street stood Charity's mother-in-law along with Mrs. Sloan, the president of the church's ladies circle. "I can get the supplies you need. I'll put them on my father's account. You can pay him whenever you're able." Her heart pounding like a big bass drum, she dropped her gaze to the toes of his scuffed boots.

Derisive laughter sent a chill up her spine. "Still little Miss Do-gooder, ain't you?"

Angered at the sneer in his voice, she lifted her head and faced him with a boldness she didn't feel. His mouth was pulled into a stiff, straight line. A long scar ran from his ear to his jaw. The scar hadn't been there five years ago. Her heart swelled with emotion. Ordinary people couldn't begin to imagine the atrocities this man had suffered. "I try to help out where I'm needed."

He took one step toward her. His gaze lowered to the front of her chest. Mercy bit back a whimper of humiliation. She'd always been ashamed of the oversized bosom nature had bestowed on her. Even tight bindings couldn't hide their size.

"Maybe you can give me what I need, lady. I've been in prison for a long time. Aren't you afraid of being near a criminal? No telling what a man like me can do to an innocent woman." His hand lifted to her cheek.

Mercy's mouth went dry. His touch was unexpectedly gentle, but his eyes were dark and without expression. Looking into his eyes was like staring into the bowels of hell. Mercy shivered. She was scared to death—not of anything he could do to her, but of the way being near him turned her knees to mush. Rarely was Mercy this close to a man—especially a strong, virile man like Pace. Her insides were trembling so bad she thought she would upchuck her dinner. But she refused to let Pace Lansing know how badly he affected her.

"We're in the middle of town on a sunny afternoon. I'm sure you aren't foolish enough to try something untoward."

"Untoward? Lady, you have no idea what I could do to you. Don't you remember? I killed a man with my bare hands." He ran the back of his finger down her cheek.

As hard as she tried, she couldn't stop the heat that turned her face crimson. All her life Mercy had had a soft spot for Pace. At times she thought she'd been halfway in love with him. Not that a handsome man like Pace would look twice at a plain woman like Mercy. "I only offered to help." She owed it to him. He'd come to her aid that one time, and she felt responsible for the chain of events that had ended with him in prison.

Pace struggled for control. Either the woman was a fool or a man-hungry spinster. "I don't want or need charity. I'm not some orphan child who needs help. And I sure wouldn't take anything from the preacher's daughter." Lord, her skin was soft. And she smelled like cinnamon and freshly baked bread.

"It isn't charity. I fully expect you to pay us back." Golden flecks flashed in her brown eyes that the thick spectacles couldn't hide. Stray strands of hair pulled loose from the tight braids that circled her head. The flush on her cheeks extended clear to the stiff white collar that touched her chin.

"You haven't changed a bit, have you? I'm not one of your poor parishioners who needs your castoffs. And I'm not the twelve-year-old you taught how to read and cipher. I don't need help from you or anybody else in this town."

"Lansing. Take your hands off my sister-in-law." The sharp male voice came from over his shoulder.

Pace dropped his hand to the gun at his hip. He spun around and faced the man who'd testified against him—the brother of the man he'd killed. The banker's testimony had caused Pace to lose five years of his life. Blakely had wanted to see Pace swing from the end of a rope. To this day, Pace still didn't know why the judge had sentenced him to prison rather than the hangman's noose. Sometimes he thought he'd have been better off dead than in that hellhole where he'd spent five long years.

"Well, if it ain't Clifford Blakely. Foreclosed on any widow women lately?" he asked to rile the man. So Blakely had married the remaining Goodacre sister—Prudence. Damn, the woman was more than ten years younger than the banker. And one of the most beautiful girls he'd ever seen.

The man tugged Mercy Goodacre close to his side. "Did he hurt you? Do you want me to call the sheriff?"

"No." Tugging her arm free, she hastily stepped away. "I was just offering Mr. Lansing some assistance."

Pace folded his fingers into his palms to keep from slapping the sneer off the banker's face. "I told Miss Goodacre I don't need her help."

"That's just as well. I don't want my sister-in-law helping the man who murdered my brother. If you need funds, you can sell that acreage you have down by the river and clear out of town. I've been looking for a place to build a new house for my wife."

Black rage exploded in Pace's chest. "That land ain't for sale to you or anybody else. It belongs to me, now and always." The five thousand acres along the river was all Pace had. His pa had settled the homestead while Kansas was nothing but Indians and a few military outposts. The one good thing Abner Lansing had done was choosing the best valley for himself. Dreaming about his home was all that had kept Pace sane during the dark days and nights in prison.

"Then you'd better get back to your own land before I call the sheriff. You aren't wanted here."

Pace took one step toward the man. Mercy caught his arm in a strong grip. "No, don't cause trouble."

He spotted the fear in the woman's eyes. She was scared he was going to hurt the banker. "I have no intention on giving Blakely a chance to railroad me again. I don't need his money, and I don't want your charity. Good day, ma'am." Struggling to control his temper, he all but ran to his horse.

The last words of the judge who'd sentenced him echoed in his head. *Son, I hope five years in the penitentiary will teach you to control your temper.* It was a hard way to learn a lesson. In only one day back in Pleasant Valley, Pace had managed to incite half the town and hurt a woman who'd meant nothing but kindness.

But he didn't want kindness. He didn't want charity. Most of all, he didn't want anything to do with a woman like Mercy Goodacre.

"Mercy, what were you doing with Pace Lansing?"

To her dismay, Mercy's sister, Prudence Blakely, was waiting at the parsonage when Mercy arrived home an hour after Pace rode out of town. Dressed in a batiste afternoon gown embroidered with pink and yellow flowers, Prudy was the height of fashion. A pert hat with feathers and a tiny veil covered her long golden curls.

"Word certainly travels fast in this town." Mercy set a box of food on the table. Her father would be home in half an hour and he would expect his dinner on the table. Without breaking her stride, she pulled out a freshly killed and dressed chicken. After the commotion in town over

Pace, Mercy wanted to prepare her father's favorite meal—fried chicken, mashed potatoes, and apple cobbler.

Her youngest sister set her hands on her hips in a manner much older than her twenty years. In the limited society of Pleasant Valley, Prudence had aspirations of becoming the social paragon. Her banker husband, Clifford Blakely, was the wealthiest man in town, and she had the largest house. In Prudy's opinion, that gave her the right to set the standards for polite society. That afternoon, Mercy had clearly broken another one of her rules.

"Clifford told me he caught you and that notorious man in a . . . a compromising position."

Mercy burst out laughing. "What in the world are you talking about? I was on a public street in full view of half the town."

"That's even worse, Mercy. Now everybody knows. That man is very dangerous. Clifford said he was touching you and arguing with you. You shouldn't want anything to do with the man who killed my husband's brother." Prudy perched on the edge of a kitchen chair. She stuck out her lower lip in a pout. That was how she always got her way with her husband. Pity the poor man.

"Clifford doesn't know what was going on. Billy only got what he deserved. He'd bullied half the town, and terrorized the women." She swallowed the lump in her throat. Nobody knew exactly what he'd tried to do to Mercy. She'd been too ashamed to even mention it to her family. Only Pace knew, and he'd gone to prison for helping her.

"Clifford says that isn't true. Billy just liked having fun."

"Ha. At other people's expense." After washing her hands, Mercy dropped the chicken on a cutting board. "I was only talking to Pace. After all, we were schoolmates together."

"Charity said you practically chased him down on the boardwalk."

The gossip mill was working overtime. "Did she also tell

you that Tim refused to open an account so Pace could buy supplies?"

"Clifford said that Tim was right in what he did. Pace is a criminal and he should just go away." Prudy flipped open her lace fan and waved it in front of her face. "What did he want with you?"

Nothing. Like all men, absolutely nothing at all. A few years before, Clifford had come to call on Mercy. One look at her beautiful young sister, and he'd forgotten all about plain, older Mercy. A year later they were engaged, and the next they married. By now Mercy had thought she'd become immune to rejection.

"Nothing. I offered to help him get the supplies he needed."

Prudy's mouth gaped. "Why?"

Why, indeed? Mercy hadn't stopped to think about why she wanted to help Pace, except maybe to ease her guilty conscience. "Because he needed help."

"Help," Prudy squealed. "Do you think you have to help everybody? Isn't it bad enough you embarrass us by spending your time with those *women* at the Ruby Slipper?"

"I teach a Bible class for the ladies who work there. Their souls need feeding just like yours and Clifford's, and Charity's and Tim's. Not to mention mine and Papa's."

"Humph!" Prudy stood and straightened her narrow skirt. With her vanity and love of pretty things, it was a good thing she'd chosen a rich man for a husband. "Why don't they just go to church on Sunday with the rest of us?"

"Would you welcome them into the services?" She quit cutting up the chicken long enough to study her sister's stern expression. "The fancy ladies and Miss Lily LaRose?"

"Clifford says they should all be run out of town on a rail. And Pace Lansing with them." Watching her younger sister was almost like seeing her mother all over again. But whereas her mother would have given the shirt off her back to anyone in need, Prudy was totally self-centered. Faith Goodacre had died when Prudy was only eight, and Mercy had stepped in and been a foster mother to both her sisters. Prudy and Charity were blond and blue-eyed like their beautiful mother. Mercy had her father's dark features.

"What a cruel, uncharitable thing to say. They have as much right to be here as any of us. Especially Pace. His father was one of the first settlers in the territory."

"Pace isn't white, you know." Prudy's smug tone angered Mercy. As usual, somebody was passing judgment on Pace.

"His mother was Indian. That shouldn't make any difference in how we treat him."

"Oh, Mercy, you've always been a do-gooder. I wouldn't be surprised if you didn't just carry Papa's dinner out to that man. It would be just like you."

Prudy meant to insult Mercy. However, her sister only succeeded in planting a seed of an idea in her mind. "I just might do that."

Two

"You've outdone yourself tonight, daughter."

Mercy smiled as her father wiped his mouth with a white linen napkin. His stomach was beginning to show the effects of good food and his nearly fifty years. He opened the buttons of his black vest. As the town's only minister, Ezra Goodacre always wore a black suit, ready for any emergency. Even while working in his cabinetry shop, he kept his coat handy. After all, he served not only as minister, but undertaker as well.

Her father had always loved working with his hands. After he'd entered the ministry, he kept his cabinetry and undertaking business. The enterprises provided a fine living for his wife and three daughters.

"Thank you, Papa. I always try to prepare your favorites."

Ezra frowned. "This fine meal doesn't have anything to do with your desire to help Pace Lansing, does it?"

Never able to lie or hide her feelings, Mercy turned her back to her father as she carried the dishes to the sink. "This has everything to do with wanting to prepare a delicious meal for my hardworking father."

"You can't fool me, Mercy. I heard how Tim refused to extend credit, and how Clifford ordered Lansing out of town." He moved to the stove and refilled his cup from the coffeepot. "Then you were seen deep in conversation with the man."

"I offered to help him get some supplies. The same as you would have done for anyone in need." Mercy dropped the plates into the dishpan. "He didn't want my help."

He eyed her over the rim of his cup. At five-foot-eight, Mercy stood eye to eye with her father. She barely came to Pace's chin. Shoving her hands into the soapy water, she wondered why she kept comparing every man to Pace.

"I'm thankful one of you showed a little good judgment. You're an impressionable young woman. You shouldn't be seen in the company of a notorious felon."

Her heart tightened in her chest. "Father, does everyone in town plan to ostracize Pace because of his past? Doesn't he deserve the chance to prove himself, to get on with his life?"

Pink tinged Ezra's round cheeks. "Yes, of course he does. If he repents of his sin, I know God will forgive him. But let the men handle Lansing. You have enough duties helping your sisters, assisting me with my sermons, and managing the books in the business."

"I only offered to help him get supplies."

"I'm afraid I agree with Clifford. Lansing should sell his land and move further west where nobody knows him. It would be best for all."

Mercy couldn't believe her normally generous father could be so narrow-minded toward Pace. "Best for the town, you mean. That way the people who'd sent him to prison won't have to deal with their consciences. The only reason they convicted him was because of Clifford. We all knew sooner or later Billy was going to tangle with the wrong person and kill somebody or get himself killed. It happened that Pace was that somebody."

In an uncharacteristic show of temper, Ezra slammed his cup onto the table. Black coffee sloshed over the rim.

"Daughter, a dozen men saw him beat up Billy Blakely. You can't deny he was guilty."

Hands on her hips, Mercy glared at her father. "It was clearly self-defense. Billy started the fight with Pace."

"That's no excuse. The Good Book says to turn the other cheek. He could have stopped the fight at any time. Lansing couldn't control his temper and a man died."

"The Word also says to judge not lest we be judged."

"He was given a fair trial. I even tried to help him. I agree with the verdict. He's very fortunate he wasn't hanged. By now, he should have learned to control his anger. However, I have my doubts about his repentance."

"The fact that he came home and is trying to operate his ranch should say something about the man."

"It says he had no place else to go. Did you know he was released a few months ago? And he's come back riding a fine horse and carrying a Colt forty-five. Clifford thinks he stole them. The mayor thinks he means nothing but trouble and the sheriff is keeping an eye on Lansing."

Mercy threw the dishrag onto the table. "Isn't anybody going to give him a chance?"

"If he stays out of trouble, he'll get along just fine." Ezra reached for his coat. "I'm going back to the shop. I have a piece I want to finish."

And get away from me. Mercy knew it was useless to argue with her father. Like the other men in town, he'd pre-judged Pace and found him guilty. "Are you working on the armoire for Miss LaRose?"

Ezra slipped his arms into the sleeves of his black coat. "Yes. I'd like to get it to her as soon as possible. Don't wait up. I may work late." One hand on the doorknob, he turned back to Mercy. "Remember what I said, daughter. Stay away from Lansing."

The screen door slammed shut. Mercy couldn't remember when her father had last given her an order or told her what to do or not to do. Instead of convincing her to obey him, the injustice of it all only made her angry. Anger made her stubborn. Stubbornness gave her determination. Determination spurred her to action. All she had to do was decide on her best course of action.

A dream startled Mercy awake the next morning. She jerked up in her bed. In spite of the cool April morning, her white batiste nightgown was drenched with perspiration. She tossed her long thick braid over her shoulder and tried to remember the dream that had so disturbed her.

Instantly, she caught a glimpse of Pace Lansing's face. Gone was the insolence and disdain. Instead, the man wore the most desolate and forlorn expression she'd ever seen on a human being. In her dream, he was a lost soul clawing his way out of hell. She shuddered. The man had just been released from the hell of a prison, and the townspeople were trying to send him back.

She couldn't just sit there and do nothing. All night she'd fought with her own conscience. How could she condemn the men in town, when she wasn't willing to sacrifice to help a human being in need.

Before she changed her mind, Mercy slid from between the covers. As soon as her bare feet hit the cold floor, she knew she had to move fast before she changed her mind. She reached inside the trunk that sat at the foot of her carved oak bed. Hidden in the toe of a baby shoe she'd hoped someday her child would wear, was her private cache.

Holding out her hand, she dropped her life's savings into her palm. Over the years she'd saved over a hundred dollars. It hadn't come easily. She'd swept floors, mended clothes, sold butter and eggs, and worked at the mercantile. She closed her hand and pressed her fist to her chest.

All her life, she'd pored over every book and magazine

she could find about the wonderful places beyond the Missouri River and Kansas borders. Places like New Orleans, Chicago, New York, and Philadelphia. She didn't dare dream about Europe or the Orient.

Once her father had taken her to Kansas City for a church leaders' meeting. The city was a marvel, and showed her that there was more out there that she wanted to experience. Since then, she'd been secretly saving every penny she could scrape together to take a trip. To see something grand and glorious. To meet new and exciting people.

Attending the 1876 Centennial International Exhibition in Philadelphia was going to be the realization of her dream. She'd already contacted the owner of a boarding-house and reserved a room for two weeks next summer. The Centennial promised to be the most exciting, thrilling, wondrous event in the one hundred years since America's birth. Mercy wanted to attend so badly she ached with the need.

The coins burned in her hand. How could she spend money on something as frivolous as a trip if a man, a human being, could starve because the townspeople refused to help him? Mercy counted out ten dollars. She thought about the meager stack of supplies that Tim had refused to advance to Pace. Adding ten more dollars to the pile, she returned the remainder to its hiding place in the trunk.

Thank goodness she'd chosen to keep the money hidden rather than put it into Clifford's bank. It would take an act of God to get him to release her funds. And if her brother-in-law had an inkling she wanted to use it to help Pace Lansing, she would have hell to pay.

She hurried through her chores that morning—collecting the eggs, feeding the chickens, and cleaning the house. Her father hadn't mentioned Pace at breakfast, and Mercy didn't bring up the controversial subject. To placate him, she baked his favorite chocolate cake. After she'd mixed up the batter, she discovered she had enough for a second cake. She wondered if Pace liked chocolate.

With her supper ready and waiting on the stove, Mercy tied a bonnet under her chin. The town was quiet that Tuesday afternoon as she entered the livery stable. Minutes later, she drove her buggy to the rear of the mercantile. She hesitated before stepping down. If only she didn't have to deal with Tim. She hoped he was in a better humor than yesterday.

Entering the rear door, she checked her image in the mirror. Her braids were smoothly twisted at her nape, and her brown muslin gown was stiffly pressed. A woven wool shawl covered her shoulders. She clutched her reticule in her fist.

Tim looked up when she slipped through the curtain and entered the store. Thank goodness, he was alone. If he made a scene, at least nobody else would know. He frowned when he recognized her.

"It's about time you got here, Mercy. Charity wasn't feeling well, so she didn't come in to the store today." He pulled off his grocer's apron and started around the counter.

Mercy swallowed her nervousness. "You should have sent for me if Charity needed help. But I had a lot to do this morning, and I've made other plans. I'll be free tomorrow." After a moment's hesitation, she slid a slip of paper on the counter. "Could you fill an order for me, please?"

He picked up the note and studied it. It didn't take much of a memory to remember what Pace had ordered. Only she doubled his list and added a few items she thought he would need.

"This is quite an order, Mercy. I thought you'd bought a fifty-pound sack of flour last week. You must be baking an awful lot of bread and cakes."

She turned away and picked up the broom. Mercy didn't want to lie, but she didn't want to tell the truth, either.

"Your sisters are really upset about yesterday," Tim said as he filled a box with an assortment of goods. "Charity went to bed with a headache last night. She couldn't even fix my supper."

"I'm sorry, Tim. Tell her I'll stop by later and take Timmy home with me." Much later, after she got back to town.

"Want me to deliver this to your house?" he asked.

She returned the broom to the corner. "No. I have my buggy in the alley. Just set it all behind the seat and I'll take care of it."

Tim lugged the heavy boxes to the rear and returned to the store. "I'll just put it on your father's account."

Now came the hard part. Ezra Goodacre had made it clear he didn't want to help Pace Lansing. It was up to Mercy to do the right thing.

"No. I'm going to pay cash. How much do I owe you?"

Her brother-in-law tilted one pale eyebrow. Tim was a naturally suspicious man and he always wanted payment right on time. "The reverend always settles his account at the end of the month. You don't have to pay now. I trust you."

"I insist, Tim. How much?"

"Sixteen dollars and twenty-four cents."

Biting her lip to keep from backing out, Mercy counted out the silver and copper coins. When she'd finished, she didn't feel nearly as good as she should by doing a good deed. In fact, she wondered why she was making the sacrifice for a man who didn't want her help.

Before she changed her mind, Mercy shoved the money across the counter. "For such a large cash order, how about throwing in some of that licorice and peppermint candy."

With a shrug, he wrapped a handful of candy in brown paper and handed it to Mercy. "Thank you, Tim."

At the wagon, Tim offered a hand up. "Mercy, this isn't for Lansing, by any chance, is it?"

"Whatever gave you that idea?" she asked, evading the question.

"For one thing, you never drive over here. And I filled a large order for you a few days ago."

"I'm helping a needy family. Tell Charity I'll be by later." She snapped the reins over the horse's back and headed out of town.

Mercy followed the road to the west, crossing the bridge over Pleasant Creek. Tiny wildflowers peeked colorful heads through the ground announcing the coming of spring. In another month, sunflowers, asters, gentians, and columbines would carpet the prairie in a glorious array of color.

Mercy loved spring, when the snows of winter disappeared and the promise of new life burst from the earth. Emotion swelled in her chest. Anything was possible in spring.

Pace's place was about ten miles out of town, past several farms and small homesteads. The smell of freshly tilled earth filled the air since farmers had begun breaking the ground for spring planting. Wheat and corn were major crops, along with hogs and cattle. She wondered what Pace planned to do with his land.

His father hadn't done much with the five thousand acres he'd homesteaded years ago. After Abner Lansing died, Pace tried to raise cattle. The L-Bar sat on some of the finest grazing land in this part of the state, as well as being blessed with a river that flowed even during dry seasons. He'd had a couple of good years before he'd been sent to prison. Since then his land had lain fallow. With a little luck and hard work, Pace should be able to make a success of his ranch.

Mercy, for one, was rooting for him. She might be the only person in the county who was.

Nearer the L-Bar the road narrowed to a rutted path. Tall blue-stemmed grasses waved in the wind as far as the eye could see on the rolling hills to the west. To the east, oaks, cottonwood, and willow grew along the river bottoms. A young doe and fawn grazed in the meadow. This was prime property—no wonder Clifford was interested in it.

She followed the path, certain she would reach the homestead. As she topped a low rise, she spied a log cabin and surrounding buildings. Neglect was evident everywhere. Fence posts tilted like drunken cowboys after a Saturday night at the Ruby Slipper. The barn door sagged on one hinge and the roof on the chicken house was gone. Except for the cattle milling in the meadow below the barn, there was no other sign of life. Pace must be out in the hills somewhere, Mercy thought, rounding up his cattle or whatever he did every day.

Carefully, she approached the cabin. "Hello," she called. Cupping her hands around her mouth, she called again. "Mr. Lansing, are you here?" No answer. She reined in at the front door. His cabin was small and old. New shingles contrasted with the old on the roof. Clearly, Pace had been making necessary repairs.

For a second, she doubted the wisdom of her trip. She'd traipsed over half the county without even considering that he wouldn't be home. Of course, he wouldn't, she reminded herself. In the middle of the afternoon, Pace could be anywhere on his five thousand acres. She considered her next move. If she returned to town with the supplies, her father would become suspicious and she'd never manage to get out here again.

"Hello," she shouted. Again the only response was the loud moo of the cow who meandered around the corner of the house.

Mercy climbed down from the high seat of her buggy. Lifting her skirt to avoid the piles of manure, she walked to the front door of the cabin. Again she called and knocked. The door creaked open under the pressure of her fist. "Mr. Lansing."

Like a burglar up to no good, she tiptoed into the house. To her surprise, the floor had been swept clean, and not a speck of dust rested on the scarred table or kitchen shelves. The bed in the corner was neatly made with a threadbare blanket folded at the foot. A tingle surged through her. This was the place where he slept. She tore her gaze away and moved to the stove. It, too, was scrubbed and shiny.

She shrugged. Maybe it was best that Pace wasn't here. More than likely he would simply order her back to town, supplies and all. Well, she'd come too far to retreat now.

By the time she'd carried the boxes and sacks into the house, her dress was damp with perspiration. She loosened the top buttons of her bodice, and fanned her heated skin. If this was her home, she would start supper for her man— a pot of beans or stew. The meal would be hot on the stove waiting for him at the end of his hard day's work. Then, later, they would sit together talking and sharing their dreams. And when it grew dark . . . Her gaze shifted to the bed. She cupped her heated cheeks with her icy palms. What an unseemly thing to be thinking. About a man like Pace Lansing of all people.

She turned to the door, eager to leave before he returned and caught her snooping around his home.

Pace spotted the buggy the instant he crested the rise behind the house. He'd had a fairly good day—until now. He'd found a half-dozen cows and calves in the bush. Then he'd been lucky enough to kill a couple of rabbits. He'd have meat for supper, if nothing else. Two days ago he'd used the last of the flour for biscuits and gravy. Then that grocer had refused him even five dollars' worth of credit.

He wasn't expecting visitors. In fact, since he'd been

back, not a single citizen had ventured as far as the homestead. And he wanted it that way. The less he saw of the townspeople, the better off they all would be.

At the rear of the barn, he dismounted and tethered his horse to the corral fence. Whoever was nosing around his cabin could be anywhere lying in ambush for him. On silent feet, he darted from tree to tree, then ducked around the corner of the cabin. So far he hadn't seen tracks or footprints. The intruder had to be inside. But if somebody meant him harm, why did they leave the wagon right in front for him to see?

He sneaked a peek in the window. Somebody was in there, all right, although he couldn't get a clear view of the trespasser. Gun drawn, he slid along the wall. The only sound inside was the scraping of footsteps on the floor.

At the door, he lifted his foot and kicked the door open. He leaped across the threshold and crouched, ready to fire. A split second before he squeezed the trigger, he stopped cold. He'd almost blown a woman to pieces.

Not just any woman—the preacher's daughter, Mercy Goodacre.

She squealed and covered her mouth with her fingers. All color disappeared from her face.

"What the hell are you doing in my cabin?"

Her gaze dropped to the gun still pointed at her heart. For once, the woman was at a loss for words.

"I . . . I . . ." She swallowed and tried again. "Will you please put that gun away, Mr. Lansing?" Hands raised, she backed away a step.

Pace got over his initial shock and glanced around the room. "Are you alone?"

She nodded. "Yes."

Slowly, he holstered the gun. His gaze locked on the frightened woman. Her skin was ashen, and a thin sheen of perspiration clung to her slender throat and chest where her gown was open to the tops of her bosom. A tiny row of lace peeked through the opening.

Heat surged through Pace. He didn't want to feel anything for this woman or any other. But he'd been too long without satisfying his baser needs. He cursed himself mentally. This was the preacher's daughter—not some dance-hall floozy.

"What are you doing here?" he repeated, none too kindly. "Snooping around my home?"

"I brought the supplies you needed." Her voice was soft and shaky.

For the first time he noticed the boxes and sacks on the table. "Woman, can't you take no for an answer? I told you yesterday I don't want or need you to interfere in my life."

The color returned to her face. "I'm not interfering."

"What do you call this?" Pace shouted. "You meddle where you're not wanted."

"I just wanted to help."

"I don't want your help."

"You've never wanted anybody's help have you, Pace Lansing? Even when you were in jail waiting for trial, you refused to even defend yourself. My father tried to help you, but you sent him away. No wonder he doesn't want to help you now." She planted her hands on her hips.

"If your father isn't helping me, where did this come from? Neither of your brothers-in-law would give me the time of day."

"From me."

"You? You got credit for me?"

"No, not exactly."

He took a step closer to her. Fury had his heart pounding. "Exactly how did you get these supplies, Miss Do-gooder?"

She squared her shoulders, unaware of the way her bosom bulged above the open buttons of her gown. "I paid for them with my own money."

"Your own money?" He closed in on her and caught her arms in a strong grip. Too late he realized his big mistake. Her flesh was soft and pliable and she smelled of fresh roses. Touching her sent a message to his body that he couldn't deal with. "What did you expect in return? I've heard about women who buy men. Especially—"

"Plain women? Old maids?" She twisted out of his grip. "Is that what you meant to say, Mr. Lansing? Well, don't flatter yourself. I'm not interested in you in that way, or in any way."

Moisture glittered behind her long thick lashes. Funny, he just noticed that her eyes were wide and expressive, gentle and mysterious all at the same time. He forced a calmness he didn't feel. "I'm sorry. I didn't mean to insult you. But I can't accept charity."

The word burned on his tongue like a Mexican chili pepper. And it was every bit as bitter. He remembered the church ladies who used to donate their castoffs to him and his mother when he was a child. Pace hated the way the other kids made fun of him for wearing their old clothes.

"It isn't charity. Think of it as a loan. I expect you to pay me back when you sell your stock."

He barked out a bitter laugh. "You must have learned that from Blakely. But I can't borrow money from a woman."

She threw up her hands. "You don't want charity, you can't get credit, and you won't accept a loan. Can you accept it as an investment? I'll invest in your enterprise and expect a profit at the end of the year."

Pace gaped at the atrocity of the idea. "You want to invest in the L-Bar? What will your father say? Does he know what you're doing with his money?"

Her eyes flashed with anger. "Let's get one thing straight, Mr. Lansing. It isn't my father's money—it's mine. I've worked and earned every cent. I'm twenty-six years old. I don't have to answer to anybody."

Except for the time she'd socked him in the stomach, he'd never seen Mercy Goodacre do the first thing to defy her father or convention. There was more spirit in the lady than he'd thought. Of course, she'd testified on his behalf at his trial, with her father's blessings. He never would have expected the preacher's daughter to display so much gumption.

"You know they don't trust me. Why do you? I could just up and leave and you'll lose your hard-earned money."

"Not if we sign an agreement. If you run out on our deal, I'll foreclose on your land."

A caustic smile slid across his mouth. "Now I know you've been taking lessons from Blakely."

"Do we have a deal?" She stuck out a small, white hand. "I'll grubstake you for a share of the profits."

Pace shrugged. He had little choice if he wanted to survive, and her offer was better than he'd expected. "Deal." Her fingers were small and fragile in his. After a brief shake, he released her. "But I won't have you interfering in my plans. You stay in town where you belong. It isn't safe for a woman to be out here, especially with a known criminal on the loose."

"All right. Just let me know when you need something. You know where I live."

He knew only too well. As a youth, he'd spent hours staring at her house waiting for a glimpse of either Charity or Prudence. Usually, the only one he saw was Mercy.

After escorting her to the buggy, he watched until she was out of sight. He still didn't like taking anything from a woman. But he was learning a cold, hard lesson. A man didn't always do what he wanted and he rarely got what he deserved.

Back in the house, he looked at what she'd brought. For a second he felt like a child on Christmas. But in his home, Christmas had never been this good.

There was everything that he'd had on the list yesterday,

only double, with more besides. Looked like those rabbits would make a fine stew with carrots and potatoes thrown in for good measure.

Lifting a white linen cloth, Pace couldn't believe his eyes. He dropped to a chair and stared. A chocolate cake, the likes of which he hadn't seen in over five years. Not since he'd attended a party at the church and stuffed himself on so many sweets, he had a stomachache for a week. But it had been worth the pain.

For long moments he studied the gift. Smooth, rich chocolate exactly the color of Mercy's eyes. He ran one finger across the top, then stuck it between his lips. Closing his eyes to savor the flavor, Pace wondered if Mercy's lips would taste as sweet.

He cursed himself under his breath. He had no business thinking about her that way. Hell, he had no business even talking to her. Or being in the same world with a decent woman like her.

Most of all, he didn't need an interfering woman in his life. He was certain that Mercy Goodacre meant trouble. And he already had more than a man could handle in a lifetime.

Three

They were all waiting when Mercy arrived home that evening.

At nearly dusk, she pulled into the livery stable with the wagon. On her three-block walk to the parsonage, her thoughts remained with Pace Lansing. She should have felt good about what she'd done, but she wondered if she'd somehow wounded the man's pride. He had made it clear he didn't want her help. He'd done everything short of throwing her out of his house.

Then, when they'd finally come to terms, something different glittered in his eyes. The look was so fleeting, she wondered if she'd imagined it. For a brief instant he had looked at her the way a man looks at a woman.

She recognized the look from watching the men who came into the Ruby Slipper. It was the way they looked at Rosie and Florrie when the girls were dressed up in their finery. Desire, passion, looks that a woman like Mercy had never received from a man.

Thanks to Miss Lily and the girls, she knew a little about what went on between men and women behind closed doors. Surely Pace wasn't interested in her like that. In fact, he wasn't interested in her at all. Her heart sank, and her footsteps slowed.

It would bode her well to remember they were now business partners. Her dream depended on his success.

As she rounded the corner, she was surprised at the amount of light that spilled from the first-story windows of the parsonage. Her father rarely returned from his shop before dark. She drew a quick intake of breath. Lost in her musings, she hadn't realized that it was nearly dark. Time had slipped away in her daydreams about a man who was the opposite of everything she wanted or needed in her life.

Her mind cluttered with thoughts of Pace Lansing, she shoved open the wooden gate and hurried up the steps. She'd lived in this house most of her life. Soon she would plant flower seeds along the walkway and porch. She made a mental note to remind her father to hire a boy to dig their garden in the rear yard.

In the foyer, she shrugged her shawl from her shoulders, and hung it on a coatrack with her bonnet. "Papa, I'll have supper on the table in a minute." She glanced in the hallway mirror and jumped when a number of faces besides her own frowned back at her.

She spun around and wondered who'd died. Tim, Charity, Prudence, and Clifford sat in a line on the davenport like crows on a limb. Dressed in his black suit with the stiff white collar making his face red, her father was in his favorite easy chair. His posture was anything but relaxed.

To her utter surprise, Miss Lily LaRose was rocking placidly in the oak rocker. Mercy hadn't thought that her sisters and brothers-in-law would be caught dead in the same room with the notorious owner of the Ruby Slipper Pleasure Palace. The lady wore her usual pink ensemble, with a wide flower-trimmed hat atop her silver blond hair. Things couldn't be too bad, since Miss Lily winked at Mercy.

Then they all spoke at once like a flock of magpies. Little Timmy's loud squeals drowned out the rest. The three-year-old broke away from his mother and darted toward Mercy, his arms outstretched. "Auntie Mercy, hold me."

Mercy wasn't sure what had happened, but she knew it was her fault. She picked up Timmy and balanced him on her hip.

Her father stood and signaled them all to silence much like he did to begin the Sunday worship. A hush fell over the room.

"Mercy Beulah Goodacre," he began. She knew she was in trouble when he used her full name. "We've been worried sick about you. You disappeared this afternoon and nobody knew where you'd gone or if you were safe. Your sisters wanted to send the sheriff after you."

Before Mercy had a chance to answer, Prudy jumped to her feet. "She was with that man. I know she was. See the guilty look on her face."

"Prudy is right." Charity joined their youngest sister and added to the tirade. "Tim said you'd bought a load of supplies with cash money and didn't even let him deliver it for you. He saw you drive off in the direction of *his* ranch."

Tim pointed a finger at Mercy. "I wouldn't extend credit, so you took it upon yourself to disregard the feelings of your entire family."

Her mouth agape, Mercy could only stare at the uproar that she'd caused by simply trying to be a Good Samaritan.

Clifford jumped up like a jack-in-the-box. "It's true, isn't it? You've been with Lansing, the man who killed my brother." His gaze dropped to her bosom swelling above the open buttons of her gown. In her rush to return home, she'd completely forgotten to refasten her frock. "I'll get the sheriff. Lansing won't get away with what he's done. He should be tarred and feathered and run out of town."

That did it. His bold insult drove Mercy over the edge of reason. "Exactly what do you think he's done, Clifford?" She marched across the room and shoved Timmy into his father's arms. Then she planted her hands on her hips, heedless of the way she looked. "For your information, not that it's any of your business, nothing improper happened between Mr. Lansing and me. I delivered the supplies to him, then I returned home. I don't appreciate you impugning my reputation with innuendoes."

"You left the mercantile at two o'clock. It's after six now," Charity added as fuel to the fire. "What were you doing for four hours?"

"Most of it was spent driving out there, and trying to locate his homestead. Surely you know me better than to insinuate that I would do something . . ." The words stuck in her throat.

"Calm down, daughter," her father said to interject a note of reason into the uproar. "We were concerned about your well-being. You're an innocent young woman. Anything could happen to a woman alone with a man like Lansing."

"You, too, Papa? You're condemning a man who's done nothing but try to mind his own business?" The injustice of it cut clear to her soul. "I was doing my Christian duty. It's our responsibility to help a member of our flock. Surely you would have done the same." She cringed at her own words. Pace would be furious if he'd heard her. To be honest, she was angry with herself.

"Mercy," Prudy shrieked. "He isn't a member of our congregation, he's a criminal. He's been in prison. What about your reputation? What will people think if you chase after a man like him?"

Heat rushed to her face and even her ears burned. "I'm not chasing after anybody. And you're more worried about what people will think about you than about me. It's your reputation that concerns you."

Prudy stomped one foot and stuck out her lips in the childish pout that always got her way. "You're just being stubborn. You don't care about any of us." She cuddled against Clifford and buried her face in his coat.

"Prudy is right, Mercy," Charity added. "You're being

selfish. I was ill today and I needed you to take care of Timmy. But you'd already run off to that man. Mark my words, you'll regret it for the rest of your life if you get involved with him."

Remorse shot through Mercy. All her life she'd worked hard to please her family. Her sisters had beauty and charm. Plain Mercy had to be brighter, kinder, and nicer than her sisters to get her parents' approval. Since their mother's death, she'd always been there for her father and sisters. The first time she'd gone off on her own, they'd all gone into an uproar.

She caught a movement behind her and remembered Miss Lily was watching the entire fray. "Are you going to reprimand me, too?"

Still seated on the rocker, Miss Lily laughed, a gentle ladylike sound. "I only came because you missed our appointment this afternoon. I brought some of the things the girls need mending." She pointed to the carpetbag at her feet.

Charity shot an angry glance at Miss Lily. "This is family business. She doesn't belong here."

Miss Lily simply smiled and fanned her face with a lace handkerchief.

Her father cleared his throat for attention. "Let's all calm down. Our Mercy is safely home, thank the good Lord. I'm sure she won't go off without telling us again, will you, daughter?"

Mercy folded her hands demurely in front of her. How had her good intentions caused so much trouble? "Yes, Papa, I'm sorry you were worried about me." She turned to Prudy and Clifford. "I apologize if I've caused you any concern. I'll be more careful of my reputation."

Prudy lifted her face and patted her eyes. There wasn't a drop of moisture on her cheeks. "Just because you're an old . . . I mean just because you're unmarried, you shouldn't go chasing after a man like him. He isn't good enough for a member of our family."

Mentally Mercy counted to ten to control her temper, and added five more before she turned to Charity. "I'll keep Timmy here tonight so you can get some rest. Then I'll be over first thing in the morning to help out in the store."

Her father's sigh of relief rang throughout the room. He wasn't a man who liked confrontations of any kind, and she knew that this evening had upset him greatly. "Let's all go in to supper. I noted that Mercy has a nice pot of stew on the stove."

"We can't tonight, Papa," Prudy said. "We have to run. Clifford and I are expecting an important businessman from the railroad for dinner tonight."

Tucking his wife's arm in his, Clifford ushered Prudy to the door. Both shot an unspoken warning over their shoulders. "Good night," they said in unison.

Tim draped his arm across Charity's shoulders. She rubbed her forehead. "I think not, Papa. I've developed a pounding headache. Timmy, kiss Mama, and listen to Auntie Mercy. I'll see you in the morning, if I'm feeling better."

Mercy kissed her sister's cheek. "I'll come by in the morning and see what needs to be done."

As soon as Tim and Charity had stepped onto the porch, Miss Lily rose from the rocker. "Thank you for the invitation, Reverend," the lady said with a twinkle in her eyes. "But my business awaits. I'd just like a word with Mercy, if you don't mind."

He nodded and stretched out a hand to Timmy. "Come with Grandpa, son. Let's see if Auntie Mercy has any more of those sugar cookies hiding in the kitchen."

Mercy picked up the valise at the lady's feet. "I'm sorry I missed our appointment, Miss Lily. Tell the girls I'll get these things back as soon as possible."

In an uncustomary flash of anger, the woman snatched the valise from Mercy's hands and dropped it to the floor. "Mercy Goodacre. I want to kick you right in the middle of your bustle. You don't owe me or anybody else an apology. You made my stomach turn the way you bowed and scraped in front of your sisters."

Shocked at the outburst, Mercy backed up as if she'd been slapped. "But they're my family."

Her expression softened as she took Mercy's hands in her gloved fingers. "But you don't owe them your life. Don't you see how they take advantage of your good nature? Of your kindness, and sweet heart? That's what concerns me about you and Pace. He isn't a bad man, but he's been through a lot in the past five years. I don't want him to take advantage of you, too." She squeezed Mercy's fingers. "You're how old? Twenty-five?"

"Twenty-six."

"It's time you followed your own dreams. Grab life by the horns and climb aboard. Don't be influenced by what anyone else wants for you—make up your own mind and fight for what you want."

Right now, Mercy had no idea what she wanted out of life. In the short term, she had visions of her grand trip to Philadelphia. Beyond that, she was at a loss.

"I don't know if I can."

The lady's blue eyes softened. "Then try to find out. You're a lovely young woman with a heart of pure gold. Any man would be lucky to have you as a wife. It's time for you to get on with your life." She shot a glance to the kitchen. "Your father, too. It's time he quit mourning your mother. For too long, you've depended on each other. It's past time to let go and embrace life."

Mercy looked down at their entwined fingers. "I'll try, Miss Lily. Truly, I'll try."

* * *

Pace felt pretty pleased with himself. The week that had started out so badly had turned around to his advantage. For the first time in years he didn't go to bed with his stomach gnawing with hunger, and his cupboards held more food than he'd ever seen. Even when his father had been living, they rarely had more than a few days' supplies in the house. Abner Lansing spent more on liquor than on food.

And he'd never tasted anything as good as that chocolate cake. He savored every crumb as if it were pure gold. Over the past week, he'd cut the cake into thin slices to make it last as long as possible. And with every bite, he thought about Miss Mercy Goodacre.

Of course, that wasn't the only time he thought about the woman. Nearly every night he woke up covered with sweat from erotic dreams about her. He shifted in the saddle to sit more comfortably. She was a meddling, interfering female who didn't know the first thing about men. The farther he stayed away from her, the better off they both would be.

At the crest of a rise, he reined in the stallion. In his absence his cattle had had free run of his pastures and had grown to a sizable herd with more hiding in the hills. He couldn't be sure how many head had been stolen or strayed while he'd been away.

Now, Pace Lansing was back. In spite of what the good citizens of Pleasant Valley thought, he was back to stay.

He kicked the stallion to a gallop. Getting the fine piece of horseflesh had been a rare stroke of good luck.

Pace had left prison with nothing but the ragged clothes on his back. To get out six months early, he'd volunteered to work as a scout for the cavalry in the heart of Indian country. After four years, six months, and twelve days in that filthy, dark prison, he would walk barefoot over hot coals to hell and back for the chance to breathe fresh air, and be outdoors again. After all, he'd already been in hell.

A sharp breeze from the north brought him out of his reverie. Since yesterday, the temperature had started to drop to an unseasonable low. He pulled his collar up around his throat.

In his work with the army, he'd become friends with the sergeant who'd been in charge of the remuda. The big stallion had been mistreated by his previous owner, and was as wild as a mustang on the range. Pace was the only one who could ride him, and when his time was up, the sergeant arranged for Pace to buy the horse from the army. Dancer was a strong horse with a lot of heart. Pace worked for a month to own the animal. He had also earned enough to buy a gun and the meager supplies that had gotten him started.

He worked the north section that day, flushing out another dozen unbranded cows. By late afternoon, he headed back to the house and a hot meal. He was a quarter mile from the cabin when he heard a strange moaning noise coming from behind a rock. Certain it was the wind, he hesitated for a second. The sound grew louder, like an animal caught in a trap, crying in pain.

Unwilling to see any living critter suffer, he turned the horse toward the sound. Drawing his gun to put the poor creature out of its misery, he dismounted and moved closer to the cleft in the rock. He'd never quite heard an animal like this before. The moans turned to sharp sobs and quick intakes of breath. It sounded almost human.

A pitiful, ungodly wail pierced through his thoughts. He'd heard the sounds of men dying before. Quickly, he shoved aside a bush and spotted the source of the noise. A body lay on the ground, bent double in pain. Long black hair was matted with twigs and dirt. His heart stopped beating. It was a woman—and she was in pain.

He knelt on the rocky ground and turned her head. Under the bruises and scratches on her face, her skin was as icy as a stone prison wall. She opened her eyes and flinched at his touch.

"It's okay. I won't hurt you."

Terror spread over her features, and her scream was nothing more than a weak squeak. Her entire body convulsed. He lowered his gaze. The woman had her hands clutched around her swollen stomach.

All the heat left Pace's body. The woman was pregnant, and in labor.

He sat back on his heels and stared. Over the years, he'd seen cows and mares give birth, but he knew little about women. She shivered, and lifted her gaze pleadingly. Pace slipped out of his jacket and wrapped it around her slender shoulders. When another pain racked her body, he knew he had to do something or she would die out here in the wilderness. So would her child.

Nobody deserved that.

"I'm going to pick you up and take you to my cabin," he said. He slid his arms under her back and picked her up. She shook so badly he had to cradle her to his chest to lift her from the ground.

"No," she muttered, the word a mere grunt.

"I'll get you some help. You need to get warm."

She jerked, and went limp. For a second, he thought she'd died in his arms. With one fingertip he touched the pulse at her throat. She was alive, just barely. Gently, he balanced her on the saddle and mounted behind her. The woman weighed so little, the extra weight was no problem for the big stallion. Pace hugged her to his chest to ease the ride. He prayed as he'd never prayed for himself that she and her baby would survive.

After a few minutes, his cabin came into view. She was still unconscious when he lifted her down and carried her to his bed. Pace stared down at her pale face. He had no idea what to do. Taking a clean cloth, he wiped the dirt from her forehead. She awoke and stared at him with pain-glazed eyes. Again she clutched her stomach.

His gaze fell to her overly thin arms. Red, raw bruises ringed her wrists. Rope burns. She'd been tied and, from the looks of her, abused.

Black fury shot through him. He remembered how his old man had beat him and his mother when he got drunk. When he was big enough to defend himself, the old man went out and beat the dog. Abner Lansing was a sorry excuse for a human being. The man who'd done this to this woman, who was little more than a girl, was the worst scum on the earth. By experience he knew there were men who preyed on the weak and helpless. If he had his way, he would tie them all together and let them gnaw at each other like starving rats.

His stomach clenched. She needed more help than he could give. She needed a doctor. He held a cup of water to her lips. She swallowed, but most of the water drizzled down her chin.

He pulled the blanket over her and tucked it in. "I'm going to get help. Just relax." She nodded, as if she understood. As he rushed out the door, he glanced back at the woman. Again she was doubled over in pain. He didn't know how long it took to birth a baby, but he knew if he didn't get a doctor, they both might not survive.

Outside the cabin, he paused and forced down his own nausea. He'd seen men die; he'd even killed a man. But seeing a woman like this was more than he could stand. He hated to take Dancer out again, but the stallion was fast and strong. After giving the animal a drink, he mounted and headed for Pleasant Valley. For the first time, he cursed the distance to the town. Not wanting to push his horse to the point of exhaustion, he cut across country, slicing the journey by half.

As he entered town, he chose the rear alley so as not to meet the sheriff or any other citizen who would delay him.

In the growing darkness pale yellow light flowed from various homes and businesses. He breathed a sigh of relief when he spotted the shingle that signaled he'd found the doctor's office. Without bothering to knock, he burst through the door.

"Doctor," he called.

The room was empty and dark. In the pale moonlight that streamed through the window, he spotted a large oak desk and bookcases lining the walls. His heart pounding out of control, he rushed through the door at the end of the narrow room. "Is anybody here?"

A long table sat in the center of the room, and a locked cabinet held a variety of bottles and vials. As he started to backtrack, another door swung open. Relief flowed through him. He stopped cold. A woman carrying a kerosene lamp stared at him with wide, frightened eyes.

"Is the doctor here? I need help."

She backed up a step. "Are you hurt?"

"No. But a woman is having a baby, and I need to get the doctor out there right away."

"He isn't here."

Impatience made him shout. "Then where is he?"

"I don't know," she said. "He's out making house calls."

"When will he be back?"

"I'm only the housekeeper. I don't set his appointments. If you'll tell me what you need, I'll tell him when he returns."

Pace strangled on his anger. He slapped his hands against his side in frustration. "I need him now."

Her gaze dropped to the gun at Pace's hip. "He may not be back until tomorrow. Sometimes he stays away overnight." She was clearly trying to get rid of him.

Aware he was wasting time arguing with the housekeeper, he marched back out into the early evening breeze. He slammed his fist into a post. Where was he going to get help? If a doctor wasn't available, he had to find a midwife or a woman.

A woman willing to help him. In the distance he spied the steeple of the church.

There was only one woman who would even speak to him. He hated to involve her in his problems. He'd vowed to stay away from her. He didn't want to ask for help.

Then he remembered the woman back in his cabin. The help was for her, not for him.

Leaping back on his horse, he raced down the alley toward the parsonage. He prayed Miss Mercy Goodacre was at home. Right now, she was his only hope.

Four

The pounding on the rear door startled Mercy out of her peaceful lethargy. She jabbed her finger with the needle and stuck the injured finger into her mouth to keep the blood from dripping on Florrie's gold satin gown. Mercy had promised to have the gown ready by the next morning for the busy Saturday night at the saloon. She'd hoped for one night without interruption.

With a sigh, she dropped her spectacles into her sewing basket. Who but her sisters or brothers-in-law would summon her after eight o'clock?

For the past week they had tormented her to death with one so-called emergency after another. Timmy spent more time with Mercy and her father than with his own parents.

Since Ezra was meeting with the church's deacon board, it was her responsibility to respond to the problem, real or imagined. Looked like poor Florrie would have to wait for her gown. Mercy had counted on the money to replace some of what she'd spent on Pace.

"I'm coming," she called. Her finger still in her mouth, she started for the kitchen. As she stepped onto the shiny linoleum floor, the door flung open. A man much larger than Tim or Clifford rushed in and nearly toppled her from her feet. A startled cry escaped her lips and only a pair of strong hands kept her upright.

Mouth agape, she found herself staring into Pace

Lansing's equally startled black eyes. Strange tingles rushed to the pit of her stomach. Her face was level with his jaw shadowed with whiskers. He looked like the desperado her sisters had accused him of being.

He backed her against the wall, chest to chest, toes touching. Her gaze followed a drop of perspiration that trailed down his throat into the faded bandanna tied around his neck. For a second her heart stopped beating.

"Miss Goodacre," he said between gasps. "You have to come with me. I need a woman—I need you."

Her breath caught in her throat. A weaker woman would have fainted dead away. Surely, the man was mad. How dare he make such a preposterous proposition to a decent woman?

"Mr. Lansing, what do you mean?" she gasped. "This is highly improper."

He backed up a step and clenched his hands at his side. "I'm sorry. But the doctor isn't in and I need help." The words came in short gasps.

She shook her head trying to make sense of his outlandish request. "The doctor? Are you hurt?"

"No, not me." He tore off his hat and ran his fingers through hair as long and black as an Indian's. "It's a woman."

Mercy's heart plunged to her feet. He'd come to ask her to help another woman. She fought back a twinge of unwanted and unfamiliar jealousy. "Where is she?"

"At my place. She's having a baby, and I think she's dying."

A chill raced over Mercy. Childbirth. The very word filled her with horror. Her own mother had died trying to birth a son. She'd never prayed harder for anyone than when Charity had gone into labor for Timmy. "I . . . I didn't know you had a wife."

His head jerked as if he'd been punched in the jaw. "I

don't have a wife. I found her in the brush and she's in real bad shape. She needs help."

"We'll get the doctor."

"I told you, he isn't in and I didn't know where else to turn." He slammed his battered hat back on his head.

"Who is she?"

"I don't know. She's Indian. Maybe she ran away from the reservation," he shouted. "Are you going to help me?" His hands snaked out and gripped her arms.

"I don't know anything about delivering a baby." The very thought turned her knees to jelly. "I'll try to find somebody who can help."

"I told you we don't have time. We have to leave now." He shook her until her teeth rattled.

Mercy didn't understand a bit of it, but she couldn't refuse someone in need. Stranger or friend, Indian or white, it didn't matter. All her life she'd been taught to help no matter the cost. A nagging voice whispered this could cost her reputation. She ignored the voice that sounded too much like her sister's. "Let me gather up a few things." He dropped his hands—and stepped away.

Motivated by the urgency in his voice, she raced up the stairs to the linen closet. She shoved clean sheets and towels into a pillowcase and, at the last second, added her sewing kit. Throwing her black wool cape over her shoulders, she met Pace in the kitchen. For a man who'd endured untold personal adversities, concern for the woman made him look young and vulnerable.

"I'm ready."

He snatched the pillowcase from her fingers. "Then let's go."

She hesitated for a second, certain she'd forgotten something important. "We have to go to the livery and hitch up my buggy."

"No," Pace said in a tone that brooked no argument.

"We'll take my horse. It'll be quicker if we bypass the roads."

"Your horse?" Her voice came out in a raspy squeak. "How?"

His hand at the small of her back, he shoved her out the door. "We'll ride double."

"Double? That's impossible. And indecent."

He grabbed her by the wrist and tugged her to the edge of the porch. "Lady, right now decency is the last thing on my mind." In one fluid movement he leaped into the saddle and tied the pillowcase to the pummel. "Now, put your foot here in the stirrup and I'll give you a hand up."

Before she could consider the impropriety of her situation, she flung her leg over the big horse's back. Her legs stretched in the most unladylike manner. She'd never straddled a horse before. With one hand she struggled to cover her bare limbs, while the other grabbed his shirt.

"Wrap your arms around me and hang on," he ordered. Hardly giving her a chance to oblige, he nudged the horse and the big stallion took off with a gallop. Her arms flew around his waist and she held on for dear life.

The horse galloped down the deserted back alley, past the mercantile and the bank. At the rear of the Ruby Slipper a man stepped through the doorway. He struck a match to a cigarette, pooling his face with a pale yellow light. In the brief instant of time, she was certain she recognized Clifford. She ducked her face into Pace's back, praying her brother-in-law wouldn't notice her.

Seeing Clifford brought to memory what had escaped her when she'd left the house. She had forgotten to leave a note for her father. It was too late to correct that oversight now.

Moments later, they left the lights and activity of the town behind. With only the moon and stars to light the way, they headed west. The wind stung her face and her hair tore loose of the pins. Her cape flew behind her like the black wings of an angel of the night. She'd never experienced excitement like this. The flight through the darkness on a huge horse, while clinging to a strong, dangerous man, thrilled her more than anything in her twenty-six years. She almost hoped the ride would never end.

Pace was all hard muscles and warm flesh. Her hands clutched his middle feeling the powerful masculinity of the strong body. She'd never touched a man in this fashion before, had never been this close to losing all sense of propriety. Every hoofbeat of the horse pressed her more intimately against his body. His buttocks rode against her stomach, her breasts pressed into his back. Even her thick layers of clothing couldn't stop the sensations that sizzled from her neck to the deepest reaches of her stomach.

Never had she felt so alive or aware of her own body as at that moment. She pressed her face into his jacket and inhaled the scent of leather, sweat, and man. Her breasts swelled and threatened to burst from their bindings.

She couldn't believe that she was riding off in the night with a notorious man like Pace Lansing. It was like an adventure from a storybook such as *Robin Hood* or *Ivanhoe*. She was certain she would awaken any minute and find it was all an impossible dream.

But the flat stomach under her fingers was solid, the wind in her face was cool, and the saddle under her bottom hurt like sitting on a bouncing rock. And the strange sensations that had her body tingling were so strong that she didn't want to ever wake up.

They flew past trees and houses. He left the road and cut through pastures and meadows. The horse splashed through a stream and leaped a low fence. When Mercy nearly tumbled from the saddle, Pace turned and glanced at her.

"You all right?" he shouted, his words carried away by the breeze.

"I guess so," she returned.

He caught her wrist in a strong grip to steady her behind him. "We're almost home."

All during the wild ride, she'd concentrated on two things—Pace's body and the way he made her feel alive and unrestrained.

Now that their journey was almost ended, she focused what she would find when she reached his cabin. Was there an ill woman, or was this some ruse to get her away from town and alone? A shiver raced up her spine as fear settled like a stone in her chest.

She had trusted him enough to go alone to his home to deliver the supplies. But that was during the day, not under the cover of night. Doubts about Pace took root in her heart. She'd been duly warned, both by her family and Miss Lily. Yet, something deep in her soul told her not to worry. Pace may have killed a man with his bare hands, but instincts told her he would never lift a finger to a woman. And long ago he'd rescued her when Billy Blakely had threatened her. Locked in his wounded heart was a knight waiting to be freed.

Silhouetted against the moonlit sky, the dark shadow of his cabin came into view. He reined in near the door. Man and horse were heaving for breath, and Mercy wondered if she would ever breathe normally again.

The instant before the horse stopped, Pace removed Mercy's hands from his waist. She trembled, not sure how she'd get down from the huge animal. "I can't move," she said.

"Just set your foot into the stirrup, and fling your leg over his rump. I'll hold you up."

Her foot found leverage, and her hands gripped his arm. He bore her weight until her feet touched the ground. Then he was beside her.

Her knees buckled under her, and if Pace hadn't been there to catch her, she would have slunk into the dirt. The muscles in her thighs felt stretched beyond ever returning to normal. Her backside was bruised until it was numb.

"I'm not used to riding astride. I don't believe I can walk," she grunted.

Pace muttered something under his breath. He slipped his arm under her knees and lifted her high against his chest. "You can sit down while I light the lamps." He kicked open the door and entered the room lit only by a thin beam of moonlight.

Mercy squealed in surprise when he plopped her onto a hard chair. "I don't think I can sit down either." Indignation rose up in her. The man had practically kidnapped her, and he was treating her like an old sack of potatoes. She opened her mouth to remind him she was a lady, when she heard a gasp followed by a low moan. At first she thought it was Pace's labored breathing, but the sound was too soft and weak to be his.

Shivers raced over her. He struck a match and touched it to the wick of a kerosene lamp. Pale yellow light touched his face dark with worry. In two long steps he moved to the far corner of the room and set the lamp on a low table.

A small figure lay huddled on his bed in a tangle of sheets and blankets. "I brought help," he said. He lifted his gaze to Mercy. "I was afraid we'd be too late, but she's still alive, barely."

Somehow Mercy found the strength to rise and walk on shaky legs across the room. A woman lay on his bed, her hands clutched to her distended stomach. Damp ebony hair was tangled around her face, and her black eyes were filled with terror. Hands shaking, Mercy touched the woman's forehead. "She's ice cold," she whispered.

"What are we going to do?" he asked.

"For one thing, start a fire and try to get her warm."

Pace moved to the fireplace and stacked it with wood. When the kindling started a weak blaze, he returned to her side.

As Mercy and Pace stared in bewilderment at her, the woman let out a weak cry of pain. Her slender body jerked with convulsions. "I don't know much," Pace said, "but I think the baby is coming."

"We need a doctor," Mercy moaned. She had been with Charity when Timmy had been born, but her duty had been to bathe her sister's forehead and grip her hands while she pushed. After the baby came, she washed and dressed him. By then, the doctor had lowered the sheet, and Charity was reaching for her son.

"Lady, we've only got each other." Without waiting for instructions, he flung the blanket from the woman's legs. Blood was everywhere on the thin sheet.

A huge knot tightened in Mercy's stomach. Frightened by the sight, she jumped to action. "Bring in the pillow-case. We need clean sheets and towels. Then heat water and get some strong soap." Mercy swallowed the bile that rose in her throat. She'd agreed to help, and she would do her best. Her gaze fell on the woman's face. Mercy gasped at the pale skin under the dark bruises and scrapes. She was very small and young—little more than a child herself. "What's your name?" Mercy asked softly.

"Na-o-mi," the answer came as a weak moan.

"Naomi, that's a beautiful name. We're here to help you. You're going to deliver a strong healthy baby."

Naomi closed her eyes. "I will die, but my child must live." The words were barely discernible.

Mercy's heart tightened. "No. You'll both live." She blinked back tears. Lifting a cup of water that sat beside the bed, she held it to the woman's lips.

Before Naomi swallowed a drop, another pain doubled her over. Pace raced back into the room and flung the pillowcase at Mercy's feet. Then he ran to the stove and stoked up a fire.

Time was running out for the woman. Mercy knew it as surely as she knew that many women didn't survive childbirth in the best of circumstances. Her own mother had been one of those unfortunate women.

While Pace put the water on the fire, she tugged the soiled sheet loose from the bed. "Pace, can you lift her a little so I can slip a clean sheet and towels under her?"

Without a word, he obeyed. Mercy grabbed her scissors from her sewing kit and cut away Naomi's filthy cotton dress. "I think the baby is coming," she said, afraid to even consider what to do next. "We have to keep her legs open to allow it to come out." Taking a moment to push down the nausea that kept her stomach churning, she removed her cape and washed her hands. Pace followed and did the same.

Seconds later, they returned to Naomi. She was very weak and hardly able to push. Pace held her legs open but kept his gaze averted. Under his tan, his skin was as pale as the woman struggling to birth a child. Mercy ran her hands over the firm stomach. She gritted her teeth. Never had she touched another woman, and she'd never seen another woman's private parts. But this was no time for modesty. Two lives hung in the balance.

Naomi was so small and weak, Mercy doubted she would be able to push hard enough to birth the child. Another weak gasp and the muscles in her stomach contracted. "I think it's coming," she said. "Keep her legs spread."

In spite of the chill room, perspiration streamed from Mercy's face. Her hands were slick with blood and water when she caught a small squirming figure in her arms.

"It's a boy," Pace said, his voice soft and reverent.

From watching Dr. Lewis when Timmy was born, she had a vague idea of what to do. Quickly, she cleared the child's mouth and gave him a smack. Instantly, he let out a loud squeal. Mercy laid him on his mother's stomach while she cut and tied off the cord.

By the time Mercy had finished tending Naomi, the woman's breathing was shallow and coming in short gasps.

She hugged her child, now wrapped in a clean towel, and lifted her gaze to Pace. Her lips moved and he leaned closer to hear. "Take care of my son," she said.

His face damp, Pace wiped his cheek with a long rough finger. "He'll be fine. So will you."

"No. I die. Swear you and your woman will care for him."

Pace glanced at Mercy. "I swear."

Mercy wrung out a cloth and wiped Naomi's sweaty brow. "Rest now. You can talk later."

In a surprisingly strong grip she caught Mercy's wrist. "You swear."

"I swear," she said, knowing she would always cherish this child she and Pace had brought into the world. Very likely she would never bear a son of her own. This baby had already won her heart.

Mercy gathered the dirty linens in her arms and shoved them aside. Exhausted and yet exhilarated beyond belief, she moved to the stove. Within a few minutes, she had a pot of coffee heating on the fire. "We have to try to get her to eat something. She looks as if she's been starved."

Pace glanced up from where he was staring at the baby. "Yes, as soon as she wakes up." He moved toward Mercy. "You did a great job, Mercy. You saved two lives. Not to mention mine. I about died of fright." Pace dropped his tough facade and looked younger than his twenty-five years.

A tiny smile touched her lips. It was the first time he'd used her given name since they were youngsters. "Not half as scared as I was."

He smiled and brushed a loose lock of hair from her cheek. "You're the bravest woman I've ever met."

Her heart skipped a beat. His gentle touch made her weak with emotion. "After you kidnapped me, what choice did I have?"

His smile widened. "You came willingly, Miss Do-gooder."

"Then I suppose I'll have to call you Mr. Do-gooder. You're the one who dragged me here."

Stroking her cheek gently, he shrugged. "That'll be a first. I'm a notorious killer, remember?"

"I'm . . ." she started to protest, when the loud cries of the baby brought her up short.

Together Mercy and Pace raced to the bed. The baby was kicking his feet and flailing his arms. Something was very wrong. Naomi hadn't moved. At first she thought the woman was asleep. Pace snatched up the baby and shoved him into Mercy's arms. He touched the woman's forehead, then searched for a pulse. His face turned ashen. The expression on his face said it all.

Naomi was dead.

Pace had seen men die. He'd killed a man with his bare hands. But to see this woman lose her life cut him clear to the core of his soul. His own mother had died in this very cabin.

Anger surged through him. It wasn't childbirth that had killed Naomi, but the brute who'd starved and abused her. He suspected she'd been running away from the man when he'd found her. It was too late now. She was free of him and his abuse.

He glanced at Mercy with the baby in her arms. If it took every bit of strength he had, the bastard wasn't going to get his hands on the baby. Pace clutched his fingers into fists. But if he ever got his hands on the man who'd done this, he would give the man a taste of his own medicine. Let him know how it felt to be bound, beaten, and starved.

Pace shivered. Was it Naomi he wanted to avenge, or himself for the atrocities committed against him in prison?

"We can't do anything for her now." He gently covered Naomi's face with the clean sheet Mercy had brought.

Across the room, Mercy bounced the baby to keep him quiet. "What about the baby?"

"I made a promise to take care of him. I intend to keep my word." From the moment he'd seen the tiny, red infant struggling for breath, something had changed inside Pace. A strange sensation had come over him—almost like a fog, or mist. His knees nearly buckled as emotion swelled in his heart. He wasn't sure what it was, but this was the closest he'd come to love since his mother had died.

"How? You have a ranch to run. A man alone can't take care of an infant."

He hadn't thought that far ahead. "I'll work out something."

The baby cried louder. "I think he's hungry. We have to find some way to feed him."

Pace was completely out of his element. He had no idea what to do next. "I have a couple of cows that have dropped calves recently. I could try to milk one."

"It's dark outdoors. You'll never get close enough. I have an idea. When Timmy was cross, Charity would wrap some sugar in a handkerchief and let him suck on it. We can also try to give him a little water. It's the best we can do until tomorrow." She shoved the baby into his arms. "Hold him while I get it ready."

"I don't know how to hold a baby." The baby was so tiny, he barely filled Pace's hands. "What if I drop him?"

Mercy glanced at him over her shoulder. "You won't."

He must have been doing something right, because the baby's cries dropped to a whimper. Had he ever been this small and vulnerable? It was a strange feeling to literally hold a young life in his hands. She spread a towel on the table and cut a sheet into squares. A few minutes later, Mercy took the baby from him.

Pace realized how little he knew about babies. He

doubted he could manage to diaper and feed a child. While she tended the baby, he went outside to take care of his horse. Truth was, he knew more about horses and cows than about women and babies. And he needed a minute alone in the darkness of the night to understand the odd emotions that had sprung up so unexpectedly.

His horse brushed down, fed and watered, and safely in the barn, Pace sank into a haystack to consider the unusual events of the day. Naomi—Mercy—a baby. How had he gotten caught in this situation?

Pace was a loner, not by choice, but by fate or whatever force guided men's lives. Thanks to a legal system he couldn't understand, he'd lost everything, including five years of his life. Now, he'd come back to claim what belonged to him—his land, his cows, his freedom, his life.

There was no place in his world for anybody. Not a friend, not a lover, not a child. But he'd given a dying woman his word, and he would do his best to keep his promise. After all he'd lost, the only thing left was his word of honor.

No closer to solving his dilemma, Pace returned to the house. He pushed open the door and stopped in his tracks. Mercy was seated near the table with the baby in her arms. Her hair had pulled loose from its stiff confines and hung in waves down her back and around her face. His breath caught in his throat.

How had he ever thought her plain? With the baby close at her breast, she was the most beautiful woman he'd ever seen. She lifted wide brown eyes to him. In that instant, something sparked between them like a bolt of heat lightning on a hot summer night. A bond formed to link them together. His stomach tightened into a hard knot, and desire slammed into him as it hadn't in a very long time.

"He's beautiful. He's part white, isn't he?" she asked.

Pace nodded. "I suppose. He has blue eyes and light hair. His mother was clearly Indian."

"He needs a name."

He filled a cup from the coffeepot on the stove to clear his thoughts. "What do you suggest?"

She thought for a moment. "Joshua. It means 'whom God has saved.' You saved his life. The name fits."

"Joshua. Good. That's what we'll call him. Is Joshua asleep?"

"Yes. If you'll spread out those towels, I'll lay him down and get you something to eat."

Seconds later, he took Joshua from her arms and laid him on the makeshift bed in a small wooden crate. The baby was so tiny and defenseless. Since his mother had died, Pace hadn't loved a single soul. He wasn't sure what he felt for this tiny stranger was love, but it was the closest he'd ever come to love. Pace sort of liked the feeling. He felt more alive than he had in years. This child had nourished a part of his soul that had shriveled and died years ago.

"You don't have to get me anything to eat. I've been taking care of myself for a long time."

Mercy smiled. "I don't mind. I'm used to doing things for my family."

He picked up a stale biscuit from that morning. "I'm not your family. You don't owe me anything."

Pain glittered in her eyes. "I know. I'm sorry I interfered in your life."

"I didn't mean it that way. Relax. It's been a long night. You must be exhausted."

She studied him for a moment before her gaze fell to the remainder of the cake beside the stove. "You didn't like the cake?" Her voice was soft and shaky.

"I loved it. I just want to make it last as long as possible. Never know how long it'll be before I get another one."

A woman like Mercy Goodacre would never understand what it was like to be hungry, or cold, or alone. She wouldn't know what it was to horde every morsel of food and make it last an impossibly long time.

"I'm glad you liked it."

"I never thanked you for the stores. If you'll draw up that paper about the partnership, I'll sign it."

"Good. I'll get some more supplies when I get to town."

Pace chewed slowly. "I don't need anything. You brought plenty." He didn't know what else to say. Silence hung like a heavy curtain between them. "Guess I'll have to bury her in the morning."

"She deserves a Christian burial. We can take her to town. My father will make a nice coffin and conduct the funeral."

"She's Indian. He won't help." His voice hardened. He knew from experience how the townspeople felt about Indians.

"That isn't true. My father isn't like that. He'll do it because it's the right thing to do."

"Reckon we'll find out tomorrow."

"We should try to find a good home for Joshua, too."

A band tightened around his chest. "Impossible. A white family won't want a half-breed, and he'd be an outcast with the Indians."

"Surely there's a good family who'll be willing to take in such a beautiful baby."

"The only people who would take him in would probably abuse him and use him for a slave."

"That's a terrible thing to say. What other choice do we have?"

Despair threatened to choke him. "Let's wait and see what develops."

"All right. I'll take him home with me until we can make a decision."

"We'll talk about that, too, in the morning."

Five

Reverend Ezra Goodacre woke at dawn. As he'd done every morning for the past thirty years, he knelt beside his bed and prayed. Although he didn't understand why, his daughter, Mercy, was utmost in his thoughts. She was a dutiful girl, and he didn't know what he would do without her. But lately, she'd shown an uncharacteristic streak of rebellion. Ever since Pace Lansing had come back to town.

After he asked forgiveness for his unkind thoughts, Ezra prayed for himself. He prayed that he wouldn't let his intolerance get in the way of being a good and true minister. There had been times since his wife's death that he doubted his calling. As a young man he'd wanted nothing more than to be the best woodworker and cabinetmaker in Sweetwater, Illinois. Then he'd fallen in love with Faith Smithson, the minister's daughter. Ezra believed his calling came more from wanting to marry Faith than from wanting to serve God. They'd moved to Pleasant Valley and started the church shortly after their marriage.

He prayed even harder for his male weakness. At close to fifty, Ezra was still tormented with the male urges he'd tried to suppress since he'd lost his beloved Faith. But more and more, he caught his gaze straying toward the widow ladies in the church. It was Miss Lily LaRose, however, who sent his pulse racing and reminded him of how lonely his bedroom had become. And she was the most unsuitable woman in the state.

The house was very quiet when he ventured downstairs for breakfast. The clock in the hallway struck seven times. Strange, he thought, Mercy usually called him for breakfast long before now. "Mercy," he called and got no answer. The kitchen was empty, and the stove cold.

It wasn't like Mercy to oversleep, but she'd been working harder than ever lately. It seemed her sisters were constantly in need of her services. He'd returned home late the night before, and slipped into his own bed without awakening her. Upstairs, he knocked on her door to no answer. Gently, he shoved the door open and found her bed neatly made as it was every day.

In the living room, the gold gown she'd been mending lay discarded on the rocker. She'd mentioned having to finish it by this morning. Her cloak was missing from the peg in the foyer. Concern replaced his irritation. Could someone have called her away during the night? One of her sisters must have sent for her and she didn't want to disturb him.

Ezra slipped into his coat and started out the door. Charity or Prudy would know what was going on. As he stepped onto the porch, he spied a figure swing around the corner and amble toward the house. For a moment he thought it was Mercy. Opening his mouth to chastise his daughter for worrying him, he shut it immediately when he recognized Cora, Miss LaRose's maid. The mulatto woman had arrived in Pleasant Valley with Miss LaRose shortly after the War. Rumor had it they'd come from New Orleans.

"Morning, Reverend," the woman said. Clad in a pretty calico dress, she flashed her usual friendly smile. Her black hair was neatly coiled in an elaborate chignon. Cora was taller than he, and as slender as a reed.

"Good morning, Cora," he returned with a tip of his hat.

"Is Miss Mercy in? Miss Lily sent me to fetch the garments she was mending for the girls."

"Mercy isn't here. I suppose she's with one of her sisters. When I find her, I'll let her know you were looking for her."

"Yes, sir. Tell her Miss Florrie will be needing that gold dress for tonight. Saturday's big business at the Ruby Slipper."

Ezra frowned. He was all too aware of what went on in the noisy saloon and Miss LaRose's part in the establishment. He didn't need Cora to remind him. "And Sunday is big business at the church."

"I know, preacher. I'll be there in my usual spot, just like every week."

Although she worked for Miss LaRose, Cora had become one of the faithful in the congregation. It hurt Ezra to realize that being part Negro, the pretty, well-spoken woman along with the few other colored in the county were relegated to the balcony. But he had little say-so in the matter. Too many of the parishioners still harbored prejudice from the past.

"If you see Mercy, please tell her I'm looking for her," he said.

A large woven basket swinging from her hand, Cora turned to retrace her footsteps. "Yes, sir. I'll surely do that."

Now he was getting worried. It wasn't like Mercy to go off and not inform him of her whereabouts. Ezra hurried his footsteps. Already that morning Main Street was crowded with wagons, buggies, horses, and pedestrians. Farmers and ranchers mingled with townspeople on the boardwalk and in the various shops. The women huddled together sharing gossip and news of the week. He nodded and called out greetings, but didn't slow until he reached Fullenwider's Mercantile. He flung open the door expecting to see Mercy behind the counter with the white apron covering her frock.

Tim looked up and waved a greeting. Charity turned from the customer she was serving and raced to her father.

"Papa, where's Mercy?" his middle daughter demanded. "She said she would be here this morning to help us and to take care of Timmy." Her words came out in a rush. Timmy tugged on her skirt, whining for attention.

Ezra picked up the child and tossed him in the air. The little boy squealed with delight. Mrs. Waterman, who'd been examining a bolt of muslin, turned and smiled. The widow had invited him for dinner at her farm a number of times, but his interest in the mother of four robust boys was purely that of a minister for a member of his congregation.

He nodded to the woman, and took Charity by the arm. "I don't know where Mercy is," he whispered. "She didn't prepare my breakfast, and I assumed she'd come to help you and Tim."

"We haven't seen her since yesterday." Charity glanced around. "She refused to keep Timmy last night, claiming she had mending for those women. She's probably over there right now."

Several women paused in their conversations and had their ears pealed. Ezra hated to have his business spread all over town by the gossips. Within minutes every word they said would be whispered from one end of the county to the other.

"No. Cora came by and she hadn't seen Mercy. She must be with Prudence."

"Or with that man," Charity sneered.

"Daughter, it won't help to malign your sister like that."

"Sorry, Papa," she said, not a bit sincere. "Prudy doesn't stir from bed before ten, but Clifford is at the bank next door. Let's go ask him." Ignoring her customers, Charity headed for the door followed by Ezra, who was still holding Timmy. "Tim, I'm running over to the bank. We'll be back in a minute."

They pushed through the crowd gathered on the board-walk and entered the bank. The stone building had been built to Clifford's specifications to avoid robberies and theft. In spite of threats in the area by the Younger and James gangs, People's Bank of Pleasant Valley remained untouched.

As usual, Clifford was at his desk in the corner, where he could watch all the activity in his bank. The sturdy oak counter stretched from wall to wall with the upper half made of thick metal bars that reached to the ceiling. Armed with a shotgun, a guard stood watch.

Although Clifford provided a luxurious living for his wife, Ezra was still concerned about his youngest daughter. His son-in-law was close to fifteen years his daughter's sen-ior. Sometimes Ezra wished she'd waited until she'd ma-tured before marrying. But Prudy had always liked pretty clothes and fine things. Even as a child she'd vowed to marry a rich man who would adore her and give her every-thing she wanted. As soon as she was old enough to realize Clifford Blakely was the wealthiest man in town, she set her sights on him. Even though Clifford had come to call on Mercy, his youngest girl wouldn't be denied. Prudy al-ways got what she wanted.

Charity shoved through the waiting customers and sig-naled for Clifford. He rose from his chair and unlocked the door that led behind the counter.

"Charity, I'm very busy. What do you want?" Pulling a gold watch from his vest pocket, he frowned. "I don't have time to visit."

"We're looking for Mercy. Have you seen her today?"

Clearly annoyed at the interruption to his business, Clif-ford shoved his hands in the pockets of his gray striped suit. "No, not this morning." He thought for a moment. "But I thought I saw her last night."

"Last night? Where?"

Clifford rubbed his freshly shaved jaw. "I was working late at the bank, and when I left, I saw Pace Lansing dash past me on that great big horse of his. He had a woman riding behind him. At first I thought it was Mercy, then I figured I'd been seeing things." He thought for a moment. "Come to think of it, she was wearing a cape just like the one Prudence gave her for Christmas. It *was* Mercy."

Ezra's heart dropped. "Mercy wouldn't have gone off with him."

Charity grabbed her father's arm. "Of course she wouldn't, not willingly. Pace kidnapped her," she squealed. "There's no telling what that man will do to an innocent woman like Mercy."

His daughter echoed his unspoken fears. Several bank customers stopped and stared. They began whispering among themselves.

"Reverend," Clifford said, his voice soft and serious. "You had better get Sheriff Jennings. He'll get up a posse and go out after that outlaw."

Certain time was running out for his oldest daughter, Ezra shoved his grandson into his mother's arms. "Yes, Jennings will know what to do."

While Pace dragged out his old farm wagon, Mercy washed Naomi's body and wrapped it in a clean sheet. Since she'd often helped her father in the undertaking business, she knew what needed to be done. As she worked, she prayed for the woman and the baby she'd left behind. Mercy had promised to care for Joshua, and it was a promise she fully intended to keep. During the long night when she'd fed, diapered, and held him, she'd fallen hopelessly in love with the tiny infant.

As best she could, she straightened her hair and clothes. Her gown was wrinkled, and during the wild ride from town, her hairpins had flown like hail behind her. After combing her long brown hair with her fingers, she braided the thick tresses and let the braid hang down her back.

She only wished she had some soft, pretty baby clothes for Joshua. Things like she and Charity had made for Timmy. Since her nephew had long outgrown the layette, she hoped Charity would donate the clothes to Joshua.

Mercy paused in her musings. She was acting as if she intended to keep the baby—to raise him as her own.

She sat down and cuddled him to her chest. His little hands touched her and his mouth rooted for her breast. "Sorry, sweetheart, but I can't help you like that."

"Like what?" Pace asked as he entered the cabin.

Heat rushed to Mercy's cheeks. She shifted the baby high up on her shoulder. "I can't hold him and get breakfast for us."

"I told you, you don't have to wait on me."

"I'm starved. It'll only take a few minutes to fry up some bacon. I made the biscuits while Joshua was sleeping." She placed the baby gently in his arms. "You can hold him for a while."

She moved to the stove and dropped the bacon in the frying pan. Behind her, Pace didn't made a sound. He was considered an outcast by the people in town, yet he'd gone out of his way to help the dying woman. Mercy's instincts had been right. He wasn't as bad as his reputation.

Last night, he'd gone out to the barn to sleep, not wanting to compromise her reputation by staying under the same roof. It was almost funny. If anybody found out she'd gone to his cabin, her reputation would be so tarnished, no amount of polish and elbow grease could shine it up again.

Pace chuckled softly and Mercy turned to see what he'd

found humorous. She'd never heard him laugh before. The sound sent a flutter to the center of her heart.

"Sorry, buddy, I can't help you that way either."

Nestled in Pace's arm, Joshua was rooting his mouth at the front of Pace's shirt, exactly as he'd done to Mercy.

Mercy bit back a smile. She set a plate of bacon and biscuits on the table in front of him. "Let me take him while you eat."

"No, I can manage. I don't suppose I'll get to see him often when you take him into town."

She folded her hands in front of her as he broke open a biscuit and filled it with crisp bacon. The look of appreciation on his face warmed her heart. It felt good to see a man enjoy her cooking. After he'd finished half a dozen, he glanced up at her. "Much better than mine."

"Thank you." She twisted her fingers together. "Mr. Lansing, I've been thinking about Joshua. Until we can find a good home for him, I would like to keep him with me." Although it may mean postponing her dream of travel and excitement, Mercy realized the infant deserved a home with the love and the attention she could give him.

He nodded. "What will your family say?"

A lot, if she knew them. But her father would never turn out an innocent child. "I can deal with them. There's always a chance I may be lucky enough to find a young couple who wants a baby."

A frown tugged at his lips. For the first time, she noticed that he had shaved and changed into a clean blue work shirt. In spite of the scar on his cheek, Pace was the handsomest man she'd ever known. "If you do, I want the right to approve or reject them."

"Yes, I understand. After all, you found Naomi and saved Joshua's life."

"I couldn't have done it without you."

"Next time we'll let the doctor handle the deliveries."

"Or the stork."

She wouldn't have imagined he had a sense of humor. For a short few minutes he had dropped his hard, austere facade and shown the real man who was struggling to find his way back from the depths of perdition. If only she could help. But it was up to Pace to work through his past and forge a future for himself.

"We had best get on the road to town. My family will be looking for me." She took the baby from Pace. After she changed his diaper, she wrapped him in clean cloths. "That should keep you clean and warm, little fellow," she said.

When she looked up, her gaze locked with Pace's. His eyes held such a longing her heart ached at the sight. She clutched the baby to her chest to keep from reaching to smooth the creases between Pace's eyes.

"You're right. We'd better head for town."

Mercy tucked Joshua under her cape to protect him from the wind and sun. They'd hoped to get to town early enough to avoid the many farmers and ranchers who made their weekly trek on Saturday morning. But the wagon needed repair, and the horses rebelled at being hitched to the traces. She was certain it was well past eight o'clock when they left the cabin.

The sky was a bright clear blue, and the grass bowed and swayed in the wind. More wildflowers had begun to bloom, and soon the prairie would be alive with color. The horses trudged along the rutted road, each step bringing her and Pace closer to the time that they would part. In spite of the sadness of the night, she'd never been so exhilarated in her life. She cradled the sleeping baby to her breast. Strange how the minister's daughter and Pace Lansing, the most notorious man in Pleasant Valley, had brought a new life into the world. She almost hated to return to her ordinary, dull life.

Three or four wagons passed them on the road to town. She recognized the people who attended the church, and others who shopped at Fullenwider's Mercantile. They stared at her so hard, she wondered if she'd grown two heads.

With every revolution of the wheels, Pace grew more and more pensive. He hadn't muttered a word since they'd crossed the boundaries of his land. Mercy, too, drifted off into her own thoughts. She dreaded having to face her sisters.

They were about a mile from town when a cloud of dust announced approaching riders. Fear clutched at Mercy's heart at the sight of a half-dozen armed men. She prayed they weren't outlaws out for death and destruction. As they drew closer, Pace pulled his gun from the holster and set it on the seat between them. He tugged the reins and the wagon slowed to a crawl.

In a flurry of shouts and dust, the horsemen skid to a stop. Mercy sagged with relief when she recognized Sheriff Jennings. With him were other men she'd known all her life. She started to call out a greeting when the sheriff leveled his shotgun at them. Pace closed his fingers on his Colt.

"Don't even try, Lansing," the sheriff sneered.

Mercy covered Pace's hand with hers. "Sheriff, what's wrong?"

Jennings ignored her and gestured with the gun. "You're under arrest. Lift your hands where I can see them."

"What for?" Pace grunted between his teeth. Slowly, his hands rose above his head.

Before the sheriff answered, Mercy's father pushed his horse through the milling crowd. "Daughter, are you all right? Did he hurt you?"

Pace glared at the posse. His face was a mask of fury and his eyes flashed murder. If looks could kill, her father would have more business than the undertaking parlor could hold.

"Father, what's the meaning of this? Why are you here? Why does the sheriff want to arrest Mr. Lansing?"

"Let's string him up right now." Jake Sackett, who ran the livery stable, waved a rope at Pace. "We should have done it five years ago."

Mercy's heart plunged to her feet. "What's the matter with you? Have you all gone mad?"

"You won't get away with this, Lansing," her father called.

That was the moment Joshua chose to make his presence known. The baby let out a loud scream. Three of the horsemen jerked back. Mercy shoved her cloak aside and jiggled the baby to stop his crying. "Look what you've done. Now you've wakened the baby."

If it was possible for grown men to faint dead away, all six would have tumbled right off their horses to the ground.

"Mercy, whose baby is that? What are you doing with that man?" Her father was first to recover his composure.

"Tie him up, Sheriff, before he gets away," Otis Kennedy called from the back of the posse, safely away from Pace.

Pace's body was rigid, and anger radiated from him like heat from an inferno. Any second he was going to explode like a spewing volcano, and after that, Lord help them all. Mercy couldn't let that happen.

She dropped her hand and snatched up the gun. Until that moment, she had no idea how a gun even felt in her hands. It weighed more than the iron poker she used to stoke the fire. "Nobody's taking him anywhere," she said, the gun pointed at the posse.

Pace dropped his gaze to the gun, and for an instant, she thought he was going to snatch it from her fingers. She was shaking so badly, it wouldn't take much effort.

Ezra stared at Mercy as if he'd never seen her before. Actually, he'd never seen her display so much passion or guts. "Mercy, put that gun down. You don't know how to use it. Somebody could get hurt."

"Then if I pull the trigger, no telling who I'll hit—you, or your horse."

"Miss Goodacre." The sheriff was the only one who hadn't turned ashen at the sight of the gun in her hand. "Let's talk this over. If you'll explain what's going on, we can all get back to our business."

"First you tell me why you're attacking us with rifles and shotguns? Why do you want to arrest us? We haven't done anything wrong."

"He kidnapped you," Otis shouted.

It was Mercy's turn to be shocked. In her arm Joshua started screaming at the top of his tiny lungs, and in her hand, the gun was weaving back and forth. "He did no such thing."

Pace snatched the gun from her fingers. "Your pa's right, Miss Goodacre. Somebody could get hurt." He shoved the gun into the holster. "As you can see, Miss Goodacre is fine. But that baby won't be unless we get him some milk." He pointed to the back of the wagon and the sheet-covered form. "Neither will his ma if we don't bury her soon."

"Mercy, what in heaven's name is going on here?" Her father took a chance and edged closer to the wagon. He studied the covered body in the bed of the wagon. His face paled as he recognized the shape of a body.

"Papa, I can explain everything. Mr. Lansing can take me to our house, then you can go with him to the undertaking parlor."

The sheriff dropped his shotgun. "Reverend, looks like you ran us all over creation on a wild-goose chase. Don't look like your girl did anything but get herself a baby and a man. I don't rightly approve, but she's your problem."

Sheriff Jennings tugged his horse into step beside Pace.

"Lansing, after you finish with the reverend, I want to see you in my office and get this whole mess straightened out."

Pace nodded and shook the reins to urge the horses to a trot.

After one long, curious look at Mercy and Pace, the men turned their horses and raced back to town. Their relief was evident. It was clear no one had a stomach for a gunfight with the notorious Pace Lansing.

Six

Mercy dreaded facing her sisters, not to mention the other ladies in town. Without meaning to, she'd broken more of their rules of proper social conduct. As she'd expected, not only were Charity and Prudence waiting at the parsonage, but Charity's mother-in-law, Mrs. Fullenwider, as well as most of the Ladies Circle. Being Saturday, they were all in town for the day.

And they'd found more excitement than Pleasant Valley had seen in a month of Sundays.

The frown of Pace's face deepened. "I feel sorry for you, Miss Goodacre," he said between his teeth. "Looks like those men didn't waste any time spreading gossip about us."

"In addition to their speculation about Joshua and Naomi." Thankfully, the baby had again fallen asleep.

"It's my fault you're in this mess. You don't deserve to be treated like this."

"I can handle them. I've done it all my life."

The instant Pace drew up in front of the low picket fence, the entire group of curious women swarmed on the wagon like cackling hens after a handful of feed.

They cast scathing glances at Pace, while struggling to get a glimpse of the baby who was tightly wrapped in Mercy's cloak. Her father dismounted and held his hands up to silence the women. "Ladies, please. We know you've been praying for my daughter's safety, and we appreciate your concern. But as you can see, she's safely home, and quite tired. You can get back to your families and business. Thank you for caring and keeping my other daughters company. I will see you in church tomorrow morning."

Not at all happy with their minister's decree, one by one they offered condolences to Mercy and walked slowly away. Charity's mother-in-law was last to leave. The woman's forbidding expression spoke louder than words. She tilted her nose in the air and gathered with the other women at the corner of the fence.

Mercy didn't know how her sister put up with being related to the harpy. As the mayor's wife, Henrietta Fullenwider not only had set herself up as the social leader of town, but also ran the local newspaper. Mercy had given the woman enough gossip to keep her hand press humming for weeks.

With an effort, Mercy tore her gaze from the women, and glanced at her father. During the slow ride into town, she'd explained the situation to him. Although he scolded her for going unchaperoned to the cabin with Pace, he'd reluctantly agreed she'd done the right thing. As a favor to her, he was willing to conduct the funeral for Naomi.

That settled, Mercy now had to deal with her sisters.

While the women dispersed, Charity and Prudence moved to the porch. Arms folded across their chests like avenging angels guarding the portals of heaven, they waited. But unlike angels, they seemed determined to keep Mercy out.

Before she caught her father's hand to step down from the wagon, Pace touched her arm. "Take care of Joshua. As soon as I finish with your father and the sheriff, I'll come back to check on both of you." He cocked his head toward the women waiting on the porch. "Good luck with them."

She nodded. "I'm going to need more than luck."

Her father helped her to the ground, then climbed up beside Pace. "I'll be back after a bit, daughter," he said. "And I'll be ready for my breakfast."

While off with Pace, she'd unwittingly forgotten about her father and his needs. And had broken another of his commandments—to have his meals on the table at precisely 7 A.M., 12 noon, and 6 o'clock in the evening. Ezra didn't know a skillet from a kettle, and could barely refill his own coffee cup. That was another transgression her sisters were sure to remind her of.

Right on cue, Joshua started crying. She hastened her steps. A grown man like Ezra Goodacre had the ability to fend for himself if he would only try. Joshua couldn't. The infant needed her.

And, she admitted to herself, she needed him. Until now, her maternal leanings had been directed to her sisters and nephew; now she had a baby of her own. Even if Joshua wasn't of her own flesh, she was determined to care for him and love him as if she'd given birth to him. She hugged the baby closer and promised in her heart to be his mother in every way that counted.

Thankfully, her sisters waited until the front door had closed behind them before they fell into their tirade.

Charity managed to get in the first word. "What do you mean spending the night with a man like that? And coming home with Pace Lansing's bastard. The entire town is in an uproar."

Heat rushed to Mercy's face. She'd known about bigotry and prejudice—all small towns had it—but this was the first time they'd aimed it at her personally. She felt just a smidgen of what Miss Lily, her girls, and even Pace faced every day of their lives.

Mercy lifted Joshua to her shoulder to quiet him. "First of all, he isn't Pace Lansing's child. His mother was an Indian woman Pace found in the bush. And second, will you please hold your disapproval and condemnation until later. Joshua is hungry. I have to change him and find a way to feed him."

Prudy narrowed her gaze on Mercy. This was abnormally early for her to be up and about on a Saturday morning, or any morning except Sunday. In deference to their father she somehow managed to show up at church not more than ten minutes late. Her hair hung in curls around her face, and she wore a simple lawn frock printed with purple flowers.

"An Indian? Are you going to be a nursemaid to an Indian's baby? How are you going to feed him?" she demanded.

"The same way Charity fed Timmy when her milk dried up. With a nursing bottle." Marching past her sisters, she laid the screaming infant on the davenport. "Charity, go tear a sheet into squares so I can change his diaper. And when you get home, gather up the clothes Timmy has outgrown."

Charity stomped her foot. "I will not help you with that . . . that man's baby."

Lips set in a determined line, Mercy stared at her sister. "Then I won't help you with Timmy." She didn't know why she'd make what was certainly an idle threat. There was nothing Mercy wouldn't do for her sister and the nephew she adored.

"Oh." Charity hesitated a second, then raced up the stairs to the linen closet.

Mercy looked up at Prudence. "Get the milk out of the well, and put it in a pot to heat. Then run over to the mercantile and get a nursing bottle from Tim."

"I'm not your servant, Mercy Goodacre. And I will not run anywhere." Prudy flopped onto the davenport to emphasize her disapproval.

Mercy gritted her teeth, not at all surprised that Prudy refused to lift a finger. As the youngest sister, they'd all spoiled the beautiful girl until she was virtually worthless.

When someone knocked on the front door, she looked up at Prudy. "At least answer the door."

"It's that woman and her maid," Prudy called as she peeked through the lace curtain.

"Then let them in." Mercy snatched the torn sheet from Charity's hands and carefully wiped the baby clean. He stuck his tiny fist in his mouth, and when he discovered nothing there, he squalled louder. His face turned purple with rage.

Prudy stepped back as Miss Lily swept into the room with Cora trailing close behind. Each woman carried a large woven basket.

"We heard you were bringing home an infant, Mercy. And we thought you may need a few things." Miss Lily ignored Prudy and smiled down at the baby. "What a handsome young man."

Mercy looked up. "I don't know how you can tell, with the way he has his face all squinched up. His mother died, and I've got to find a way to feed him." She jiggled the baby, and his cries dropped to a pitiful whimper.

"That's why we're here. Cora went to the mercantile and purchased a few things we thought you would need— clothes, blankets, a nursing bottle, and cans of Borden's milk." She took a large basket from her maid's hands. "Heat up some milk, Cora. Mix it with a little water and syrup. This little fellow is starving."

The maid grinned. "Yes, ma'am. I'll have it directly."

Emotion welled up in Mercy's heart. Friends had come to her aid without question while her own family refused to help a tiny, defenseless baby. "Thank you, Miss Lily. I'll pay you back."

"Oh, fiddle. You'll do no such thing. It's just a little gift for the newest citizen of our town." She winked and reached out a finger to Joshua. He took the soft manicured finger and tried to pull it into his mouth. "And everybody knows how much I appreciate men."

Mercy giggled, while her sisters scowled from across the room. Prudy settled on the rocker, and Charity stood behind her.

Miss Lily ignored the women who obviously didn't want her there. "Now, Mercy, let's get a gown on this little fellow, and you can tell me why everybody is going around saying that Pace kidnapped you."

The way Miss Lily smiled, Mercy didn't at all object to explaining the entire situation to her friend. Miss Lily would never criticize anybody. She'd been the recipient of more than her share of reproach from the "good ladies" of Pleasant Valley.

"Pace found a dying Indian woman in the bush. When he realized she was in labor, he came to town for help." She slipped a soft white gown over Joshua's head. He protested the clothes and yelled louder. "Doctor Lewis wasn't in, so he came and got me. Believe me, I went with him of my own free will." She shot a meaningful glance at her sisters. Their grim expressions hadn't changed one iota. A sudden thought struck her. "How did everybody know I went off with Pace? What made them come looking for us?"

Miss Lily slanted a glance at Prudy. "Your brother-in-law claimed he saw Pace when he was leaving the bank last night. He thought the woman with him looked like you."

The bank? Mercy was certain she'd seen Clifford leaving the Ruby Slipper. "I didn't see him," she lied. It wouldn't do to plant suspicion in Prudy's naive mind.

To her relief, Cora returned with a glass bottle filled with milk. The instant she brushed the rubber nipple against Joshua's lips, he opened his mouth and sucked like a greedy little calf.

"We were lucky to save Joshua, but his mother was too weak from hunger and neglect." Her voice dropped to a soft, reverent whisper. "I asked Papa to give her a decent burial."

Charity gasped. "He can't bury an Indian in our cemetery."

Mercy had taken about all she could stand from her sisters. "Why not? Her people were here long before ours. It would be wrong to deny an innocent woman a burial because of some stupid prejudice."

"It's just wrong, that's all."

She turned her attention back to the baby. Her father was the minister. Let him handle his own business. She prayed that Pace would be able to control his temper in the face of the town's intolerance. He hadn't wanted to come into town, and had only done so at Mercy's insistence. Now he was the one to be subjected to the bigotry of the narrow-minded people.

Within minutes the bottle was empty. His stomach full and his bottom clean, Joshua fell fast asleep. "I'd best put him down and get my father something to eat. He should be back soon, and I wasn't here this morning to get his breakfast."

Cora stood over them, a wide grin on her face. Her golden eyes sparkled. "No need to bother, Miss Mercy. I brought a basket full of food. The reverend won't go hungry."

Tears burned at the back of Mercy's eyes. "How can I ever thank you? And I haven't even finished with Florrie's dress."

"You can thank us by taking good care of that little boy. And I'll tell Florrie to wear something else tonight." Miss Lily brushed another finger across the baby's fuzzy scalp. "You be sure to bring this little man along when you come for the Bible study on Monday. The girls will spoil him rotten."

"Yes, ma'am." She held Joshua to her shoulder. The baby let out a loud burp and returned to sleep. "The sign of a satisfied male."

Covering her mouth to conceal a grin, Miss Lily exchanged glances with Cora as they strolled toward the door.

"Miss Mercy sure don't know anything about men, does she?" came Cora's softly accented voice from the porch.

Miss Lily laughed softly. "Not a bit."

The hairs on the back of Pace's neck prickled. They were watching him. From the instant he'd ridden into town, all gazes were on him. After five years of having armed guards constantly staring at his every move, he should have been used to it. That was only one of the things he hated about coming to town. He felt as much a prisoner here as in the penitentiary.

So far he'd managed to keep his temper under control. He'd been tempted to bash a few heads when a couple of the men spit on the ground as he drove past. It wasn't the reverend seated beside him that kept him calm, but the memory of Mercy with Joshua. He wouldn't be any help to them if he landed in jail. After finally gaining his freedom, he would die if he had to go back behind bars again.

The gossip was flying. He could see them whispering behind gloved hands. None were actually bold enough to say anything to his face. Inside the mortuary that the preacher ran from his woodworking shop, a deep sadness overtook Pace. Dutifully, he helped saw the pine boards, and nail them into a box. All the while he remembered his mother's death.

The Lansings had always been considered outcasts—as much because of his rebellious behavior as having an Indian mother. Abner Lansing was known as a drunk and bully, so he was never welcome in town. Without money for a proper funeral, Pace buried Dancing Brook himself. He'd made a box out of scrap lumber and buried her on a knoll above the house. The few prayers he'd learned as a child served as her funeral.

He wanted better for Naomi.

"I'll pay for the funeral, Reverend, as soon as I sell my cattle this fall. I'd appreciate you extending credit until then."

The minister looked up after they'd laid the woman's body in the box. His expression was as solemn as any undertaker's. "She was too young to die. Just like my Faith. We lost her in childbirth, too, only my son didn't survive."

"I'm sorry."

Reverend Goodacre nailed the lid on the box. "There won't be any charge. I often do this in memory of my wife."

Pace hated to take charity, but by the expression on the minister's face, it wouldn't do to argue. He suspected the man was as stubborn as his daughter about his good deeds.

"I'll make the arrangements and we'll bury her at noon," the preacher said.

"Thank you, Reverend. I'll meet you back here after I speak to the sheriff."

"Sorry about the misunderstanding, Lansing, but I'm sure you can appreciate my concern when my daughter was missing." He rolled down his sleeves and shrugged into his black jacket. "I would like to have a word with you in private. Later, we may not have a chance to talk man to man."

The minister stood before Pace, stretching to his full height that barely passed Pace's chin. But the man had a presence that made him look twelve feet tall. "Yes, sir?"

He rubbed his jaw as if searching for the right words. It wasn't hard to figure out what Reverend Goodacre wanted to say. *Stay away from my daughter,* came to mind. Along with, *You aren't welcome in Pleasant Valley.*

"I want to talk to you about Mercy." He shoved his spectacles up his nose. It was amazing how much Mercy resembled her father, only in a soft, feminine way.

"Sir, I want to assure you that your daughter was entirely

safe with me. Nothing untoward happened, and her virtue is intact."

Staring straight into Pace's eyes, the man seemed to be searching for the truth. "Yes, I believe you, but I'm afraid that you've started gossip that will be very difficult to stop. All they know is that Mercy rode off with you, and that she returned this morning with a baby in her arms. They will surely figure that it can't be hers, but it could be yours."

Pace felt the old familiar heat rise in his chest. "The baby can't be mine. Simple numbers will tell them I was in prison when he was conceived."

"I'm aware of that. But that doesn't negate the fact that Mercy spent the night alone with you in an isolated cabin. Her reputation is at stake."

And yours. Somehow Pace managed to bite back the words. "Reverend, I'm sorry about that. But it was a matter of life or death. We were grateful to be able to save the baby."

"Mr. Lansing, I'll do my best to find a good home for the child. However, I am going to ask you to stay away from my daughter. She's an innocent young woman, and she isn't used to dealing with men."

He gritted his teeth and curled his hands into fists to keep from hitting something. "Men like me, you mean." Clearly Mercy hadn't mentioned their agreement to her father. Perhaps she'd already changed her mind about their partnership.

"Yes. She's led a rather sheltered life, and she sees nothing but good in people."

"Believe me, Reverend, I have no intention of doing anything to cause Miss Mercy any distress."

"Good, I'm glad you see it my way."

"Yes, sir. But I feel a responsibility to the baby. I would like to visit with Joshua from time to time."

"I'm sure that can be arranged. Until he moves into

another good home, I'll see that you have ample time to see the child."

That was more than he'd hoped for. But far less than he wanted. Somehow the thought of not seeing Mercy cut a path clear to the center of his chest. He cursed his own needs. The woman was a meddling female who didn't know her place. He should be glad to be rid of her. Her father was just echoing his own sentiments. But hearing the censure in his voice burned like a hot poker in Pace's gut.

Nobody had to remind Pace that he wasn't good enough for her or any of the town women. He'd told himself the same thing for years. Mercy Goodacre was the minister's daughter, an innocent if he'd ever seen one.

"Yes, sir. After the funeral, I won't see her again."

With the baby tucked in a blanket-lined basket, Mercy entered the cemetery behind the church. Pace dropped a shovel of dirt on the ground near a hole in a far corner, away from the other plots. Her heart skipped a beat. He looked so lonely and sad. So alone.

Her father at her side, she approached slowly. When Pace spotted them, he tossed the shovel aside and wiped his hands on the legs of his mud-stained denims.

"Reckon it's ready, Reverend," he said. His gaze shifted from the hole in the ground to the baby in the basket. "How's Josh?"

"Dr. Lewis examined him. He said we did a good job, and the baby is strong and healthy. He did tell me that it isn't good for a newborn to be outdoors, but Joshua was already a seasoned traveler. I thought it was important that we bring him to his mother's burial."

Her father checked the hole, then nodded. "Let's begin." Opening his Bible, he moved to the plain wooden box.

Side by side, Mercy and Pace stood near the open grave. As Mercy shifted the basket on her arm, her crocheted shawl slipped from her shoulders. In a flash of movement, Pace caught the soft garment and returned it to her shoulders. His strong fingers lingered for a moment. Flutters settled in the pit of her stomach. Then, just as quickly he dropped his hands and stood ramrod straight. He took off his hat and twisted it in his fingers.

They had to be an odd sight, Mercy thought. The day seemed normal enough. Sunlight filtered through the leaves above them. In the distance the rattle of wagons and pounding of hoofbeats signaled a normal Saturday in Pleasant Valley. Tim was serving his customers, and Clifford running his bank. She was almost sure Prudy had taken to her bed with a headache. But for Mercy, the day was anything but normal. This was the strangest day in her life. Her gaze shifted to the man at her side.

Only two mourners, three counting Joshua, had come to pay their respects to the deceased woman. The curious stared from outside the fence. While eating his breakfast, her father had complained that he'd had to fight a couple of the deacons to allow the Indian to be buried in the cemetery. In the long run, he'd won the argument. However, the usual caretaker refused to dig the grave. It had been left to Pace to provide a place for Naomi to rest. Mercy swiped the tears from her eyes.

"Ashes to ashes, dust to dust." Ezra's solemn voice brought Mercy back to the sad occasion.

She'd heard the ceremony many times and could repeat the prayers from memory. Except for her mother's death, no other had touched her so deeply. In spite of his austere exterior, she suspected that Pace was equally moved.

When Joshua started to wiggle, Pace reached out a hand. "It's okay, boy," he whispered, rocking the basket from side to side.

Before long, the ceremony ended and Ezra signaled to

Pace. Together they gripped the ropes and lowered the casket into the ground. By the time they'd finished, tears flowed freely down Mercy's cheeks.

Ezra said a final prayer, and turned to leave. He took Mercy by the arm and left Pace to cover the coffin. She glanced back over her shoulder. "Please come to the house when you finish, Mr. Lansing."

Pace shifted his gaze to her father, as if seeking approval. "For a few minutes. Then I have to get back to the ranch."

A new emotion settled in her chest. She suspected that after today, she would see little of Pace if anything at all. It shouldn't bother her, but it did.

Pace washed the sweat and dirt from his face and arms in the trough at the rear of the church. By the time he'd patted the last shovel of dirt on the grave, the spectators had dispersed. It was hell being the object of disdain and curiosity, but by now he'd gotten used to it. He hated subjecting Mercy Goodacre to the meddlesome people who were supposed to be her friends. As long as he stayed away from her, she would soon live down the blot on her reputation.

To get to the preacher's house, he chose the long way around. He followed the path through the woods that ran behind the alleys and away from the houses. He'd already caused enough trouble for an innocent woman.

In addition to wanting to see Joshua, he had unfinished business with Mercy. They needed to sign an agreement to seal their partnership. Pace hated to depend on anyone, but since he'd already accepted the supplies, she needed a paper to protect her interests.

A band tightened in his stomach as he approached the parsonage. He tied off the horse at the back fence and strolled up the garden path to the house. The newly tilled soil smelled of manure and earth. A hen dashed from under the porch and clucked at the intrusion. Pausing for a minute, he studied the place the reverend had provided for his family. It was quite a contrast from the one Amos Lansing had built.

The two-storied house sported a fresh coat of paint, and the shutters were a shiny green. Smoke curled from the chimney.

Neat flower beds bordered the porch, and a climbing vine curled its way clear to the roof. In a few months, tomatoes, peppers, and other vegetables would probably ripen in the garden. If he knew anything about Mercy, rows of flowers would be intertwined with the food.

He couldn't stop the grin that broke across his face. Sunflowers. She would plant the huge yellow flowers that followed the progress of the sun. They grew wild on his pastures, and he always looked forward to the summer when they brightened even the gloomiest day. The memory of sunflowers had kept him sane during his dark years in a filthy cell.

Shaking his head to clear away the dismal thoughts, he hurried to the porch. He knocked on the door and slapped the dust from his hat.

The door swung open to reveal the minister standing on the threshold. "Come in, Lansing. Mercy and the baby are in the parlor."

"Thank you, sir," he said, carefully wiping his boots on a small rug.

In the middle of the kitchen, the table was set with plates, cups, and several covered dishes. His mouth watered at the smell of fresh bread and strawberry jam. He hadn't had either in so long, he could barely remember the taste.

Mercy sat on the rocker with Joshua nestled against her bosom. The minister took the seat at a rolltop desk, leaving Pace standing in the middle of the parlor.

She smiled at him, and all the gloom and sadness of the

day flew away like dry leaves in the wind. "Would you like to finish feeding Joshua while I pour the coffee?"

"I can't," he began when she rose and shoved the baby in his arms.

"Of course you can. It's quite simple. Just hold the bottle so the nipple is full at all times. When he finishes, lift him to your shoulder and let him burp."

"What if I hurt him?" The baby weighed next to nothing, and Pace felt big and awkward. Josh's little legs and arms were no bigger around than a man's fingers.

She shoved him toward the rocker, and arranged baby, blanket, and bottle in his hand. Her touch was gentle, her hands like silk against the roughness of his skin. A spark, much like lightning, flashed between them. His stomach tightened. He'd already spent too much time with this woman, and with this baby. If he had a lick of horse sense, he'd hightail it back to his ranch as fast as the wagon would carry him. Some long-forgotten emotion had him rooted to the spot. Pink colored her cheeks, and she jerked back her hands as if she'd been singed.

"I'll call you when the coffee is ready," she said, her voice slightly breathless.

For his part, his throat was so tight, he couldn't utter a sound.

Left alone with the preacher, Pace concentrated on the baby in his arms. For the briefest of instants, he wished Joshua was his son, that this was his home, that Mercy . . . He forced the wayward thought away. It wouldn't do either of them any good to let his imagination run wild. These were dreams he should never entertain for even an instant.

Reverend Goodacre turned to his desk and began to write. Pace watched the baby suckle, his cheeks bulging like a chipmunk. His blue eyes were wide open and his little arms flailed in the air. Joshua clearly didn't understand why he was wrapped in so many clothes. A little ruffled cap covered his head, a long gown covered his legs, and overall, he was wrapped in a blanket. Pace was tempted to remove it all and let the baby enjoy the freedom of the fresh air.

"Is he done?" Mercy asked.

Pace started. He hadn't heard her enter and was surprised to hear her voice. "I think so."

Hoisting the baby to her shoulder, she gently patted his back. After he burped, she lay him in the quilt-lined basket. "We can set him on the table so we can watch him while we eat."

"Eat? I didn't expect you to prepare dinner for me," he said. In spite of his words, his stomach growled with hunger. The aromas coming from the kitchen made his mouth water.

With the basket in her hand, Mercy led the way to the kitchen. "Father, would you like to join us?"

The minister glanced up from his desk. "I'm not hungry. I'll get something later."

Pace was slightly surprised that the preacher allowed his daughter to be alone with a notorious criminal. Mercy set the basket on the table and placed a plate of sliced ham, applesauce, and rolls in front of him. She opened jars of strawberry jam and apple butter and filled a cup with fresh coffee. His mouth watered at the sight. The last time he'd eaten food like this had been at an Independence Day picnic six years ago. Everybody in town had been invited, and he'd stuffed himself until he couldn't walk.

She settled on the chair opposite him and bowed her head. He followed suit. He'd never prayed before a meal either. When she whispered, "Amen," he lifted his gaze.

For a long moment he stared at the food in front of him. He was torn between shoveling down the food as fast as possible before it was snatched away, and hoarding it for later. Years in prison had ruined what few table manners he'd ever had.

"I'm sorry that's all we have ready, Mr. Lansing. Cora

and Miss Lily brought the ham and rolls over this morning. If I'd had time, I could have prepared a much nicer meal."

He'd never seen a nicer meal. "It looks wonderful, Miss Goodacre."

"Then eat up. There's plenty more on the stove."

"Thank you, ma'am."

Following Mercy's lead, he spread the linen napkin on his lap and quietly sipped his coffee. Pace forced himself to use the fork and knife, instead of his fingers, to eat slowly and savor every bite. When the plate was empty, she didn't hesitate to refill it. Only when he couldn't hold another bite did he hold up his hands to stop her. The platter was empty, the rolls were gone, and the jars of preserves were empty.

"That was delicious, Miss Goodacre. I don't believe I've ever had better."

A flush colored her cheeks, making her look young and pretty. "I've prepared a basket for your supper."

"You didn't have to do that. You've given me enough already."

"I haven't given you anything. You need to eat well to keep up your strength. You have to work that ranch and make a profit on the cattle." She smiled and his heart slammed against his chest.

"That reminds me. I think we should sign an agreement. Something to protect your investment."

Surprise glittered in her eyes. "I don't need a paper. I trust you."

"Your brother-in-law would advise you to get everything in writing."

"I haven't told Clifford or anyone else. This is strictly between you and me. And I want to keep it that way."

"I would feel better. Can you get a sheet of paper and a pen?"

"Certainly."

Together they formed the words of the agreement. In

exchange for providing the supplies, she would receive a share of the profits from the cattle.

"How much?" he asked.

"Half."

"Half?" He swallowed hard. And she said she hadn't talked to Blakely.

"All right," she said. "Forty percent."

"Twenty."

"A third."

"One fourth. That's top dollar."

She stuck out her hand. "Deal."

While she filled in the amount, he breathed a sigh of relief. He'd expected her to demand at least a third. The bank would. Clearly she hadn't discussed it with her brother-in-law.

As he signed his name under hers, she grinned like a cat who'd caught a fat mouse. "Excellent, Mr. Lansing. I thought you would insist on no more than a tenth. I've struck a real bargain."

Seven

Joshua's basket in one hand and a carpetbag containing the mended garments in the other, Mercy trudged down the dusty street toward the Ruby Slipper. She yawned, wishing she could spend the afternoon in bed instead of teaching the Bible study.

Overall, the baby was good, but at two weeks old, he demanded food every three hours, day and night. With the added responsibilities of Joshua, and trying to keep up with her other duties, Mercy found herself tired most of the time. Her sisters had become more demanding than ever, and her father refused to lift a hand to help.

Slowly, she climbed the rear stairs to the living quarters above the saloon. Nobody paid much attention to her controversial mission. The deacons and church leaders had reluctantly agreed to allow the Bible study. That was only because it kept the scarlet women from soiling their pure sanctuary.

Mercy often wondered how many of the sanctimonious deacons spent their Saturday nights enjoying the favors of these same women, then bowed their heads the following morning.

Not that anybody could have stopped Mercy from her mission. She liked Miss Lily, Cora, and the other women who came and went at the Ruby Slipper. In a way, she was as much an outsider as they. Most women her age had husbands and families. Miss Lily had made these girls her family, and she'd generously included Mercy into her inner circle.

More than once she'd heard men whisper that Miss Lily ran one of the best establishments in Kansas. To work for her, she required her girls have regular medical examinations, and adhere to a strict hygienic program. She also demanded that they attend the weekly Bible study. This outing was often the highlight of Mercy's week.

Although Rosie and Florrie were younger than Mercy, in experience they were years older. They often shared humorous stories about their adventures and customers—always being careful not to mention names. Miss Lily would have their hides if they carried tales out of school.

She shoved open the door and entered the narrow hallway. The door to Miss Lily's private apartment was ajar. Mercy called out before stepping into the sitting room. No one answered, and the only sound was Joshua's cooing. She set his basket on the red velvet davenport.

Mercy loved teaching the Bible study, as much for the luxurious surroundings as for the religious aspects. The fringed lampshades, the gold flocked wallpaper, the satin drapes looked more like a salon in Paris or New York than a saloon in the dusty Kansas town.

Opening the carpetbag, she tugged out the gowns she'd spent the past night mending. She shook out the gold gown and studied the tiny stitches in the side. "Isn't this beautiful, Joshua?" she asked, grinning at the baby.

He stared up at her and shoved his fist into his mouth. Clearly this male was unimpressed. Just as Pace was unimpressed with Mercy. Since he'd left town after signing the papers for their partnership, she hadn't seen hide nor hair of the man. Every time she heard a noise at the rear door, she looked for Pace. He was constantly on her mind, and truth be told, in her heart.

On a long sigh, she sank to the brocade chaise lounge. "Would he notice me if I wore a dress like this one?"

Joshua cooed louder, as if agreeing with her statement.

Mercy glanced around to make sure she was alone. The bar was open, but the real action didn't begin until after five o'clock, leaving Miss Lily time to do her paperwork, and the other girls a chance to rest.

Her gaze dropped to the gown. Florrie was about Mercy's size, and when the other woman wore the gown, the men couldn't take their gazes off her. Would Pace notice Mercy if she wore the gold gown?

Shoving the door closed, Mercy hurriedly tore open the buttons of her blouse and slipped out of her skirt. The muslin petticoats fell to the floor in a heap. Clad only in her corset and chemise, she stepped into the slender garment. She stuck her arms through the narrow straps that held the front from sagging clear to her waist.

In front of the mirror, she studied her image. Beaded with gold and black bangles, the gown was all wrong for Mercy. Several inches of white camisole showed above the bosom and the split up the side showed more leg than a decent woman would allow. Tears burned behind her eyes. She looked like a poor duck pretending to be a swan.

"Miss Mercy, what are you doing?"

She spun around and faced both Florrie and Rosie grinning from the doorway. Each woman wore a thin wrapper over a loose chemise. Florrie's red hair was tousled from sleep, but her green eyes sparkled with humor.

"I'm sorry," Mercy said, wishing the floor would open up and swallow her alive. Never had she felt such a fool.

Rosie moved into the room. "With just a little help, you'd look a sight better than Florrie in the gown."

The other woman laughed. "We'll see about that."

Before Mercy could move, both women swarmed over her. Rosie grabbed her braids and within seconds had the long hair flowing down her back. "Stop," Mercy protested. "I'll give back the gown."

Florrie reached for her camisole, and tugged it over her head. "What in the world is this?" She ran a finger under the bindings covering Mercy's bosom.

A tear crept down Mercy's cheek. "Stop. They're too large and embarrassing."

Both Florrie and Rosie stopped to stare. "Honey, you're going to hurt yourself," said Rosie. In an instant, the woman grabbed a pair of scissors from a low rosewood table and slashed through the rags.

Humiliated at the size of her breasts, Mercy tried to cover them with her hands. As she struggled with the two dance hall women, the door flung open.

"What is going on in here?" Miss Lily planted her hands firmly on her hips. "Rosie? Florrie? Mercy?" In a flounce of a flowing silk tea gown, she entered the room. Cora followed, carrying a tray containing a teapot and cups.

"We just wanted to see how Miss Mercy looked all dressed up in something besides those gray and brown things she always wears. Doesn't she look beautiful?"

Struggling to cover her bosom with the gold gown, Mercy dropped her gaze to her feet. "I'm so sorry. I didn't mean any harm."

Miss Lily crooked a finger under Mercy's chin. She studied Mercy like a piece of goods for a new gown. "Stand up straight," she ordered.

Afraid to do otherwise, Mercy straightened her shoulders. To her surprise, the gown didn't slip and fall. Miss Lily, Cora, and the other two women converged on Mercy at once. They pulled and yanked, they brushed her hair, and shoved something into her scalp.

"She has beautiful hair," said Rosie, "though you wouldn't know it by the way she wears it twisted into those awful braids."

"And this figure. It's a crime to hide it under those awful rags."

Mercy didn't dare move or protest. She blinked back tears. Why were they trying so hard to embarrass her like this? Not even her sisters had ever seen her so unclothed. Her awful big bosoms were barely covered by the fabric, and her corset cut off her breath.

Just when she thought she couldn't bear the humiliation another second, Miss Lily held up her hands. "Excellent. See what you think, Mercy?" Tugging her by the hands, the two dance hall girls placed her in front of the cheval mirror.

Too ashamed to lift her gaze, she covered her face with her hands. Gently, Cora tugged at her wrists. "You look beautiful."

Taking a deep breath, she lifted her gaze. At first glance, she didn't recognize the woman staring back at her in the glass. Long brown hair flowed like a dark veil, and a single lock curled over one breast. She stretched out a hand to make sure it wasn't some kind of trick mirror. This couldn't be Mercy Goodacre. Pink cheeks and shiny eyes stared back at her. In the glass she spied the faces of the four women standing behind her. Their wide appreciative smiles gave her courage to lower her gaze.

The hated oversized bosoms swelled above the low neckline like fine porcelain globes. Her waist was nipped in as neatly as her sister's, and with the slightest movement one long leg showed through the slit in the skirt of the gown.

Her fingers touched the mirror, just to make sure she wasn't mistaken. It really was her. And she was rather comely. "I look rather nice," she whispered.

The four women laughed. "Nice?" Miss Lily asked. "My dear, I could make a fortune off your looks. Innocent and alluring, the men would be eating out of your hands."

Mercy bit back a moan. What would Pace think? Would he like her if he saw her like this? Would he even notice?

She forced a smile for their sakes. "I feel like a little girl playing dress-up."

Laughing, Miss Lily sauntered over to the chaise and slithered down to the seat. "We didn't mean to embarrass you, Mercy. But it's time you quit hiding your looks and let the world see you for the lovely young woman you are. This doesn't suit you, but there's no reason you can't wear your hair down, and show off your figure with the right clothes."

"And throw away these God-awful bindings." Florrie tossed the strips of cut sheet into the trash. "Men like women with nice bosoms." She winked at Rosie. "I bet even Pace Lansing would notice you then."

If possible, Mercy's face turned even redder than before. "Why do you say something like that?"

Miss Lily shot a warning glance at the woman. "She's only funning. Why don't we get on with our Bible study?"

Mercy looked down at her lack of proper apparel. "Like this?"

Rosie laughed. "We're in our wrappers. What difference does it make?"

It made a lot of difference to Mercy. Dressed in the gold gown, she felt like a sinner, a wanton—a desirable woman for the first time in her life. But not like a prayer meeting leader.

"I have to change," she whispered.

Picking up Mercy's discarded clothing, Cora gestured to the bedroom door. "I'll help you, Miss Mercy."

"Thank you."

Mercy hurried through the doorway. What had ever possessed her to try on the gold gown? She'd started something she would never live down. Yet, she couldn't deny that she enjoyed feeling beautiful, and being admired.

With Cora's help, she removed the lovely gown, and reached for her camisole. She slipped it over her head. Without the bindings, her breasts pressed against the soft fabric. Lifting a questioning gaze to the maid, she opened her mouth to protest.

Cora shook her head. "You don't need those bindings, Miss Mercy. Let Mr. Lansing know you're a woman."

Heat raced from her forehead to the tips of her toes. "I . . . I don't want him to notice me."

"Sure you do. All ladies like to be admired by the men they care for." With swift expert hands, the maid helped Mercy into her blouse and skirt.

"Pace?"

"Or some other man. You're pretty enough to have your choice."

Mercy ducked her head. "I'm not pretty."

The maid threw up her hands in surrender. "I give up." Cora picked up the gold gown and started for the doorway.

Reaching out a hand, Mercy stopped her. "Cora, wait. May I ask you something?" Tilting one shapely eyebrow, the woman waited for Mercy to continue. "Do you think he would go to the May Day dance with me?"

Cora's dark eyes grew soft with understanding. "I can't say, Miss Mercy. But you'll never find out unless you ask him."

"Ask him?" She clutched her chest, now much larger than an hour ago. "A lady can't ask a gentleman out. That's a man's place."

"Honey, if you wait on him, you'll be waiting a mighty long time. After all Pace Lansing has gone through, I doubt he even wants to come into town. But he owes you a favor or two."

"I don't want him to do it because of any supposed obligation. I want him to want to be with me." Mercy snapped her mouth shut. Already she'd revealed more to the maid than she'd admitted to herself.

"Sometimes a woman has to just reach out and grab what she wants." With a toss of her head, Cora returned to the sitting room.

Left alone, Mercy thought over what the other woman had told her. How could she ever get the courage to ask a man out? And if by some stretch of her imagination Pace agreed to attend the party, what made her think he would dance with her? The only other time a gentleman had called on her had been when Clifford had taken her to the social. To her utter humiliation, he'd danced every dance with Prudence, leaving Mercy standing with the other spinsters and widows.

She dropped to a edge of the huge feather bed to catch her breath. After all the times she'd been to the sitting room, this was her first glimpse of the lady's private boudoir. If she thought the sitting room was luxurious, this room was like something befitting Marie Antoinette.

A large bed sat between two windows draped with rose silk and white lace to match the canopy that hung from rods above the bed. Dozens of lacy pillows of every size and shape rested on the pink silk counterpane. Her gaze shifted to the large armoire. She'd seen it many times in her father's shop, while he'd lovingly carved the oak into the beautiful piece of furniture. To see it in a lady's boudoir, however, gave it an entirely different look. It was almost as if a part of her father lived here amid these opulent surroundings.

That thought was almost as strange as her inviting Pace Lansing to the May Day dance.

Female laughter and a baby's cries snapped Mercy out of her musings. In her imaginings, she'd forgotten all about Joshua, and the reason for her visit to the saloon.

She rushed into the sitting room, to find the two dance hall girls entertaining Joshua with a silly song, while Miss Lily bounced the baby on her lap. Cora entered from the hallway, a glass bottle of milk in her hand.

"This is what the little man needs," she said.

When Mercy reached for the infant, Miss Lily shooed her away. "I'll take care of him, while you start the Bible study. These two heathens need all the religion they can get."

Mercy smiled and reached into her bag for her Bible and notes. The other women settled on chairs and folded their hands demurely in their laps. Except for their lack of decent apparel, they looked as pious as Sunday School class members sitting in the church.

A half hour later, Mercy could hardly keep her eyes open. The words blurred on the page, and she yawned so wide, everybody in the room giggled. "Oh, excuse me, please. That was terribly rude of me," she said.

"Let's just finish with prayer, and you can get along home," Miss Lily said.

Mercy nodded. A few minutes later, she bowed her head in a soft "Amen."

After kissing and petting Joshua, Florrie, Rosie, and Cora left Mercy with Miss Lily. The woman placed the now sleeping baby in his basket. "Mercy, you look exhausted. Have you been getting your proper rest?"

"I'm fine. It just takes getting used to a baby's schedule. Soon he'll be sleeping through the night and things will get better."

"Dear, are you still working at the mercantile?"

Mercy nodded. She needed the money she earned from Tim as well as from mending to help Pace and replenish her stash. "A little, when I find the time."

"Are your sisters still making their outrageous demands? And of course you do everything for your father." She stood and shook her finger at Mercy. "When are you going to stand up for yourself and quit letting them treat you like their servant?"

"I defied them when I offered to help Pace and by taking care of Joshua. I really don't want them angry at me. They're my family."

Miss Lily draped an affectionate arm across Mercy's

shoulders. She turned Mercy to the chaise lounge. "Lie down here and rest."

"As long as Joshua is sleeping, I suppose I can take a nap."

"Nobody will disturb you, and after you rest a little, you can go on home."

The rose brocade chaise looked a lot more inviting than the stairs or the walk home. Or the further demands from her sisters if they found her. "If you don't mind, I think I will."

"Good," she said. "I'll call you in plenty of time to prepare your father's dinner."

"Thank you, Miss Lily. You're a real friend."

Giving Mercy a shove toward the chaise, Miss Lily flashed a wide smile. "You're always looking after everybody else. It's high time somebody started looking after you."

Mercy returned the smile. All her adult life she'd wished for a man she could look after and who would look after her. She sank into the chaise. Could Pace Lansing be the man she'd been looking for? As Miss Lily tiptoed from the room, Mercy closed her eyes and dreamed about Pace.

Charity showed up at the parsonage the following morning with Timmy in tow. As soon as the three-year-old ran into the kitchen, he looked for Joshua. The little boy thought the baby was some kind of toy and he chattered away as if Joshua understood every word.

"Would you like some breakfast?" Mercy asked her sister. "How about you, Timmy?" She refilled her father's coffee cup. He thanked her with an absentminded nod, hardly lifting his gaze from his Bible.

"We've already eaten," her sister answered. By her haughty tone, Mercy knew her sister hadn't come on a social call. Either she wanted something, or Mercy had once again broken another rule of social convention.

"Surely Timmy would like one of my muffins. How about it, honey? Want a muffin?" She held the freshly baked treat toward her nephew. For just a brief instant, she wondered if Pace would enjoy hot muffins with his breakfast. As quickly as the thought struck her, she willed it away.

The little boy snatched it from her fingers. "Can Josh have one, too?"

She laughed. "He's too small." Picking up her tow-headed nephew, she snuggled his belly with her nose. "When he gets as big as you, you'll have to share."

In a huff, Charity snatched the child from Mercy's arms. "I've already given you Timmy's outgrown clothes."

"The worn-out ones. If you have another child, you'll have all new things anyway. If it hadn't been for Miss LaRose's generosity, he would be wearing nothing but torn sheets. Or swaddling clothes."

Setting her son on the floor, Charity narrowed in on Mercy. "How long do you intend keeping Pace Lansing's b—"

"Don't say it, Charity. Don't even think such a horrible thing. Joshua is not Pace's child. He was still in prison when the baby was conceived." For one of the few times in her life, she stood up to her sister. "And if it were true, you certainly can't hold it against an innocent child."

Charity sniffed, and tilted her chin. "Doesn't the Word say that the sins of the father will be visited upon the sons? Didn't Pace kill Billy Blakely?"

Fury welled up in Mercy. "That's horribly unfair. Billy got what he deserved and Pace paid for what he'd done. You certainly can't condemn this baby for what happened five years ago."

"Girls!" Ezra slammed his Bible shut and glared at his two daughters. "You aren't children to carry on like snarling cats. Charity, you can't blame the baby for what his parents have done. And Mercy, I also want to know what you intend to do with the child? Are you trying to find a good family for him?"

Mercy shifted her gaze to the baby in his basket. Dressed in a soft flannel gown, he flailed his arms for attention. "Not yet. He's so small, I want to make sure he's healthy before I give him up." Her voice trailed off. Truth be told, she loved the baby, and she'd sooner cut out her heart than let him go.

Her father reached over and touched Joshua's hand. Instantly the baby clutched Ezra's rough finger in his tiny fist. "I suppose you have a point. I would like to christen the child, though. Give him a Christian name."

"I'd like that, too, Papa," she said, blinking back tears. As stern as he tried to be, she saw the softening in his eyes whenever he looked at Joshua. Did the child remind him of the son who'd died in childbirth?

"You don't mean to bring this half-breed into our church?" Charity said with as much indignation as her mother-in-law, who'd already made her opinions clear to the entire town as well as the church board.

Ezra slanted an authoritative glance at his second daughter. "Charity, it is the Lord's house, and I am the minister. I believe that it's only right and proper to christen all the babies into the faith. Mercy, we'll do it as soon as you wish."

She threw her arms around her father's neck. "Thank you, Papa."

Charity sat down with a huff. "You've certainly gotten your way."

"Sister, did you come over here this morning just to ridicule me?" Mercy set her hands on her hips and glared at her sister.

"No. I want to know why you never showed up at the mercantile yesterday like you promised."

"Oh." Mercy had forgotten all about her promise.

"Then Tim saw you sneaking down the rear stairs of the

Ruby Slipper at suppertime. Everybody is talking about you."

She frowned at her sister. "Everybody? Or just you, Mrs. Fullenwider, and Prudy? After the Bible study, I was so tired, I fell asleep on Miss Lily's chaise."

"In that place? Mercy, anything could have happened to you. All kinds of men go in and out of there, day and night."

"Mercy, I agree with your sister on this point." Her father returned to his coffee. "I allowed you to teach the Bible study because I believe these women deserve to hear the Word as well as any other citizen in our town. I've been rethinking my position. It may be best if I personally take over that particular duty."

Both Mercy and Charity stared slack-jawed at their father. "But Papa," Charity responded first. "That would be even worse."

"Yes, what would the deacons say?" Mercy added.

Ezra gathered himself to his full height and stared down his daughters. "If anyone thinks teaching lost souls would tarnish my reputation, then they had best call another minister. As long as I'm here, I'll teach my classes and strive to obey my calling."

"But Papa, you can't go into that place." Charity turned pale.

"You're right, daughter. They can come here, to the parsonage. Mercy, will you contact Miss LaRose and make the arrangements?"

Mercy had never been prouder of her father. "I'm sure Miss Lily and the other ladies will appreciate your efforts."

"You girls can visit without me. I'm on my way to the shop. Miss LaRose ordered a bureau to match the armoire I delivered last week. That woman keeps me hopping."

Biting back a smile, Mercy planted a quick kiss on her father's smoothly shaved cheek. She wondered if more than furniture making was going on between the unlikely couple of the minister and saloon owner.

Lily was kind-hearted and generous, yet it seemed implausible that anything lasting could develop between the pair. Ezra was stuck in his ways and adhered to a strict moral code. Free-spirited Lily's past was a mystery. Mercy had learned that she and Cora had come from New Orleans, but nobody knew much more about the ladies. Still, Mercy liked Lily. As strange as it seemed, she believed that the lady would be good for Ezra. It was high time her father found a woman to love and to love him in return. Miss Lily LaRose just might fill the bill.

As soon as Ezra left the kitchen, Joshua began to fuss. Mercy lifted the baby to her shoulder and patted his back. Timmy climbed onto a chair to press his face to the infant's. Joshua cooed, soothed by the gentle swaying and the boy's soft words.

With their father out of earshot, Charity turned on Mercy with another line of attack. "You want to keep that baby, don't you?"

A knot tightened in Mercy's chest. She'd fallen in love at first sight, and her feelings grew stronger every time she touched the baby. "Charity, look at me. I'm twenty-six years old, past the age when most women marry. Chances are I may never marry and have children of my own. I feel as if God gave me this baby, and I want to do what's best for him. If the right family comes along, I'll consider letting them have Joshua. Otherwise, I'm willing to raise him as my own son."

"Mercy, you're a fool. You can't take in every stray that comes your way."

She squared her shoulders. "That may be true. But Joshua isn't a stray puppy or cat. He's a child and he deserves all the love I can give him."

"Are you going to give up working at the mercantile?"

"No. I need the money I earn to support myself and

Joshua. It isn't fair to expect Papa to support us. If Tim doesn't mind my bringing the baby, I'll be there tomorrow after I serve Papa's breakfast."

"I suppose he won't mind. Tim needs help, and you know more about the stock and keeping the books than either of us." Charity tugged her son by the hand. "By the way, would you mind taking care of Timmy on Saturday night so Tim and I can attend the May Day dance?"

Mercy's spirits plunged to her feet. For once in her life she wished she could be included in the festivities. But as usual, the old maid sister was relegated to the outskirts of the party to mind children and serve food. "I suppose so. I've promised to bake a cake, but I'll be glad to keep Timmy here with Joshua."

"Thanks, Mercy. Got to run. See you tomorrow."

Timmy pulled away from his mother's grip. "Timmy want to play with Josh."

Charity lifted her gaze questioningly to Mercy. "Can he stay?"

In that instant, Mercy came to a decision. She decided that unless she wanted her life to go on in the same old humdrum manner, she had to take Cora's advice and reach out for what she wanted. Although she wasn't sure exactly what she wanted, she knew Pace Lansing was part of the answer. "Not today, honey. Auntie Mercy has some errands to run. You can play with Josh tomorrow."

Eight

This time Tim's only reaction to Mercy's order was a frown and grumble or two. He managed to curtail his criticism as he loaded her wagon. She didn't bother to lie or offer an explanation. Without a doubt, Tim understood the supplies were for Pace Lansing.

With Joshua asleep on the seat beside her and the supplies in the back, Mercy snapped the lines and guided the team toward Pace's home. Besides replenishing his goods and delivering another chocolate cake, she had two other excuses for the visit.

First of all, she wanted to inform him about the christening, of her father's wish to baptize the baby and give him a name. Almost as important, she wanted to remind him of the May Day dance.

A lady would never dream of inviting a gentleman to escort her, but there was no harm in letting Pace know about the dance on Saturday.

This time she brought paper and pencil to leave a note just in case he wasn't at the house. In a way, she almost hoped he wouldn't be there. Writing a note was much safer than risking embarrassment and rejection.

She halted the wagon at the door to the cabin and called out. "Mr. Lansing, are you here?" Standing, she surveyed the ranch. Everything looked much as on her last visit, except that more cattle grazed in the pastures, and the fence posts were standing upright. "Yoo-hoo, Mr. Lansing?"

A moment later, a bare-chested figure appeared from the dark interior of the barn. At the sight of him, her heart fluttered like a flag in a windstorm. She bit her lip to quell the strange sensations. Pace tugged off his gloves and shoved them into the rear pockets of his denims. As he walked purposefully toward her, he slipped a faded shirt over his head and buttoned it at the neck and wrists. He swiped a faded red bandanna across his face, then tied it at his throat.

Long strides ate up the distance between them in a few heart-stopping seconds. A scowl turned his mouth down at the corners, and his face was dark as a thunderhead. Regardless of his stern expression, Pace Lansing cut a fine figure of a man. Broad of shoulder and long of limb, he was enough to make a spinster's heart churn like a tornado in full fury.

Certain she'd made a mistake in returning to his ranch, Mercy controlled her instinct to turn tail and race back to town. A man like Pace wouldn't look twice at a woman like Mercy. In coming to him, she was opening her heart to rejection and pain.

"Miss Goodacre," he said, touching his fingers to the brim of his hat. "What are you doing here?"

"Nothing like getting right to the point, is there, Mr. Lansing?" Nervousness added an edge of sarcasm to her voice. She lifted the basket where Joshua was coming awake after sleeping the entire trip.

"Forgive my bad manners, ma'am. It's been a long time since I've welcomed polite company." His gruff tone faded when he spotted the baby. "How's Josh? Is anything wrong?" Reaching up, he took the basket from her. With his free hand, he offered her a lift down. His touch was strong and firm on her fingers, and she couldn't deny the current of awareness that shot through her.

"Joshua is fine," she said as her feet hit the dusty ground. She shook out her skirt in a futile effort to shake off her agitation. A blind man could see he didn't welcome her presence. Snatching the basket from his hand, she jerked her head toward the buggy. "Would you mind unloading the boxes?"

His gaze shifted to the load in the space behind the seat. "I didn't ask you for any more supplies. I have plenty left."

She bit her lip to control an angry retort. Nobody, man nor woman, had ever evoked such strong emotions in her. She'd defied convention and her family to help a man who clearly didn't appreciate her efforts one bit. "And chocolate cake?"

A light glimmered in his eyes, but was blinked away so quickly, she wondered if she'd imagined it. "Since you're already here, reckon I'll have to accept them."

"Mr. Lansing, we're partners, remember? I'm doing my share, so you're able to do yours."

"Yes, ma'am," he muttered. "I'm out in the bush every day rounding up my cattle. I've branded some, and put them back out to pasture. We should have a good herd to sell this fall."

"Good," she said, mentally calculating how much she would need for her trip to Philadelphia. "Do you mind if we go indoors? I don't like keeping Joshua out any longer than necessary."

Pace picked up a large box and led the way to the cabin. He kicked open the door and nodded for her to enter first. As before, she found the interior immaculate, if sparsely furnished. She set Joshua's basket on the table and lifted him from his blankets. The baby stretched his arms and whined, a signal that meant he wanted two things—milk and a changing. While Pace carried in the remainder of the supplies, she changed the baby.

"Would you like to hold him while I heat his milk?" she asked.

After a second's hesitation, he stretched out his hands. "I won't hurt him, will I?"

"I don't think so. Just don't drop him."

One big hand under the baby's bottom and the other supporting his head and shoulders, he weighed Joshua like a sack of sugar. "He's grown, hasn't he?"

Mercy stoked the fire and set a small pot on the stove. "Yes. He eats every three hours, and already he's outgrowing his newborn gowns."

"Miss Goodacre, I hope you're keeping track of how much you've spent on Joshua. I'll take care of his needs when I sell the cattle."

"That isn't necessary, Mr. Lansing. I agreed to care for him, and I'm able to provide whatever he needs."

The line of his jaw tightened and the scar stood out like a flash of lightning against the night sky. In her rush to judgment, she'd severely wounded his pride. After the horrid things that had happened to him, all Pace had left was his pride. She couldn't take it away from him.

"All right, if you insist," she said before he opened his mouth to argue. "But I've gotten a lot of help from Miss LaRose, and my family. I'll keep track of the expenses for you."

"Thank you for taking care of him. I hope he isn't too much trouble for you." His voice softened.

"He's no trouble at all." Pouring the milk into the glass nursing bottle, she checked the temperature on the inside of her wrist. "Would you like to feed him?"

With a negative shake of his head, he handed the infant back to her. "Would you like some coffee? Or a slice of that cake?"

"Coffee, please, if it isn't too much trouble."

"I haven't stopped to eat, and that cake looks mighty tempting."

For just once in her life, Mercy wished a man would look at her the way Pace was gazing at the cake. It was a look of hunger, of desire, and pleasure. She shoved her spectacles up her nose and studied the baby in her arms. Mercy knew she was stalling, too afraid of rejection to state the business that had brought her to the ranch.

Without a word, he placed a cup of dark coffee in front of her, and cut himself a large slice of cake. "Sure you don't want cake?"

"No, thank you."

An awkward silence settled between them. The baby's noisy sucking was the only sound in the small room. Pace ate a large slice of cake, then shoved a leftover biscuit into his mouth. Mercy chanced a glance around the cabin. He'd set the boxes on the board beside the stove. From what she could tell, his supplies were low, and he truly needed the things she'd brought.

She draped a napkin over the shoulder of her simple white shirtwaist and lifted the baby to burp him. Pace's gaze followed her every movement. He reached out a hand and patted Joshua's back. Their hands brushed, and he jerked his fingers away.

At that moment, Joshua let loose with a loud burp and spewed milk all over the protective cloth. She yelped, the baby gurgled, and at the same time soaked his diaper and Mercy to boot. He flailed his arms and legs as if proud of his accomplishment. Pace gathered the soiled cloth, his hands brushing her bosom in his effort to help. Grabbing a clean rag, he stared at the growing damp spot on her front. His hands stopped inches away, unsure what to do.

The dampness soaked through the white shirtwaist and her batiste camisole clear to her bare skin. Thanks to Cora's suggestion, Mercy had shed the bindings, leaving her full breasts loose under her garments. Under his gaze her nipples tightened into buds, pressing against the damp fabric. His eyes darkened and tingles raced over her. For a brief instant she saw desire in a man's gaze. Just as quickly he snatched the baby from her arms and flung the cloth at her. Spinning on his heel, he held the dripping baby over an empty pail.

Embarrassment spread a crimson stain over her face. She pulled a handkerchief from her pocket and mopped at the dampness; for little good it did. Decent women didn't show their bodies as she'd accidentally done. Standing, she snatched up her shawl and effectively covered the embarrassing display. "I'll take him now and change him again."

Pace handed over the baby, averting his gaze from the front of her bodice. She'd wanted Pace to notice her, but not like this.

"I'll fetch a clean shirt, you can't go out wet like that."

Replacing Joshua's wet garments with dry, Mercy placed him in his basket to sleep. Pace handed her a clean, but worn chambray shirt. "I'll go outdoors while you change."

"Thank you," she murmured. Quickly, she removed her soiled blouse and slipped the shirt over her head. The shoulders sagged down her arms, and she rolled the sleeves to her wrists. She lifted the soft, worn material to her face. The shirt smelled of soap and sunshine. Wearing his shirt left her feeling slightly wicked. A part deep inside liked the sensation. Not that she would dare do anything improper. She bit her lip. Everything she'd done since Pace had come back to town had astonished even her. Leaving the garment hanging outside her skirt, she again wrapped her shawl around her shoulders.

After stuffing her and Joshua's soiled garments into the basket, she glanced around. With nothing left to do, she knew she should leave before anything else happened. Yet she couldn't go without getting to the real point of her visit.

She moved to the door and tugged it open. Pace was standing beside the horses, examining their coats. He spun around when he heard her approach. He shot a quick glance at her, before dropping his gaze to his scuffed boots.

Mercy wasn't prepared for the pain when he looked away. She was tempted to slink away and never see him again. However, she'd come too far to leave without at least giving her plan a try.

He followed her back into the house, and picked up his cup of cold coffee. Mercy cleared her throat, and struggled to bolster her confidence. "Mr. Lansing, I wanted to ask you something."

"I'm in your debt. What is it?"

"It's about Joshua." She swallowed hard and rushed ahead. "My father wants to baptize the baby. You know, give him a name—godparents. It's part of our faith. And since he's living in my father's home, it's only right that we agree to the ceremony. But I didn't want to do anything without your permission."

"Hold on, Miss Mercy. I don't cotton much to religion and I'm not sure I believe in your God the way you do." He brushed a hand over his jaw. "But if you think it's best for Joshua, I'll go along with it."

Her breath came out in a rush. "Thank you. We would like to do it this Sunday, if you don't mind."

"Sounds good."

Now came the hard part. "I would like you to come to church and stand up as his godfather. And if you don't object, I want to be his godmother."

His mouth turned down into a frown. "Church? Sunday? I haven't stepped inside a church since I was a young child." He let out a humorless laugh. "Imagine the good people of the congregation when they see a convict in their midst."

"Everybody has a right to attend church. It would be wrong to keep anybody out."

"Any sinner, don't you mean?"

"Saint or sinner, there's room in the church for all."

He propped his hips against the counter, crossing his long legs at the ankles. She lifted her gaze and followed his movement. His denims stretched across his groin, emphasizing his maleness in a way that made her pulse race. Quickly she glanced upward to his impossibly wide shoulders and arms now crossed over his chest. A muscle twitched in his jaw.

"All right, Miss Goodacre. I suppose I can go along with you. If I slip into the back, maybe nobody will notice me."

Mercy doubted that. Pace Lansing would stand out like a wolf in a flock of white lambs. "Thank you." She wiped Joshua's mouth with a napkin. "Would you like to hold him again before I leave?"

Pace's eyes softened when he looked at the baby. "Sure." He lifted Joshua to his wide shoulder, and stared down into the tiny face. "You be a good little fella for Miss Mercy. She's sure got her hands full."

"You're a good boy, aren't you, Joshua?" She repacked Joshua's basket. In a few minutes, she would be on her way back to town. It was now or never. "Mr. Lansing, since you'll have to come to town on Sunday, perhaps you could come in on Saturday evening. We're having our annual May Day dance, and you could spend some time with Joshua."

"I don't dance, and I'll be busy. I'll see Josh on Sunday."

Just like that, he'd rejected her without even realizing what she was asking. A lump formed in her throat, but Pace would never know how much he'd hurt her. "I see. I had best be getting back to town." Carefully, she returned the infant to his basket. Joshua was already halfway asleep.

Pace carried the basket to the wagon. "Thank you for the supplies, Miss Goodacre. I'll see you in church on Sunday."

After setting the baby on the seat, he gripped Mercy's elbow to help her up. Since it would be grossly rude to pull away, she accepted his help. His hand lingered on her elbow a second longer than necessary. Mercy bit back a moan, and tugged out of his grip. As much as she wanted to touch him, have him hold her, he'd already made his choice—and it didn't include her.

Wishful thinking and girlish dreams were for the young, not twenty-six-year-old spinsters.

"Good day, Mr. Lansing," she said. With a curt nod, she headed back to town and her solitary life.

Pace watched the buggy until it disappeared behind a grove of trees. He wanted to kick something, and rewarded his baser instincts by booting a large stone. All he'd managed to do was hurt his toe in the worn soles of his boots. It didn't help his conscience one bit.

He'd hurt her, he knew by the look in her eyes. The woman had been nothing but good to him. She'd supplied food when the rest of the town would have let him starve to death. Thanks to her, Joshua was a strong healthy baby. Without her help he would have been forced to give up the child and maybe sell off part of his land. The only thing she'd asked was to baptize the baby. And for him to attend a dance. With her.

A time or two he'd attended the town socials. The younger Goodacre girls were very popular and rarely sat out a dance. Mercy, on the other hand, usually served the punch or tended the younger children.

Although he wished he could help her, being seen in the company of a man with his reputation would do her more harm than good. Pace was more an outcast now than five years ago. Surely somewhere there was a decent man who would see her good heart and want her. She sure deserved better than Pace Lansing.

Angry at himself, he returned to the house. True, he'd begun to run low on some commodities, but he could survive on a lot less than she'd brought the first time. Carefully, he removed the various cans, sacks, and fresh produce. In one box he found homemade jelly and freshly baked bread. Hers. Like the chocolate cake, things she'd made with her own hands for her family.

Pace sank to a chair and weighed the bread in his hand. His mother hadn't learned how to bake anything except biscuits and hardtack. And in his years of incarceration, he'd been lucky to get anything before the rats carried it away.

Cursing himself for showing such weakness, he tore off a piece of the loaf and shoved it into his mouth. He closed his eyes, enjoying the soft, sweet bread. The woman sure could bake. He wondered if the rest of her cooking was as good.

Realizing he'd wasted enough time, he shoved to his feet. His gaze fell on a white cloth draped across the other chair. He picked it up, and rubbed the soft fabric between his fingers. It was Mercy's embroidered handkerchief. She'd forgotten it when she'd left. Pace lifted it to his face and inhaled. It smelled of rosewater and . . . He squinched his face. Like sour milk the baby had spewed on her front.

A moan came from deep in his throat as he remembered how she'd looked in the wet blouse. The soft, transparent material had given him an unwanted view of her camisole and breast. It had taken all his self-control not to reach out and weigh the full globe in his hand. His groin tightened at the thought of the dusky tip pressing against the white thin material. He ached to touch her, press his lips to her sweet flesh, feel her soft body against his.

He curled his fingers into fists, the nails digging into the palms. It had been so long since he'd had a woman, he was fantasizing about the only person in the world who had befriended him.

A string of curses erupted from his lips. He threw down the handkerchief and stomped from the house.

The farther he stayed away from her, the better off they

both would be. But the idea of not seeing her brought a strange twinge to his heart. With an angry snort, he returned to his chores. By fall, he would sell the cattle and get the blasted woman out of his life forever.

Nine

"Auntie Mercy, can I have another piece of choc'lit cake?"

Mercy wiped the smudges and crumbs from her nephew's face with a linen napkin. "I think you've had enough for now, little man."

The sound of fiddles, a banjo, and even the tinkle of the piano drifted out the open doors of Fullenwider's Feed and Grain. For the past few years Horace Fullenwider had donated the use of the large barn for the annual May Day dance. The way the mayor strutted around, his thumbs in his suspenders, one would think he was the king throwing a ball for his subjects.

Timmy set his small fists on his narrow hips. "It ain't for me. It's for Josh." He gestured to the baby, gurgling and cooing a few inches away.

With a small laugh, Mercy ruffled the little boy's blond curls. At first, she'd planned to stay home with the baby and Timmy. However, after arguing with herself for three days, she'd decided to attend the festivities. Just because Pace Lansing had rejected her offer, was no reason to hide away like a recluse. To spare herself the embarrassment of being one of the few women under sixty without an escort, she had spread a blanket on the grass near the grove of trees. Here they were close enough to hear the music, yet far enough away to allow Mercy to nurse her shattered dreams.

For the biggest social event of the year, she wore a new lavender gown, one she'd remade from Prudy's rejects. It had taken a lot of work to alter the bodice, since without the bindings, her bosom was much larger than her younger sister's.

Flashing his most charming smile, Timmy settled on Mercy's lap. He twisted his pudgy fingers in her loose curls. "But Auntie Mercy, you make the best choc'lit cake in the whole town."

"Maybe even the whole wide world."

At the sound of the raspy male voice, Mercy jumped. Her heart thumped against her chest. Flutters raced up her spine. A long shadow fell over the blanket. She dared let her gaze move to the man towering over her. His scuffed boots were polished to a shine and clean denims stretched over muscular legs.

Pace hunkered down beside her, and brushed a crumb from the corner of Timmy's mouth. "So you like chocolate cake, too, huh cowboy?"

The boy ducked his head into the crook of Mercy's shoulder. He giggled and tugged on her hair. Pace reached over and untwisted the boy's fingers from the curly tresses. Gently, he stroked the hair between his fingers. Her pulse pounded, but she didn't dare move. Being this close to a man— to Pace—was too precious to want to break the spell.

She looked up at him. The hard angles of his face softened in the thin beam of moonlight that filtered through the trees. His mouth tilted at one corner, the half smile of a man afraid to reveal himself. A man who'd had little to smile about in his life. Mercy found the gesture more endearing than the full wide grin of any man she'd ever known.

"I like your hair like this," he said. "It's so shiny and bright, like the sparkle of moonlight on the water."

A tremor raced over her. Her breath caught. "What are you doing here?" she asked in a soft whisper.

"I thought you invited me."

"I didn't expect you." Warmth settled in her chest.

He dropped the lock of hair and let it fall over her shoulder. "I went by your house, then I came here looking for you."

"Why?"

"To apologize." He shoved back his battered hat, revealing eyes as dark and unreadable as the night sky without stars.

Was that all he wanted of her? The joy at seeing him faded like yesterday's roses. "You don't owe me an apology." Timmy shifted on her lap and reached out to Pace.

"You're wrong, Miss Mercy. I owe you my life and this baby's."

So he'd only come because he felt guilty. Not because he wanted to be with her, but because of an obligation—to pay a debt. That hurt worse than being alone.

Pace caught Timmy and settled him beside Joshua on the blanket. "How's Josh enjoying the party?"

"All right, I guess," she said around the lump in her throat. "I was getting ready to take him back home. He shouldn't be out too long."

"Can't you stay a little longer? I just got here."

Mercy wanted nothing more than being with him. If only he wanted her as much. Not just to fulfill some kind of duty he felt toward the person who had befriended him.

"I suppose. Would you like something to eat? The ladies have outdone themselves."

He glanced toward the crowds in the barn. "Do you suppose they'll welcome me to eat at their table?"

"You're a part of the town. You have as much right to be here as anybody else."

His crooked grin disappeared. "If you want this party to end early, just let me show my face in there."

Sick and tired of the way the town treated Pace, she
shoved to her feet. "I'll fetch you a plate. Keep an eye on
Joshua." She grabbed her nephew's hand and tugged him
toward the open doors. Feeling Pace's gaze on her, she
gave her hips a little swing, imitating Florrie's and Rosie's
walks. The girls knew how to attract men, and it was time
Mercy followed their leads. Head held high, and bosom
thrust out, she felt as decadent as on the afternoon she'd
returned home wearing Pace's shirt instead of her own
white shirtwaist. Fortunately for her, nobody had been
home to criticize her.

She nodded to Mrs. Fullenwider, who manned the
punch bowl, making sure none of the robust cowboys decided to add spirits to the drink. Mercy's father stood near
the food-laden table, his head bowed toward the widow
Weatherman. Ezra appeared to be listening, but his gaze
drifted over the dancers. His glance fell on Mercy and he
nodded a greeting.

"Hey, Drampa," Timmy yelled. "Auntie Mercy is going
to get some choc'lit cake."

"Don't eat too much, Timmy. You'll get a tummyache,"
Mrs. Watterman said.

"It ain't for me, it's for—"

"Me," Mercy cut him off.

"Mercy, where's the baby?" her father asked, concern
in his tone. Over the past week, he'd softened considerably
toward Joshua. Often he offered to hold the baby while
Mercy heated the bottle.

She tilted her head to avoid the truth. "I left him with
somebody." Hurrying away, she picked up a plate and
filled it with an assortment of meats, potatoes, and sweets.
With Timmy tagging along behind her, she waved to Charity and Tim and continued toward the door.

"Dance, Miss Mercy?" The mayor stopped her with a
hand on her arm.

With a sad smile, she glanced at her sister's father-in-law.

Every year, Horace Fullenwider felt obligated to dance with every lady in town. His was always her one and only dance, except of course when her father or brothers-in-law felt sorry for her and dragged her onto the dance floor.

"Thank you, Mayor," she said. "But I promised Charity I'd look after Timmy, and I have Joshua outside."

"Next time then." He tousled Timmy's hair and turned to search out another spinster or widow on which to bestow his benevolence.

When she returned to the blanket, Pace was seated cross-legged with Joshua nestled in his lap. The sight touched her clear to the bottom of her soul. He lifted his gaze and so much need glittered in his eyes, Mercy grew weak. The big lonely man and the orphaned child needed each other. They needed her—she needed them.

Shoving aside the emotions that churned within her, she handed him the plate without speaking. Timmy passed over the silverware and napkin. "Thank you," he said.

"Can I have a bite?" the child asked, settling on Pace's knee.

"Let me take Joshua," she offered. Slowly, she lowered herself to the blanket.

"It's okay. I can handle both these little fellas."

Pace tore his gaze from Mercy and focused on his plate and the two children in his lap. When he'd watched her walk away, he'd about burst his britches. He wanted to settle that swaying bottom against him and bury his hands in those full breasts. How had her father ever let her out of the house looking like that? The lavender dress made her skin as creamy as sweet milk, and with her hair flowing around her shoulders, she looked much younger than her twenty-six years. He pulled his thoughts from the woman and the lust that could lead to nothing but trouble.

The little boy took pleasure in snitching cake from the plate, while Josh gurgled and waved his arms. Mercy reached over and adjusted the cap on the baby's head.

Her fingers brushed his knee as gently as the touch of a feather. Fire shot to the pit of his stomach.

Coming here had been a big mistake. He'd debated with himself for three days before giving in to his conscience. He bit down on a piece of roast beef. Hell, conscience had nothing to do with it. Plain and simple he was lonely and wanted to be with people—with Mercy.

"Is something wrong, Mr. Lansing?" she asked.

Aware of the scowl on his face, he tempered his emotions. "It's delicious, Miss Goodacre." He glanced at her face. The food wasn't nearly as luscious as those lips that smiled up at him. With an effort, he schooled his features.

"Let me take Joshua. He'll be asleep in a few minutes."

This time when she reached for the baby, her hands lingered even longer on his leg and her breast brushed his arm. How he managed to remain seated, he had no idea. Blood pulsed through his veins with a force that left him weak. Thank goodness for the darkness. Taking a long deep breath, he managed not to embarrass himself. Without Josh in the way, Timmy shifted in his arms and dropped his head on Pace's shoulder.

"Reckon this little fella will be joining Josh in dreamland."

He watched the way she cuddled the baby, then kissed his forehead, and laid him on the blanket. Emotions swelled in his chest. Being with her was almost like belonging. He inhaled the sweet clean baby scent of the child. Rollicking music floated on the breeze and voices and laughter came from the barn. Yet, as always, Pace Lansing was relegated to the shadows of life, an outsider.

The child's breathing deepened and his head nodded. When Mercy reached for her nephew, Pace shook his head. "He's comfortable." He enjoyed the weight of the child in his arms, and it kept him from making a fool of himself with Mercy.

She nodded and placed a light blanket over Timmy. "I wonder what he's dreaming about?" she asked wistfully.

"Probably your chocolate cake."

Her gentle laughter added fuel to the fire in his blood. "And what do you dream about?"

"Nothing." The word came out in a harsh rasp.

"Surely you dream about something. Everybody has dreams."

It wouldn't do to tell her every time he closed his eyes he saw her. After tonight, he probably would never sleep again. "My ranch. Breeding cattle and horses."

"What about a wife? Children?"

That was just what a woman would wonder. At twenty-five, Pace knew better than to dream about things beyond his grasp. "I don't have time to court a woman or waste time trying to woo some maiden. Besides, who would want a convicted felon?" He softened his tone and changed the subject. "What about you? What do you want more than anything?"

She lifted her gaze to the stars. Moonlight sparkled in her eyes. "I want to travel to the ends of the earth. I want to see new places, meet new people, enjoy new experiences I've only read about in books."

"That's a mighty tall dream."

"I've been saving my money for ages. Next year I'm going to the 1876 Centennial International Exhibition in Philadelphia." With a charming tilt of her head, she grinned at him. "That's why you have to work extra hard to make your dream come true. Our dreams are all tied up in those silly cows."

Pace couldn't help smiling back at her. "I'll do my best, Miss Goodacre. And I'll pass the word along to the cattle."

She bent her legs and rested her chin on her knees. "I know you will, Mr. Lansing."

For long moments he studied her. Mercy Goodacre may not be as beautiful as her sisters, but her inner beauty shone brighter than the North Star on a clear night. It amazed him that no man had ever noticed. His gaze shifted to the figures inside the barn. She belonged inside enjoying the party rather than outside keeping company with children and an outcast.

He remembered all too well the way she'd been treated by the men in her younger days. Billy Blakely had been the worst of all. Pace had caught Billy with Mercy behind the livery. Billy had shoved the helpless woman against the barn door, his hands groping the front of her gown. When she'd fought back and screamed for help, Billy had twisted her arms behind her back and stifled her shouts with his mouth. He'd laughed and said he intended to find out what she was hiding under her skirts.

Pace had seen his pa treat his mother like that. Something snapped in his brain. He ordered Billy to leave Mercy alone. Hateful, and full of meanness, Billy threw Mercy into his arms and called her an Indian's whore.

For years, Pace had watched Billy terrorize younger boys and animals. They'd fought a number of times, and the hatred was mutual. This time he wouldn't let the bully get away with mistreating a woman. The fight started in the back alley, and didn't stop until Billy fell against the corner of a horse trough. He hit his head and died instantly. Mercy had testified at his trial that Billy had started the fight. She'd kept Pace from the hangman's noose, but he'd spent five years in prison.

Looked like after all this time the men in town didn't treat her any better. They were a pack of fools, every one.

Pace picked Timmy up and placed him beside Joshua. The boy mumbled something, but returned to sleep immediately. Lifting his gaze, Pace found Mercy staring at him. In that instant, he felt as if she could see clear into his soul. Her eyes reflected the need that had been gnawing at his gut since he'd spotted her with the children. She swayed gently in time to the music.

In one quick movement, he stretched to his feet. Before he changed his mind, he reached out a hand. "I'm not very good, but would you honor me with this dance, Miss Mercy?"

Shock fluttered over her face. Quickly, she blinked it away and grinned. The look was so soft and open his heart pounded against his ribs.

"I'll check my dance card, Mr. Lansing." She opened her hands as if looking at a book. "You're lucky. This dance is open."

Taking his offered hand, she allowed him to tug her gently to her feet. Instantly, she went into his arms. For the briefest instant her breasts pressed against his chest. Just as quickly, she pulled away.

Carefully adhering to the rules of propriety, Pace set his right hand on her waist, and clutched her other hand in his left. They stared at each other for a long awkward moment. "I hope I don't step on your toes."

She placed her fingers on his shoulder. Standing toe to toe, the top of her head reached the middle of his chin. His big, scratchy palm swallowed up her small, soft hand. Although at least six inches of space separated their bodies, Pace felt the heat as if he were in front of a roaring fire. He liked being touched, being needed. Being wanted.

He took a tentative step to the left, hoping not to tangle his legs in her skirt. She followed his lead, her shoe touching his boot. On the grass, their steps were inexperienced and slow. They moved back and forth, in unsure movements. Pace had only danced a time or two, and had almost no sense of rhythm. Mercy didn't seem to mind. She kept up with him, following his steps as if he were an expert dancer.

None of that mattered. He liked holding her, touching her. Inhaling the fragrance of her hair was sweeter than the smell of the wildflowers that grew in his meadow. In the distance he heard voices, and realized that the music had stopped.

Reluctant to let her go, he slowed his steps. Mercy tilted her face and her gaze met his in the pale light. Her pink tongue darted out and moistened her lips. Nothing had been as inviting as those pink, full lips. Hunger surged through him. He needed to kiss her, to learn if her mouth was as sweet and soft as it looked.

He released her hand and slid his fingers up her arm. When she didn't protest, he tightened his hold at her waist. Her fingers moved to his nape. The touch of her flesh against his sent a tremor through him. As he nudged her closer, he realized that she was shaking.

"I won't hurt you, Mercy," he murmured against her hair. The soft loose strands whispered against his cheek.

"I know you won't, Pace."

The trust in her voice brought a catch to his throat. He inched closer to her, until her breasts pressed into the front of his shirt. Her soft whimper urged him on. His mouth met hers, with a light brushing of lips to lips. He didn't dare move faster. Holding his lust in tight rein, he touched her as gently as he would Joshua.

Pace set his hands on her back, the flesh soft and warm under her gown. He savored her lips like a man biting into the first ripe strawberry of the season. She tasted sweeter, purer, better than anything he'd dreamed about. The touch of her soft breasts against his chest sent another shock of desire through him. His body burned with unfulfilled need.

He kissed the corner of her mouth, and ran his tongue over her lips. His mind spun with the pure joy of being with Mercy. Even her name evoked pleasure. On her own, she shifted to get closer into his embrace. His arms tightened, drawing her flush against him.

Unable to stop himself, he slanted his mouth over hers, in a kiss full of the passion he could no longer control.

She stiffened momentarily, then relaxed and returned the kiss. Wanting more of her sweetness, he nudged his tongue against the seam of her lips. Her teeth barred the way to the deeper recesses of her mouth. He didn't force her, but enjoyed the touch of her lips, the pressure of her breasts, and the feel of her stomach against his pelvis.

An inner voice warned him to stop while he still had the strength. But she felt too good to quit. It was like his first taste of freedom. He wanted to savor every second, every ounce of her. She was a healing balm to his aching soul.

The kiss went on, and his knees grew weak with need. He wished they were alone so he could bury himself into her warmth.

Somewhere in the back of his mind he heard the voices, loud voices, angry voices. Lost in the wonder of the kiss, he ignored the warning in his brain.

A hand clutched his shoulder, shoving him away from the woman in his arms. "Get your hands off her." A man's angry voice penetrated his dazed mind.

He stumbled for a brief second before his instincts took over. Jumping back a step, he curled his hands into fists. The instant before he swung, Mercy grabbed his arm. "Stop, don't fight."

Pace shook the fury out of his eyes. His gaze fell on three men and two women—Mercy's entire family staring at him as if he had just committed murder. Or worse.

"You won't get away with it this time, Lansing." It was Clifford Blakely's voice, with the same threat he'd made five years ago. His threat had cost Pace years of his life. "We'll string you up like we should have when you murdered Billy."

Mercy sobbed, and stepped smack in the middle of the melee. Her father reached for her, but she brushed him aside. From the blanket came a baby's high-pitched squall, and a child's whines.

"My baby, what have you done with him?" Charity moved past her husband and picked up her child from the ground. "Don't cry, Timmy. The mean man won't hurt you."

"Papa, what are you doing?" Mercy asked.

"Taking you away from this man. Did he hurt you?" Turning his ashen face to Pace, he shook his fist. "How can you do this to my daughter?"

Pace lifted his hands in surrender. He'd been wrong to touch her. It was his fault and this time he would pay.

Mercy swiped tears from her eyes. "He didn't do anything to me."

"He compromised you. We saw him attacking you," Tim said between his teeth.

"How can you accuse him of something like that? He was kissing me."

Both women gasped. "And you let him?" the other sister, Prudy asked. "That's even worse."

A crowd gathered. The sheriff shoved his way toward him.

"Why not?" Mercy shot back. Her next words knocked him clear off his feet. "We're engaged to be married."

Ten

Mercy looked around to see who had uttered those outrageous words. Who would dare say something so startling and shocking? Then she realized the words had come from her own mouth—through lips warm and tingly from Pace's kisses. Even the darkness couldn't hide the shocked expression on every face.

Especially Pace's.

It was wrong to lie, to trap Pace into something he didn't want. But it was the only way she could think to save him and protect her reputation. Sheriff Jennings had already drawn his gun, and with Clifford inciting the crowd, anything could happen.

"Engaged?" It was her father who recovered first.

"To him?" Her sisters spoke in unison.

"The man who killed my brother?" Clifford shouted.

Aware things could get worse, Mercy sidled up to Pace. "Yes, Pace asked me to marry him. And I said yes." To his credit, Pace didn't protest. He tucked her arm in the crook of his elbow. A reluctant suitor at best. A trapped man in truth.

"You're lying," Tim added to the foray.

Pace tightened his grip, clearly trying to control his temper. "Are you calling my betrothed a liar?"

She sagged with relief at his willingness to go along with the ruse. Later, when they were alone, she could explain, and give him a chance to get out of the outrageous situation.

Her father turned white. He reached out and took her hand. "Daughter, are you sure this is what you want?"

"Yes, Papa." She caught a glimpse of Pace's stoic expression. "It's what I want."

"Sir, I'm sorry I didn't ask your permission first," Pace said. "Would you mind if I take Miss . . . Mercy home and we can discuss this in private?"

The rabble around them grew louder. A series of gasps and snorts erupted from her friends and neighbors. Nobody could believe that a man would want plain, old maid Mercy Goodacre. Or that she would be interested in a man like Pace Lansing. She could already hear the "I told you so," for a wedding that will never take place.

"Papa, do something," Charity said, jiggling Timmy to quiet his sobs.

At that moment the commotion woke Joshua. His loud squalls drew Mercy's attention. Shoving away from Pace, she picked up the baby. At her side, Pace took the infant from her arms and lay him against his chest.

Prudy caught Mercy's arm. "First you embarrass us by helping this criminal, then you take in his bastard, now you say you're going to marry him. How can you do this to us?"

Mercy shot an angry glance at her sister. "I haven't done anything to you. It's my life, and it's about time I started living it my way."

Her sister pulled out a lace handkerchief and turned into her husband's shoulder. "Now, now, love. Don't cry," Clifford said in an effort to console his young wife. "You never talked to your sister like that before you got involved with him."

"Mercy." Pace's husky voice whipped through the confusion. "Let's get the baby home. We can talk later."

"Yes. Let's go where we can be alone."

"Alone? With him?" Charity shouted.

"Aren't you tired of putting on a performance for the entire town?" Mercy whispered to her sister. "Your mother-in-law has enough gossip to keep her tongue oiled for months."

"It's your fault." Charity turned away.

"Mercy is correct," her father said. Using his pulpit voice, he addressed the crowd. "I'm taking my daughter home so we can straighten out this affair. Please let us through."

When her sisters started to follow, her father gave them his sternest glare. "Everybody go home. I want to see Mercy and Lansing alone. We'll explain everything tomorrow after church."

Taking a second to snatch up the blanket from the grass, Mercy returned to her father's side. He caught her elbow and urged her toward the parsonage. Pace fell into step at her side. His face was void of expression.

Whispers followed them out of the yard and down the street. A glance over her shoulder showed a company of curiosity seekers trailing behind. For an evening that had started out so perfect, it had turned into complete disaster.

And by her foolishness, she'd stuck Pace smack in the middle of everything. He'd made it abundantly clear he didn't want to get married. Now, she'd put him in a precarious position and embarrassed herself to boot.

It was all her fault. She'd all but lured him into her arms. A decent woman wouldn't have kissed him like that. Or entice him to dance with her. Or invite a man in the first place.

With every step toward home, her spirits sagged until they dragged behind her like shackles weighing her down. Instead of blaming Pace, they should blame the woman who'd tempted him to sin.

What made it worse was the fact that they hadn't done anything wrong. Nothing that other courting couples didn't do every day. However, they weren't courting, and they certainly weren't a couple.

She wished she could talk to him, explain why she'd told such a bald-faced lie. It would serve her right if he didn't speak another word to her as long as she lived.

When they reached the house, Joshua was awake and hungry. Pace followed her father into the parlor, while Mercy prepared a bottle for the infant. She hated what she'd done, but at the time she couldn't think of another way out of the problem. Clifford had been gunning for Pace since Billy had died, and he would have gladly carried through with his threat.

Mercy bit her lip. She'd been responsible for that incident five years ago, and now she had once again put Pace in harm's way. If only she had a few minutes alone with him, she could explain her plan.

From the kitchen, she tried to hear what was being said in the parlor, but she heard nothing. Ezra's booming voice was silent. Thankfully, he was waiting for Mercy before raking Pace over the coals of hellfire and damnation.

Once the baby was changed, she settled on the rocker to feed him. Standing with his fingers tucked into the rear pockets of his denims, Pace stared out the window. His big revolver rested at his hip. Her father sat in his favorite chair with his Bible in his lap.

Mercy's heart was pounding like a tom-tom. Fury was clearly written on Pace's face. She'd made a complete and utter fool out of both of them. After what seemed an eternity, Joshua finished his feeding. He stared up at her, waving his arms, wide awake and ready to play.

Ezra tore off his spectacles and set his Bible aside. Their short reprieve was over. Yet, Mercy had no idea what to tell her father.

Pace was first to break the awkward silence. "Sir, I apologize for what happened tonight. You were right, I was completely out of line. I should have asked permission to call on Miss Goodacre. It was all my fault. She didn't do anything wrong."

Mercy couldn't believe he was willing to take the blame for her folly. "No, Mr. Lansing. I was at fault."

Her father swung his gaze from Mercy back to Pace. "Lansing, you compromised my daughter's reputation. I think it would be best for her if we plan the wedding as soon as possible."

In spite of the baby in her arms, Mercy leapt to her feet. "Papa, how can you say that? You know I wouldn't do anything indecent. And Pace was a perfect gentleman."

"Regardless, half the town saw you. Your sisters are furious and we both know Clifford is gunning for Lansing. It wouldn't take much for him to get up that lynching party."

"Sir, I'm ready to do the right thing by your daughter. I would be honored to have her hand in marriage." Pace glanced at her, then dropped his gaze to the baby in her arms.

"When do you plan to be married?"

"As soon as Miss Goodacre can make the arrangements."

Everything was getting out of hand. She would have to think of something fast, or Pace would be trapped in a marriage he didn't want. "Papa, we need time. I want a decent betrothal—a year, at least. To make plans. To prepare a trousseau."

Pace shot a hard glance at her. "Anything you say, Miss Mercy."

Her father stood and stuck out his hand. "Young man, I want you to know you're getting my jewel. Be good to my daughter, or you'll have to answer to me."

To his credit, Pace accepted her father's ultimatum without comment. "Yes, sir."

"Since that's all settled, I think we had best get that little fellow to sleep. He's got a big day tomorrow." Ezra looked up at Pace. "You are planning to stay in town for the christening tomorrow, aren't you, Lansing?"

"I promised your daughter I would stand up as Josh's godfather."

"Good night, then. I have to prepare my sermon." He moved to the door and held it open. "We'll see you at church tomorrow."

"Good night, sir." Pace touched his finger to the brim of his hat. "Miss Mercy."

Ezra closed the door with a decisive click and set the lock. Pace's boots thudded on the wooden porch. She watched through the lace curtains as he disappeared into the darkness.

"After you settle the baby, we can work on my message, daughter. Considering the events of this evening, we had best prepare the most inspiring sermon on forgiveness and compassion this town has ever heard."

Tears burned at her eyes. Her father had accepted the scandalous situation with more grace and understanding than she deserved. She only wished she'd had a minute alone with Pace to explain her plan. They could pretend a betrothal, and after a decent period, she would break it off. He would be blameless, while she took the reproach of the town.

She snuggled Joshua to her breast, wishing their engagement had been real. For a few short minutes tonight she'd felt desired, needed. Then her euphoria had burst like a soap bubble in the wind.

And Mercy was alone with only his kisses burning on her lips to warm her lonely heart.

A thin stream of early morning sunlight filtered through the newly green leaves of the overhanging branch. Pace woke with a start. As always, he came fully alert and rolled to his feet in one quick movement. At the same instant, he snatched his gun from its holster. Since his release from prison, he always kept the weapon within arm's reach.

Self-preservation taught a hard lesson. Even as a child, he'd been a light sleeper. It wasn't unlike his old man to sneak up on him in the dark and take out his anger and frustration on Pace.

Alert for any out-of-the-normal sound, he backed up a step and studied his campsite. His horse whinnied and champed the grass, a blue jay skittered in the oak over his head, and a squirrel scurried up the trunk. Ordinary sounds, ordinary activities, in what was certain to be an extraordinary day.

Rather than go all the way back to his homestead, he'd bunked down beside the Pleasant River, a half mile from town. A bedroll on the ground was a sight better than being somewhere he wasn't wanted. After washing up in the cool clear water, he ate some of the bread Mercy had left for him a few days ago.

He'd slept little the past night—heck, he'd slept little since Mercy Goodacre had burst into his life. If wanting the woman didn't haunt his sleep, then worrying about her did.

Now he'd gone and gotten engaged to her. He knew why she'd done it. It wasn't concern for her own reputation at being caught with him. Over the past weeks she'd proved she didn't care what people thought of her. Her concern was to do right and damn the consequences.

Pure and simple, she'd done it for him. To save his worthless neck. He had little doubt that her brother-in-law would have succeeded where he'd failed five years ago. If it hadn't been for Mercy sacrificing herself, he could right now be swinging from a tree with the buzzards stripping his flesh from his bones.

Despair seeped clear to his soul. He couldn't support himself—how was he going to provide for a wife and baby?

If he could hold her off until fall, things would be better. After he sold his cattle, they could make plans.

As he rinsed his cup in the water, he caught a glimpse of the man staring back at him. With black hair, much too long, he looked more Indian than white, and a night's growth of whiskers gave the appearance of a desperado.

He changed into a clean shirt, then covered his head with his battered hat. In spite of his meager efforts, Pace Lansing was a sorry picture of a man.

By the height of the sun in the sky, he knew it was close to time for the church service to begin. It took only a few minutes to ride to the church and tether the horse apart from the others in the grove of trees near the building. He waited until after the bells rang and the congregation had sung the first hymn before he slipped into the rear pew.

As expected, the other worshippers gave him a wide berth. Heads turned and nervous voices whispered through the building. In the front row, Mercy remained ramrod stiff with her gaze straight ahead. Joshua's basket rested on the seat next to her.

The gray-haired woman playing the piano stumbled over the notes. He couldn't blame the people. This was the first time a Lansing had ever darkened the doors of a church. From the pulpit, Reverend Goodacre spotted him. To the man's credit, he didn't skip a beat of the hymn.

By the time the second song began, the doors swung open, slanting a strong stream of sunlight down the center aisle. Prudence and Clifford Blakely swept in as if they owned the world. The couple shot angry glances at Pace before continuing to the front pew and squeezing in with Mercy, Charity, and Tim.

Pace struggled to concentrate on the service. He didn't dare move a muscle for fear it would be misinterpreted. After the singing, he rose with the congregation for prayer. He sure needed his share. The preacher's sermon spoke eloquently on love, forgiveness, and compassion. More than once, Pace was tempted to slink out the rear door. The words of understanding were as much for him as the people of Pleasant Valley.

At the end of the sermon, Reverend Goodacre announced that he had the great honor of christening a new member into the body. He motioned for Mercy to carry the baby to the front, then called Pace forward. Around him the whispers grew louder. Indignation rang like bells through the congregation. In their opinions, Pace Lansing had no business desecrating their church house. He hesitated for a second. Then when Mercy glanced back, the pleading in her eyes convinced him to do the right thing. He couldn't leave her to take the heat alone.

Slowly, he rose from the seat. His hat in his hand, he forced one foot in front of the other until he reached the spot where Mercy awaited him. The tense lines in her face softened as he stopped at her side. A tiny smile brightened her face. He dropped a glance to the baby. Joshua wrinkled his face, as unhappy with the situation as Pace. The infant wore a long white gown, decorated with lace and ribbons and a fancy bonnet. He waved his arms as if begging for relief. Pace knew exactly how he felt. Given half a chance, Pace would snatch Joshua and run as far away from the judgmental town as he could get.

But he knew he would do no such thing. After all Mercy had done for both of them, standing at her side for the ceremony was the least he could do.

Reverend Goodacre cleared his throat and began. Pace studied on every word, wanting to know exactly what he was promising in front of his few friends and many enemies. It all seemed simple enough—he and Mercy were promising to take care of the child. He'd already promised Naomi. The minister prayed over the baby, then took Joshua from Mercy's arms. Joshua let out a squall that could be heard a mile away. Snickers came from the children in the congregation, along with their parents' hushing.

A flush crept over Mercy's face, and she glanced at Pace for help in quieting the baby. Joshua sounded as if somebody was sticking him with a pin. No matter how much she tried to quiet the baby, he only screamed louder. Desperate to help, Pace took Joshua from the minister and jiggled him for a moment. In an instant, the crying stopped, and the infant waved his arms with glee.

"Perhaps it would be best if you hold him, Mr. Lansing," the minister said. He signaled Pace and Mercy closer to the small basin perched atop a polished oak pedestal.

Mercy's arm brushed Pace's as she untied the ribbons of the bonnet. Warmth sizzled between them. He squelched the unwanted feelings that swelled within him whenever he got anywhere near this woman.

The minister scooped a handful of water and sprinkled it on the baby's head. "Joshua . . ." He hesitated and looked from Pace to Mercy. "I forgot to ask his last name."

"Lansing," he answered without thinking. Behind him the shocked noises ranged from gasps to downright snickers, and a few loud "I told you so's."

In defiance to the censure of the townspeople, Pace squared his shoulders and tilted his chin a notch. He chanced a glimpse at Mercy and spotted the high color on her cheeks. Yet in spite of bearing the reproach of her friends and relations, she nodded to her father.

Reverend Goodacre bore his own shock well. The man scooped another handful of water and continued the ceremony. "Joshua Lansing, I baptize you in the name of the Father, and of the Son, and of the Holy Spirit." When the last drop of water was wiped from his head, the baby bellowed loud enough to wake the dead.

"I think he's hungry," Mercy said, taking the baby from his arms. Joshua quieted when Mercy stuck a small cloth knot into his mouth. The baby sucked noisily on the sugar wrapped inside. Together, they moved aside while her father dismissed the service. As the congregation eased from the building, a number of people cast disparaging glances at them. Mercy's own sisters turned away with a loud "humph," and refused to look at her. Pace curled his fingers into his palms to keep from wiping the sneers from her brothers-in-law's faces. If they hadn't been in church, Pace would have shown them a thing or two about snubbing a woman as good and sweet as Mercy. Heck, he was tempted to do it anyway.

When they were alone, Cora Davis, Miss LaRose's maid, approached from the balcony stairs. Pace knew who she was, but he'd had little contact with the woman in the past. Her eyes sparkled and her grin widened when she touched the baby.

"Didn't look like the young man was too fond of the water," Cora remarked. "Just like all little boys. Never knew one to like baths."

Mercy smiled for the first time since the fiasco last night. "Actually, Joshua loves his baths. He gets as much water on me as I get on him," she said.

Cora brushed one finger along the baby's cheek. "I reckon he gets bigger every time I see him." She looked up at Pace. "Congratulations, Mr. Lansing. You've done a fine thing giving the boy your name. Someday he'll grow up as big and strong as his godfather."

"Thank you, ma'am." Pace set his hat back on his head. "And give Miss Lily my thanks, too. Miss Goodacre says you've both been right kind to Josh. We both appreciate your help."

"You're most welcome." The lady turned to Mercy. "I suppose we'll see you tomorrow at the Bible study. I hear tell your father is taking over for you and he'll be having it at the parsonage from now on. We surely hope you'll be there with Joshua. The girls have been arguing all week about who's going to hold him first."

Pace wanted to check his hearing. Mercy and the ladies of the Ruby Slipper were friends? And they attended Bible study at the reverend's home? Things sure had changed in Pleasant Valley. Yet, for him, things had remained the same. The people still mistrusted him, they still thought of him as a killer, and he didn't have a friend in the world.

Except Mercy Goodacre, and she was too good to even bid him the time of day. That she would save his hide by sacrificing herself for him burned like a hot branding iron to his chest. If anything, he deserved to be tarred and feathered for what had nearly happened between them— for what he wanted from her.

After bidding them a good day, Cora moved to shake hands with the reverend at the door. Pace took one last glance at the baby, and tipped his hat. "I'd best be running along, too, Miss Mercy." He'd already spent too much time with this woman. And too much time with his own thoughts about her.

Mercy snaked out a hand and stopped his hasty retreat. "I assumed you were staying to have dinner with my father and me."

"I can't, ma'am. I have chores to get to."

"But you have to eat." She lowered her voice. "We have things to discuss."

His gaze fell to her hand, small, white, and soft against his dark skin. "I'll go along with whatever you and your father say."

"It isn't that simple, Mr. Lansing. I have to talk to you, to explain my plan."

He jerked his gaze to her face. "Plan? What are you talking about, Miss Goodacre?"

She opened her mouth to answer, but snapped it shut. Her gaze shifted past his shoulder. From the corner of his eye, Pace glimpsed her father striding toward them.

"Are you ready to take that little fellow home, Mercy?" Reverend Goodacre tickled Joshua under his chin.

Joshua chose that moment to spit out the rag and let out another ear-splitting howl. How could a baby that small make so much noise? he wondered.

Mercy wrapped the baby in the blanket and lifted him to her shoulder. "He's hungry, let's go on home." She paused at the front pew. "Mr. Lansing, will you be so kind as to carry the basket. I have my hands full."

"I'll take it, daughter," her father offered, his hand meeting Pace's on the wicker handle.

"Mr. Lansing can handle it, Papa. I've invited him to have dinner with us."

Ezra Goodacre released his hold on the basket. "Aren't your sisters and their husbands coming to our home?"

"No," she answered, lifting her voice to be heard over the baby's squalls. "They have other plans. So it will be just the three of us."

Pace swallowed down his uneasiness. He'd never been welcome at the tables of polite society. He had little, if any, manners, but he knew enough to understand it would be rude to refuse the invitation. Caught as he had been the past night, Pace could do nothing but follow silently behind the reverend and his daughter.

For a man who wanted to be left alone, Pace suddenly found himself surrounded with people. He was engaged to the preacher's daughter and tied to an infant. And under the scrutiny of the entire town.

Fate or somebody was playing a strange trick on him.

Pace Lansing felt himself being drawn into a net from which there was no escape.

A tiny piece of his heart wanted nothing more than to surrender. Another part warned not to expect too much. He would never be anybody but Pace Lansing, convict, outcast, half-breed.

And he'd best not forget it.

* * *

With dinner finished, and Joshua asleep on a blanket, Mercy served coffee to her father and Pace on the porch. From the looks of him, Pace couldn't wait to escape back to his homestead. As she set the tray on a low wicker table between the men, she caught a glimpse at the uncomfortable expression on Pace's face.

"Sit down, daughter," her father said. "I think we need to have an understanding."

She swallowed down her own embarrassment. It was her fault they were all caught in this predicament.

If only she hadn't invited Pace to that foolish dance. If only she hadn't led him on.

If only she hadn't fallen in love with him.

"Yes, Papa." Mercy willed her cheeks not to pink at the thought.

Her father sipped his coffee, then pierced Pace with a stern stare. "Young man, I'm not quite sure how things got out of hand with you and my daughter. But the facts remain that in front of the entire town, you've asked for her hand. As her father, I intend to see that her honor is preserved." He paused and glanced over at Mercy.

"Papa, I wish you would let me explain."

Pace stood and slapped his hat against his thigh. "Miss Mercy, I think we should listen to what your father has to say. He was kind enough to give his permission when we embarrassed him in front of his friends and neighbors."

Put that way, Mercy knew it would be foolish to try to change the course of events she'd started with her lies. Later, alone with Pace, they could make plans for their breakup.

"Thank you, Lansing," her father said. "I hope you aren't planning to rush into anything. After all, you haven't been keeping company very long."

"No, sir. If it's all right with you, I want to wait until the fall. When I sell my cattle, I'll add a room to the cabin for

Miss Mercy and Joshua. It isn't much, but I promise I'll never hurt her or the baby."

Ezra stiffened his shoulders. "I should hope not. If I suspected such a thing, I would personally take a horse whip to you."

"Papa," Mercy exclaimed. "How can you say such a thing? You've always been against violence."

Ignoring her outrage, her father continued his discourse. "Where my girls are concerned, I don't believe in turning the other cheek. Young man, you realize her sisters and brothers-in-law will also be watching you."

"Yes, sir. Along with the sheriff and half the town. The other half doesn't know me."

Her father ran a finger under his high stiff collar. His Adam's apple bobbed in his throat. "You can keep that in mind if you try to disgrace my daughter in any way."

Pace edged closer to the steps. He looked as if Ezra already had the horse whip in his hand. "I gave my word, sir. I wouldn't do anything to dishonor Miss Mercy. I'll provide for her as best I can."

Mercy bit her lip to keep from crying out. In all this discussion, nobody had mentioned any kind of affection. Not even her father. Did he, like everybody else, consider her unworthy of a man's love? A familiar ache settled in her heart.

"Papa, I think you've given Mr. Lansing enough instructions. May I have a minute alone with him?"

Ezra stood, and stretched out a hand to Pace. "When can we expect to see you again, young man?"

Taking the proffered hand, Pace set his mouth in a hard line. "I'm not sure when I can get back into town, sir. I'm still rounding up my stray cattle, and I'm pretty busy."

"The Word says we're to honor the Sabbath. I'll expect to see you in service next Sunday. And since you're planning to marry my daughter, it's time for the entire family to get together and make peace." By the tone of his voice, her father would brook no argument. He rarely made demands on his family, but church attendance was a priority with him.

"I'll try to make the meeting." Pace pulled back his hand and settled his hat on his head. "Thank you for dinner, ma'am, sir. It was nice. Tell Josh goodbye for me."

"Mr. Lansing, I'll walk you around the house to your horse." She glanced back at her father. "Papa, will you kindly keep an ear out for Joshua? I'll only be a minute."

She fell into step beside Pace along the walkway to where his horse was tethered. He seemed in an awful hurry to get away from her. Not that she could blame him. In the little time she'd known him, she knew that Pace valued his freedom above all else. And she was about to take that freedom away from him.

"I'm really sorry, Mr. Lansing, about the mess I've gotten you into."

"Not your fault. I was to blame for what happened last night. I should be thanking you for saving me from the necktie party those men had in mind." He stopped at the fence and glanced down at her. "You sacrificed yourself for me."

A knot twisted in her chest. "No, I was as much to blame. But I won't force you to go through with this charade. I have a plan."

He wrinkled his brow. "What kind of plan?"

She glanced around to make sure nobody could hear them. Her father had wandered back into the house, and the nearest neighbor was nearly a quarter of a mile away. "To be perfectly honest, nobody wants this marriage to take place, but we've all been caught up in this thing like a tornado. If you try to break it off, my father would be offended, and Clifford wouldn't hesitate to carry out his threats."

"What do you want to do?"

"We can keep up the farce for a while, then I'll tell

everybody that I've changed my mind. If I break off the engagement, nobody will be able to blame you. You'll be the innocent party. We can both get on with our lives. I'll take a trip, and everybody will forget what happened."

A muscle twitched in his jaw and his hands curled into fists. "Miss Mercy, it would be wrong to fool your father like that. I gave him my word. Right now, that's all I have left. I intend to honor my commitment."

Her stomach sank clear to her toes. More than anything she wanted to marry. But not without love. And Pace didn't love her. "You'll have no choice if I refuse to marry you."

"Your father won't allow you to dishonor him like that. And I know Blakely will find a way to blame me. Like it or not, we'll be married in the fall."

Caught in a trap of her own making, Mercy tilted her chin. "Why don't you go along with my plan? You don't want a wife. And I'm not ready to marry."

"Looks like I'm about to get one, and a baby to boot. I made a promise to your father, and I'll keep it." He loosed the reins of his horse.

"What if I refuse to marry you?"

"Then you can just watch me swing from a rope. 'Cause that's what will happen if anybody thinks I've done anything to hurt you or cause you to change your mind."

Her spirits plummeted further. "I never meant for any of this to happen. I'm so sorry."

"I don't blame you for wanting to get out of the deal, Mercy. I'm not much of a bargain. You sure as heck could do better."

She touched his arm, feeling the hard, stiff muscles under her fingertips. "That isn't the reason. I just think a couple should marry for love."

His sad, dark eyes locked on her. "Love? I don't even know what love is. I never had love, and I never wanted love. From what I've seen, love makes a man weak, makes him do foolish things. There's no place in my life for love."

He swung into the saddle and gazed down at her. "I know you have your dreams, and I can't give you what you want. If you're determined to cancel the arrangement, I won't stop you. Do whatever you think is best."

Best? For whom? If she carried out her plan, Pace could be hurt. If she broke off the engagement, she could be the laughingstock of the town. If she married him, she would have to give up her dreams of travel and seeing the world. Worse still, if she married him without love, her heart could be broken. Joshua needed them both. That left her little choice but to carry the engagement through to marriage.

"I will." She hugged her arms to ward off a sudden shiver. The heat of the afternoon did little to warm the chill that settled in her heart.

As Pace rode off, she thought about his warning. He'd as much as told her not to get her hopes up. He didn't love her and never would. She felt as if he'd stomped on her heart and left it crushed in a pile of dust.

Along with her dreams.

Eleven

Miss Lily LaRose timed her departure from the Ruby Slipper to arrive at the parsonage at precisely two o'clock. Against the wishes of his deacon board, Reverend Goodacre insisted on moving the Monday afternoon Bible study to his home. And it was his decision to replace Mercy as the teacher.

The idea held distinct possibilities for Lily. For years she'd been trying to catch the widowed minister's eye. She'd ordered enough furniture from him to furnish all the upstairs rooms at the Ruby Slipper. In his late forties, the man was still attractive, in his own stern, staid manner. But thinking about him was like blowing bubbles into the wind. Whatever made her think a decent man like Ezra Goodacre would be interested in a soiled dove like Lily LaRose?

Head held high, she led her small procession straight down the boardwalk of Main Street. She twirled her pink lace parasol and smiled at Mrs. Fullenwider at the doorway of the mercantile. As always, the mayor's wife refused to recognize the women she considered beneath her. Lily controlled the impulse to tell the woman just how the cow went down the road. But for too many years she'd lived on the outskirts of polite society, and she knew nothing she could say would change her status in the community.

As owner of the Ruby Slipper, she was the town's madam

and saloon keeper. Of course, this wasn't her real ambition in life. For now, she rather enjoyed relieving the arrogant males of their money. Men like Mayor Fullenwider, who held his "council meetings" in the back rooms at the Ruby Slipper. If he won at the weekly poker game, he was certain to spend an hour upstairs with Rosie. Even his son was an occasional visitor, as were a large number of the men of Pleasant Valley. The Reverend Ezra Goodacre being the exception.

Through the windows of People's Bank, she caught a glimpse of Clifford Blakely behind his desk. The arrogant banker was the most hypocritical of the lot. Wouldn't his pretty little wife be shocked at the things he did with Florrie several times a week?

Cora walked proudly at her side, unintimidated by the townspeople. Lily glanced over her shoulder at Florrie and Rosie trailing behind. The girls held their Bibles tightly to their bosoms. Anyone who didn't know better would think them young ladies out for an afternoon stroll. Lily's mild threats had persuaded them to button their simple cotton afternoon gowns to their throats. However, she hadn't been able to convince them to leave the rouge and lip color behind. Even now, the buttons had somehow come loose, showing an immodest amount of white bosoms. She would see that the buttons were again fastened by the time they entered the minister's home.

Her heart beat faster as she turned the corner and the parsonage came into view. She chided herself for her foolish thoughts about the minister.

"Reckon Miss Mercy and Mr. Lansing will actually go through with a wedding?" Cora asked.

Lily shrugged, causing her lace shawl to slip down her arms. "I wonder about that myself. I can't think of a more mismatched couple." Except herself and the reverend, she added to herself.

"I don't agree," her maid said. Cora was her most faithful friend and companion and she always spoke her mind. They'd escaped together from New Orleans in the confusion at the end of the War. Lily had saved Cora's life after she'd been severely beaten by her Creole lover, and Cora had more than once saved Lily from a violent man. "I think they're perfectly suited."

"Cora, Pace is an ex-convict and Mercy is a sweet, innocent young woman."

Cora shifted the basket on her arm. "They're both lonely souls who belong together. Mercy and Pace love Baby Joshua and they both need a home and somebody to love them. It's only a matter of time before they fall in love with each other."

Lily laughed. "Cora Davis, I didn't know you were such a romantic."

She leaned closer and lowered her voice. "If Miss Mercy gets married and leaves the reverend, he might decide to look around for a wife. Don't think I haven't seen the way he glances at you when he thinks nobody is watching."

"Wishful thinking on your part." Lily flipped open her fan and cooled her heated face.

"We'll just have to wait and see what happens."

Not one to get hopes up when she knew they would only be dashed by reality, Lily glanced back at the girls. "Come along. It's nearly two. Time for the Bible study."

Rosie shot Florrie a sly glance. "Yes, ma'am. We don't want to keep the reverend waiting, do we, Florrie?"

"We surely don't. I think he's rather comely, don't you?" the other woman responded.

"In a princely sort of way. Makes you wonder what he's like in bed." Rosie giggled and nudged her companion.

"Girls! That's no way to speak about our minister. He's a man of the cloth." Lily gave up trying to ignore their irreverent banter. More than once, the girls had flirted openly with the minister. Being a true gentleman, Ezra remained aloof and always kind.

"He's a man, ain't, I mean isn't he, Miss Lily?" Rosie patted her red curls and threw back her shoulders, revealing even more of her ample bosom.

Florrie tossed her head in laughter. "Last time I looked at his trousers he appeared to be one."

Cora rushed ahead to open the gate, leaving Lily to deal with her impudent employees. "That's enough." She spun around and speared the girls with a stern stare. "Button your gowns, and watch your mouths. If you don't behave, I'll throw both of you out. We'll see how you like working the back rooms at the Red Dog." The threat of working in the saloon at the other end of town quieted their banter.

"Yes, ma'am," they said in unison. In spite of their instant obedience, Lily noted the glint of rebellion in their smiles.

Flashing them another warning glance, she continued through the gate and up the porch steps. Before she had a chance to knock, Mercy appeared at the door.

"Good afternoon, Miss Lily." She stepped aside and allowed the entourage to enter. "Come in, Cora, Rosie, Florrie. Papa is waiting for you in the parlor."

Reverend Goodacre stood as the women strolled into the parlor. He removed his eyeglasses and slicked his hair back from his forehead. Lily curled her fingers around her fan, itching to comb through his thick thatch of graying hair. "Good afternoon, Reverend, Mercy," she said in greeting. Funny the way her throat constricted every time she addressed the minister. For a worldly woman who'd experienced more than many women twice her age, Lily didn't understand her reaction to the rather ordinary preacher with three grown daughters.

"Are you ladies ready for our studies?" he asked, gesturing to the davenport and chairs set in a circle.

"Yes, sir," Rosie answered. "We even read the scriptures Mercy assigned us."

Cora passed the basket to Mercy. "Before we get started, you can take this into the kitchen."

Mercy studied the covered goods inside. "What is it?"

"Some of my gumbo for your father. I remember how much he liked it when he delivered the armoire to Miss Lily."

"It wasn't necessary to bring anything, Cora," Mercy said. "But we do appreciate it. I've been so busy lately with Joshua, I've been neglecting Papa."

"Speaking of the little man," Lily asked, "where is he?" She settled in the seat nearest the minister's large over-stuffed chair.

"Sleeping, thank heavens. But don't worry, he'll wake up soon enough and demand everybody's attention."

The reverend cleared his throat. "I think we should begin before he wakes up and interrupts our study."

Rosie and Florrie jostled for a position on the sofa. "I get to hold him first," Rosie whispered. "You held him last time."

"You don't know anything about babies," Florrie retorted.

"I know males, and what they like," the other girl shot back.

"Ladies," Lily commanded. "Open your Bibles to today's lesson."

Ezra's face pinked in the most charming way. He adjusted his black coat and returned to his chair. The man was clearly ill at ease with a room full of women, three of whom didn't dare darken the doors of his sanctuary. Cora had started attending the church as soon as they'd moved to town, and she refused to let anybody intimidate her into staying away.

"We're studying the life of King David," Mercy said as she eased into the rocking chair. "The ladies are quite fascinated with his life."

"Yes, I can imagine," the minister said under his breath.

"Today we'll learn how Bathsheba tempted David and caused all kinds of problems for him."

"Papa, I've studied the scriptures, and I don't quite see things that way." Mercy shoved her eyeglasses up her nose. Lily wished the young woman would get rid of the glasses and begin to wear brighter colors. The brown homespun did nothing for her except make her blend in with the furniture.

"What do you mean, daughter?" Ezra frowned, unhappy about having his word disputed.

Lily was forced to add her piece. "I believe I understand, Reverend. Bathsheba didn't tempt David to sin. She was minding her own business when he went up on the roof and spied on her. He lusted after something he couldn't have—a woman who belonged to another man."

"Miss LaRose, I've studied the scriptures quite extensively. It's quite clear that Bathsheba was bathing and she tempted the king to sin."

"Papa, Bathsheba was in her own home, you can't blame her for going about her daily routine." Mercy gestured to the verse in her Bible.

Heat sparkled in the minister's eyes as he warmed to his subject. "You certainly can't deny that the woman committed adultery." He slanted a rather shy glance at Lily. A tinge of pink surfaced to his cheeks. "And she was made to suffer for her sin."

Lily shifted in her chair. As much as she cared for the staunch man, he would never see her as anything except a fallen woman—much like Bathsheba. He had no idea that he was preaching to Lily, or that she had paid greatly for her sins.

Not to be outdone by Reverend Goodacre's harsh declaration, Mercy leaned forward to confront her father. The young woman had always shown a bit of spunk, but lately she'd defied convention and the wrath of her family to do what she thought was right in helping Pace and teaching the Bible class. She'd certainly won Lily's love and respect, as well as the affection of her girls.

"David paid a harsh price, too, for taking another man's wife and having Uriah killed," Mercy stated flatly.

"Yes, yes, you're both right. Let's get on with our study. We'll learn how God forgave David, and he'll forgive others, also."

The remainder of the study passed without controversy while the minister extolled the Word. Cora hung on every word, while Florrie and Rosie looked rather bored. By the time he dismissed them with prayer, Lily wondered if this would be their first and last meeting. However, as he closed his Bible, Ezra stood and grinned rather timidly. "Be sure to study the next few chapters for our lesson next Monday. I'll expect another lively discussion."

Lily's mouth gaped open. "We certainly will, Reverend. And of course we greatly appreciate your taking your time to feed our souls. I hope you'll allow me to make a donation to the church on our behalf." She reached into her handbag.

He held up his hands to stop her. "Miss LaRose, it's my duty to do whatever is necessary. And that pot of gumbo Cora brought is payment enough."

Her heart warmed more by the man's smile than the study, Lily stood and stuck out her gloved hand. "Thank you, Reverend Goodacre."

His touch was strong and firm. As their hands touched, Lily wondered about the real man behind the stiff black suit. Could he be as passionate about a woman as he was about his vocation? Would he ever fall in love again? A rope tightened around her chest, nearly cutting off her breath. Not with a woman like Lily LaRose, an inner voice shouted. From all she'd heard, his first wife was as near to a saint as a woman could get, while Lily was considered the handmaiden of Satan. No, she would never get to know the man of whom she was fast becoming fond.

Their hands locked together, she lifted her gaze to his. His brown eyes sparkled with something she'd never seen there before. Affection, interest? Then just as quickly it disappeared and he tugged his hand free. In spite of the warm afternoon, a chill raced over Lily. She hugged her lace shawl close to her shoulders. When she glanced from the minister, she was aware of the other four women with their gazes locked on her.

With a proud tilt of her chin, she turned to leave. One thing no man had ever stolen from Lily LaRose was her pride. That, plus a few tattered gowns were all she'd taken from New Orleans ten years ago. The gowns had long ago been tossed out, but the pride remained.

"Let's go, ladies," she said. "Reverend Goodacre and Miss Mercy have to get back to their chores."

Florrie stuck out her lower lip like a petulant child. "Aren't we going to get to see Joshua? I wanted to hold him for a little while."

As if he heard the woman's complaint, the baby let out a yell. Everyone, including the minister, started laughing.

"I'll get him," Mercy said. "It's time for his feeding."

"It's my turn," Rosie stated. "Florrie fed him last time."

While Mercy fetched the infant, the girls bickered back and forth in a friendly good-natured way. Lily hoped she could soon find good husbands for them. Cora had taught them how to cook, and the basics of running a household. They'd learned how to manage their money, and both would go into marriage with a handsome dowry. The girls loved children and would make two lucky men fine wives. If the men were able to get past the girls' reputations and see them for the warm, loving women they were.

Lily settled back on the davenport. Her heart sank. In the last ten years she'd been courted by rich men and poor. The only one to interest her, however, was the one she could never have. Ezra Goodacre returned to his chair. While the girls and Mercy fussed over the baby, he cast an occasional glance her way. Then his gaze would drift to the photograph on the mantel. Her gaze followed his.

The young blond woman in the picture stared forward without a smile. She was quite pretty and very young. Prudence looked exactly like her mother. Faith had died giving birth to a baby who also didn't survive. Since then, the reverend hadn't seriously courted any of the widows and spinsters in town. It was clear no woman would live up to the memories of his wife.

Lily returned her glance to him. Interest glittered in his gaze whenever he looked at her. Clearly he was lonely. As lonely as she.

On a sigh, she told herself that for him she would break her own hard-and-fast rule not to take customers. If he ever felt the need, she would open her arms, her heart, and her bed to the man.

All given freely, and with love.

Twelve

Pace argued with his conscience all week. He owed Mercy a lot. More than he could repay. Whatever troubles hounded him now, he had brought on himself. He had killed Billy Blakely. He probably would have been hanged if she hadn't come to his defense. Since his return, she'd helped him when everybody else would have run him off on a rail. When he needed someone to care for Joshua, she'd been there, giving freely of her time and money to take care of another woman's baby.

All he'd given her in return was trouble. Because of his impropriety they'd been caught in a compromising position and forced into an engagement neither wanted. Her idea might work. If she broke off the betrothal, they both might be able to get on with their lives. Their separate lives.

As he rode into town late the next Saturday afternoon, he wondered about his own life. He'd come to like being with her and Joshua. The baby was important to him—the child he'd never thought to have. He'd surely never dreamed of having a woman like Mercy Goodacre in his life.

At first he hadn't planned to obey her father's dictates to attend church the next day. But his need for nails to repair the house and barn made the trip into town necessary.

This time he didn't have to beg for credit. Pace was able to stand up like a man and pay for his purchases. Mayor Fullenwider at the hardware store stared at him suspiciously when Pace forked over the cash. Pace nearly laughed out loud at the merchant's expression. The mayor probably thought Pace had robbed a bank or something. Everybody knew he was flat broke and that Mercy Goodacre was grubstaking him.

He jingled the coins in his pocket. Lord, it sounded good. And he felt good, too. A nester passing through had needed a heifer and Pace had sold him one with a newborn calf. The man didn't have much cash, so they bartered with some goods the man could spare. Not that Pace had much use for a silver-plated brush and mirror set. But he'd taken it with the thought that he could sell it or, better still, give it to Mercy.

The woman on his mind, he wandered toward the mercantile. The streets were crowded and noisy with people and animals. A tinkling piano rang from the open doors of the Ruby Slipper. For a second he considered going into the saloon for a cold beer. Then he thought about what he owed Mercy, and decided to save his few coins.

As usually happened when he entered the store, the other customers stepped aside to make room. Mercy stood in front of a row of shelves, stretching on tiptoes to reach a can beyond her fingertips. He reached a hand over her head, and pressed the tin can into her hand.

"This what you're looking for?" he asked.

Startled, she jerked back, ramming her shoulder into his chest. "Pace, you scared me," she said.

His arm around her waist to keep her from falling, he gazed into her golden brown eyes. "Sorry, ma'am. Just wanted to help."

She was warm and soft, and smelled of peppermint candy. Her hair had come loose from her bun, and stray tendrils touched her ears and pink cheeks. "Thank you."

She clutched the can of peaches to her bosom. "What are you doing here?"

He glanced around the store, and saw that all action had stopped and everybody was watching him. "Can we talk later? What time do you quit?"

"In a few minutes." Her gaze dropped to his arm still firmly attached to her waist. Reluctantly, he loosened his grip. "If you can wait, you can walk me and Joshua home."

Pace nodded. A sense of being needed, of belonging, spread over him like a warm blanket. "Where is the little fellow?"

"Over behind the stove," she said. "He'll be waking up any minute."

Moving away from her, he scanned the space for the baby's basket. Josh was still sleeping, so Pace wandered the store. He took in the merchandise he hoped to buy when he was able to sell his cattle—a new halter and blanket for his horse, a brand new Stetson hat, and something nice for Mercy.

Mercy returned to the counter and added the peaches to a box of goods. The lady bid good day, and left with her purchases. Only a handful of customers remained, mainly farmers talking together, catching up on the news rather than buying anything. And of course, the two old men playing checkers.

The bell over the door jangled, and Pace slanted a glance at the newcomer. The man was a stranger to town, but he easily recognized the type. Dressed in a blue cap with the Cavalry insignia, he wore the dirty blue pants of a man recently released from the military. A large Colt revolver hung from his hip, and a drizzle of tobacco juice ran down his chin. He'd seen more of this type than he cared to ever encounter again.

The stranger's narrowed gaze shifted back and forth, taking in the entire room in a single glance. Former soldiers often took jobs as prison guards, since they were cruel, hard men full of hatred with nowhere to go after their discharge. A shiver raced up Pace's back. He stood stock-still and instinctively slipped into the shadows.

The man stomped to the counter and slammed his fist onto the wooden board. Where the heck was Fullenwider? Did the shopkeeper often leave Mercy alone to deal with the rough men who came into town looking for trouble?

"May I help you, sir?" She took a step backward.

"Ya jest might, little lady." He scanned her face then dropped his gaze to her bosom.

Pace took one step toward them but checked himself. It wouldn't do any good to cause trouble in the store. Mercy's family already had the worst opinion possible of him.

"I'm looking for a woman. I figure somebody in town might of seen her." He spit a wad of brown juice on the floor, missing the spittoon by a foot.

"There are a lot of women in town. Why don't you ask over at the Ruby Slipper, they might be able to help. Or you can try the Red Dog Saloon."

The stranger glanced around, catching the gazes of the men. One by one they looked away. "Most folks get into the mercantile sooner or later. Figured you might have heard about her. She's Indian, about so high." He moved his dirty gloved hand up Mercy's arm to her shoulder. "Goes by the name of Naomi."

Mercy's face turned deadly white. "No. I haven't seen an Indian woman."

His hand tightened on her arm. "Well, if I can't find my woman, guess I'll have to take another one. You'll do jes' fine. She was too skinny anyway. I like my woman nice and plump. Like a tasty hen."

Deadly fury swamped Pace like a bolt out of the blue. This was the man who'd abused Naomi. The man responsible for her pain and death. Now he dared touch Mercy. In a flash, Pace leaped on the man, snatching him by the front of his shirt, and slamming him against the wall. Cans and jars rattled. "Leave the lady alone. If you want Naomi, I'll take you to her."

"Pace," Mercy called. "What are you doing?"

In a burst of rage he tossed the man onto the floor. "Taking him to his woman."

The stranger shoved himself up and reached for his gun. Just as quickly, Pace kicked the weapon from his hand. The man yelled in pain. "Who the hell are you? I didn't mean no harm."

Around them the farmers and their wives backed away. "He's Pace Lansing. He's a convict. He killed a man." The words echoed in the now quiet store.

"You touched my woman. That's what you did." Pace picked up the gun and shoved it into the waistband of his denims.

Tim Fullenwider appeared as if by magic. "Lansing, get out of here. Haven't you caused enough trouble for Mercy?" Tim placed his arm around Mercy. She clutched her cheeks with her palms.

Pace shot an angry glance at the storekeeper. The man didn't try to defend his sister-in-law, and he'd shown up a few minutes too late to do any good.

"I'm going." Grabbing the stranger by the collar of his shirt, he hauled the man to his feet. The man smelled worse than a billy goat on a hot summer's day. "I'm going to take him to Naomi."

The spectators moved aside, making an aisle through the store. Pace shoved the man in front of him, nearly lifting him off his feet.

"You know where she is, just tell me," the man yelled stumbling to stay on his feet.

"I'll show you."

Fury propelled Pace to force the man in front of him down the middle of the dusty street. Horses shied, and wagons pulled to the side to let them through. The curious followed a dozen yards behind to see what kind of excitement they could find. They fully expected to see the notorious Pace Lansing kill a man. But they were going to be disappointed. This sorry piece of dung wasn't worth a bullet it took to put him out of his misery.

"Hey, where are you taking me?" the filthy varmint shouted, fear in his voice. As they neared the cemetery, the man cowered with fear.

In spite of the parade on his heels, Pace didn't slow his pace. Inside the fenced graveyard, he continued to the newly dug grave, not yet covered with grass. There he shoved the man facedown on the ground. "Here she is. Naomi." Pace pulled the man's shaggy hair so his face was level with the name on the wooden cross.

If the man was pale before, his ruddy face blanched like new fallen snow. "She's dead? Who did it? I'll kill him."

"You did, you dirty son of a boar hog. You beat her and nearly starved her to death. She's buried here." Pace released his grip and the man fell to the ground.

He scurried away on all fours, as if afraid of what Pace would do next. Pace wasn't sure how much longer he could hold his temper in check.

"What about the kid?"

Lowering his voice so only the man could hear, he whispered, "Right in there with her." There was no way he would ever let this brute get his hands on Joshua. "Take my advice and get out of town."

"Who do you think you are?"

Again he grabbed the man by the front of his shirt and lifted him off the ground. "I'm Pace Lansing. Don't you know I killed a man with my bare hands?" Unable to control his hatred, Pace pulled back his right hand, ready to wield just a bit of what Naomi had received. The instant before his fist struck home, a voice stopped him.

"Pace, don't." Mercy grabbed his arm, tugging with all her weight and strength. "He isn't worth it."

Shocked back to reality, he tossed the man aside like a sack of garbage. "You're right. He isn't worth the effort." Still clutching his arm, Mercy guided him toward the gate.

The crowd that had been watching the whole episode parted like the Red Sea before Moses. When they had reached the gate, Reverend Goodacre and Sheriff Jennings blocked their path.

"What kind of trouble are you starting now, Lansing?" the sheriff asked, his gun drawn and ready.

Shoving Mercy behind him, he faced the lawman eye to eye. "That renegade was trying to hurt Miss Goodacre. He's the one who killed Naomi."

"You can't prove that, mister. She was my woman and she ran away. I don't know what happened to her after that." Now that he saw help, the stranger staggered toward the sheriff. "He didn't have no cause to hit me."

"It doesn't look as if you've been struck," Reverend Goodacre stated in his booming preacher's voice.

"I admit I wanted to, but I didn't hit him." Pace slanted an angry glance at the man.

"What's your name?" asked the sheriff.

"Denby, Ham Denby." He brushed the loose dirt off his shirt.

"What are you doing in Pleasant Valley?"

Denby backed away from the lawman. "Looking for my woman. This man says she's dead."

"Was she Indian? Young?" The minister glared angrily at Denby.

"Yeah."

"He's right. I buried her myself."

"I think it's best you make your way back to where you belong," Jennings stated in no uncertain terms.

"Okay. I'll leave at first light." He glanced over his shoulder at Pace. "If my woman is dead, I don't need to stay in this sorry town."

"Just see that you leave." Jennings watched as Denby

staggered toward the heart of town. "Lansing, stay out of trouble." With the warnings ringing in the air, the sheriff led the procession back to Main Street.

When Pace was finally alone with Mercy and her father, he brushed his hands against his pants to wipe off the filth of handling the man. "Reckon I embarrassed you again." His heart sank at the distraught look on her face.

Mercy bit her lip, her chin trembling. "Do you think he's Joshua's father?"

"Could be. There's no way to know for sure. I ain't going to ask him to find out. No telling what a man like that would do with a baby. As far as anybody is concerned, the baby is mine."

Reverend Goodacre took his daughter by the arm. "I agree with you, Lansing. Joshua is better off with us until you and Mercy marry."

"Yes, sir. By the way, where is Josh?"

Mercy hurried her footsteps. "I left him with Charity. He's probably giving her fits about now."

By the time they'd reached the corner of Main and Jefferson, Charity Fullenwider and her husband Tim met them. Their son tagged at his mother's skirt. "Where did you run off to, Mercy? This baby has been screaming his head off since you left." She looked up at Pace. "I should have known he was causing trouble again." Charity shoved the whimpering baby into Mercy's arms.

Mercy nestled the baby against her shoulder. Josh stopped crying instantly. "It wasn't Pace's fault. That man came into the store and started the trouble. Pace came to my rescue."

Tim caught his wife's hand. "I don't care who's at fault. I've got a store to run. Let's get back so we can close up."

Charity tugged her hand free and set her fists on her hips. "Mercy, I wish you would marry him so people will stop talking about you. Prudy and I can hardly hold our heads up. Papa, you've got to do something."

"I will, daughter," the minister said in a soothing voice. "Let's talk about it on the way back to the mercantile. Lansing, will you please see Mercy and the baby home. I'll be along directly."

"Yes, sir."

Mercy glanced to her side at Pace. He was so tall and stalwart, so strong and brave. He'd jumped to her rescue when Tim had cowered in a corner. He'd accepted a stranger's child when others would have sent the baby to an orphanage.

"Do you think he'll try to get Joshua away from us?" she asked, her voice a husky whisper.

"Not likely. A man like Denby doesn't have any use for a kid. He wanted the woman."

"I hate to think of what he did to her. She was so young and pretty."

Pace's normally stoic expression shifted into a dark scowl. "Any man who would hurt a woman doesn't deserve to live. One day he'll get what's coming to him."

The utter hatred and malice in his voice sent a shiver up her spine. So far Pace had managed to control his temper, but would he be able to in another encounter with Denby? Fortunately the sheriff would see that the despicable man left in the morning. Until then, she would see that Pace remained safe.

"Will you stay in town for church tomorrow?" she asked.

"I suppose so. It's what your father wants."

In spite of her anxiety for Pace, Mercy was glad he had enough regard for her father to respect his wishes. "You're welcome to stay with us. We have lots of room."

"No, thanks. I wouldn't know what to do in such a fine house. I'll camp out down by the river."

Her heart sank with disappointment. She wished she

could spend at least a little time with the man she was supposedly engaged to. "You can stay for supper with us."

He stopped at the gate that led to the house. "I appreciate your offer. But you've already done enough for me."

"I haven't done anything. I'll pack you a piece of the chocolate cake I baked this morning."

If Mercy didn't put a light in his eyes, her cooking did. That hurt. Just once, she wished a man would look at her the way Pace looked at her chocolate cake.

She handed Joshua over to him. "Hold the baby while I pack you a basket."

He looked slightly flustered with the squirming baby in his arms. Mercy rushed ahead and entered through the kitchen door. "This will just take a second." She sliced a piece of cake and set it on the table with a cup of coffee. In Pace's arms, Joshua cooed and waved his arms. Her heart tripped. Being with him and the baby felt so natural, as if they really belonged together. As if they were a family. But that was never to be. In a short time, she would break the engagement and free him from his commitment.

While he played with the baby, she wrapped some bread, meat, an apple, and a large piece of cake in a napkin. Then she heated milk for the baby and prepared his nursing bottle. Sensing it was mealtime, Joshua yelled to let them know he was ready to eat.

"Thank you kindly, Miss Mercy. I'd best be seeing to my horse. I left him down by the livery." He started to hand over the baby when Mercy shoved the bottle into his hand.

"Hold on a second, Mr. Lansing. I forgot to give you something." Hurrying up the stairs, she retrieved his now clean and ironed shirt from her bureau.

When she placed it in the basket with the food, he lifted a startled gaze to her. "What's that?"

"Your shirt. I appreciate you lending it to me."

"You didn't have to wash and press it." Pace stood and handed over the baby.

"It's no trouble. We have a laundry lady who comes once a week." She didn't mention she'd washed it herself rather than let Mrs. Oslo see the big blue shirt that clearly wasn't her father's. That bit of news would have spread more fuel on the fire already shooting from the gossips' tongues like flames from a dragon.

Mercy lifted Joshua to her shoulder. "Tell Pace we'll see him tomorrow at worship," she said.

He brushed a long tanned finger over the infant's downy hair. "Be good for Miss Mercy and look after her while I'm gone."

The softness and caring in his voice brought Mercy's head up with a start. Could he care for her, just a little? Warm black eyes met soft brown ones. Her breath caught in her throat. Longing and need glittered like diamonds in his look. His gaze fell to her mouth. She parted her dry lips and moistened them with the tip of her tongue. More than anything she wanted to feel his mouth on hers, to know again that brief moment of passion they'd shared outside the dance.

His hand stroked slowly down the baby's head and rested lightly near Mercy's throat. Ever so gently, he brushed the backs of his knuckles across her cheek. Heat sizzled through her, and she felt as if even her bones were melting under his touch. She stared at his mouth, his lips full and inviting. When he lowered his head, she stretched to meet him halfway.

The instant before their lips met, a noise from the front of the house drew them up short. Pace jerked away. "Someone came in," he whispered, his voice husky and raw.

"My father," she sputtered, barely able to catch her breath.

In a burst of speed that left Mercy's head spinning, Pace dashed toward the door.

"Pace," Mercy whispered loudly. "Take the basket."

He grabbed the package she'd prepared, and darted through the rear door as Ezra meandered from the parlor.

"Did I hear you talking to somebody?" he asked, slipping his arms from his coat.

"Just Joshua," she murmured. "I'll get your supper as soon as I change him."

His gaze shifted to the empty cup and plate still on the table, but he didn't say anything. "We have to prepare tomorrow's message as soon as supper is over."

Color raced to her face. Her father knew Pace had been there; he could hardly have missed the closing of the back door. She was thankful he had chosen not to say anything.

"Yes, Papa. I'm sure it will be as inspiring as last Sunday's."

After Mercy had washed the dishes and cleaned the kitchen, she settled in the parlor to assist her father. While they discussed the Scriptures for the next day's sermon, she gently rocked Joshua in the cradle she'd borrowed from Charity. Although she managed to hold a coherent conversation, her thoughts were on Pace. Where was he? Was he comfortable? Did he have enough to eat? She prayed he wouldn't do anything foolish, like going after Denby.

The baby fell asleep and her father dozed off with his Bible on his lap. Loud pounding on the door jerked her to her feet. She couldn't imagine what was wrong, or who would be knocking on their door after nine o'clock.

She strolled to the door and peeked around the lace curtain. A dark shadow stood just outside the dim light from the windows. Pace? she wondered. Something must surely be wrong.

Tearing open the door, she jumped back when a man's

rough hand shoved her aside. She squealed and her father jerked to his feet.

"Where is he?" Denby shouted.

"Who?" She moved toward her father for protection.

"My kid. The one Naomi had. I want my son."

Thirteen

From his makeshift shelter in the Goodacres' wood shed, Pace kept a diligent watch over the house. He'd started for the river, but some instinct warned him to keep an eye on Mercy.

He saw the figure march up to the door. For a second he thought the man was either Fullenwider or Blakely, or one of the men from town looking for the reverend.

Mercy's piercing scream warned him otherwise. Something was wrong. He took off at a run and vaulted onto the porch. Through the open doorway, he spotted Denby in the middle of the parlor waving his fists at Mercy.

Reverend Goodacre shoved his daughter behind him, facing the man with all the protective instincts of a father. "Get out of my home before I send for the sheriff."

"If you want my kid, you can pay me for him." The man started toward the cradle where Josh was sleeping.

Pace's temper exploded with the force of a land mine. He grabbed the man by his shoulder and spun him around. In one movement, Pace smashed his fist into Denby's sneering face. The man staggered backward. He hit the wall and slid to the floor. Instantly Pace was on him. His knees at Denby's chest, he slammed his fist into the man's face. Eyes bulging in his head, Denby tried to fend off Pace's blows. But Pace was fueled with fury. The words "I want my kid" roared in his head, knocking out all sense of time and place.

One voice managed to penetrate his violence-dazed brain. "Pace, stop. You're going to kill him. Don't. I need you. Joshua needs you."

Mercy tugged at his shoulder; her father grabbed his arm. The man under him twisted and bucked, trying to free himself from Pace's grip. Pace shook his head to clear away the red haze that had gripped him.

"Lansing, let him go." The preacher's sharp tone snapped him back to reality.

Pace lifted his fists, surprised at the blood on his knuckles. He glared down at the man's battered face. Had he done this? Had he lost control and couldn't stop himself? For a second his mind had shot back to five years ago, and the face he was pounding was Billy Blakely's. His hands trembling, Pace rose to his feet, towering over the injured man.

Denby struggled to his feet, and staggered against the wall. He wiped his hands across his split lip. Black and purple bruises were visible under a thick stubble. Eyes glittering with hatred, he glanced from Pace to Reverend Goodacre. "You can't stop me from taking what's mine."

The words poured kerosene on the fire that Pace was trying to stamp out. He took a quick step toward the man. Mercy jumped between him and the pitiful excuse for a man. "Pace, don't."

"There's nothing here that belongs to you," Pace stated, wiping the sweat from his brow. He picked up his hat that had flown off during the fight.

"They told me Naomi had a kid before she died." Denby spit out a broken tooth and a wad of blood. "The preacher's daughter has the baby."

"That's my son," Pace stated in deep, flat voice. There was no way he would let the bastard take the baby, or sell him. "Naomi's son died. This boy is mine."

Denby looked to Reverend Goodacre for confirmation. "Is that true?"

The minister swallowed; his Adam's apple bobbed and his face turned red. "If Lansing claims the child, I can't say otherwise."

Pace sagged with relief, and Mercy gripped his arm. "You heard him. Get out of here, Denby. If I see you around here again, I swear I'll kill you."

"Pace!" Mercy gasped. "Don't say that."

He advanced toward the man, but stopped short. Hadn't he already caused enough trouble for Mercy and her father?

Reverend Goodacre shoved against Denby's back. "Get out of my home. If you ever show your face around here, I'll have the sheriff throw you into jail."

Denby staggered toward the doorway. "You ain't heared the last of this."

"I certainly hope we have, young man. Stay away from my daughter and my home." The minister gestured to the doorway. He followed Denby onto the porch and remained there until the man had disappeared down the street.

From the open doorway, Pace spotted the spectators watching from the shadows. Didn't the people have anything better to do than spy on Mercy and her father? Without a doubt, every word and action would be spread throughout the entire county by morning.

He turned to Mercy, surprised at the weary look on her face. She snatched off her spectacles and brushed a finger under her eyes. His heart swelled with an emotion he'd never felt before. The feeling was so foreign, he didn't know what to do next.

"He wants to sell Joshua." Her voice dropped to a husky whisper.

Not knowing what else to do, he opened his arms and drew her close to his chest. "I won't let that happen. Josh belongs with us. I'll do whatever I have to do to protect him." She was soft and warm, and smelled of rose water. Heat stirred in him.

"He's gone." Reverend Goodacre's deep voice came from the doorway. His hard gaze bore into Pace and Mercy. She pulled away, a flush on her face.

"Thank God," Mercy whispered. Moving across the room, she glanced down into the cradle. "You'll be safe here, little fellow. Papa and Pace will see that nothing happens to you."

The minister studied Pace for a long moment. "Lansing, how did you happen to get here so quickly?"

He twisted his hat in his fingers. "I was worried that Denby would try something. I decided to spend the night where I could keep an eye out for you."

Ezra drew himself up to his full height, barely past Pace's shoulder. "Did you think I couldn't protect my household?"

Aware his strong-armed tactics had insulted the minister's manhood, Pace felt obligated to explain. "Yes, sir, I mean no, sir. I just feel that this is all my fault. I didn't want anything to happen to you, or Miss Mercy or Joshua."

"Papa, Mr. Lansing only wanted to help us. We should be grateful."

"I suppose you're right, daughter. That man meant nothing but harm for us." The minister turned to the kitchen. "Would you care for a cup of coffee, Lansing? My daughter has some cake left."

The offer tempted Pace to stay—to enjoy the warmth of the family. However, he knew the minister was only being polite. "No, thank you, Reverend. I've caused enough trouble for Miss Mercy as it is. I'll be on my way."

"Mr. Lansing." The worried sound of Mercy's voice stopped him with his hand on the doorknob. "You're more than welcome to stay with us. We have lots of room."

"Again, I have to refuse, ma'am. I'll bunk out in the wood shed."

Settling his hat on his head, he continued out the door. A quick glance over his shoulder showed Mercy silhouetted in the doorway. Under his breath he cursed the needs she inspired in his body—the longing in his soul. And he cursed the circumstances that would forever keep them apart.

Mercy lay awake most of the night worrying about Pace. Joshua usually slept through the night, but she got up and checked on him anyway. Fear of losing the baby had robbed her of much-needed rest. Assured the child was well, she stared out the window. The night was very quiet, with only the sounds of night insects and the hoot of the owl who inhabited the wood shed to break the silence.

Was Pace out there somewhere, watching the house? Somehow, she felt safer knowing he cared enough to stand guard against trouble. After her eyes had adjusted to the darkness, she studied the shadows among the trees. Under the large oak that offered shade in the summer and protection from the wind in winter, she spotted a tiny red glow of the tip of a cigarette. Even as she watched, it disappeared.

In the darkness of night, she let her mind wander to the man who'd come to mean more to her than she dared even admit to herself. Butterflies danced a reel in her stomach whenever he came close to her. She hugged her arms to her chest, remembering the way he'd opened his strong arms and invited her into his embrace. Nothing she'd ever experienced in her life compared to the way he made her feel.

The night at the dance when he'd kissed her had more than fulfilled a maiden's dreams of romance. To be held and kissed by a man brought out all the longings she'd tried to bury—all the feelings she'd tried to deny. If only things were different. She'd lied and told her father they were engaged, but she had to give Pace a chance to get out of the arrangement. No matter how much she loved him, it wasn't fair to trap a man that way.

With the faint glow of dawn on the horizon, Mercy turned from her vigil to wash and dress for church. She reached into her wardrobe for her brown plaid Sunday gown, but her fingers bypassed it in favor of the pretty frock with the purple flowers she'd worn to the dance. For a minute, her common sense debated with her femininity. When she heard Joshua stirring, she grabbed the closest garment. She wasn't surprised to see she'd picked out the pretty lawn gown that Pace had admired.

The instant she'd finished fastening the tiny buttons, the baby let out a loud squeal. Picking him up to keep from waking her father, she realized she hadn't had time to twist her hair into its usual bun. The brown tresses lay heavily around her shoulders.

Unable to finish her toilette, she concentrated on the infant. With a skill learned of necessity, she changed his diaper, washed him, and dressed him in a clean gown. Wrapping him in a blanket, she carried him to the kitchen for his morning feeding.

The hungry baby took only minutes to empty the bottle of milk. His stomach full, and his diaper clean, she placed him in his basket while she prepared breakfast.

Once the coffee was made, she opened the rear door and searched the grounds for Pace. Surely he deserved hot coffee against the chill of the early morning. "Mr. Lansing," she called in a loud whisper. When no answer came, she ventured into the yard. She checked the spot under the oak, where she'd thought she'd seen him, but found no sign he'd even been there.

Fear gripped her heart. What if something had happened to him? What if Denby had attacked him during the night? Lifting her skirt against the dew-dampened grass, she moved on silent feet toward the wood shed. Her dress boots left a path of footsteps in the moisture. The soft whinny of a horse carried on the breeze. Pace's stallion? she wondered.

At the lopsided door of the wood shed, she paused to catch her breath. Afraid of what she would find, she shoved the wooden door open an inch. A thin streak of daylight slanted across the dirt floor. "Mr. Lansing?" she whispered, her words raspy and low.

As she took one tentative step across the threshold, the door jerked open. Mercy found herself face to face with a pistol.

She gasped and her hand flew to her mouth. Past the hand holding the gun, her gaze leveled on a bare male chest. He was big and muscular, his face lost in the shadows of the shed. Her knees grew weak, and she would have crumbled to the ground if his hand hadn't stretched out and clutched her upper arm.

"Mercy, what the hell are you doing?"

"Pace?" she squealed. "You scared me half to death."

"Yeah. Well, I didn't know who was sneaking around the shed at this time of morning." He returned the gun to the holster at his hip.

"I . . . I just wanted to know if you'd like some coffee." Her eyes adjusting to the dim light, she studied the half-naked man before her. His skin was bronzed, the color of the rich warm birch her father used to fashion cabinets and chests. She'd never been this close to a man in this stage of undress. The heady feeling brought a catch to her throat.

He stepped away from her and snatched up the clean shirt she'd given him the day before. "I'll come up to the porch as soon as I finish washing," he said, turning away from her.

Her gaze lingered on his strong back. She yearned to

reach out and touch his skin, to learn for herself the texture of his flesh. Only when she took one small step closer did she spot the thin white lines that crisscrossed the wide expanse of flesh. Scars. Pain lashed through her. Pain for the untold agonies he'd suffered at the hands of other men.

He spun around and tugged the shirt down over his chest. "Ugly, ain't they?" he asked as if he could read her thoughts. "You should have seen them a year ago." His voice was as cold and hard as the ice that formed in the dead of winter. And his eyes were every bit as bleak.

"I'm so sorry." Unable to pull her gaze from him, she spotted the marks at his throat and both wrists—scars made by shackles or ropes. Reminders that he would always bear of his years in prison. A constant reminder of her part in the incident that had caused him to lose five years of his life.

"They're healed. They don't bother me. But I'm afraid the ladies don't think much of my looks."

"That isn't true," she whispered.

His gaze swept over her, touching her eyes, her lips, then settled on her long disheveled hair. He reached out a hand and twisted a shiny brown lock around one finger. "Are you afraid of me, Miss Mercy?"

Tingles raced over her from his gentle touch. "No." She shoved her hands into the pockets of her apron to keep from reaching out to him. He was the handsomest man she'd ever seen—a man any woman would be proud to call her own.

He slid his fingers along her nape, his thumb stroked her throat. "You should be. Most women won't get within a stone's throw of me. With a bit of pressure I could break your windpipe."

The threat hung in the air between them. But Mercy wasn't frightened and it didn't change the feelings in her heart. "I don't believe you want to hurt me." At least not physically. What she feared most was his power to destroy her soul and spirit.

"No, I could never hurt you." His touch gentled, his thumb stroked her tender skin. He lowered his face, and she was certain he was going to kiss her. Warmth radiated from his body. "Miss Mercy, where's the baby?"

That was the last thing she'd expected him to ask. She jerked away, snapped out of her daydreams by his words. Aware that Joshua could even now be screaming his head off, she felt the color rise in her cheeks. "I left him in the kitchen. I didn't intend to be gone so long." Her concern for Pace had chased all other thoughts from her mind. "Please come up to the house for breakfast."

"Thank you, ma'am." He fastened every button, effectively covering every scar and mark. Then he tied a bandanna at his throat.

Halfway across the lawn, she glanced back over her shoulder. He remained in the doorway, his wide shoulder propped against the wall. "We're having hot cakes," she called back.

"Hope you got lots of syrup."

She smiled. "Maple."

Once back in her kitchen, Mercy leaned against the door to catch her breath. She brushed her hand over her nape where moments ago Pace had held her captive. Letting out a long sigh, she realized that he'd long before captured her heart.

With Pace at her side, Mercy greeted the church members on the path leading to the white frame building. Although some spoke a curt greeting, most steered clear of Pace. He'd been very quiet, as if he was completely out of his element. Mercy hated putting him through any discomfort, but they had to keep up appearances until she could break off their betrothal.

As she'd expected, her father was polite, but aloof during breakfast. After eating, Ezra excused himself and left for the church. He liked to arrive early to open the windows and welcome the flock.

While Mercy had completed her toilette, Pace kept Joshua company. To her surprise, he'd also washed the dishes, and straightened the kitchen. Inside the sanctuary, Pace steered Mercy to the rear pew. "In case Joshua cries," he said. Her sister, Charity, shoved Timmy ahead when he tried to stop and talk to Mercy. They settled on the front pew with the Mayor and his wife.

Mercy was grateful to remain in the rear. She didn't want everybody in the church staring holes into the back of her head. She sat, and Pace set the baby's basket between them. As the bells began to toll, her father walked down the center aisle, his black Bible in his hand. Mercy always felt a thrill when she watched her father take his place in the pulpit. He wasn't classically handsome or tall like Pace, but she often thought he looked exactly as God would look. Ever since childhood, she'd been proud to be his daughter.

The pianist struck up a chord, and Ezra picked up a songbook. A commotion at the rear door brought his head up. His gaze turned stormy. One by one, heads swiveled to see what was causing the disruption. Murmurs droned like swarming bees. Mercy's heart slammed against her ribs as Sheriff Jennings marched down the aisle to the front. Two men armed with shotguns guarded the door. Mayor Fullenwider leaped up and met the sheriff at the minister's side.

"What do you mean disrupting my church service, Sheriff?" her father asked.

Mercy reached over and clutched Pace's hand. He was ramrod stiff. She sensed that if she hadn't been with him, he would have bolted and run.

Jenning's gaze slid over the congregation and settled on

Pace. Mercy's pulse raced. Something was very wrong. She felt it clear to the center of her soul.

"I'm looking for Lansing," the sheriff announced.

Pace stood, and settled his hand on the gun at his hip. "I'm right here, Jennings. What do you want?"

From the corner of her eyes, she saw the two armed deputies level their shotguns at Pace.

"Don't try anything. You're under arrest." Jennings moved down the aisle. Shock left Mercy immovable.

"What for?" her father managed to say.

"Murder."

Gasps and whispers grew louder. Accusations, reproaches, and fingers pointed at Pace.

"No," Mercy jumped up and moaned.

The deputy snatched the gun from Pace's holster. "I didn't kill anybody," he said between his teeth.

Jennings faced Pace eye to eye. "We found Denby's body in the alley behind the Ruby Slipper. He looked like he'd been beaten to death."

Pace clamped his mouth shut and glared at the sheriff.

"Half the town saw you fight with him. Not only at the cemetery but at the preacher's house last night." Jennings reached out with a pair of manacles toward Pace.

Mercy watched his face turn pale. After all he'd gone through, she doubted he could survive this kind of indignity again. Yet the man refused to speak in his own defense.

She couldn't let this happen. She wouldn't let them take him to jail. True, he'd fought with him, and now Denby was dead. However nobody deserved it more than a man who would kill his woman and try to sell his own son.

"When do you figure he died?" she asked.

"Denby left the Ruby Slipper at about one o'clock. Nobody saw him after that. I figure you were waiting for him in the alley and finished what you'd started earlier."

Mercy clutched Pace's arm. "He didn't do it." Mercy wasn't certain where Pace had spent the night, but she would sacrifice her life to save his. She loved him that much.

The sheriff turned his gaze to Mercy. "How do you know, Miss Mercy?"

"Because he spent the night with me."

Mercy clutched Pace's arm, silently begging him not to contradict her. Without words, she knew he wouldn't survive jail, if the townspeople let him get that far. They were constantly watching to see him make a mistake and prove them right.

"Daughter, you didn't," her father said, his voice full of pain and reproach.

Her heart clenched. In helping Pace, she'd hurt her father and her family. Charity appeared at her father's side, while Mrs. Fullenwider and the other ladies whispered among themselves.

"Mercy, do you mean you spent the night with this outlaw?" Charity demanded, her face strawberry red.

Pace twined his fingers with hers. "No, ma'am, she didn't."

"Who's telling the truth here, Lansing or Miss Mercy?" Sheriff Jennings glared at both Pace and Mercy.

"You don't have to protect my reputation, Pace," Mercy said, praying she wouldn't be struck dead for lying in church. "I don't care if they know we were together. We didn't do anything unseemly, we only sat and talked."

"Talked?" Charity squealed. "It doesn't matter what you did. You spent the night unchaperoned. Mercy Goodacre, you're a disgrace to all of us."

At that moment two other figures pushed through the doorway and stepped right into the middle of the melee. Mercy groaned. Prudy and Clifford would make matters worse.

"What has Mercy done now?" her youngest sister asked.

"She says she spent the night with that murderer." Charity pointed an accusing finger at Pace.

Anger emanated from Pace like heat from an inferno. He shook off her hand and took one step toward the sheriff. "I didn't kill that man, and Mercy hasn't done anything wrong. She doesn't deserve this kind of treatment."

"Neither does Pace," she added to his confession.

By the looks on their faces, nobody except her father believed a word of it. "Enough," he announced. "If my daughter said she spent the night talking with Lansing, then I believe her. Sheriff, if you aren't here to worship with us, I would appreciate you taking your deputies and leaving my church."

Jennings shoved his gun back into his holster. "If Miss Mercy vouches for him, I suppose I'll have to go along with the alibi." He turned his attention to Mercy. "I hope you know what you're doing, ma'am. This man is dangerous. Call me if you need help." Reluctantly, he passed the revolver back to Pace.

More than anybody, Mercy knew about the dangers Pace posed. Dangers to her heart, not to her person. That was the worst kind of peril.

Ezra turned his righteous indignation to the congregation. "If you will regain your seats, we will begin the worship." Then he pointed a finger at Mercy and Pace. "And since you've already announced your betrothal, we'll conduct the marriage ceremony following the sermon."

Fourteen

Mercy wished the roof would fall in on her or that the earth would swallow her alive. She'd really done it this time. Not only had she made a spectacle of herself, she managed to entangle Pace in her schemes.

"But, Papa," she protested.

Her father shot a hard glance that effectively silenced her. From a lifetime of living with him, she knew better than to argue when he came to an absolute decision. And he'd made up his mind not to tolerate her rebellious behavior any longer. Time after time she'd ignored his advice. Mercy had only herself to blame for the predicament in which she found herself.

Trouble was, she'd gotten Pace tangled in the same web. At the stares of the congregation—many of the same people she'd known all her life—she grew hot with embarrassment. Several of the women from the Quilting Circle leaned their heads together and snickered behind their hands as if agreeing that the only way Mercy Goodacre could get a husband was in a shotgun wedding.

With the sheriff stationed at the end of the aisle, and two gun-toting deputies at the door, nothing could be truer. She glanced over her shoulder and spotted Cora Davis slip down the stairs and out the door.

Pace folded his arms over his chest and set his feet apart. So far he hadn't even glanced at her. She wouldn't blame him for hating her. Tears burned behind her lids. Neither of them had any choice but to go along with the marriage ceremony. Chancing a glance at him, she pleaded with her eyes for forgiveness.

This time he dropped his gaze and stared at her. Surprise, amazement, and a hint of gratitude glittered in the midnight depths of his eyes. His lips moved and he breathed the words, "I'm sorry."

If it were possible to feel any worse, Mercy's spirits hit rock bottom. She knew he was sorry. Sorry to be trapped in a marriage he didn't want. Sorry to be tied to the plainest woman in town. Some choice he had—a wedding or a hanging.

The pianist struck a chord, and one by one, the people turned their attention back to the minister. Mercy's sisters and their husbands resumed their seats, sending scathing glances her way. The singing, the prayers, the sermon all buzzed in her head like the roar of thunder. At Pace's side, she stood, she sat, she knelt, she waited.

When her father concluded his message on love and compassion, several heads turned toward Mercy and Pace.

"I'd like to ask all of you to remain as I unite my daughter, Mercy, and Mr. Pace Lansing in holy matrimony." Clearly, he wasn't happy about the situation, but as always, the minister did what was right and proper. "Will both of you please come forward?"

Pace caught Mercy's elbow. "Ready?" he whispered.

She nodded, her throat too tight to utter a sound. Leaving Joshua asleep in his basket, she stepped past the sheriff into the aisle. The sheriff touched her arm.

"Are you sure you know what you're doing, Miss Mercy? Did he spend the night with you?" Jennings asked, his words for Mercy's ears only. He was offering a way out for Mercy, but a trip to the gallows for Pace.

That wasn't going to happen. "Yes," she managed to say.

Pace stared at her, then shifted his gaze to the armed men guarding the doorway. This surely wasn't the way she'd envisioned her wedding day. She had a reluctant groom, the sheriff as a witness, and armed guards as bridesmaids.

On leaden feet, she moved to the front of the church. Her father's face was a mask of misery. Pace's expression was unreadable, and her sisters looked like harpies ready to heap damnation on her and Pace.

Her father began the ceremony. From being witness to numerous nuptials over the years, she recognized the abbreviated version of the marriage rites. It took all her willpower not to crumble to the floor in a heap of tears and misery.

"Do you, Mercy Goodacre, take this man, Pace Lansing, as your lawfully wedded husband? Do you promise to honor and obey him as long as you both shall live?" The question echoed in the silent church.

Mercy hesitated for an instant, debating within her heart if she was doing the right thing for Pace and her. From the rear of the church a baby's squeals urged her to speak from her heart. "Yes," she said in a full firm voice.

Turning to Pace, her father continued. "Do you, Pace Lansing, take this woman, Mercy Goodacre, as your lawfully wedded wife? Do you promise to honor and cherish her as long as you both shall live, so help you God?"

Pace tightened his grip on her elbow. "Yes, sir."

Did anyone else notice that her father had omitted the word "love" from the vows?

Ezra glanced at Pace as if looking for the ring. When he realized that Pace hadn't had time to get a ring for her, he continued. "By the powers vested in me, I now pronounce you husband and wife. What God hath joined together, let no man put asunder." Her father's voice broke. "You may kiss the bride."

The dam of tears in her eyelids burst, flooding her face

with moisture. There was no turning back. From this moment on, her life would be irrevocably linked with a man who didn't want her.

Pace bent his head and placed a quick, chaste kiss that landed halfway between her mouth and chin. Then he shook hands with her father. "I'll take care of her, sir. I swear."

"I love you, Mercy," her father whispered.

"Thank you, Papa." She clung to her father's shoulders as if clinging to the last sliver of her childhood. It suddenly struck her that she was no longer his daughter to be cherished and protected. He'd effectively handed her over to another man—a stranger she barely knew. A man she'd lied for and whom she wasn't sure could be trusted.

She was no longer obligated to prepare her father's meals and run his household, or be at her sisters' beck and call. From now on she would perform those chores for her husband. As well as duties she'd heard whispered among Miss Lily and her girls.

"You'll be fine, daughter. I'll be watching out for you." Ezra patted her gently on the cheek.

She pulled away from her father and looked up at her new husband. Pace watched her through lowered eyelids. Mercy had no idea what to do next. If she expected congratulations from her friends and family, she was sadly disappointed. Prudy and Clifford turned up their noses and strutted to the rear of the church. Charity sank to the pew and fanned her face. Tim hovered over her. Whispers raced through the congregation.

Joshua let out a squall, pulling Mercy out of her stupor. "The baby," she said. Lifting her gaze, she spied Joshua bouncing in Cora Davis's arms.

"I guess he's really our son now," she said.

Clutching her arm, Pace ushered her down the aisle. They'd managed to reach the rear pew when a lady clad in pink shoved the deputies aside and strutted into the church.

If Pace's presence had caused a flurry, Miss Lily LaRose swept through the church like a full-blown Kansas tornado. The lady stopped inside the doorway and waved her parasol in Sheriff Jennings's face.

Silence fell like a heavy curtain, attention tuned to the woman who'd never darkened the doors of the church before. "Jennings, you fool. Is this any way to conduct an investigation? What do you mean marching over here and accusing an innocent man of murder?"

Mercy and Pace glanced at each other, then stared wide-eyed at the commotion.

"What are you talking about, Lily?"

"When you found that man's body, you just rushed to judgment and came to the wrong conclusions. You hurried to the church and tried to arrest Pace Lansing. You didn't bother to question me, or to even glance at the balcony above the Ruby Slipper."

"No. I knew that Lansing had been fighting with Denby, and he killed the man."

Lily slammed her pink lace parasol into the lawman's chest. "Last night, I had that despicable Denby thrown out of the Ruby Slipper for trying to attack one of my girls. Later, he attempted to climb the trellis up to the balcony. I heard the sound of shattering wood, but I didn't see anything from my window. The fool was drunk and fell to his death without assistance from anybody. Of course, you, like the rest of this town, jumped to judgment." She waved her arms toward the congregation. "And the wrong conclusion, as usual." So far Miss Lily hadn't so much as raised her voice.

The sheriff's face turned red. "Can you prove any of this?"

"Are you calling me a liar?" Her tone turned deep and husky; her eyes flashed fire. Only a fool would argue with the woman, and Jennings was certainly no fool. It was well known that Miss Lily gave the lawman free drinks and sometimes the favors of her girls.

"No, ma'am. I'll check with Doc and see if he can tell us how Denby died."

"You should have done that before accusing Mr. Lansing of murder." With a wave of her hand, she dismissed the sheriff. The lawman slammed his hat back on his head and stalked out the door. His deputies followed at his heels.

Lily faced Mercy and Pace. Anger disappeared and a wide smile brightened her face. "I understand congratulations are in order." Reaching out a gloved hand, she clutched Mercy's fingers in hers. "I hope you'll be happy."

What a wish for a wedding day, Mercy thought. Nobody was happy about this marriage. Not the groom, the family, the town, nor the bride.

Mercy's stomach dropped to her feet. She'd lied to protect Pace. If only she hadn't opened her mouth and stuck her foot in it. If she hadn't forced him into this situation, he would be a free man. Miss Lily had come to his assistance fifteen minutes too late.

"Thank you, Miss Lily," she murmured. So far the most notorious woman in town was the only one to offer a bit of kindness.

"Mr. Lansing," the lady continued. "Take good care of Mercy and Joshua." She lowered her voice and poked a finger into Pace's wide chest. "Or you'll have to answer to me."

For the first time since the whole farce had begun, Pace's expression changed. A tiny smile tugged at one corner of his mouth. "Yes, ma'am. And to half of the town."

People Mercy had known all her life drifted past her. Some nodded, others gave a brief halfhearted congratulations, but most just stared at her as if she had sprouted horns and a tail.

At the door, her father shook hands with his flock and thanked them for coming. With Tim holding their son, Charity tilted her nose into the air at a perfect forty-five-degree angle. "I hope you don't expect us to throw you a party," she said.

Her sister's harsh declaration cut straight through to Mercy's heart. "No, Charity. I don't expect anything out of you."

Tim hesitated for a second. "I suppose Lansing won't let you work at the mercantile any longer."

Mercy shrugged and glanced at Pace. He tightened his grip on her elbow. "Mercy can do whatever she pleases."

His words told her how little he cared about her. "We'll talk about it later," she said, unable to keep the utter misery out of her voice.

Seconds later, only Mercy, Pace, Cora, and Miss Lily remained in the church when her father returned. He looked at the small assemblage. "We have some things to discuss. Let's retire to the parsonage where we can talk."

"Miss Lily, would you and Cora like to have dinner with us?" Mercy asked.

"Thank you, my dear," the lady said in her soft drawl. "I plan to make sure Jennings follows through with his promise. I don't want him causing trouble for you newlyweds."

Cora smiled over the baby's head. "If you need me to take care of this little fellow while you honeymoon for a few days, you just let me know," she offered.

Heat rushed to Mercy's cheeks. She hadn't even thought that far ahead. Pace, too, blushed at the woman's offer. "We'll keep the baby with us." Mercy reached for the child she loved as if she'd given birth to him.

Miss Lily brushed her fingers across the infant's head. "The offer is always open." She glanced at the minister, then back to her maid. "Come along, Cora. We have a business to run, and a sheriff to keep in line."

Pace picked up Joshua's basket and followed the women out the door. With her father at her side, Mercy watched her new husband. She brushed her thumb across her bare ring finger. She'd always dreamed about her wedding, and about the gold band that would link her with the man she loved. How strange to think she had married. Certainly, she would awaken any second and find out it had all been a dream. She prayed the dream wouldn't turn into a nightmare.

Ignoring the stares of the people, Pace walked beside his new wife and father-in-law toward the parsonage. He should be happy to finally have what every man wanted—a wife and family. To his own surprise, though, he wasn't angry or terribly upset. Once again, Mercy had stepped in and saved his neck. He owed her, but she didn't deserve the poverty and deprivation he offered. He'd expected to have some time to get things settled before marrying. Before accepting the responsibility for Mercy and Joshua.

While he fed the baby, Mercy prepared their noon meal. Her father said little, and Pace supposed the minister had problems getting accustomed to a son-in-law who was an ex-convict.

Reverend Goodacre cleared his throat to draw Pace's attention. "Lansing," he said. "This has all come up so suddenly; are you prepared for a wife?"

"I can't give Mercy as fine a home as this, but the cabin is clean and weatherproof. I'll add a room for her before the winter." Pace forced himself to remain calm, not to feel intimidated by the well-educated and respected preacher.

At that moment, Mercy entered the parlor. "Papa is right. This came up so suddenly, I don't have anything packed. Would you object if I remained here for a few days? Just to make arrangements, to pack, to hire a housekeeper for Papa?"

Pace let out a sigh of relief. A few days' reprieve would

give him time to get accustomed to the idea of a wife and family. "If you think that's best, I have no objections. Take all the time you need."

"Thank you. Please come into the kitchen—our dinner is ready."

The aromas wailing from the kitchen made Pace's mouth water and his stomach growl. He'd never eaten better than since he'd become friends with Mercy Goodacre.

His breath caught. No, as of an hour or so ago, she was Mercy Lansing—Mrs. Pace Lansing. One advantage of this marriage was having a woman who could turn a plain piece of beef into a mouth-watering delight. But it held a whole lot of disadvantages. Mostly for Mercy.

After the minister pronounced the blessing, few words were exchanged at the table. It seemed that nobody had anything to say, each lost in his own thoughts. Pace worried how he was going to support a family. When he'd returned to town, the last thing he'd expected was to take a wife. And the last woman in the world he would have considered was the minister's daughter.

Mercy's thoughts were written on her face. Her concerns were similar to his. A killer was the last person she'd expected to marry. From the few times he'd kissed her, he knew she was inexperienced with men. Every time she glanced at him, he spotted the anxiety in her eyes. She was worried about being alone with him. About how he would treat her in bed.

He tightened the grip on his fork. Just the thought of being with her sent heat to the pit of his belly. As he watched the play of uneasiness in her gaze, he made a vow to let his needs go unfulfilled. No matter what it cost him, he wouldn't dirty the pure, sweet woman with his carnal needs. She was too good for the likes of Pace Lansing.

With every passing minute, the silence threatened to smother him. The minister rarely glanced his way, his gaze on the roast beef and potatoes on his plate. The man was clearly troubled for his daughter's future. Not that Pace could blame the man. If he had a daughter like Mercy, he wouldn't let a man like Pace Lansing within a hundred miles of her.

When Pace couldn't hold another bite, Mercy produced an apple pie. She insisted that he have a piece. He couldn't deny that having her as a wife would be an advantage. She had to be the best cook in the county.

While her father retreated to the parlor and his pipe, Pace helped clear the table. Their first time alone, and still they hadn't spoken more than a dozen words. After setting the dishes in a tin pan, Pace reached for a soft white rag. At that same moment, Mercy reached for the same strip of cloth. Their hands collided. She jumped back as if she'd been struck.

"I'm sorry," he said.

"I'm the one who's sorry," she whispered. "I'm sorry my father forced you into something you didn't want."

He shrugged. "There's no use blaming anybody. He just did what he thought was best for your reputation. It was my fault that I let my temper get the best of me last night. If you hadn't stopped me, I would have killed Denby then and there. Jennings wouldn't have had any choice but to arrest me. And you couldn't have stopped him."

She covered his hand with hers. "I know this is uncharitable, but he deserved to die. But I'm glad you didn't kill him."

Her hand was so soft and warm, he wondered how it would feel to have her touch him, really touch him. As quickly as it came, he shoved the thought aside. "Thanks to Miss Lily, you know you didn't marry a murderer."

"Pace, I never doubted you."

His heart swelled with emotion. "Thank you for trusting me."

She lifted her head to him. Her mouth was pink and inviting, her eyes offering more than he deserved. He wanted to kiss her and he knew she wanted it also. He lowered his face and opened his mouth. Their lips were a breath apart when he remembered his promise.

This was wrong. He couldn't do it. He refused to defile this woman. And to try it here in the parsonage with the minister in the next room. "I have to go," he said, his voice raw with need.

"But aren't you going to spend the night here?"

"No. I have to get back to my spread."

Her skin paled, and her smile was forced. "Yes, I understand."

He was sure she didn't. But he had to get away from her before he did something they would both regret. "I have to check on the stock."

She nodded her approval. "Do you mind if I continue to work at the mercantile until I move out to the cabin?"

"You can do whatever you want. You don't have to ask my permission."

"Thank you." She turned back to the table where the remains of their dinner waited. "Can you wait a moment while I pack a basket for you?"

"That isn't necessary. I have lots of food left."

In an uncustomary show of temper, she set her hands on her hips and glared at him. "Pace, like it or not, I'm your wife. And a wife's duty is to take care of her husband's needs. I want you to have some of the roast and fresh bread. Remember, we're still partners. You gather the cattle, I'll provide the meals."

He locked gazes with her. Fire glimmered in her golden eyes. He wondered what kind of passion lurked deep inside the woman who was normally so meek, everybody walked right over her. The way she stood up to him pleased him more than he dared let show.

"I'm sorry for my bad manners. This is all so new, it's going to take some getting used to. I appreciate the meal. You're a fine cook."

"Thank you." Turning away, she placed thick slices of meat into a basket along with a loaf of bread and half the apple pie. "When will you get back to town?"

"I'm not sure. I want to check for cattle in a small canyon at the edge of my land. It may take a while to round them up and get them branded."

"Meanwhile, I'll start packing my things to move out to the cabin. It shouldn't take long to find a housekeeper for my father."

"Take all the time you need. I'll be busy out in the fields for a while." He set his hat on his head, and took her hands gently in his. Her small fingers were nearly lost in his palms. Pace stared at the finger that should hold his ring, that was bare of jewelry. Abruptly, he dropped her hand, too embarrassed to face his shortcomings. "If I don't see you before next week, tell your father I'll try to make the worship on Sunday."

Sadness covered her like a heavy veil. "Goodbye, Pace."

"Goodbye, Mercy."

Fifteen

Mercy's package in his hand, Pace left by the rear door. As he strolled across the lawn to where he'd tethered his horse, he thought about Mercy and their untimely wedding. She sure deserved a lot better than she got in a groom. The very least she deserved was a ring.

Instead of heading out of town, he turned toward the Ruby Slipper. More than once, Miss LaRose had come to his assistance. She might be willing to help him again.

Since the saloon was closed on Sunday, he climbed the rear stairs and knocked on the door. After several minutes, Cora answered. "Mr. Lansing? We're closed today."

"Yes, ma'am, I know." He removed his hat. "Could I see Miss LaRose for a moment?"

She glanced behind her as if struggling to come to a decision. "Come in. I'll ask her."

He waited in the dimly lit hallway and stared at the closed doors. Gleaming floors were covered with a narrow strip of carpet, and flocked wallpaper decorated the walls. The scent of perfume hung in the air. This was his first visit upstairs, never having had the money to spend on the pleasures offered in the rooms. In fact, only on rare occasions had he even enjoyed a beer downstairs.

Moments later, a door opened at the end of the hallway. Cora signaled him to come forward. Twisting his hat in his hands, he moved slowly toward where the woman waited. She gestured him into a fancy sitting room, and closed the door behind him. The fragrance of roses greeted him.

"Come in, Mr. Lansing," Miss LaRose said from her position on a long one-armed settee. "Please have a seat."

The room was dimly lit with only a few candles to guide the way to a small velvet chair. He sure hoped his weight wouldn't snap the flimsy legs in two. "Thank you." A thin sliver of afternoon sunlight edged around the brocade drapes.

"Would you care for some tea?"

"No, ma'am."

She sipped from a flowery china cup in her hands. The lady had changed from her pink dress, and now wore a lacy wrapper of some kind. Miss LaRose was a beautiful woman, who knew just how to attract men. Her smile was warm, and inviting. "What brings you to my establishment? Didn't Cora tell you we're closed for business today?"

"Yes, ma'am. That isn't why I'm here." He swallowed his nervousness at being alone with the madam. "I want to thank you for standing up for me today."

Brushing her fingers along her flowing skirt, she gestured with her beautiful, slender hands. The front parted, revealing slim, white legs. He quickly averted his gaze. "Think nothing of it. I hate to see the whole town condemn you for something you didn't do."

"How can you be so sure?"

She set down her teacup. "I'm not. But I like Mercy. I don't want her to think she married a murderer."

He frowned. "At least you're honest. But aren't you afraid I'll hurt her?"

"No. You aren't an abusive man. You might kill a man with your bare hands, but you'd never strike a woman. You'll protect Mercy with your life if need be."

Until Mercy had come into his life, nobody had ever showed that kind of confidence in him. "I would."

"I'm glad. She deserves a good husband."

His heart twisted. "That's why I came to see you. I didn't have a chance to get her a ring. I doubt if I can buy one in town. Do you know where I can order one for her?"

She stared at him for a long moment before answering. For a second, he was afraid she'd laugh him to scorn. "Do you have the money to buy a ring? I understood you were looking for credit a few weeks ago."

"I sold a cow and calf to a nester passing through. He gave me some money. I don't have much."

"I may be able to help you."

In a sweep of pink silk, she strolled across the room to a bureau. The gown clung to her body, and draped over her womanly curves. Pace wondered how Mercy would look in a garment like that. The pink would make her skin glow, and the soft material would enhance her shapely body. Just thinking about it sent a fever through his body.

Seconds later, Miss LaRose returned to the settee with a small wooden chest in her hands. "Sometimes when men start losing at poker, they don't stop until they've gambled away everything they own. I have several rings and pocket watches I'll never be able to sell." She dropped a small ring into his hand. "This would look lovely on Mercy's finger."

He'd never seen anything so pretty. Engraved flowers wound around the thick gold band like the roses that grew in Mercy's garden. She would love it; she deserved the best. But in reality, the ring was far more expensive than he could afford. Reluctantly, he offered it back to Lily. "Thank you, but this is much too expensive."

The diamonds on her fingers glittered as she waved him off. "How do you know? We haven't discussed price."

"Ma'am, I'm not stupid. A ring like that doesn't come cheap." Determined not to embarrass himself further, he pressed the ring into her palm.

She stroked the ring with the tip of one finger. "No,

they don't. But I have no use for a wedding band. You need one, and I think Mercy deserves the best." When he opened his mouth to protest, she pointed a finger at him. "I owe Mercy a debt of gratitude. Of all the people in this town, she is the one who cared enough to conduct a Bible study for me and my girls. The fact that she had a shotgun wedding must have caused her a certain amount of distress, especially with her sisters looking on. They've done nothing but ridicule and look down on her for not having a husband. A beautiful ring would ease some of her pain, and show them that she didn't do too badly in the husband department either."

"I didn't think of that. You're right. She's been nothing but good to me and Josh and she deserves a lot more than I have to offer."

The lady's eyes turned icy blue. "I won't argue that point. But you're married now, as the preacher said, for better or worse. Having a ring will make her more acceptable to the other women in town and maybe show her family that things can work out fine."

Pace swallowed what little pride he had left and stretched out a hand. "How much?"

Her pink lips pulled into a small frown as she named a price. It was much lower than he'd expected, but still more than he owned. "But you don't have to worry about paying right away. We'll set up a payment plan. You can pay me when you sell your cattle in the fall."

He weighed the gold ring in his hand. At the rate he was spending the money he didn't have, he'd never get out of debt. But he owed Mercy even more—he owed her his life. "Deal," he said, although reluctantly.

"Would you care for a drink? Something stronger than tea?"

"No, thank you. I'd best get back to my spread."

She covered his rough hand with her soft one. "Aren't

you going to give that to Mercy? I have a feeling she could use it."

With a smile, he shoved the ring into his pocket. "After that I'm going home."

Lily watched the man hurry through the doorway and into the hall. Now that she was alone in her boudoir, she returned the jewelry box to the bureau and securely locked the drawer. When she looked up, Cora was staring at her. The maid picked up the china pot and poured herself a cup of tea. After all they'd been through together, Cora knew to make herself at home. To the world, they were mistress and maid; in private, they were best friends.

"You gave him the ring?" Cora asked, knowing the answer.

"I sold it to him."

"For a lot less than it's worth."

Lily walked to the window and pulled open the drapes. From her location, she had a clear view of Pleasant Valley. The little town was quiet as families spent the day together. It was too beautiful a Sunday afternoon to be sequestered in her room. Yet, here she was, a prisoner of her own making. "I have a dozen more expensive. Mercy didn't even have a plain gold band."

"Why that one? I didn't think you would ever get rid of Etienne's ring."

Cora handed Lily a fresh cup of tea. She smelled the drop of brandy her friend had added. Right now, she needed the extra fortification. "It's time I buried the past. I guess I was only holding on to it to torture myself. I should have thrown it into the Mississippi River before we left New Orleans."

"That little ring fed us more times than I can remember. Seems men lose their concentration in a poker game when a widow puts up her wedding ring."

She smiled at the few good memories connected with the ring. Etienne had been a gambler—handsome, charming, and he'd swept her off her feet. She'd given up her position as a schoolteacher and followed him up and down the Mississippi, going wherever he could find a card game or roulette wheel. When her husband died, the gold ring was the only thing he hadn't gambled away. "If any luck comes with the ring, I hope Mercy has lots."

"You should have been there for the wedding. I'd have thought Pace would be the one to bolt and run, but it was Mercy who kept glancing at the door."

"I suspect that deep down that man wants a wife and family. He just needed a little nudge toward the altar."

Cora laughed. "With a shotgun."

"Some men just don't know what's good for them." She set the cup aside and returned to the window.

"You're not thinking about the reverend, by any chance?"

"Not a chance." Only Cora suspected Lily's feelings for the minister. "How would you like to live in San Francisco?"

Golden brown eyes widened in surprise. "San Francisco? One place is as good as another to me, but I thought you liked it here."

"I'm getting restless. After I find husbands for the girls, I can sell this place for a nice profit. We can start that school for young ladies that we talked about. Maybe we'll find you a husband in San Francisco."

"No, thank you. I've seen too much to want to tie myself down to a man."

Sadness settled in Lily's heart for her closest friend. She knew only too well what Cora had experienced at the hands of an abusive man. The beautiful mulatto had been raised and educated to be a rich Creole's mistress. At fifteen, she'd been set up in her own apartment in New Orleans' French Quarter. The man used and abused Cora, and at eighteen, she'd been beaten and left for dead. Lily found the beautiful young woman and nursed her back to health. When the Creole tried to reclaim his property, he met with a back alley accident. Cora and Lily hightailed it out of New Orleans on the first steamboat. On that day Nellie Parker died and Lily LaRose was born.

She'd taken up where Etienne had left off—going from riverboat to casino to saloon, wherever she could find a sucker willing to bet money on the turn of a card. In a high stakes game in St. Louis, she met the owner of the Ruby Slipper. After the man had lost all his cash, he'd put up the deed for the saloon. Lily had won the pot, and for the past eight years she and Cora had called the little town of Pleasant Valley, Kansas, their home.

"We could open the school here. The town is growing, and the girls here need refinement, too."

"From brothel to finishing school? I afraid we'll have to start over where nobody knows us."

"I suppose you're right. California sounds promising."

"Very promising."

Lost in her own misery, Mercy nearly missed the noise in the parlor. Since Pace had left her alone earlier, she remained in the kitchen wallowing in self-pity. Recognizing her sisters' voices, she dried her eyes. She didn't feel like company, and she certainly didn't want to face her holier-than-thou sisters.

Hurriedly, she splashed cold water on her face and pasted on a smile. After greeting their father, Prudy and Charity stomped toward the kitchen. "Well, well, hiding in here?" Prudy asked. She fluffed the lace ruffle at the low neckline of her embroidered lawn gown. "Where's the blushing bridegroom?"

"Don't tell me he's hightailed it out of here already?" Charity's snide remark added to Mercy's misery.

Mercy squared her shoulders and faced her sisters. "Pace had to get back to his spread." She turned to the stove to avoid their snobbish glances. "Would you like some apple pie?"

"No. We have something to tell you."

"What?" By the looks on their faces, the news wasn't good for Mercy.

"Do you really think your husband left town this afternoon?" Charity stuck a finger into the pie and licked it clean.

Before Mercy could respond to the cruel accusation, Prudy spoke up. "He lied to you. We saw him climb the stairs outside the Ruby Slipper and go into that woman's private quarters."

"You must be mistaken." Mercy's heart sank. Not because he'd lied to her, but that her sisters had caught him.

Charity tilted her nose. "No, we aren't. He was there, as big as life going into that woman's bedroom."

"He probably went to thank her for coming to his defense."

"I did." The three women jumped as heavy male boot-steps entered the kitchen. Pace shot an angry glance at her sisters, before settling his gaze on Mercy. "I had another reason, too."

Mercy thought her sisters would faint dead away when Pace glared at them. They shrank back against the table, as if afraid he would strike them.

Alerted by the commotion in the kitchen, her father appeared in the doorway. "What's going on in here?" he asked.

Pace caught Mercy's hand and faced Ezra with her at his side. "Sir, I'm glad you're here." Shocked at his action, she stood there mouth agape. What if he had changed his mind about marrying her? What if he wanted to ask her father to have the marriage annulled? She couldn't bear any more humiliation.

"I thought you'd left, Lansing. What brings you back?" Ezra asked.

"I'd like for you to complete the wedding ceremony." He dug into his pocket and fished out an object. "I have a ring for my wife." Lifting her left hand, he held it toward her father.

He could have knocked her over with a feather. Her mind went blank, but her spirits soared. "Where did you get it?"

"I bought it for you. I want my wife to wear my ring."

"This is ridiculous," Prudy said. "You're already married."

Charity nudged her younger sister. "Be quiet."

"This is highly unusual," their father said. "But I suppose there's no harm in repeating the part of the ceremony I skipped over. Come into the parlor."

"Thank you, sir," Pace said. For her part, Mercy's throat was so tight, she couldn't utter a sound.

Seconds later, she and Pace stood in front of her father, her sisters at her side. This was more how she'd envisioned her wedding, not the one in church with the armed deputies on guard.

The minister repeated the ceremony, and when he reached the part where Pace would place a ring on her finger, he paused and smiled at Mercy. "Place the ring on her finger and repeat after me."

Mercy's hand was trembling so badly, Pace had to grip her fingers to shove the thick gold band into place.

"With this ring I thee wed," her father said.

Pace's voice dropped to a deep rasp as he repeated the vow.

Mercy barely heard a word that followed. She'd never been happier in her life. Pace must care for her. Why else would he have gotten the ring? She stared at the ring as if she'd never seen one before. Actually, she'd never seen anything prettier than the flowers engraved in the gold. Charity had a plain gold band, and Prudy's was only a little fancier. Mercy's new husband had come through with a winner.

When Pace kissed her briefly on the cheek, she snapped out of her stupor. Only then did she realize she was crying. "Thank you, Pace," she whispered.

He nodded, then abruptly stepped away. "If you'll excuse me, sir, I want to get back to work."

"You're family, Lansing. My house is always open to you." Her father stuck out his hand.

Pace accepted the gesture. "Thank you, sir. I'll be back in a few days to see Mercy and Joshua."

Mercy clutched her hand to her chest. She loved him so much, she wished she could tell him, show him how much she cared. But she knew he wasn't ready. Too much had happened too quickly.

He looked down at her, a new tenderness in his eyes. "Goodbye, Mercy. I'll see you soon."

Her sisters whispering behind their hands, Mercy watched her groom leave.

He would come back, she knew it. She would prove to Pace that he needed a wife.

That he needed her.

Sixteen

After two weeks of marriage, Mercy had spent a grand total of ten minutes alone with her husband. Pace had come to town the past Sunday for the church services, but had left before the last "Amen" echoed through the congregation.

She pulled the freshly baked rolls from the oven and thought about her husband. A twinge tugged at her heart. She was married, but she didn't feel married. Living in town with her father hardly suited her dreams of blissful matrimony. Her wedding night had been spent in her own lonely, maiden's bed.

Every woman wanted to be loved and cherished. And Mercy was no different.

Lost in her thoughts, she let the dishrag slip and burnt the tip of her finger. Dropping the pan on the stove, she shoved the injured finger into her mouth. She'd gotten up early to bake an extra batch of bread and rolls to take with her.

Mercy had endured all she could take of the snickers and reproach of the local women—her sisters being ringleaders. While working in the mercantile, she'd been the subject of more than her share of sympathetic glances. It was time for Mercy Lansing to take her rightful place as a wife.

So she'd taken matters into her own hands.

Mrs. Whitehead had agreed to come in three times a week to cook and clean for her father. The laundry lady would still pick up and deliver the wash, and on Fridays and Saturdays when Mercy came into town to work in the store, she would see that things were running smoothly at the parsonage.

The rest of her time Mercy would be where she belonged, with her husband and their adopted child.

Her bed and furniture, plus her trunks and Joshua's things, were loaded on a flatbed wagon she'd hired from the livery. Lemuel Smithers would drive the wagon after church.

Although he wasn't happy about her plans, her father had no choice but to agree. Pace, however, was a different matter. Since he hadn't been in town for the past week, she hadn't been able to discuss her plans with him. He would just have to face the facts that she was his wife and it was about time she took her place in his home.

It didn't matter that his cabin wasn't as fine as her father's home. With a few feminine touches, like curtains, rag rugs, and hot meals, the place would be a cozy haven for a family.

She planned to break her news to Pace when she met him in church later that morning. Carefully, she packed the rolls in the box with the ham, jars of preserves, and other food she'd put up the past year. One thing was for sure—they would eat well. Better than Pace had in years.

Hurriedly, she prepared breakfast, then went upstairs to call her father and tend Joshua. Her stomach tightened into knots at the idea of leaving home for the first time. But it couldn't be helped. Her place was with her husband. A husband who didn't want a wife, but was stuck with one anyway.

The thought of spending time alone with Pace was both exciting and frightening. What would he expect from her? The knots in her stomach turned into aches. From overhearing Miss Lily and the girls, she had a vague idea of what happened between men and women in bed. They seemed to think it was fun, that they enjoyed men. Well, some men anyway. More than once she'd overheard Prudy and Charity complain about the demands of their husbands. Mercy was more than a little confused. Still, she'd made her choice, and she would just have to live with it.

A few hours later, she sat on the rear pew in church with Joshua in her arms. So far, she hadn't seen hide nor hair of Pace. The congregation was in the middle of the second hymn when a shadow slanted from the doorway. Her heart rate quickened, then slowed when she recognized Prudy and Clifford making their entrance. Her sister didn't even bother to glance her way.

Her gaze remained on her sister's stiff back while she sang the words to the hymn from memory. Pace had never been this late; surely he wasn't coming. Disappointment coiled around her heart.

As Miss Audrey at the piano pounded out the final chorus, Mercy felt movement at her side. She didn't have to look to know that Pace had finally shown up. Whenever he came close to her, she felt the electricity that always sparked between them. Joshua leaped in her arms, as if he, too, was glad to see Pace. The baby reached out his hands. Pace set his hat under the bench and took the infant from Mercy.

She relaxed against the hard wooden pew her father had made years ago. At least she wouldn't have to surprise Pace by showing up at his place unannounced.

The worship seemed to drag on forever. Even seated on the rear pew, Mercy spotted the occasional superior glances aimed at Pace and her. She stared right back at them. Nobody in this town was going to look down their long noses at her and her family.

Finally, her father called on Mayor Fullenwider to pray the benediction. Joshua came awake at the loud voice invoking God's blessing on the town. When he finally said "Amen," Mercy sighed with relief. The hardest part of her day was yet to come.

Pace returned the infant to his basket. "He'll soon be outgrowing his bed. I can't thank you enough for what you're doing for the boy."

Her heart sank at the way he continued to treat her like a stranger, instead of as a wife. That situation was soon coming to an end. If she had her way, she would soon be his wife in every sense of the word. "I do it because I love him." She didn't add that she would do anything for Pace, too, because she loved him.

"I still appreciate everything you've done for me and Josh." He bent down and retrieved his hat and settled it low on his forehead. "I'd best be leaving. Reckon I'll see you next Sunday."

She caught his sleeve and tugged him away from the aisle now crowded with people leaving the building. "No, Pace. You'll see me long before then."

His jaw tightened into a hard line. "What are you talking about? I have too much work out on the spread to spend time here in town."

"You won't have to. I'm going home with you today."

Pace felt his jaw drop. He wasn't sure what Mercy was talking about. "You can't go with me. What about your father? Your job at the mercantile?"

Hands set firmly on her hips, she lifted her chin. "Pace, I'm your wife, and it's time you face the music and treat me like one. As for my father, I've made arrangements for his care. And I can work at the store on Friday and Saturday, when Tim is busiest."

He glanced to the side and saw her sisters waiting at the end of the pew. The pitying stares aimed at Mercy fueled his anger toward the self-righteous women. Mercy was better than the whole lot of them put together. She'd already suffered enough because of him. "Are you sure this is what you want?"

"Yes. Lemuel Smithers has his wagon loaded with my things. I'll drive my own buggy with Joshua, and you can ride beside us."

How could he disregard the pleading look in her golden eyes? Moisture glittered behind her eyeglasses. "Okay. The cabin still ain't much."

"It will do just fine for us."

He was caught as neatly as a grizzly in a bear trap. The way he saw it, the only way out was to chew off his own leg. Either that, or accept his fate. How bad could it be? The woman wasn't bad to look at, she was kind, and she sure could cook. She'd already done more for him than he could repay. If she wanted to play house, he had no choice but to go along with her plan.

Pace picked up the baby's basket and eased his way to the door. While he continued down the steps and into the sunshine, Mercy stopped to talk to her sisters. Behind his back, he could hear them arguing with Mercy. Probably trying to get her to change her mind. He stopped a ways from the other people. Part of him wished they would be successful—that they could convince her to remain in town where she belonged. The other part, the carnal man inside him, wanted her in his home, in his bed.

His gut tightened. No, that would never do. Mercy was good and pure, a virgin and a lady. But he wasn't sure how he was going to live with her in the tiny cabin and keep his body under control. Whatever it took, he promised himself to try.

Moments later, the object of his musings appeared on the narrow porch that fronted the church. She ducked her head and touched her handkerchief to her eyes. He tightened his grip on the basket handle, wishing he could wrap his fingers around the necks of the harpies who'd caused her tears. Then, with the stiff posture that would

do a queen proud, she stepped lightly down the steps. After a few brief words with her father, she lifted her gaze.
It took a moment before she spotted him waiting in the
shadow of a large oak. She greeted a number of her friends
and neighbors, as she worked her way across the yard.

"Mr. Pace?"

The soft feminine voice came from behind him. He
spun around and met Cora Davis's knowing gaze. Her
smile was strained. He touched a finger to the brim of his
hat. "Ma'am?"

The woman brushed a finger across the baby's cheek.
"We're going to miss this little fellow at our weekly Bible
study." She lifted her gaze and met his boldly. "Miss Mercy
means a lot to all of us. You better be good to her."

Over the past weeks, he'd had threats and warnings from
half the town. Did they think he was such a brute that he
would do anything to hurt her? The very idea cut like a
knife to his heart. "Yes, ma'am. I understand."

"I surely hope you do."

After another glance at the baby, Cora headed toward
town. Pace took a deep breath of air. A wagon loaded with
household goods pulled into the yard. Lemuel Smithers
tugged the reins and stopped the team.

"Pace," Mercy said in her soft voice. "Are you ready?"

No, he wasn't ready. He wasn't ready for a wife. He
wasn't ready for a family. He groaned. Ready or not, it was
too late to run.

"Yes, ma'am. Looks like an awful lot of stuff in that
wagon." Too much for his tiny cabin. And all reminders
of how little he owned to provide for a family.

Pink colored her cheeks. "Just a few household goods.
Things we'll need."

His gaze shifted to a polished bureau and the bed with
a soft feather mattress. Did she expect to share her bed
with him? Did an innocent like Mercy have any idea what
that meant? He sincerely doubted she knew about desire

and lovemaking. The few times he'd kissed her she'd responded shyly. But he sensed an underlying passion that had never been tapped. His gut tightened with a need that he would never fulfill.

"Then I suppose we'd better head out to my spread," he said in a voice harsher than he'd planned.

She bit her lip, as if holding back a sob. "Yes. I'd like to get the baby settled in our home." Taking Joshua's basket from his fingers, she strolled quickly to her buggy waiting in the shade of the oaks.

Pace shrugged, and moved toward his horse. "I'll tie up behind and drive your buggy." He paused. "If you don't mind."

"That will be fine. In case Joshua wakes up, I'll be able to take care of him."

Moments later they left the churchyard, the livery wagon following behind. From the corner of his eye, he spied the reverend and several church members watching them leave. Mercy turned and waved to her father, who lifted his hand and waved back. The look on the minister's face spoke volumes. He couldn't blame the man for being concerned for his daughter. *Don't worry, preacher, I won't touch her against her will. I'll remember my vows, and before I let anything happen to her, I'll deliver her to your house and turn myself in to the sheriff.*

It was nearly dark by the time Mercy had the cabin resembling her idea of a home. She'd hung curtains, covered the table with a cloth she'd embroidered for her trousseau, and prepared a pot of stew for their supper. Joshua lay in his cradle, kicking and cooing, happy to be well fed, warm, and clean.

She moved to the window looking for Pace. He'd left the cabin immediately after he'd helped Lemuel unload the wagon and set up the furniture. Her heart twisted.

Without meaning to, she'd hurt his pride. When he reached into his pocket to pay the wagon driver, Mercy had stopped him since she'd already paid for the man's services. Moments later, he'd gone out to look after his livestock.

One thing was sure about Pace Lansing: He might have been short of funds, but he was sure long on pride.

Now, she was waiting. And she was getting sick and tired of being ignored by her husband. Her gaze shifted to the bureau and trunks that crowded the cabin. She'd arranged her things in the drawers, and had left room for Pace. Not sure what to do, she lifted his small stack of clean shirts and underwear to place them in a drawer. As she arranged the garments in a row, she spotted something strange wrapped in a cloth.

As uneasy as a child sneaking a cookie from the jar, she glanced around as if she was doing something illegal or wrong. Thinking it was a gun or something covert, she carefully unwrapped the cloth. Her breath caught in her throat as she gently touched a silver-backed brush and mirror. Both were exquisite, as pretty as anything she'd ever seen. But where did they come from? The items weren't something a man like Pace would possess. Could he have stolen them? After all, she knew he didn't have any money, and he certainly wouldn't keep something that could be sold or traded for supplies.

He'd mentioned selling a cow and calf to a farmer passing through. Maybe he bought the gift for Mercy. Her heart sank. No. If he intended it for her, he would have already given it to her. Not wanting to be caught snooping in his things, she tucked the brush and mirror back where she'd found them.

She sat on her bed now covered with the double wedding ring quilt she'd stitched the past winter. She brushed a hand across the pillows. Would he share the bed with her? The thought both thrilled and frightened her.

Mercy swallowed her discomfort and returned to the window. There wasn't much he could do outdoors after dark. Unless he was avoiding her. Common sense said she should have discussed moving in before taking matters into her own hands. But left to Pace, she would probably shrivel up and grow old in her father's house before he came after her.

Miss Lily and Cora had given her an important piece of advice: Make yourself indispensable to a man, let him believe he can't live without you, and he'll always be yours.

How could she do that if he didn't even want to be in the same house with her?

Her spirits dragged the ground like a snake's belly. She wiped the dampness from her cheek. Well, Mercy, she told herself, you may be in his house, but it looks like you'll still be sleeping alone.

When the door flung open, she jumped and covered her heart with her hand. She hadn't seen him approach. He stomped the mud from his feet, then stepped across the threshold. His gaze locked with hers.

Momentary surprise in his dark eyes was quickly swept away. The look he shot her was unreadable. His black hair was damp and swept from his forehead like the wings of a raven. A day's growth of whiskers shadowed his jaw. Her heart thumped against her ribs. Shaded by the night and the dim light of the kerosene lamps, Pace could have posed for the painting of Satan that decorated the pages of her Bible. In that instant, she wondered if she'd made the mistake of her life.

His dark gaze shifted from her to the stove, where the pot of stew simmered. "Reckon you got yourself all settled in," he said in a voice flat and devoid of emotion.

She wrapped her bravado around her like a heavy cloak. "Yes. I hope you like what I've done. The cabin was nice, but I wanted some of my things around me."

He merely shrugged, as if it didn't matter what she did. "Something smells good."

At least that was one way she could please her husband. If nothing else mattered to him, he liked her cooking. It might not be the way to his heart, but at least she could do him some good.

"I put on a pot of stew. It's ready."

The table was already set with the dishes Mercy had placed in her hope chest years earlier—along with linens and the baby things that Joshua now wore. She spooned up the stew, along with fresh biscuits. Pace stopped on his way to the table and spoke briefly to the baby. As usual when Joshua spotted Pace, he lifted his arms and squealed for attention. And as always, Pace didn't disappoint the infant. He took the baby from the cradle and cuddled him in one big arm.

Mercy smiled at the sight of the pair she'd learned to love more than she ever thought possible. It didn't matter that she wasn't loved in return. Her love was enough.

"You shouldn't spoil him like that, Pace," she said, mildly chiding him. "Joshua will expect you to pick him up whenever he sees you."

"As if you and your father haven't already spoiled him." He sat at the table and settled the baby on his lap.

"We just gave him all the love the little fellow deserves." She took the chair opposite him, candles glittered between them. Flames danced in his dark eyes as he studied her. He deserved love, too. Only he wasn't ready to accept it. "How are you going to eat with Joshua in your arms?"

"He's nothing. I can manage with one hand."

Mercy's appetite deserted her. The look on his face had her stomach fluttering. She spotted a hunger in his gaze, a longing that he tried to hide from the world. Something that she was certain nobody else had ever seen. When he blinked, the look was gone, replaced with his usual stoic expression.

She dropped her gaze and shoved the food around her bowl. A different hunger lingered in her heart. Just like Pace, she longed to be loved—she deserved to be loved.

Her gaze shifted to her bed. After they had spent the night together in her bed, he would feel how much she loved him, how much she wanted to make him happy.

The dinner passed quickly. Soon after she'd washed the dishes, she took the fussy baby from Pace and readied him for bed. Unaccustomed to the new surroundings, Joshua took longer than usual to settle into a sound sleep. When he finally fell asleep in his familiar cradle, Mercy swallowed her own trepidation and began to prepare for bed. She reached into her bureau and retrieved a white nightgown.

"It's getting late. Would you like some milk or something before we go to bed?" Holding her nightgown in front of her, she lifted her gaze to Pace.

He turned from where he'd been staring out the window. His gaze drifted slowly over her. A flush crept under his whiskers. He shoved his hands into his pockets, drawing the front of his denims tight across his pelvis. Mercy avoided looking at the bulge evident there.

"Mercy, I . . ." His voice faded. After a deep breath he started again. "Where's my bed?"

"Your bed?" At his harsh question she jerked back a step. "I took it down. I thought . . . you would . . . that we would . . ." Oh, Lord, had she again offended him? This time by wanting him to share her bed? Her throat tightened, and the sinking feeling returned to her stomach. "My bed is big enough for both of us." Her voice was a whispered squeak.

"I decided to sleep in the barn. That way I won't disturb you and Josh when I get up in the morning."

"But I always rise early. I'll fix your breakfast."

He turned his back and shoved some of the biscuits and ham into a sack. "I'm leaving early to round up some more of my cattle. You don't have to bother with me."

"I shoved the mattress under my bed," she said, her heart shattered by his rejection.

She stood aside as he tugged the lumpy, straw mattress from where she'd stored it away. It wouldn't do any good to argue, or to further humiliate herself. Pace clearly didn't want her.

He stopped at the door and glanced back at her. "Good night. I suppose I'll see you in a day or so."

Biting her lip to keep from calling him back, she nodded her assent.

"Be sure to bolt the door. Don't open it for anybody but me."

"I'll remember. Good night, Pace." She followed him to the door and watched as he made his way to the barn. On the night she'd expected to be held and loved, she was once again alone.

With every step he took, Pace cursed himself a thousand ways. He called himself every foul name he'd ever heard, and he'd heard plenty in prison. He'd hurt Mercy. The pain was evident in her eyes. She didn't deserve to be hurt. She sure didn't deserve to be married to him.

And with each step he ached for her. Ached to bury his hands in her sweet-smelling hair, yearned to snuggle his face in her soft, full breasts, longed to mate his tormented body with hers.

She'd brought that big soft feather bed, and expected him to share it with her. If he turned to her she wouldn't deny him his husbandly rights. Mercy was raised as a dutiful woman, one who did what was expected of her. But she had no idea what was expected of a wife. What he could do to her.

He was scared to death he would be like his pa. He remembered the times the old man had taken his mother when they thought Pace was asleep. He'd heard the grunts, like a pig or a hog rooting in the dirt. Not really knowing what was happening, Pace covered his ears with his thin pillow to drown out the noise. But nothing drowned out his father's angry reaction or the sound of his pa slapping his mother. Even as a child, Pace knew that was wrong.

Later, the old man's loud snoring would vibrate through the house. More than a few times, he'd heard his mother's sobs and he knew the act had hurt her.

Pace had determined not to be like his father, and the few times he'd made love to a woman, he'd been careful not to hurt her. So he'd hurried and taken his pleasure, then left immediately. Mercy deserved better than that. She deserved better than him.

He dropped the worn mattress on a pile of hay. The smells of the barn were far different from the aroma of rose water and talc that surrounded Mercy. And the snorts of the horses a far cry from her soft words and the whimpers of the baby.

Sharing a barn with the animals was where he belonged. Where a son of Amos Lansing belonged. He'd promised the preacher he wouldn't hurt his daughter. But he'd rot in this hell of his own making before he eased the pain in his loins with an innocent like Mercy.

Again taking up his litany of curses, he headed for the creek behind the barn for a dunk in the cold water.

Seventeen

Three days later, Mercy wasn't any more a wife to Pace than when she'd married him. She'd done her best to make him realize she was an asset to him. Every morning, she rose early and prepared a breakfast he didn't even show up to eat. And every evening, she cooked a fine dinner. The only time he darkened the doors of the cabin was to enter and shovel down his meal. Then he rushed back to the barn as if he couldn't get away from her fast enough.

Mercy didn't know what else she could do to please her husband. Joshua must have sensed the tension in the small cabin, for he cried and whimpered all night and into the next day. Nothing she did would soothe the child. By nightfall, when she still hadn't seen any sign of Pace, she wondered if she should just hook up her buggy and take the baby to the doctor in town. As far as she could tell, Joshua wasn't ill. His forehead was cool, he was clean and fed, yet nothing she did consoled him.

Added to her own strained situation, her concern for the baby had her nerves frayed. The only time he quieted was when she had him cradled to her breast. That made preparing the evening meal difficult. Not that Pace would notice if she served him slop. He ate so fast, he hardly tasted his food.

She slipped into her white nightdress and curled up in

her bed with the baby. Propped against the carved oak headboard, she closed her eyes to rest. As long as she held him or rocked him, Joshua was content. The instant she put him down, he let out a squall that shook the dust from the ceiling.

Although she missed adult conversation, she was grateful for the infant's company. Tending to his needs filled the void in her heart—that big gaping hole left when Pace walked out every night. Uninvited tears rolled down her cheeks. He wasn't coming back tonight. As she dozed off, she wondered if he would ever return.

The baby grabbed a fistful of her unbound hair and yanked. Mercy jerked awake. As she tried to untangle his fingers from her hair, she heard a knock at the door. Confused, she glanced at her strange surroundings. For a second she wondered why her room looked so different. Then she remembered. This wasn't her father's home, but her husband's. And it was his voice calling her from behind the locked door.

"Mercy, are you awake? Are you okay?" Pace asked, his voice deep with concern.

"Pace?" Setting the baby in the center of the bed, she swung her feet to the floor. Barefoot, she padded across the room.

"Yeah. I wanted to make sure everything is all right before I go back to the barn."

She couldn't let that happen. Her husband at least deserved a hot meal after a hard day's work. "No." She slipped the latch and pulled the door open. "I mean, you have to eat. I have your supper on the stove."

He backed up a step. His gaze narrowed on her white nightdress, then snapped back to her face. "I didn't mean to disturb you."

"You didn't. I was . . ." How to tell him she was waiting up for him, hoping, praying he would return? "I was worried about you."

"There's no need. I'll just take a bowl out to the barn."

With a boldness that surprised her, she caught his arm and drew him into the house. "This is your home. I don't want to run you out."

Pace stared at Mercy as if he'd never seen her before. He knew she had spirit, like a frisky filly out of the barn for the first time. In her virginal, lace-trimmed nightdress, she looked more like an angel than a woman. The material draped over her breasts, the tips dark against the white material. His gut tightened and the pain nearly doubled him over.

Coming to the house had been a mistake. But he had to know she was all right. That the baby was fine. He turned away, moving to the stove.

Who was he trying to fool? He wanted to see her. Now he wished he hadn't. As appealing as she was in the dream that had kept him awake night after night, the flesh and blood woman was enough to tempt a saint. He'd managed to reach the table when the baby's cries stopped him.

He jerked to a stop and spun around. Joshua was lying in the center of the bed, waving his arms and legs. His face was red as a cardinal's breast. In a few short strides Pace reached the infant. His mouth open, his eyes wide, Joshua quieted as abruptly as he'd started crying. The baby lifted his arms and smiled.

With a sigh of relief, Pace brushed a rough finger along the child's cheek. "Hey, little man. You being good for Mercy?"

"No," Mercy said from behind him. "He's been fussy all day."

"Is he sick?" Pace asked, careful not to look at Mercy. The baby's cries had temporarily cooled his burning lust. Now, at the sound of her voice, he was harder than ever, and even more determined to get out while he could still walk.

"No, I don't think so. But if he keeps it up, I might take him into town and let the doctor look at him."

"Do what you think best."

"I'll see how he is tomorrow. Come to the table, your supper is ready.

Pace backed away from the baby. If he could make it to the table and sit down, maybe Mercy wouldn't notice the bulge that strained the fly of his pants. He hadn't taken two steps when Josh let out a howl louder than the scream of a train whistle. This time Pace couldn't resist picking up the baby. Josh quieted, and made a noise that sounded like laughter. "He wanted me to pick him up." He looked at Mercy, amazed at how this tiny baby had manipulated him.

"We must have spoiled him. He wanted to be held all day."

With a shake of his head, Pace tried to return the baby to the bed. Again Josh let them know of his great displeasure. "I give up. Reckon I'll have to hold him while I eat." Thankfully, thinking about the baby had distracted Pace from his own carnal needs. He only wished Mercy had the good sense to put on a wrapper over her gown. The woman clearly had no idea of the effect she had on him.

Josh seemed perfectly content to be held while Pace ate his supper. Mercy filled a plate with thick slices of tender beef and rich gravy over creamy mashed potatoes. After he'd finished the meat, he sopped up a biscuit with gravy and held it to the baby's lips. Pace smiled as the child opened his mouth and sucked greedily on the soft bread.

"Pace," Mercy said, laughing, "babies can't eat biscuits."

"This little man is hungry, and he knows good chow when he sees it. I think he's jealous since all he ever gets is milk." Pace glanced up at the woman hovering over them. He could see the golden tips of her eyelashes often hidden behind the thick eyeglasses. He'd been so intent on her body, he hadn't noticed she wasn't wearing the spectacles. And her body was so close to his, he felt her heat and smelled her sweet flowery soap.

"Look, you got gravy on his mouth." She leaned forward and touched the baby's mouth with the corner of a napkin.

Pressed so close, her breast brushed his arm. Fire shot through his veins. The flames exploded like dynamite clear through to his groin. All his effort to cool his ardor was lost in her nearness. He jerked upright. The movement only pressed his arm tighter against her softness. His spoon clattered against the bowl.

The tip of her breast hardened, like the hot point of an arrow against his skin. Heat branded him. He didn't dare move. Only the baby on his lap kept him from filling his hands with those full, firm globes.

Her hand stilled, and her voice trailed off. For a moment, they were frozen in time—her body so close, her face inches from his, her hair flowing freely around her shoulders. Even Josh stopped squirming and stared up at the adults who were lost in each other. Their gazes locked, and the longing in her eyes took his breath away.

With a superhuman effort, he pulled his gaze away. He was already about to bust his britches; another second and he would do something they would both regret.

Knees weak, Mercy couldn't move. She didn't know what had happened to her in those few brief seconds. Something blossomed in her stomach, like spring flowers opening to welcome the warmth of the sunshine. Her breasts swelled against the hard muscle in his arm. She'd never known her skin could be so sensitive. Pace's smoldering dark eyes filled her sight, lye soap and leather on his skin filled her nostrils, and his harsh breathing filled her ears. Desire drained her mind of coherent thought. She longed to sift her fingers through his thick, black hair.

Mercy didn't want to think, she wanted to feel. Her body grew warm and fluid. In that tense moment, with Pace inches away, she knew she loved him as she would never love another man. She had to make him hers, tie him to her the way a woman possesses a man—as his wife in every sense of the word.

Her gaze locked with his. He wanted her. She saw the way his pupils dilated, flames glittering in the depths of his soul. Mercy dropped her head, afraid to break the contact. Inches away from his mouth, she parted her lips and offered herself—heart, soul, and body.

His warm breath brushed her skin, and she closed her eyes and waited. Then in a movement that took her by surprise, Pace shoved away from the table and jerked to his feet.

Stunned by his abrupt movement, she staggered against the table. Her face turned crimson. In that instant her hopes were dashed as if doused by icy water. He couldn't have shocked her more if he'd struck her.

How could she embarrass both of them with her wanton behavior? He didn't want her. What made her think any man could want a woman shaped like a cow? A woman who should be old enough to forget silly, girlish dreams.

Pace shoved the baby into her arms. "I've had enough," he said. His hard angry voice rifled through her chest.

He'd had enough. Enough of her—a woman he'd never wanted in the first place.

Joshua wailed at the sharp words and quick movement. He grabbed a handful of Mercy's hair and tugged. The pain didn't hurt nearly as much as the ache that tore at her heart.

"I'd best leave." He shoved his battered hat back onto his head, and raced toward the door. The man couldn't get away from her fast enough.

As he reached the door, she made a decision. If he didn't want her around, she would simply give him his wish. "I think I should take the baby to the doctor. I'll leave first thing in the morning."

Without turning, he said, "That's fine. I'll hitch up your buggy before I leave. Stay in town as long as you want."

Mercy's heart plunged to her feet. Not only didn't he want her in his bed, he also didn't want her in his house. She swallowed her pain. For all he cared, she could have stayed with her father forever.

He slanted a quick glance over his shoulder, his gaze hot and needy in spite of his actions. Then he set his jaw and stalked through the doorway, slamming the door shut behind him.

She cuddled the baby close to her chest and forced her feet to remain in place. As if he sensed her distress, Joshua cooed and made smacking noises with his mouth. She sank to the bed and let her tears flow.

Pace stood outside the door for long minutes before he was able to move toward the barn. From inside the cabin, he heard the soft sounds of a woman's sobs. He'd hurt her. Mercy had been nothing but good to him, and he'd hurt her feelings. Damn, but women were thin skinned. A moan escaped his lips at the thought of her skin. It was soft, white, and inviting as hell. He'd wanted her with all the fire and passion in his soul.

In the brief moments that she'd been so close that he felt heat from her flesh, he'd almost broken his vow and taken her. It would have been so easy. And he knew that she wanted him, too. Not that Mercy understood anything about what she was asking for. She was an innocent, a virgin, who had no idea of what a man's lust could do to her. What he could do to her.

He gathered his courage and returned to the barn. It was best for them both that she return to town. He never should have allowed her to come to the cabin. But how could he stop her? She was his wife. True, he'd married her to save his own neck, but the marriage was legal and binding. He didn't know how much longer he was going to be able to resist her. Even now he was on the brink of going crazy with lust. There was only so much a man could take, and he was at his wit's end.

A little time apart would be good. It would give him time to set his resolve and garner his strength without facing the temptation of a willing woman.

He ran a shaky hand over the stubble on his jaw. Only God knew what it cost him to make this noble gesture. God? God had nothing to do with it. This kind of torture came straight from the depths of hell. Punishment for all the sins he'd committed.

The past Sunday Reverend Goodacre had preached on "Reaping what you sow." Well, Pace was raking in a bumper crop. And he couldn't do a damn thing about it.

Mercy drove her buggy into town at about noon the next day. By the time she'd washed herself and the baby, Pace had her horses hitched to the buggy for her. She'd insisted he come in for some breakfast before she left. After all, it was the least she could do for her husband. He didn't want her affection, but he certainly enjoyed her cooking.

To her surprise, he rode beside her until the streets of Pleasant Valley came into view. When she'd protested that she didn't need him, his eyes had darkened with pain. It felt good to let him feel a little bit of the rejection he'd given her. Then she repented that she'd hurt him. Nobody knew more about rejection than Pace. He'd lived with it all his life. Although it wasn't necessary, she accepted his offer, and allowed him to escort her into town. Actually, she did feel safer with her husband at her side. And she definitely liked the idea of being his wife.

After a brief farewell, more to Joshua than to Mercy, he turned back toward the ranch. As she drove down

Main Street, she was amazed at the amount of activity in the various stores and shops. Men lounged on the board-walk outside Fullenwider's Hardware Store. Ladies carrying baskets of goods shared news and barely lifted a hand in greeting to Mercy. She smiled and let them enjoy their gossip—probably about her and Pace.

Tinkling music poured from the open doors of the saloons. The Ruby Slipper was open for business. Her gaze shifted to the saloon. She caught a glimpse of a black horse in the alley behind the buildings. At the fluttering in her chest, she willed her foolish heart to quiet. It seemed everything reminded her of Pace and the way she reacted whenever he came near. She knew he wasn't anywhere in town. He could hardly wait to return to the homestead.

Well, she'd cried her last tear over him. Once she'd gotten over her initial pain, she would set a plan into motion. Pace Lansing had rejected his wife for the last time. She knew exactly where to go for help. Miss Lily and the girls were experts in handling men. They would know exactly how to handle a reluctant male. Pace didn't have a chance.

Although Joshua seemed better, she decided to have him checked by the doctor anyway. As she'd expected, the baby was in excellent health, and probably spoiled. Her father was happy to see her, and said that she was welcome to stay as long as necessary. He hadn't wanted her to leave in the first place. Mercy assured him she could only stay until Sunday. She needed to help Tim in the Mercantile during his busy days.

The moment the shopkeeper realized Mercy had returned, he sent his delivery boy after her. Charity was at home with Timmy, and he desperately needed help. Thankful to be needed, Mercy gladly spent the rest of the day at the mercantile. Not only was she able to earn enough for their supplies, but she enjoyed seeing her friends and neighbors, and sharing a touch of gossip. However, she wasn't naive enough not to realize that over the past weeks, she'd been the main source of gossip for the wagging tongues of the town.

Although she missed Pace like crazy, it was good to spend a quiet evening with her father. They discussed his message for the next Sunday, and he clearly enjoyed playing with Joshua.

Close on to nine o'clock, someone rapped lightly on the door. Easing himself from his favorite chair, Ezra went to see who was summoning him at this hour. To the surprise of both of them, it was Sally Anders, a young girl Prudy was training as her personal maid.

"Reverend, sir," the girl bobbed her head, and performed an awkward curtsy. "Mrs. Blakely wants Miss Mercy to come to see her. She's feeling right poorly tonight."

Mercy stepped forward. "Did she see the doctor?"

"Yes, ma'am. He gave her a tonic, but she wants to see you." Sally backed up a step, remaining in the shadows of the porch.

Duty to her sibling warred with her responsibility for Joshua. Mercy glanced at the baby asleep in his basket. Although she hated to take him out into the night, she had little choice. "Tell Prudy I'll be right there."

"Thank you, ma'am," the girl said. With another curtsy, Sally took off at a run toward the edge of town.

"Papa." Mercy turned to her father. "Has Prudy been sick long?"

Ezra shook his head. "I doubt if it's anything serious. You know how your sister likes attention. She's been upset that you haven't been here to look after her. I think she misses her big sister."

Mercy stared at her father. This was the first time in memory that he'd criticized his youngest daughter. He'd always given in to Prudy's whims and wishes. Mercy realized it wasn't that he loved one of his daughters above the others, he simply had no idea how to handle three girls on his own. Since his wife's death, he'd turned over the rearing of his girls to Mercy, although she'd been little more than a child herself.

On a long sigh, Mercy moved toward the baby. "It's time Prudy grew up and accepted her role as Clifford's wife. She has to understand that I have my own responsibilities to my husband and family." Although it sounded reasonable, Mercy knew her sister wouldn't take criticism well. She was more spoiled than the infant sleeping in the basket.

"Easier said than done, daughter," her father muttered. When she reached for Joshua, he stilled her with a hand to her arm. "Leave him sleep. I'll keep an eye on him."

"Are you sure, Papa?"

"Of course I am. I've changed more than one diaper in my time. And this little fellow needs to get acquainted with his grandpa."

Pleasure wafted over her that he was willing to accept Joshua as part of his family. She flung her arms around his neck and kissed him soundly on the jaw. "Thank you."

Pink tinged his smoothly shaved cheeks. "Run along and see what your sister wants."

Mercy grabbed her knit shawl. "I won't be late."

A few minutes later, Mercy lifted the brass knocker on her sister's polished front door. Clifford had done well by Prudy, building her the finest house in town. Seconds later Sally opened the door, a grateful look on her face. Mercy suspected that her sister had given the girl a hard time.

"Come in, Miss Mercy. Mrs. Blakely is waiting for you in her room, I mean her boudoir."

"Thank you, Sally." An elegant Oriental carpet muffled the sound of Mercy's footsteps as she climbed the curved staircase. Slowly, she entered her sister's room at the top of the stairs. Prudy was lying under a thin sheet, her back propped against the headboard of her tester bed. The room was decorated in soft pastels, lace, and ruffles—a woman's boudoir. Mercy was well aware that Clifford slept in the room on the other side of a closed door.

The second Mercy stepped across the threshold, Prudy whined, "Sister, thank God you're here." Tears flowed down her cheeks.

Over the years, Mercy had seen this performance so many times, she was immune to her sister's feigned distress. "What's wrong this time, Prudy?" she asked, unable to disguise the disapproval in her voice.

"I have one of my headaches, and you're the only one who can make it better." Prudy shifted on the mattress to make room for Mercy.

Her younger sister had been plagued with headaches since their mother's death. Mercy didn't doubt that they were real, but she was certain they were brought on by stress or whenever Prudy didn't get her way. She picked up the silver hairbrush from the dresser and sat at her sister's back. Slowly, she slid the brush through Prudy's long blond curls. It never ceased to amaze her how both her sisters had gotten such beautiful golden hair, while Mercy's tresses were dark brown and straight as a board. "I know, darling," she said to soothe the younger woman. "I'm here now. Just relax and tell me what happened."

"I wish you hadn't married that old Pace Lansing. You know how much I need you here."

So that was the problem. Prudy missed her unpaid servant. Dropping the brush, Mercy began the second part of the treatment—gently massaging her sister's temple and forehead. "I'm sorry, darling, but it was about time I had a husband and family of my own."

Prudy relaxed against her sister. "I know. You deserve a wonderful life. But Pace took you away, out to that old ranch. And I've been worried about you. Can't you live here in town?"

This was the first time her sister had expressed any kind of concern for Mercy. "Honey, I have to live out at my husband's homestead. Pace isn't the villain he's been made out to be."

"Mercy, I've been married for over a year, so I know what men want from a woman." She shivered, and Mercy knew it wasn't an act. "I know how demanding they can be, how they constantly want to . . . you know, do it. How they're always pestering you. Coming into your bed when all you want to do is sleep."

Wouldn't her sister be shocked to know that so far Mercy and Pace hadn't come close to doing "it"? Under her fingertips, Mercy felt her sister begin to relax. "Prudy, it's part of a husband's rights."

"I hate the way he grunts like a bull and the way he gets his sweat all over me. I have to hurry and take a bath afterward." Prudy's voice dropped so low, Mercy had to strain to hear. "Now he wants me to have a baby."

"That's wonderful. You don't know how much I love Joshua and what a joy he is."

"But you didn't have to get big and fat as an ugly old heifer, or to have him pulling at your bosom for milk. I'll lose my shape, and I'll look like . . ." She stopped just short of saying "you."

Mercy wrapped her arms around her sister to ward off a chill. She knew her sister didn't mean the insult. Prudy was once again the frightened child she'd comforted in the middle of the night when she awoke with nightmares.

"I remember when Mama died having a baby, and the way Charity screamed in pain when Timmy was born. Even that Indian woman died from having her baby." Prudy turned and clung to Mercy as if to life itself. "I don't want to die."

Her sister sobbed heart-wrenching tears. She'd never seen her this genuinely upset. She wanted to remind Prudy that she was an adult woman, and it was time she accepted the responsibilities of marriage. Not just managing a big house, and having pretty clothes, but the other side, too.

Instead, she offered what comfort she could. "Sweetie, calm down. All women don't die when they have babies. If they did, there wouldn't be any women left in the world, and no children. But you should have known when you married that your husband would want a child."

"I thought Clifford was different. I thought he would be happy with just me." She hiccuped and clung tighter to Mercy.

"Hush now, honey. It's only natural for a man to want a child. It's just too bad they can't have it themselves." She felt Prudy calm. "If they had to have children, the world would have ended thousands of years ago."

Mercy smiled. "You're right about that. Just think, you might have a little girl who looks just like you. She'll be beautiful with blond curls, and you can buy the prettiest dresses."

The idea of spending her husband's money calmed Prudy more than anything else. "And I'll have to get a whole new wardrobe—all the latest fashions, of course."

Patting her sister's back, Mercy wondered how her sister had gotten so selfish. Of course, she accepted part of the blame. Mercy had given in to her youngest sister's every whim when she knew better. Against her chest, Prudy's breathing slowed, and she knew her sister was on the verge of sleep.

"You're right. Having a baby wouldn't be so bad after all." Her words drifted off and her head bobbed.

Slowly, Mercy eased her sister back to the pillows. She looked so young and innocent in her white silk gown, her hair spread on the pillow, her skin pale and almost translucent. No wonder she'd always gotten her way. She was so beautiful, she could have had any man she wanted. But something about the way she talked gave Mercy pause to wonder if her sister had made a mistake in marrying Clifford Blakely. Was she truly happy? The man was older, and much too worldly for a young woman like Prudence.

However, there wasn't much a sister could do. Mercy had husband problems of her own. Exactly the opposite of Prudy's. Whereas Clifford wanted his wife in every sense of the word, Pace didn't want Mercy at all.

Certain Prudy would sleep peacefully now that the headache had eased, Mercy slipped quietly from the room. She hoped she'd also helped erase some of her sister's distress over bearing a child. Mercy hugged her shawl to her chest. More than anything, she wanted to make love with Pace and have his baby.

Lost in her thoughts, Mercy descended the stairs and entered the darkened foyer. As she reached for the door, a hand clasped her arm. She jumped back with a squeal. "What?"

"Don't be frightened, dear sister. I just want to talk to you before you leave," Clifford said from behind her. "Come into my study."

He clutched her arm with more force than necessary and led her down to the hallway toward the rear of the house. She struggled to pull away, but he only tightened his grip. "I have to get back to Papa's. I left Joshua with him."

"This will only take a few minutes. I'm worried about Prudence."

So was Mercy. Perhaps she could reason with her brother-in-law, help him to better understand her sister's fears and concerns.

Once inside the mahogany-paneled den, Clifford released her arm and slid the door closed. She rubbed her arm, surprised at the lingering ache from his fingers. On the large desk a single lamp cast a pale yellow glow on the room. Beside it a thick, brown cigar was propped on a crystal ashtray. A sheaf of papers, a pen, and a silver letter opener waited for attention. Uneasiness skid down her back. She reached to turn up a wick in the lamp, when once again Clifford caught her wrist.

"Leave it," he said, his voice husky. "My eyes are tired from all that reading."

This time he released her immediately and moved slowly across the room to a sideboard. "Would you like a drink? Brandy? Wine?"

Mercy folded her hands in front of her skirt. Something was definitely wrong. Never had she seen her brother-in-law anything but impeccably attired. Tonight his shirt was wrinkled, and his collar missing. Even his usually slicked back hair was tousled. "No thank you, Clifford. You know I don't indulge."

He filled a snifter with a liberal amount of the amber liquid and held it up in a mock toast. "Did you know that your eyes are nearly the color of brandy?" Taking a step closer, he reached out a hand and snatched her eyeglasses from her nose. "Of course, most men don't notice when you're wearing those awful things."

Fear curled ugly fingers around her heart. "Give me back my glasses," she said, trying to hide the tremor in her voice. Her brother-in-law had always been the perfect gentleman, the staid banker who doted on his young wife. Tonight he wasn't himself at all.

He dropped the spectacles on the desk. "You know, dear sister, you've somehow gotten much more attractive in the past few weeks. Is that what marriage to Lansing has done for you? Has that rutting bull brought out the heat in you? Made you more a woman?" His body pressed against her, trapping her against his desk.

Her stomach retched at his filthy implications. "Move away, Clifford. I want to go home."

"Not yet." He downed the remainder of his liquor and tossed the glass toward the fireplace. The crystal shattered on the stone hearth. "Not until I find out what you gave Lansing while you've kept it from all of us. He killed Billy when he tried to sample your wares."

A chill raced over her body. "You knew that your brother tried to rape me?"

Clifford let out a deep, evil laugh. "Rape? Billy didn't have to resort to rape to get a woman. He told me he wanted to do you a favor. To teach you what it's like to be with a man."

Bile rose up in her throat, and she struggled not to vomit. The man who'd once asked to call on her had condoned his brother's attempted attack. It was only Pace who had come to her rescue. "Get out of my way."

"Now that you're Lansing's whore, you don't have to play all innocent and pure. I just want what Billy didn't get, what you've been giving to that breed all along." He shoved his hips into hers; his arousal pressed into her stomach. His hand shot out and cupped her breast. Cruel fingers twisted the nipple. "You've got such nice, big breasts. Not like those little knots on my wife's chest."

Pain shot through her chest at his cruel touch. His other hand circled her back, holding her tight against him. "You're either insane or drunk." The liquor on his breath made her gag. She twisted her head when he attempted to kiss her. His mouth landed at her throat. Bracing herself on the surface of the desk to get away from him, her hands made contact with a sharp object. From the corner of her eye she spotted the letter opener.

"I'm neither, sweet Mercy. I'm just aching to sink into your softness. You owe me. While I'm stuck with your skinny sister who won't even let me near her bed, Lansing is lying with you day and night."

She lifted a hand to strike at him. Clifford was quicker and stronger than she'd thought. He caught her wrist and twisted her arm behind her back. "Don't try that again. You'll like it if you'll just relax."

Frightened, she attempted to reason with her brother-in-law. "Stop. Your wife is upstairs. What if the servants hear you?"

"I sent them home, and Prudy is asleep by now. She never comes in here." His breath came in sharp gasps.

Mercy closed the fingers of her free hand over the letter opener. Her heart was pounding so hard, she was certain it would burst through her shirtwaist. She struggled to retain control. If she panicked, he would surely rape her. That would start a string of tragedies that would end in more than one death. Pace would find out and come after Clifford. One of them would die, and the other would probably swing from the end of a rope. It would also ruin her entire family. She had to stop that from happening.

"Pace will kill you."

"You won't tell him. You won't tell anybody. Who'll believe a half-breed's strumpet over a respected banker?"

His hand moved from her nipple to the center of her blouse. With one quick tug, he tore open the buttons, exposing her entire chest to his view. Her breath caught in her throat. His mouth came down on the flesh above her camisole. Sharp teeth nipped at the soft skin.

Desperate, Mercy realized she didn't have the physical strength to stop him. She remained still and bit her lip to keep from crying out. The pain in her arm was excruciating, but she couldn't let him know he had the upper hand. His head came up, and she couldn't believe the wildness in his eyes. He was more animal than human. He growled like a wolf stalking a weak little lamb. But Mercy wasn't a weak lamb.

"Kiss me," she whispered to distract him. Meanwhile, she shifted to reach the letter opener.

Clifford lifted his head, victory written in his expression. "It's about time you realized you can't fight me. You're like a bitch in heat. You need a man to mount you and tame you."

Instantly, he covered her mouth with his. Nausea threatened to weaken her. As he attempted to slip his tongue into her mouth, he relaxed his hold on her arm. She managed to put a few inches between their bodies, enough room for her hand to bring the letter opener between them. Mercy had never hurt another human in her life, but too many lives were at stake. She jabbed the sharp point into his ribs.

Startled, Clifford let out a yelp like a wounded dog, and jerked up his head. "Let go of me now," she said between her teeth. "Or I swear, I'll carve your heart out like a worm from a rotten apple."

His eyes narrowed. For an instant, she was afraid he would snap her arm. She pressed the sharp tip into his shirtfront; a drop of blood trickled down the white linen. Mercy didn't know how long she could keep up her bluff. He must have read the determination on her face, however, because he stepped away and dropped his hands.

"I didn't mean to offend you, dear sister," he said, using the coddling voice that make her sick. "I thought you would enjoy a gentleman after having to endure Lansing's vile advances."

Mercy wasn't fooled by his smooth talk. She didn't dare drop the knife. Snatching her eyeglasses from the desk, she backed toward the door. "No gentleman treats a lady like that. If I ever hear of you hurting my sister, I swear I'll cut out your heart and feed it to the hogs."

"Lady?" He laughed, a wicked evil sound. "You're a whore like your friends at the Ruby Slipper. You sold yourself to Lansing for a marriage license, and your sister sold herself to me for a few gowns." He took one staggering step toward her.

"And you sold your soul to the devil a long time ago." She reached for the doorknob and twisted it with the hand still numb from his cruel grip. "Keep away from me, Clifford, or I'll shout your sins from the rooftop."

He touched the blood on his shirt. A string of curses burst from his lips. "And I'll tell everybody that you came here and offered yourself to me for money. They all know you were lying with Lansing before you were married. Who's going to believe that a man married to the most beautiful woman in town would want her plain older sister?"

His words cut through her like shards of glass. He was right about that. Nobody would believe her—except her father and Pace. And she couldn't tell either man. Jerking the door open, she darted into the dark hallway. Thankfully, Clifford didn't try to follow her. With trembling fingers, she twisted the key in the front door and escaped to the safety of the outdoors.

Only when she'd run halfway home did she feel the cool evening breeze on her exposed bosom from where her shirtwaist was torn. She'd lost her shawl sometime during the struggle, but she still clutched the letter opener in her hand.

A drop of Clifford's blood darkened the tip.

Eighteen

Pace awoke with a jerk. In one quick movement he sprung to his feet. He listened to the night sounds—the distant howl of a coyote, the deep mooing of the cattle, the occasional hoot of a barn owl. All ordinary noises. Nothing unusual, nothing that should have disturbed his sleep.

By the thin beam of light that filtered through the window curtains, he studied the newly furnished cabin. Mercy's touches were everywhere.

Even in his dreams.

He dropped back to the pallet on the floor, and folded his hands under his head. That was it. For the past few nights he'd slept in the barn, leaving Mercy to her privacy. He'd thought that would make her happy, that she would prefer not to be bothered by him. Yet she seemed upset every night when she carried his sorry body to the barn. If she only knew what it cost him to leave a sweet-smelling woman and bunk down with the animals.

His gaze fell on the big bed that took up far too much of the cabin. He'd touched it, running his fingers over the quilt she'd made with her own hands. If he'd had any sense at all, he would right now be lying in it, snuggled in its warmth and comfort. Instead, he'd opted to sleep on his thin straw mattress on the floor.

Pace called himself every kind of fool. But to sleep in

her bed was to smell her fragrance, to imagine her sweet soft body, and wonder how she would feel wrapped in his arms, with his . . . He moaned aloud. Those kinds of thoughts would cause him nothing but trouble. And another sleepless night.

By then, he was convinced sleep wouldn't come. He missed her, and he missed the baby. They'd become far too important in his life. That wasn't good for them and it wasn't good for him. Since it was close to sunrise, he figured he might as well get up. He pulled on his trousers, and slipped his arms into a shirt. Even his own clothes smelled like Mercy—like her soap and sunshine.

He turned up the lamp and filled a cup from the coffeepot on the stove. At the first sip, he spewed the cold, bitter brew from his mouth. With his thoughts on Mercy, he'd clean forgotten to stoke the fire and warm it up. Every morning she made fresh coffee, and prepared a breakfast he was too much of a coward to enjoy. He'd done his best to stay away from her, and all he'd succeeded in doing was making himself and her miserable.

Sinking into a chair, he tore off a chunk of the bread she'd left. Again, his thoughts wandered to her. How was she getting along in town? Was her father glad to see her? What about her sisters? A frown tugged at his mouth. Were they taking advantage of her goodness as usual? And her brothers-in-law? They didn't have any use for Pace, and he didn't have any use for them. Especially Blakely.

It wasn't just because the banker had tried to get him lynched when Billy died; it was more than that. Years ago he'd heard rumors about the man. How he'd ruined more than one young girl, and refused to marry her. Why Prudence married the man was beyond him. Probably all that money, most of which had been left to him by his father, who'd made a fortune during the War. Most of it, he was certain, was illegal.

The Blakelys thought they could do anything they

wanted and get away with it. When Billy had harassed Mercy, Pace couldn't stand by and let him hurt her. He wasn't sorry Billy was dead; he was sorry that Mercy had been involved.

A shiver raced over him. If any man touched his wife, so much as looked at her cross-eyed . . . Pace didn't even want to think about what he would do.

He jerked on his boots, and slammed his hat on his head. At least Mercy was safe in town. Nothing would happen to her there.

Mercy was torn with indecision.

Although she had no intention of revealing what Clifford had attempted the night before, she couldn't stop the tremors that tore at her stomach when he entered the store the next afternoon. She hadn't slept a wink last night. At daybreak, she was tempted to hitch up her team and hightail it back to the homestead and her husband. Only that would make everybody question her actions. And she couldn't come up with one plausible excuse.

Clifford had nerve, strolling in as if he were the most righteous creature under God's blue heaven. Today, he was his usual dandy self, immaculately clad in an expensive gray suit and sparkling white shirt. A stickpin with a diamond the size of her little fingernail winked from his black silk necktie.

The man had the unmitigated gall to smile and address her as if he hadn't tried to attack her the night before. "Good morning, dear sister," he said in his slimy, oh-so-kind voice. "How are you on this fine day?"

She grunted a nonanswer, and continued to tally the previous day's receipts for Tim.

Not to be ignored, Clifford inched closer to the counter. "And how's that fine young baby?"

He didn't give a fig about Joshua, Mercy, or anybody else's welfare. "Fine," she muttered.

"In case you're interested, Prudence is much better today. I suppose seeing you last night was the medicine my sweet little wife needed to cure what ailed her." He plucked a long cigar from his pocket and snipped off the end. "She asked me to invite you to dinner tonight."

"Tonight?" Mercy hesitated. She'd rather eat in a pigsty than spend one minute with Clifford. "Sorry. I have other plans."

Her brother-in-law eyed her through hooded lashes. His gaze lowered to her chest, and he gave a nearly imperceptible nod. Her stomach clenched. Under her gown and petticoats, her knees trembled. She shook, not with fear, but pure, honest anger. Anger at the nerve of the man, and at herself for letting him affect her this way.

"Surely you won't decline to have dinner with us. We've both missed you since you've moved out of town." He struck a match to the cigar. "Tim and Charity are coming. Your sisters will be disappointed."

It would snow in Kansas in July before she darkened the doors of his home again. Prudy could just come over to the parsonage if she wanted to see Mercy. "Sorry, Clifford, I won't be able to make it. Now, if you'll excuse me, I have work to do."

Before she could step away, he caught her arm. She cringed at his touch. "You know, I could use a smart clerk like you at the bank. I'll pay double what you get from Tim."

All the money in the world couldn't entice her to be alone with her duplicitous brother-in-law. "I'm happy here." She dropped her gaze to her arm where his fingers dug into the flesh. The night before he'd left dark marks. She refused to endure any more of his abuse. "Get your hand off me," she whispered.

"Sorry, sister," he said with a sly grin. "I hope you'll

reconsider. Lansing can't support you and his bastard. Someday you'll come begging for what I've got."

She jerked out of his grip. At that moment, Tim stepped through the curtained doorway from the storeroom. "If you'll excuse me, *dear brother,* I have to get back to work. Give Prudy my love." She rubbed her arm to wipe away his unwanted touch. Mercy didn't understand why she'd never seen through Clifford's facade before. He was as phony as the false fronts on the town's businesses. Nice to look at, but without strength or substance.

Tim stretched out a hand. "Clifford. I didn't hear you come in."

The banker shook the merchant's hand. "Just having a little chat with our dear, sweet Mercy. You know, she gets prettier every day."

"Mercy?" Tim stared at her as if he couldn't agree, but was afraid to disagree.

Clifford winked and laughed, more sneer than humor. He was funning, making Mercy the brunt of his joke.

She'd thought she despised him last night, but that didn't even compare to the loathing that drove her into the storeroom. As the men shared another laugh and indulged in male humor, she tore off her apron, picked up the sleeping baby, and darted through the rear doorway. Tim could take his accounts and tally them himself. Or let that contemptuous banker do it.

Needing to get away, she rushed into the alley. Oh, she was good enough last night—attractive enough, so he said—for Clifford to force his unwanted attention on her. Today, he mocked her when she turned down his proposition. Who knew how many other women he'd accosted? Poor Prudy, she thought, her heart aching for her youngest sister. To be stuck for life with a man like Clifford was worse than prison. No wonder Prudy was sick all the time.

In spite of the summer's heat, a shiver raced over Mercy. She vowed to keep what had happened her secret. It would destroy her entire family if they learned that Clifford was a lecherous goat. The respected, wealthy banker wasn't half, no he wasn't one-fourth the man poor, ex-convict Pace Lansing was.

Not wanting to go home and face her father, or chance a meeting with any of the ladies from church, Mercy headed to the one place she could find solace. To the one person in whom she could confide. The one woman in town who wouldn't condemn or accuse her. She headed down the back alley and stopped at the rear stairway that led to Miss Lily LaRose's private quarters above the Ruby Slipper.

Since it was early afternoon, the saloon was relatively quiet. The bar was open, and the bartender was serving drinks. But the ladies didn't start working until later that evening. They usually slept until past noon, while Cora and Miss Lily handled the business affairs. She hoped her friend wouldn't be too busy to visit.

At the head of the stairs, she knocked lightly on the door. Joshua was stirring in his basket, and would soon awaken. That would mean a bottle and changing. She glanced around. Perhaps it would be better to go home and take care of her responsibilities. Just as she turned to retreat down the steep stairs, the door swung open.

"What do you want?" Cora demanded.

Mercy jerked up her head and stared at the woman she'd called her friend. She bit back a sob. After all she'd been through, the unfriendly welcome tore at her heart.

"Miss Mercy, or should I say, Mrs. Lansing. I'm sorry I treated you so poorly. I declare, I didn't recognize you." Cora took the basket from Mercy's hand and urged her into the hallway. "I thought it was that pesky Johnson girl. She's always hanging around, looking for a handout. She wants to come to work for Miss Lily, but I told her we don't need any more help." Her skirts swishing on the long, thick carpet, Cora led the way toward Miss Lily's private suite. "In fact, Miss Lily is thinking of selling the Ruby Slipper and heading to San Francisco."

"That's so far away. Doesn't she like it here?" Mercy hurried to keep up with the taller woman's strides.

Cora glanced at Mercy for a moment before she opened the door. "She likes it just fine. Especially a certain gentleman, whom shall remain nameless."

A gentleman? Mercy's head spun at the thought. She'd hoped that her father would notice the lady for the person she was, not for what she did for a living. And more than a few times, she noticed the way Miss Lily looked at the minister. Such an unlikely couple. Even more diverse than she and Pace.

"Miss Lily," Cora called as she entered the ornate suite. "We have company."

"Mercy, how nice to see you." Miss Lily rose from her desk and reached out a welcoming hand. "And how's that young man we all love?"

"Joshua is just fine, though a little spoiled, I'm afraid." She caught both of the woman's soft hands in hers, suddenly aware how rough her own had gotten in a few weeks. She jerked back her hands and shoved them into her pockets.

"That's only natural with two doting parents, plus your father," Lily remarked as she perched on the edge of the chaise. Nobody sat or moved more gracefully than Miss Lily. The hem of her pink silk wrapper pooled around her feet like the petals of a flower.

Cora lifted the baby from the basket. "My, he's almost outgrown that carrier. I reckon he'll be crawling and walking before we can blink an eye."

Joshua squirmed and cooed at the attention. "He eats all the time," Mercy said. "I think he's hungry again."

"I'll take care of him while you and Miss Lily visit. The girls will be fighting to hold him." Propping the infant against her shoulder, the woman left the room and closed the door softly behind her.

"Sit down, Mercy, and have some tea." Lily gestured to the cushion beside her.

"Thank you." Mercy settled on the cushion. Now that she'd come, she wasn't sure why she'd wanted to burden her friend with her problems.

After filling a delicate china cup with tea, Lily handed it to Mercy. "Now tell me, what's gotten you so upset?" Her voice hardened. "Has Pace done something to hurt you?"

Mercy jumped. How in the world did she know something was wrong? "Oh, no. Nothing's wrong. Pace has been nothing but . . ." Her voice trailed off to a whisper. "Good."

Lily hooked a finger under Mercy's chin and forced Mercy to look into her face. Staring into the older lady's deep blue eyes was like staring into the heavens. And she suspected that those eyes had seen far more of hell than most women twice her age. Mercy felt as if Lily could read her thoughts.

"You can't fool me, Mercy. I know you too well. You're the most open and honest person I've ever met. Something's happened, and I want to help."

Mercy tore her gaze away in a struggle to regain her thoughts. This was the chance she needed to get some advice on how to handle her husband. Of course, she would never reveal what Clifford had tried to do. She stood and paced across the thick carpet. Miss Lily lived a luxurious life. The sitting room was as elegant as the lady herself.

As she turned to face the lady, her gaze fell on something shiny on the desktop. She paused. The silver mirror and brush looked familiar—exactly like the set she'd discovered among Pace's things.

She bit her lip to keep from crying out. That *had* been

Pace's horse she'd spotted behind the Ruby Slipper yesterday when he'd escorted her into town. He'd given the beautiful gift to Miss Lily. No wonder he didn't want anything to do with her. He was in love with another woman.

It all became clear. He hadn't wanted to marry her. And didn't Cora say that Miss Lily was interested in a certain man she refused to name? Of course she couldn't tell Mercy that man was her own husband.

To be betrayed by her friend hurt worse than what her brother-in-law had attempted. Her thumb brushed the ring on her finger. She nearly doubled in pain. He'd gotten the ring for her finger from his lover.

Mercy set her teeth and vowed not to make a fool of herself in front of the other woman. "Nothing's wrong. But I really must get home. I'll go fetch Joshua from Cora."

Before she could leave the cloying confines of the room, Lily stopped her with a gentle hand to her shoulder. "Mercy Lansing, you aren't going anywhere until you tell me what's wrong. Have I done anything to offend you? Is it Pace? Or one of your sisters or brothers-in-law?"

She wanted to shout yes to all three. Instead, she squared her shoulders. "No. Pace has been . . ." She couldn't lie another minute. Her marriage was a farce. Her life was in shambles. Her heart was breaking into a thousand tiny pieces. Unable to hold back, she covered her face with her hands and let out a heart-wrenching sob.

Wrapping her arms around Mercy's shoulders, Lily urged her back to the settee. Her touch was warm and loving, almost like a mother's. But Lily wasn't her mother—she was a rival for her husband's affection. Taking a deep breath, Mercy managed to regain a bit of composure.

"I'll give him an annulment," she said, willing to sacrifice her marriage so the man she loved could be happy.

"Why would you want to do that? What has Pace done? If he's hurt you, I'll horsewhip that man myself."

Mercy shoved out of the other woman's embrace. How could she put on such an act? "You should know. You're his lover."

Lily leaped from the seat as if she'd sat on a tack. "Lover? Pace?" She stuttered for a moment, then glared at Mercy with fire in her eyes. "Where did you get such a foolish idea? You silly goose, don't you know I'm in love with your father?"

"My father? But Pace . . ."

"Pace is a friend because he's your husband. I've helped him a time or two for your sake. Your friendship means the world to me. I think about you like the daughter I never had."

"But he came to see you. He gave you the brush and mirror."

"Is that what this nonsense is all about? That was payment for the ring."

"He said he got the ring from you."

"I sold him the ring because I knew it would make you happy. He isn't interested in me. He's trying the best he knows how to be a good husband to you."

Her heart sank further, as if hitting the floor hadn't stopped it. "But he doesn't want me. He hasn't even touched me once."

"He hasn't made love to you?" Lily's blue eyes grew dark with fury.

Mercy shook her head. "He kissed me a time or two, but that's all. When it's time to go to bed, he sleeps in the barn."

"With the other jackasses," she muttered.

A tiny smile curved Mercy's mouth. She'd been wrong about her friend. Then she remembered what else Lily had said. "You're in love with my father?"

"For as much good as it does me. It looks like we're in the same boat. The men we love are immune to our charms."

She took Lily's hand. "I'm sorry I misjudged you. I think Papa likes you, but he doesn't know what to do."

"Well, there isn't much we can do about my situation, but I believe I can help you with yours. I have a wedding gift that's just what you need."

Lily moved toward the bureau and retrieved a package from a drawer. The box was wrapped in pink paper and a large satin bow. She placed the present on Mercy's lap.

"Miss Lily, it's too beautiful to open." Carefully, she slid the ribbon from the box, and tried not to tear the paper. She lifted the lid and shoved aside thin tissue paper. At first she thought it was an ivory scarf. When she lifted the silk, she discovered a beautiful gown and wrapper. Her cheeks heated at the sight of the gown that was little more than two strips of sheer fabric held together with ribbons along the sides and at the top. She held it up for closer inspection. "You can see clear through it."

Lily laughed at the shocked expression on Mercy's face. "Of course. That's the idea. But the wrapper is much more modest. Honey, when Pace sees you in this, he'll think he was caught in the middle of a tornado."

How Mercy wished that were true. "But it's much too expensive and fine for me."

"Nonsense. You've been good to my girls and me. We wanted to do something special for you."

Mercy felt her confidence building. "But I don't know what to do. What if he runs out to the barn again?"

"Then you follow on his trail. Don't let him get away." Lily flashed a secret smile.

"But what'll I do if I catch him?"

Lily shook her head. "I don't believe you'll have to do much. He's a virile young man who can hardly resist a lovely young woman who offers herself so willingly."

"I'm not pretty or shapely. What if he still doesn't want me?"

"Honey, you're prettier than he deserves, and you have

a figure that makes a man forget his own name. It's all in how you use it. And I'm just the lady to teach you."

For a half hour or so, Lily shared a few simple "secrets" with Mercy—ideas on how to get her husband into her bed, and how to keep him there. More than once, the heat of embarrassment colored her face. She'd never even imagined the things the lady told her she could do for her husband. Or what he could do for her. When she murmured she would die before she would touch a man, Lily reminded her that if she wanted to save her marriage, she'd better be willing to learn a thing or two about men.

In that short period of time, she learned things that she was certain neither of her sisters had known before marriage, or perhaps after, and that few "nice" ladies ever considered. Miss Lily assured her that respectable women didn't just talk about these things—they actually did them.

Mercy was a quick learner, and she took every word to heart. After being rejected by her husband time and again, she was desperate. And desperate situations called for desperate measures. Now all she needed was opportunity and courage to put the plans into operation.

When she left the saloon later that afternoon, she was armed with the beautiful silk nightgown, and reassuring words of encouragement.

Of course, she knew she wouldn't have a chance to put her plans into motion until she returned to Pace's cabin. And that wouldn't be until Sunday evening. He'd promised to meet her at worship. She'd gotten the impression that he expected her to remain with her father, rather than return with him. He was in for one big surprise, she thought. By Sunday night, she wouldn't only be with him, he would be in her bed.

The next days passed slowly for Mercy. She avoided contact with Clifford, although Prudy wondered why Mercy refused to visit her at her own home. Mercy used Joshua and working for Tim as an excuse. Besides, she wanted to spend time with her father.

It still surprised her that Miss Lily had revealed her feelings for the minister. Sometimes she thought that men were the most thick-headed creatures on God's green earth. How her father didn't recognize the signs, she would never know. The lady was constantly ordering furniture from him, and she already had a houseful.

Not that Pace was any better. His skull must be the densest of all. There wasn't much Mercy could do for her father and Lily, but she intended to get through to Pace once and for all.

On Sunday morning, she took a seat near the rear of the church. She cringed when she saw Clifford and Prudy prance into the church, like the king and queen of England greeting their loyal subjects. Mercy bit her lip to keep from accusing her brother-in-law of being the biggest hypocrite in Pleasant County, or maybe the whole state of Kansas. How dare the man try to attack her, then act as if he were as holy as an angel?

With Joshua in her arms, she stood for singing, and bowed her head in prayer. All the while she kept one eye peeled on the door. To anyone watching, Mercy was the most devoted of the flock. Her prayers, however, were that Pace would show up. By the end of the second hymn her prayer was answered. Pace slipped into the pew and sat beside her.

"Sorry I'm late," he whispered. "My horse threw a shoe, and I had to get him to the blacksmith."

Brushing a gentle hand along his arm, she nodded and smiled sweetly. "I knew you wouldn't disappoint me."

When Joshua spotted Pace, he stretched out his arms and wailed. Pace took him from Mercy, and bounced the infant on his knee. Ready to put her lessons into practice,

Mercy tucked her arm in his and pressed against his side. Pace shifted slightly to give her room, which only bolstered her determination not to let him get away. She remained locked next to him. Remaining near at all times was lesson number one.

At the end of the worship service, they wandered to the front lawn. Mercy didn't let Pace get one step away from her. She greeted friends and neighbors, and forced them to acknowledge Pace as her husband. Prudy lifted her hand in greeting, but Clifford avoided even eye contact. That was just as well. If Pace knew what had happened, there would be hell to pay.

Mercy had previously informed her father that she was leaving immediately after church, and that he should feel free to accept the dinner invitations that were always extended by the various families. At the front door, she kissed her father goodbye, and continued toward her buggy with Pace.

He stopped abruptly when they were beyond earshot of the other folks. "Mercy, is something wrong?"

She lifted her gaze and gave him a puzzled look. "What ever do you mean?"

"Did something happen? You haven't let go of my arm since I entered the church."

A lot happened, but I'll never tell you. She bit her tongue to hold back the truth. "You're my husband, and I like being with you." Her fingers dug into the muscles on his forearm. He stiffened, but didn't pull away.

He seemed confused, and he eyed her suspiciously. Joshua chose that moment to remind them of his presence and lack of attention. He let out an ear-splitting yell, then gurgled as if it were all in great fun. "You missed your daddy, didn't you, boy?" Mercy asked, brushing a finger along the baby's smooth face.

Again, Pace was taken aback. He looked as if she'd knocked him on his head with a two-by-four. His mouth gaped, but no words came out. "I missed him, too," Mercy remarked to the baby.

Mercy smiled at how well her plan was working. Lily had said she should keep him a little off balance, just enough to get through his thick skull. As they reached her buggy, he curtly disengaged his arm from her grip. Then he shoved the baby into her arms. "I have to get back to the ranch. Have a good day."

This time she felt as if *she* had been struck with that same two-by-four. "What do you mean?"

"You're going to be spending some time with your father." He reached for the reins of his horse, tied to the rear of the buggy.

Sick to death of being shoved aside, she faced him eye-to-eye, toe-to-toe. Only the baby separated their bodies. "No, I'm not staying here in town. I'm your wife, for better or worse, and I intend to honor my commitments." She shoved Joshua back into his arms. "I'm going home with my husband and baby."

"You can't."

She folded her arms and refused to accept the child. "That's a baby, not a ball to be tossed back and forth. You mean to say you don't want me." Her well-laid plans were tumbling around her like a straw hut in a windstorm. It hurt to think her husband still didn't want her.

He shook his head. "It isn't that. It's just that I'm out on the range all day. I'm not there to look after you. You're safer here in town."

Safer? With men like Clifford Blakely lurking in the shadows? She'd rather take her chance with a rattler that at least lets you know when he's about to strike. "Pace, are you going to make a scene? People are beginning to stare."

He glanced at the various people who were straining to hear. "No. You can damn well do as you please."

"Good." She lifted her skirts and climbed into the high buggy seat without assistance. "It pleases me to go home where my things are. Where my bed is and where my husband lives." Without a backward glance, she snapped the whip and the horses took off at a gallop. She could just imagine the shocked look on Pace's face as he was left eating her dust and holding the baby.

Nineteen

What the hell was wrong with the damn woman?

Pace tucked the baby into his shirt to keep his face free from the swirling dust. She'd taken off and left him staring after her while half the town looked on.

Well, she wasn't going to get away with making a fool out of Pace Lansing.

The baby cradled in one arm, he mounted his stallion. He spurred the horse and took off after Mercy. Joshua cooed and happily waved his arms in delight. It didn't take long for the horse's strong stride to catch up with the buggy.

He pulled alongside her and yelled, "Stop this thing right now."

She glanced at him, but ignored his orders.

With every pounding hoof of the horse, his anger grew. The woman was absolutely crazy. He couldn't grab the reins while holding the infant. Protecting Joshua took all his concentration.

About a mile outside town, she slowed the buggy, but kept right on going. Again he shouted at her to stop. This time, she tugged at the reins and halted the team. He breathed a sigh of relief. He'd been scared to death the baby would be hurt.

She stood and reached out her hands. "Wasn't that fun,

Joshua?" she asked as she took the child from his arms. "You like riding with your daddy, don't you?"

Pace handed over the baby, and glared at Mercy. From her perch in the buggy, she met him eye-to-eye. He bit his tongue until she tucked the baby into his basket before letting loose a string of curses that left her cheeks pink and her eyes flashing murder.

"Are you finished, Mr. Lansing? Have you exhausted your supply of profanity? Or do you wish to call me a few more names no lady should be forced to hear?"

He opened his mouth, then snapped it shut. She was right. He'd made a complete ass out of himself. Properly chastised, he removed his hat and swiped the back of his hand across his forehead. "Sorry. Reckon church didn't do me much good."

"Obviously."

"Have you come to your senses? Are you ready to go back to your father's home?"

"Actually, I have finally come to my senses, and I'm going home with my husband."

That was exactly what he was afraid of. The woman was as stubborn as a mule. "I told you, I won't be able to protect you."

"Teach me how to shoot and I'll protect myself."

"I'm your husband. Didn't you promise to obey me?"

She stuck out her jaw. "I'm glad you finally realize I'm your wife. Didn't you promise to cherish me?"

He couldn't deny she was right. "I will, after I get the cabin ready." Truth was, he had to get his libido under control, and steel himself against her allure.

"It's fine the way it is."

"It isn't good enough for you."

"I'm not complaining. Why should you?"

Arguing was getting them nowhere. Clearly, she'd made up her mind to go home with him. A tiny part of his heart quivered at the thought. Did she like him, just a little? He couldn't send her back to her father's. It would humiliate her to be packed off like unwanted baggage. Mercy deserved better than that.

"You win. We'll have to make the best of this situation."

She dropped to the seat and retied her bonnet under her chin. Her jaw quivered, but she didn't make another sound. Like a heartless beast, he'd again hurt the woman who'd only been good to him. But he didn't know how he was going to stay in the cabin with her and not share her bed. There was only so much a man could stand. The odor of horses and cows were a poor substitute for a sweet-smelling woman. And a prickly straw pallet couldn't compare with a soft feather mattress.

Joshua let loose a familiar squeal. "He wants you," Mercy said in a weak, trembly voice. "He likes riding. I reckon he'll be riding before he learns to walk."

Pace glanced at the child and realized he only wanted attention. "Leave him be. He needs to exercise his lungs."

For a moment he thought she would argue, but instead, she picked up the reins. Pace took them from her hands. "I'll drive the rest of the way home." In a few quick movements, he had his horse tethered to the rear of the wagon, and he climbed up beside her.

She moved aside to give him as much space as possible. Earlier she'd clung to him like glue; now she couldn't get far enough away from him.

Women. He didn't understand them at all.

Mercy didn't know what she'd expected of Pace, but she wasn't prepared for more rejection. As he drove across the bumpy path to the cabin, she tried to bolster her courage. Miss Lily's instructions raced over her brain.

She'd formed a plan in her mind. After a delicious dinner, they would both put the baby to sleep in his cradle. Then she would let down her hair and don the beautiful nightdress. She bit her lip to keep down her trepidation. She was set to follow him all the way to the barn if necessary.

Under her cotton gloves, her hands began to sweat. What if it didn't work? What if after all her plans, he still didn't want her? Over and over she'd thought about the things Miss Lily had told her. Men liked to be touched, they liked a woman to pursue them, they . . . oh, Lord, her shoulders sagged. What if Pace wasn't like other men? What if she made a complete and utter fool out of herself.

His gaze slid over at her. Quickly, she looked down at Joshua, who'd quit fussing and had fallen asleep.

"Is something wrong, Mercy?" he asked.

"No, the baby is fine. You were right, he doesn't need to be held all the time." She hugged her arms. Women liked to be held, too, but only by the right man. She shivered at the way Clifford had tried to hold her. His touch left her chilled to the bone. She knew it would be different with Pace, if only he would want her the way she wanted him.

"I meant you. Are you ill?"

"I'm fine, too," she lied. She was as nervous as a hen staring into the eyes of a chicken hawk. It wasn't right to keep secrets from her husband, but if he found out about Clifford, all hell would break loose. Her husband already hated her brother-in-law, and it would take just a word from her to seal all their fates.

He leaned forward and braced his elbows on his knees. "What did the doctor say about Josh?"

Thankful for the change of subject, Mercy took a deep breath. "Joshua is perfectly healthy. He's growing and he's larger than most babies his age."

"Then why does he cry all the time?"

"He's spoiled. But he's fine. I'm fine. You're fine. My father's fine. My sisters are fine. The whole world is fine."

Her voice rose to a shriek. Ashamed of her irrational behavior, she covered her face with her hands.

Pace tugged the reins and the team came to a halt. He cupped her shoulders and turned her to face him. "Mercy, did something happen in town? You're sure acting strange."

She lowered her hands and blinked back tears. Pace would never know the truth about what had happened between her and Clifford. Neither could she tell him how he'd hurt her by his lack of caring. "I'm just tired from working in the mercantile, and taking care of Joshua. And I've had to handle my father's accounts." True, she'd gotten little sleep in the past nights, but she generally handled more chores then these with even less rest. "I'll be all right once we get back home."

He patted her gently, as if he had no idea how to comfort a woman. "Try to take it easy. You don't have to fix my meals, and I'll see that Josh gets to sleep early tonight."

His attempt at kindness was almost her undoing. "Thank you. But I'm your wife, and I'll perform my duties." All of them, she added to herself. Cooking, cleaning, and sharing his bed.

"I'll try not to be a bother. You have your hands full with the baby."

"You're no bother, Pace. You're hardly ever in the house, and you can do most everything I can."

A crooked grin curved one side of his mouth. "I can't bake a delicious chocolate cake."

She returned his smile. Leave it to something as simple as a tiny compliment to make her feel better. "Is this your way of asking if I've brought one with me?"

A soft growl rumbled from his stomach. "Did you?"

"Yes. I'm starved, too. Let's get home and you can see what else I've brought for our dinner."

He released her and clucked to the horses. "Lordy, me,

Miss Mercy. You'll have me fat as a pig before you're through with me."

Contentment slid over her like a warm summer rain. She tucked her arm in his, eager to put her plan into motion. By the time she got through with Pace, he would be purring like a contented kitten in her bed.

True to his word, Pace spent most of the afternoon taking care of Joshua. The baby loved the attention, and Pace seemed to enjoy the child. Who would have thought a man so big and rough could be so gentle with an infant? Joshua took great delight in being tickled and tossed into the air. Pace even took Joshua outdoors to visit the animals.

Mercy followed at their heels, and helped Pace point out the various plants, flowers, cattle, and the rabbits and squirrels that scurried to hide in the woods. She carried a jar of lemonade and slices of cake. At the edge of the river, she sat on a large stone, and offered the treats to Pace.

At first, he seemed surprised, but settled beside her to enjoy the beauty of the sunset. So far, everything was working according to her schedule. Her husband was well fed, he was at peace, and so caring for the child, it make her heart sing.

Now, if only she could get him to pay that kind of attention to her.

With the purple glow of twilight hovering over the cabin, Pace rocked Joshua to sleep in his cradle. After his busy day, the baby fell asleep immediately. He'd started sleeping all night, and Mercy prayed that he wouldn't waken until morning.

As Mercy struck a match to the lamp, she wondered what would happen next. She'd already fed Pace, and she couldn't very well offer more food. Neither could she grab his arms and toss him on her bed.

Pace glanced around the cabin, looking as uneasy as she felt. "I reckon I'd best get out to the barn."

"Why, Pace? It isn't right for you to have to sleep out there with the animals. I feel as if I've forced you out of your own home."

He glanced over at the bed, then back at her. Quickly he shifted his gaze to the door. "I told you I don't want to be any trouble for you."

"There's enough room for both of us." She stretched out a hand and gently brushed his arm. He stiffened under her touch. Her stomach sank. What if Miss Lily was wrong, and Pace didn't like her touch? "Besides, I get lonely in here. Can't we sit together and talk?" She bit her lip and cast her eyes downward. "And sometimes I get kind of scared all alone." It wasn't quite true, but she'd also been told that men wanted to be needed to protect their women.

"I suppose I should stay close for you and Josh." Even as he spoke, he moved toward the door. Mercy was almost afraid she'd lost the war before the first battle was fought. "I have a few chores, but I'll be back shortly."

She nearly sagged with relief. Her strategy had to work. Her marriage depended on her winning this war.

Hurriedly, she removed her calico frock. She hung it in the armoire that crowded her side of the cabin. She removed her eyeglasses and took a few moments to run a washcloth over her face and arms. The French milled soap left a soft, feminine fragrance on her skin. Her petticoats and corset joined the gown. When she'd stripped down to her chemise and drawers, she paused to reconsider. She caught a glimpse of herself in the bureau mirror. Doubt about her mission made her weak in the knees. It was now, or never, she thought, as she removed the beautiful silk nightgown from the tissue and held it in front of her. It would look ridiculous with the undergarments. But how could she remove them and be naked under the sheer garment? What would Pace think? Would he consider her a wanton, a fallen woman?

Or would he appreciate her as much as Miss Lily had promised he would?

It was a chance she had to take. She couldn't remain married to him and never be a real wife.

Not giving herself a chance to change her mind, she tore off the undergarments and without even glancing at her naked body, she slipped the nightgown over her head. The tiny ribbons did little more than keep it up on her shoulders and closed at the sides. Only then did she dare glance at the image in the mirror. The dusky tips of her breasts pressed against the near transparent silk, and the dark shadow below her stomach was visible. Hurriedly, before Pace caught her in such reckless dishabille, she slipped into the wrapper and tied it at her waist.

During the long day, tendrils of her hair had escaped the confines of the many hairpins. Before she could change her mind or reconsider her actions, she removed the pins and shook out the heavy tresses. A few quick strokes of the brush, and the hair draped over her shoulders like a dark lace veil. Only then did she dare return her gaze to the mirror.

For a moment, Mercy didn't recognize the woman who stared back at her. In the dim light, she was a different person. The ivory silk brought out the glow in her fair skin, and her hair gleamed like satin.

Why, she was almost pretty. If only Pace thought the same.

She heard a noise outside the door, and nearly panicked. Reciting Miss Lily's instructions in her head, she darted for the bed and caught the headboard like clutching a lifeline. The hinges on the door squeaked, and her waiting was over.

* * *

Pace paused before he stepped through the doorway. Gut feelings told him he was making a mistake by coming back to the cabin. He'd hurried through his chores, feeding the horses, checking on the cattle, and took a few minutes to wash the day's dust from his face and arms. He wished he'd taken the time to douse himself in the cold river. The way Mercy made him feel, it was the only thing that could cool his blood.

But part of him wanted to be with her. Not that he would allow himself any intimacy. No, he'd truly missed her and wanted just to look at her and listen to her cultured voice.

He smiled at the memory of the day. Something inside his chest swelled. It had been one of the nicest days of his life. Playing with the baby, and sharing the dessert with Mercy beside the river gave him a sense of peace and of belonging that he'd never experienced. Was this how other men lived? How normal married couples spent their time? It wasn't anything like how his parents had lived. He couldn't ever remember his father touching him, except with a belt or fist. Pace's life had been hard and without love. He vowed to give Josh all the love and attention that had been lacking in his own life.

What about Mercy? Didn't she deserve love? And could Pace learn to love her? If only he had some indication that she cared a little about him. She'd been good, but as the preacher's daughter, she'd been reared to be kind to the unfortunate. He frowned. Was that how she viewed him? The husband who had been forced upon her. The man she didn't want.

He knocked lightly, not wanting to take her by surprise. A soft, hesitant voice bid him enter.

Shoving the door open, he entered the dimly lit room and quickly bolted the door behind him. Pace took a deep breath before he dared face his wife. When he turned, he stopped dead in his tracks.

The kerosene lamp that been trimmed, and several tall,

slender candles cast long shadows on the walls. Almost afraid of what he would find, he let his gaze drift slowly around the room. Joshua was sleeping soundly in his cradle, his deep even breathing the only sound in the room. For a second, he wondered what had happened to Mercy. Then he spotted her standing at the far side of her bed.

His heart leaped into his throat. In a long white gown, she looked like a ghost, or an angel. Whichever, she was too beautiful to be real.

Her dark hair was loose and a long strand draped over her shoulder and curled around her breast. The front of the ivory wrapper parted, revealing another garment underneath.

He took a tentative step toward her. His mouth went dry, and sweat broke out on his upper lip. A surge of desire knotted his stomach. The lust he'd tried so hard to control threatened to double him over. He should have turned and run back to the barn with the other animals. But something compelled him forward. He couldn't have left if all the gold in the world had lain outside his door for the taking. Mercy was far more valuable to him than his own life.

She moved across the floor toward him. The candlelight danced on her hair, and her skin glowed like the wings of a dove. He tried to speak, but the words stuck in his throat like a ball of cotton. Need swelled in him, chasing all of his previous admirable thoughts from his mind. The only thing he knew was that he wanted her. More than he'd ever craved food, drink, or rest, he needed Mercy's warmth to make him whole. To heal his soul and to take away the pain of constant rejection.

For an instant, he wondered if the light was playing tricks, and that she really didn't have that look of desire in her eyes. Then when she stretched out a finger and touched his cheek, he was lost.

"Pace?" Her voice was a breathless whisper in the silent room.

He closed his eyes, struggling to regain a smidgen of control. If he let himself go, she would probably run screaming from the cabin, and he would have to shoot himself because he'd hurt her. Her hand trembled and his was no calmer. "Mercy, do you know what you're doing? Get under the covers before something happens you'll regret for the rest of your life." She had no idea of the pain it cost him to choke out the words.

Unshed tears made her brown eyes shiny. "Yes, Pace, I know what I want. I want to be your wife." Her touch burned his skin like a branding iron. "Come to bed with me." The words were so soft, he had to strain to hear.

His gaze shifted from the woman to the bed. The patchwork quilt had been thrown back, and snowy sheets and pillowcases beckoned. On leaden feet, he took a step forward. This couldn't be real. He must have hit his head and he was dreaming this. No woman as enticing as Mercy could actually want a half-breed, ex-convict in her bed.

She stepped in front of him. The tall candle on the bureau bathed her in the soft glow. Her chin was trembling, and her shaky hands reached for the tie on her wrapper. Pace watched without moving. He felt as if his feet were nailed to the floor. The belt fell away, and the front of the garment parted. Full, white breasts overflowed the top of the nightdress, if that was what it was called, and dusky nipples thrust against the silk. The material was so sheer, not one line of her body was hidden from view. He couldn't take his eyes off her, and he couldn't speak. He felt more like a youth viewing his first unclothed woman, than a mature man with his wife.

Wife! The word echoed through his brain. Mercy wanted to be his wife in every sense of the word. And he could fly through the air like a bird easier than denying her. Surely she didn't know what she was doing. Biting his lip against the pain in his groin, he had to explain the reality of marriage. The part she didn't understand.

"Mercy, you don't know what you're asking."

"Yes, I do."

"You're a virgin, you can't possibly understand."

No words had ever come harder. Yet, she deserved the chance to change her mind.

"I understand that I want you as my husband. In every sense of the word." Though soft, her words had the strength of her convictions. The same way she'd repeated her marriage vows with confidence and certainty.

She slipped the wrapper from her shoulders, letting the ivory silk pool at her feet in a puddle of molten silver. The nightgown was little more than two scraps of silk tied together at the shoulders and sides with ribbons. He would swear on his mother's grave that no man had ever seen Mercy so unclad. Yet she didn't seem shy, or afraid.

"You can't possibly want me."

She carried his hand to her face and kissed the palm. Fire raced up his arm and settled right in the center of his chest. His body was aflame with desire, but his heart was warm with peace.

"Pace, I've never lain with a man, and I want you to be my first—my only."

God help him, but a man could only take so much. He'd reached the end of his hard-earned patience and self-control. Her face was tilted toward him, and her arms opened to welcome him. He had to take her before he went crazy with hunger.

He hesitated a moment longer, trying to consider his options. He wanted his wife; she wanted him. It should be so simple, yet some hidden fear held him back. What if his naked body frightened her? He was certain she'd never seen an unclothed man and his body was far from perfect. Scars marred his back, and he didn't think he could bear the sight of fear or loathing in her eyes. Yet he couldn't deny her. He couldn't deny himself.

"Let me snuff out the candles," he said, in an effort to gain time to control his libido. In the dark she wouldn't see his ugliness to frighten her, and he wouldn't risk losing control by viewing her beauty.

Pace was trembling with need. If he didn't take her soon, he would die. But he didn't want to rush her. He had to give her a chance to get used to him.

Mercy bit back a cry. Was this his excuse not to sleep with her? Or did he want darkness so he wouldn't have to look at her? For just once in her life, she wished a man thought her beautiful, desirable.

She'd gone through so much trouble to get him to her bed. Miss Lily had told her not to let him refuse. "If that pleases you," she whispered, embarrassed by her boldness.

Not sure what was proper, she remained in place. He snuffed out the candles on the bureau, then turned to gaze at her. His eyes turned dark and unreadable in the shadows. "I suppose we should leave a few lit in case Josh wakes up."

Mercy nodded. Pace dropped to a chair and tugged off his boots. Seconds later, he stretched to his feet. She didn't know if she should watch him. The one time she'd seen him partially unclothed, she'd had to control her urges to reach out and touch him. In spite of the scars on his body, he was a beautiful man—a man to make a woman proud.

He tugged the shirt from his trousers and loosed the buttons. Facing her, he slipped it over his head and dropped it to the floor. Despite the shadows, his chest looked even wider and more muscular than she remembered. Heat surged through her. The unusual sensation she felt whenever he kissed her settled in the private place between her thighs. "You're beautiful." The words came from somewhere deep in her heart.

Jerking up his head, Pace stared at her. Mercy resisted the urge to hide her nearly naked bosom with her hands. She couldn't go through with this. He didn't want her.

He reached out a hand to her shoulder. "I'm covered with scars and my skin is like the bark on an oak." His fingers connected with the thin ribbon, and it slipped down her arm. The breath caught in her throat. She couldn't breathe or move. She swayed slightly; her bosom brushed his chest.

She lifted her gaze to his. With a loud groan, he covered her lips with his. The kiss was hard and demanding, sucking the thoughts from her mind and the will from her body. His hands tightened, and he pulled her hard against his body. Her head was swimming. She slipped her arms around his waist, brushing her fingers along the marred skin of his back. Tears rolled from her eyes for the man who'd suffered more than any human should ever have to endure.

When the moisture reached their mouths, he pulled back. "I'm sorry, Mercy, I didn't mean to hurt you."

Tightening her grip, she refused to let him go. She wanted him too badly to stop. "You're not. I've waited so long for this."

He brushed his fingers along her shoulders and the other ribbon slid away. The front of the gown gapped. His hands were shaking as he tugged at the bow. As if by magic, the garment fell away, leaving her naked to his view. It took all her courage not to run and hide. When he dropped his head and kissed her gently on the swell of her breast, her knees buckled under her.

Before she slumped to the floor, he swept her up in his arms and laid her on the bed. He knelt over her, with one knee on the bed. The feather mattress sank under his weight. "Mercy," he ground the words. "Are you sure? Tell me now, and I'll go out to the barn." His face was in the shadows, but she heard the need in his voice.

Mercy's heart tightened. She'd never wanted anything with the intensity that she wanted him. "I'm sure, Pace. Be my husband."

He let out a loud whoosh of air, as if he'd been holding his breath for a long time. Turning his back to her, he loosened the buttons on his trousers. Afraid he would change his mind, she waited, and prayed.

Mercy had never been naked in front of a man, but she felt no shame, no modesty. Pace was the man she loved, and she was ready to give herself fully to him. He'd already taken her heart and soul, only her body remained for him to possess.

When he turned and faced her, she held her breath in anticipation. In the pale candlelight, he was little more than a shadow. Silhouetted by the dim light, the breadth of his shoulders, and the narrowness of his waist showed a man to make even a maiden's heart beat faster. In spite of Miss Lily's information on the male body, she was unprepared for the power and beauty of his masculinity. She wondered if she was woman enough to take all of him.

He dropped to the bed and stretched out beside her. With one rough finger, he brushed a lock of hair from her face. "You're very beautiful, Mercy. I swear, I'll never hurt you."

She couldn't believe he'd called her beautiful. But she understood it was only in the heat of passion that he'd said the words. "I know you won't hurt me, Pace. Just love me." The plea came straight from her soul. If he couldn't love her with his heart, he could love her with his body. That was enough for Mercy.

His hand stroked gently across her cheek, and down her neck. When he reached to top of her breasts, she felt the warmth of his touch spread down to the very center of her body. Her breasts swelled, the nipples tightened into hard peaks. His mouth followed the path of his hand, sucking, nipping lightly, sending sensation after sensation over her body. He covered her with kisses as soft and sweet as touching a baby. She thought she would swoon dead away from sheer pleasure.

Although his hands were rough and callused from hard work, his touch was gentle. Yet it excited her more than anything in her life. Her skin was on fire, her body shivering with need. She loved him, and the words hovered over her lips. He levered himself above her, and covered her mouth with his. His tongue met hers in a sensual mating that foretold of things to come.

He slid his hand between their bodies, and lifted off her. "I can't wait, please don't be frightened."

She bit her lip in anticipation, as their bodies mated. Again he kissed her, and she forgot to be frightened. Tension disappeared, and her attention centered on the wonderful way he made her feel. As he thrust forward, he swallowed her sharp cry of pain with his kiss. She jerked, and he stilled his movements.

For a second, she worried that he would stop, that she'd done something wrong. She wrapped her arms around him and anchored his body to hers.

He ended the kiss and pressed his abrasive jaw to her soft skin. His ragged breathing tickled her skin. "Please don't stop," she whispered, her own breath coming in short gasps.

Moving slowly and deeply, he continued, until Mercy was certain that heaven couldn't be any better. Just when she thought she couldn't take any more, he gave one final thrust, and sagged on top of her. Flutters of sensation rippled from her core outward to every inch of her body. She'd never dreamed anything could be so wonderful. In spite of the tenderness of her body, she knew she'd been well loved. Her thoughts were spinning, her heart overflowing with emotion.

"Am I hurting you?" he asked, his voice husky.

"No, don't move." She stroked his sweat-dampened back, her own body moist from exertion.

His muscles were tight and slick, and her fingers brushed over the hard scarred ridges. A tear rolled from the corner of her eye. She wished that she could take away his pain, that being with her could give him back some of what had been stolen from him.

After another brief kiss, he rolled to the side and slipped his arms around her. "I'm too heavy for you."

She rested her head on his shoulder. "Thank you, Pace. That was wonderful."

He pressed his lips against her hair. "I should be thanking you. You've given me a gift, something I don't deserve."

Again she resisted revealing her love for him. Although he'd bedded her, she knew it was too soon to reveal her true feelings. Men didn't always feel the same things as women.

"Pace, you've been good to me and Joshua. And I want to be a good wife to you."

She felt his smile in the near darkness. "You're a wonderful mother to the baby." His hand cupped her breast, and she felt something hard against her leg. "I hope I didn't hurt you too bad."

"No. It wasn't nearly as bad as my sisters said. And Miss Lily warned me that it was only like that the first time."

He lifted his head and stared down at her. "Miss Lily told you." He chuckled softly. "So that's where that silk gown came from. That woman has been giving you instructions."

She buried her face in the crook of his neck. "I wanted to please you."

"Oh, you've pleased me, wife. More than a sinful man deserves. You've offered heaven in the middle of my hell." He kissed her then, expressing what he couldn't say with words. His love was there, only he wasn't ready to tell her.

She knew he cared. It was only a matter of time until he told her.

Until then, Mercy would take what her husband had to offer, and give all the love in her heart.

Twenty

It was all her fault. Blast Mercy. Blast Lansing, too. And his pompous father-in-law who doomed them all to hell's fire and brimstone every Sunday morning.

Clifford Blakely downed the expensive whiskey. He rather enjoyed the way the booze burned all the way from his throat clear down to his stomach. It'd taken some doing to get the bartender of the Red Dog Saloon to pull out his best. Not that his best was anything like the French brandy and Irish whiskey in his cellarette at home.

He hated the Red Dog Saloon's dirty floors and that painting over the bar. With so much smoke and soot, he barely recognized the image of a naked woman reclining on a couch. He blinked. Darn if the voluptuous female didn't look like his self-righteous sister-in-law, Mercy, who'd turned him down to be Lansing's whore.

This joint had none of the ambiance of the Ruby Slipper. The bar was second-rate at best, as were the girls who sold their wares day in and night out.

As for the girls, their brassy hair and overripe bodies didn't compare to Rosie and Florrie and their sleek young figures. Cloying perfume that barely concealed carelessly washed bodies mingled with the odor of spilled beer and rotgut whiskey. He was tempted to pull out his linen handkerchief and cover his nose.

Under normal circumstances, he wouldn't be caught

dead in a place like this. After all, he was a wealthy banker, a respected member of society, and darn good looking if he had to say so himself.

The woman, he believed her name was Stella, sidled up to him. She knew who he was, and she knew he had money. Money he was more than willing to spend for a turn in her bed. In fact, in the mood he found himself in, he needed two women to ease the ache in his groin.

And he had only one person to blame. He dropped his glass and immediately it was filled. The woman knew exactly what a man needed.

Not like his wife. Not like Mercy either. Every time he thought about her with that bastard, Lansing, he got mad. And he got hard.

She was giving Lansing what she'd kept from him and from Billy. She'd said that Billy had attacked her. It was all a lie. The bitch had been laying Lansing all along, and Billy just wanted to get a little piece of what she gave to that half-breed.

So did he. That night in his study, he could have taken her. If she hadn't threatened him with his own letter opener, he would have laid her right there on the floor. He could just picture her writhing under him while his sickly little wife slept upstairs in the bed he'd given her.

"Something else you need, honey?" Stella slid her hand lower on his waist, nearly touching the part that demanded attention. "I've got everything you want."

He lifted his gaze and studied the woman. A few years ago, she might have been pretty. But too much booze and too many men had taken a heavy toll. "Not now, Stella. I just want to drink for a while."

Her hand dropped a few inches. She smiled and brought her lips to his ear. "You need a woman. I'm ready and available."

"Later." He had to get a lot drunker to bed this woman. Catching her wrist, he twisted until she jerked away.

She rubbed her wrist. "You didn't have to hurt me."

Tossing down another drink, he glared at her. "Don't touch me unless I tell you to."

He straightened in the chair and glanced around the dingy saloon. It was past midnight. The piano player was still going strong. He would continue as long as the drinks kept flowing. Three strangers stomped through the bat wing doors and stopped to look around.

Clifford started. For a second he thought the one in the middle was Lansing. The man was about the same height, and had dark hair. There the resemblance ended. This man was a few years older, and harder. He dropped his gaze to the drink Stella had poured and swirled the amber liquid around the glass.

He remembered when he'd decided to keep company with Mercy. She wasn't pretty, but he'd thought she would make him a fine wife. Her body was built to bear and feed children. The plain woman would have been satisfied to have a husband, and he knew she wouldn't object when he wanted to bed her. She didn't know what a real man could do for her. Now she was giving Lansing what should have been his.

Instead, he'd been attracted to her younger sister. From the first, Prudy had seduced him with her beauty. He'd dropped Mercy and courted Prudy. He rather liked the way the other men envied him whenever the beautiful woman was on his arm. And he enjoyed watching her smile and cheer when he gave her little gifts. The bigger and more expensive the present, the more she gave of herself. It had taken a diamond ring and a big house to get into her bed. He'd thought he had gotten the perfect wife.

Now, his perfect woman had headaches every time he came near her bed. Unless he had some trinket, or promise of a new gown or something else she craved, he slept alone in that hard, masculine bed.

His gaze dropped to the deep valley between Stella's soft

breasts. Again, he visualized Mercy, and how she'd looked that night. She was hot and ready, even if it had taken Lansing to heat her up. He thought about her legs wrapped around the half-breed, the two of them sweating and grunting like pigs. His own wife couldn't wait to shove him off her before he could finish, and rush to wash in her dressing room.

It was Mercy's fault that Lily LaRose had banned him from Florrie's bed. After she'd turned him down, he'd needed relief, and had sought out the whore. He paid her plenty for her favors, and sometimes he liked to take charge—show who paid the bill, who was boss, who could buy whatever he wanted. He'd never planned to leave bruises, but everybody knew that was part of the life of a strumpet. Lily had no business treating him like an ordinary cowboy. He was Clifford Blakely, president of People's Bank.

He shoved back the chair and stood. "Let's go," he told Stella. The woman hesitated a moment, then leaned heavily on his arm. Her room was in the rear of the bar, a small, dark, and smelly crib. He closed his eyes and forced himself to move toward the bed. If he wasn't so horny, he wouldn't be caught dead in this place.

The whore shut the door, and moved closer. He'd chosen her because she had dark hair and big breasts. If he closed his eyes, he could see Mercy's face. Stella reached out and touched his jaw.

"I'll make you happy, Mr. Blakely. You'll never want to see the Ruby Slipper again."

He narrowed his eyes on the woman. What did she know about his habits, and where he spent his time? "What are you talking about?" He clutched her wrist and twisted her arm behind her back.

She gasped in surprise. "Everybody knows that Florrie is your favorite. That's only because you've never bedded

Stella." Pressing closer, she rubbed her stomach against his swollen member.

"Bitch!" He shoved her to the bed. "I said don't touch me."

Eyes wide with shock, she stared up at him. "But . . ."

"And keep your mouth shut." He pulled out a silver coin and shoved it down her gown. "It's yours, but you'll keep quiet and don't move." In the same movement, he shoved the gown from her breasts. When she went to cover them, he slapped her hands away. "I want to look at them."

While she watched, he carefully removed his coat and draped it over one of the two chairs that made up the sparsely furnished room. A lopsided bureau rested against the wall.

"Take down your hair," he ordered.

By the time he had his trousers unbuttoned, her hair was spread across the dingy pillows. Her dress sagged to her waist, and the skirt was pulled to her knees. A hint of fear glittered in her eyes. That was good. The whore should be afraid. She should know her place.

The haze of alcohol dulled his brain, but not his performance. Stella's features faded, and Mercy's eyes stared up at him. A welcoming smile took his breath away. The bitch wanted him. She spread her arms inviting him to her bed.

He fell on her, and buried his face in her breasts. They were soft and full, the kind to fill a man's hands and his mouth. His hands squeezed and kneaded, then when he couldn't wait any longer, he tore up her skirts and buried his hardness into her softness.

"I've got you now, and you won't get away." He drove hard, shoving into her with a vengeance. She cried out, and he covered her mouth with his. She deserved it; she needed to learn who was in charge. She'd never fight him again.

When he tore his mouth from hers, he moaned deep in his throat. "You're mine now. Lansing can go to hell."

In another hard thrust, he spilled his seed deep inside her. Sweat poured from his face, and his linen shirt was damp from exertion. None of that bothered him. He'd really shown her. The woman beneath him squirmed and shoved against his chest. Clifford opened his eyes, and shook the fog from his brain.

For a second the dingy surroundings confused him. Then he studied the woman lying under him, and his stomach nearly revolted. "You're not her." He lifted his hand and slapped her across the face. His fingers left red welts on the startled whore's cheek.

She covered her cheek with her hand. "No, and I'm not your wife either." With more strength than expected, she pushed, and he rolled off her. "Next time, it'll cost you double if you want to play games." Swinging her feet to the floor, she pulled the low-necked gown over her bosoms and straightened her wrinkled skirt. The coin he'd paid her clattered to the floor. Quickly, she scooped it up and tucked it into her pocket. "Time's up, banker. I've got customers waiting."

Furious at the woman's smug grin, he heaved himself from the bed and grabbed her by the arm. He flung her back on the bed and straddled her middle. His hands circled her neck, and her eyes bulged as he applied pressure. It wouldn't take much to cut off her air, and watch her die. She gargled and tore at his fingers. "Listen, and listen good. You're not going to tell anybody what went on here tonight. Nobody. Understand?"

She nodded, her face blanched white with fear. Lord, he enjoyed the look on her face. He couldn't wait until he saw that same fear on his dear sister-in-law's face. "Stay here until I'm gone. Wait ten minutes before you return to your customers."

Again, she nodded. When he released her, she rubbed her throat with her fingers. Fear mingled with anger in her eyes, but she remained on the bed and didn't move.

Quickly, he buttoned his trousers, grateful for the relief. He ignored the woman as he slipped his arms into his coat sleeves, and after combing his fingers through his hair, he left the room and the whore behind.

The music had died down when he returned to the bar. Many of the customers had left, and only a handful gathered around the bar. A few girls remained, the ugly ones who couldn't get a customer unless he was stinking drunk.

Clifford hurried past the bar toward the door and the crisp night air. A few feet from the door, the three strangers blocked his path. If they were planning to rob him, they'd picked on the wrong man. He reached for the derringer tucked into his pocket. He might not hit them all, but one of the bandits would die.

"Your name's Blakely?" the tall dark-haired man asked.

He nodded, and closed his fingers on his gun. "What's it to you?"

"You know a man called Lansing? Pace Lansing?"

"I might."

"Hear tell he's your brother-in-law, and there ain't no love lost between you. Reckon you can tell us where we can find him?"

"Why do you want to know?"

The other men closed around him. "We're old friends, and we want to get reacquainted."

Clifford smelled trouble. He also sensed a way to get even with Lansing, and turn the tables on him. These men were up to no good. And if he could get them to help him, in a short while he could get it all—Mercy and that prime piece of property along the river. He eyed the three men. Clifford knew opportunity when he saw it, and here it was staring him in the face.

"Come over here where we can talk privately," he offered. "I think we may be able to do business."

Twenty-one

Pace awoke the next morning with a peace he'd never felt before. He'd lain awake most of the night simply enjoying the warmth of the woman beside him. He was afraid that if he fell asleep, he would wake to find it all a dream—that he would wake on that hard straw bed alone.

To his utter delight, Mercy was very real. So real her passion had left him awed. When he'd turned to her the second time, she'd been eager and aggressive in expressing her needs. Afterward he'd feigned fatigue so he wouldn't wear her out or make her sore.

He cuddled with her under the quilt. Early morning coolness penetrated the walls of the cabin. He didn't know what bit of good he'd done in his life to deserve this woman. She'd been more than any man could want in a wife. Her cooking had put inches around his middle, her love had tended the baby, and she'd eagerly welcomed him into her bed. Never in his twenty-five years had he ever slept on such a fine feather mattress with cool, clean sheets. If it was all snatched away from him today, he had this night to hold in his memory.

Across the room, Joshua stirred in his cradle. The infant waved his arms and cooed. Wanting to let Mercy sleep, Pace tiptoed across the cool floor and picked up the baby. Soon, Josh would want to be fed and changed. Until then,

Pace delighted in holding the child—the son of his soul, if not of his body.

As he sought to return to the bed, he spotted Mercy propped up on an elbow watching him. The quilt was tucked to her chin, and he knew that all she was wearing was a smile. He'd forgotten about his own nudity when he'd risen from the bed. Now, with her watching him in the growing dawn, he felt his cheeks heat.

"Bring him over here. Lay him between his papa and mama." She patted the mattress beside her.

At her words, something swelled in his chest. He was the baby's papa and Mercy his mama. They were the only parents he would ever know. And he vowed on Naomi's grave that he would be as good a father as the baby deserved.

Pace slid under the covers and lay the baby on his chest. Life had never been this good. He and Mercy played with Josh and he could swear the baby was giving his approval to their relationship. But as usual, Josh wanted one thing more than he wanted to play—food. He started to whine, making his needs known.

Mercy glanced down, and pink tinged her cheeks. She was too shy to show herself naked in broad daylight. He found it nice that a woman could be so passionate during the night and so shy during the day.

He lay the baby on the bed and swung his feet to the floor. A hint of bashfulness struck him. Picking up his trousers, he pulled them on. Then he lifted her gown and wrapper from the floor. His rough fingers snagged on the smooth silk. After seeing a woman in this garment, was it any wonder he'd been swept away with lust?

She took the offered garment and sat on the opposite side of the bed. Her back was smooth and white, and it took the baby to keep him from running rows of kisses down her spine. But looking didn't hurt—much.

As she lifted an arm to slip it into the wrapper, he spotted purple and black marks on her upper arm. His heart sank. He reached out a gentle finger. "I didn't mean to hurt you, Mercy. I'm sorry."

She shot a glance at her arm, and quickly averted her gaze. "You didn't do that. It happened in town."

"How? Did somebody grab you and hurt you?" Fury welled up in him. He'd seen enough brutality in his life to recognize the marks left by a man's fingers. Whoever had hurt his wife would pay a high price.

"No, of course not." Hurriedly, she slid her arms in the garment and tied it securely at her waist. "I was just clumsy and bumped into a shelf in the mercantile. It's nothing for you to worry about."

Turning her attention to the baby, she picked him up and carried him back to the cradle.

Relieved that he hadn't caused her the marks, he studied his wife in the growing morning sunshine. Although she was completely covered, the soft material did little to hide the swell of her breasts or the fullness of her hips. Even after what they'd shared during the night, he grew hard simply looking at her.

"While you tend the baby, I'll see to the animals."

"Will you be long?" she asked, a hint of worry in her voice. Did she wonder if he would leave her alone as he'd done every other day since they'd been married? No way. Pace Lansing may be uneducated, but he was no fool.

"No. I'll be back for breakfast," he said, snatching up his shirt. "And I've decided to stay close to the cabin today." He didn't add that he intended to spend most of that time in her bed.

"Joshua usually goes right to sleep after his bottle."

He stretched and yawned. "I might need a nap myself."

The smile she gave him warmed his blood like a spark on dry kindling. "Would you mind if I joined you?"

"I'll think about it." He raced toward the barn, feeding the animals the last thing on his mind. He felt like jumping and singing. The world looked fresh and clean today, and Pace Lansing had it all in the palm of his hand.

When Mercy had set out to seduce her husband, she hadn't expected it to be quite so successful. In her wildest, most exciting dreams, she hadn't imagined that people could make love so often, or enjoy it so much. In the two nights and one day since they'd become lovers, she gave up counting the times and ways they'd made love.

Pace had spent the past day with her and the baby. To their delight, even Joshua cooperated with them. He ate, slept, and seemed happy to get their occasional attention. As she slowly opened her eyes the next morning, she wondered what delights the new day would bring. Since Pace had lost a day's work, she was certain he would get back to his chores. After all, they couldn't spend every waking moment in bed. Could they?

Pace was at the table, tending the baby, when she rolled over toward him. "Good morning, Mr. Lansing," she said. Although she was still a little shy at having him see her naked, she didn't flinch at his total nudity. The man's body was magnificent and she enjoyed looking at him. She loved him, every muscle, every pore, every hard inch of him. Even the part she'd never even imagined to see in broad daylight.

"Mrs. Lansing." He nodded toward her. "Did you sleep well?"

A silly question, considering neither of them had gotten more than three consecutive hours' sleep in the past two nights. "Very well, sir, and you?"

Their formal, polite tone brought a grin to his face. "Fine. Although I may need a nap this afternoon—to refresh myself." His gaze drifted over her, touching her through the thin sheets. Hunger glittered in his eyes, and she knew that it wasn't food he craved.

A wave of heat washed over her, warming that private place that nobody had touched until Pace. She wanted him. Again. Mercy didn't know how such a thing was possible. Even Miss Lily hadn't warned her about this. She'd heard about men having strong sexual appetites, but women? From what her sisters had told her, it was a wife's duty to oblige her husband, but that was normally once a week or so. Naturally, she wasn't expected to like it. Women who enjoyed such couplings were considered hussies, wantons, Jezebels. Mercy bit her lip to hold back her laughter. In a short time, she'd become all of those and more.

"Do you see something humorous about naps?" he asked, a smile on his lips.

"Not at all. I may be quite fatigued by then, and have to join you." Reaching for the wrapper she'd dropped on the floor the night before, she said, "I had best prepare your breakfast, or you won't have strength to perform . . . your chores." Snuggling the sheet to her chest, she stuck her head over the edge of the bed. Where had the thing gone?

"Looking for this?" From across the room, Pace held the silk garment between two fingers.

"Yes. Will you please hand it to me?"

"You'll have to come and get it." For a man who'd rarely smiled until a few days ago, Pace had suddenly taking to teasing her.

Tugging the sheet free, she wrapped it around her naked body like a toga. She padded across the wooden floor barefoot. "Now, may I have my wrapper?"

Seated beside Joshua's cradle, he looked up at her. He stroked the silk between his fingers and lifted it to his face. "It feels as smooth as your skin, and it smells like you." In a movement that took her totally unaware, he snatched the end of the sheet and pulled it from her body.

Aghast, Mercy stood in a bright beam of sunlight, naked before her husband. His eyes turned dark and she knew that if it weren't for Joshua beginning to fuss, he would carry her right back to bed. Instead, he planted a kiss right in the valley between her breasts, and dragged his tongue to her navel. Her body reacted as swiftly as his. Only his was there for all to see.

"I think I'd best get dressed." He moaned and slipped on a clean pair of denim trousers.

"I'll have breakfast in a few minutes," she said as she just as quickly donned the robe and fastened it tightly at her waist.

"Don't hurry. I'll see to the animals while you feed Josh."

But hurry, she did. Mercy missed Pace, although she knew he was only a few hundred feet away. She chastised herself for being so greedy. Didn't she realize that he had chores? That if he didn't round up his cattle, he would never get his ranch on a firm footing. It was important to both of them that the ranch become successful. Especially now that they'd married. She touched the ring on her finger. She was his wife in every sense of the word and she loved it.

The morning passed quickly. While Pace went about his business, she tended his house and took care of Joshua. Pace returned to the cabin for the noon meal, and by the gleam in his eye, she suspected he was ready for his "nap."

As he ate his fried ham and fresh biscuits, he jostled Joshua on his knee. Somehow, he'd learned to eat with one hand while managing the baby with the other. "Think this guy will go to sleep soon?" He studied her across the table.

A tremor raced over her. Her body's reaction was expected. Her breasts tingled, and the tips pressed against her gown. She lost her appetite for food, but wanted her husband more than ever. "He's been awake all morning, so he may settle down in an hour or so."

"I suppose I should get back to work." His gaze dropped

to the child. "This guy doesn't look sleepy at all. I'll check out the cattle in the south pasture." He stood and placed the baby in her waiting arms. In an unusual move, he kissed her briefly on the lips. He groaned and brushed his large hand over the infant's fuzzy head. "Go to sleep," he ordered in a gruff voice.

Mercy laughed, and Joshua cooed. "I'll cook beans and ham for supper, if that's all right with you."

He smiled down at her. "Woman, anything you give me is better than I deserve."

She wanted to tell him that he deserved all the best that life had to offer. Her words were cut off when Joshua let out a loud squeal. He'd waited long enough for his meal.

Pace turned toward the door, and stopped abruptly. His smile faded, and a grim expression crossed his face. "Somebody's coming." In a quick movement, he strapped his gun to his hip, checked the cartridges, and picked up the shotgun that rested beside the door.

Fear washed over Mercy. "Are you expecting trouble?" she asked, afraid of the answer.

"Never can tell. I like to be prepared." He glanced out the window and spoke without looking back at her. "Three riders, strangers to these parts. Stay in here and don't come out unless I call you."

Thanks to Sheriff Jennings, there hadn't been much trouble with Indians or outlaws in years. However, gangs still roamed the countryside and it was better to be safe than sorry. "All right. I won't make a sound." She cradled Joshua close to her chest, and stuck his nursing bottle in his mouth.

Pace broke open the shotgun and shoved in two shells. He snapped it closed and placed it on the table in front of Mercy. "If anything happens, shoot first and ask questions later."

Apprehension shivered over her. "I've never handled a gun, I can't shoot anybody."

"Mercy, I don't have time to argue. If it's your life or his, shoot. Bolt the door behind me."

Without warning, he opened the door and stepped onto the narrow porch. He pulled the door closed behind him.

The baby in one arm and the gun in her hand, Mercy moved to the window. She didn't recognize the men who rode up. Moving to the side, she watched where she wouldn't be seen.

His past had caught up with him.

Pace settled his hand on the gun at his hip. He resisted the urge to pull it from the holster and take the advice he'd given Mercy. The men rode slowly, their hands on their reins, or where he could see them. Clearly they meant no threat. Not yet. Still, he knew troublemakers when he saw them, and Morrow was the worst of the lot.

"Ho, Lansing." The tall dark-haired fellow in the center rode forward.

"Morrow. Thought you had a couple more years in prison."

"Got pardoned."

Pace nodded, surprised that an inmate as mean as Morrow would get out early. "What are you doing here?"

"Is that any way to greet your old cellmate? We're passing through, and looking for work. Hear tell you're starting up your spread and you could use some hands." Morrow leaned forward, his cold eyes shifting to check out the ranch.

Pace didn't trust the man for a second. But he didn't have anything to steal, that much was obvious. And the men couldn't know about Mercy. A chill raced up his spine. If they found out about his wife, there was no telling what men like these would do.

"Don't have any work, or money to hire hands. You'd best move on to greener pastures."

The other two hadn't spoken, but they were studying the countryside. "Mind if we water our horses, and rest under those trees over yonder?" the shorter of the men asked, in a voice husky with a deep Southern drawl.

Morrow nudged his horse closer. Pace stood his ground. No way were these men going to get near the house and Mercy. Thank God she'd obeyed his orders and remained hidden in the cabin.

"You can camp by the river. There's lots of water and shade." Pace gestured toward the grove of trees that grew behind the barn. If he could get them away from the house, he could protect his wife and child. There was no telling what these men had in mind.

After another studious glance at the cabin, the men nudged their horses in the direction he'd indicated. Only when they'd disappeared into the trees did he release the breath he'd been holding.

He knocked on the door and signaled for Mercy. "It's me, Mercy. Open the door." As quickly as he slipped inside, he set the bolt. "Pack up some things for you and Joshua. I want you to go into town and spend a few days with your father."

She sent him a quizzical glance. "Why? Who are those men?"

"I'm not sure of two of them, but the leader is a man named Morrow." He hated involving his innocent wife in his sordid past. "I knew him in prison. He's mean, and he means trouble."

"Trouble? I heard him ask you for work."

"That skunk has never done a lick of honest work in his life." He took the baby from her arms and laid him in the basket. "Just do as I say. You've got to leave. Get packed while I hitch up your buggy."

She caught his sleeve in her fingers. "But I don't want to leave you. What if something happens to you?" The pain and fear in her eyes touched him to the core of his soul. Nobody had ever cared for him the way this woman did.

"Nothing's going to happen to me, but I want you and Josh safe in town. I'll fetch you home as soon as they leave." He hadn't meant to speak so harshly, but he had to make her understand the danger these men posed for her.

"If they're so bad, come with me."

"I won't run from trouble. Those pigs will burn this place to ashes if I leave. And I won't let them think I'm a coward."

From the look on her face, he knew she didn't understand. What woman understood a man's need to protect what was his?

"What am I going to tell my family? I spend more time with my father than with my husband."

"I don't care what you tell them, just get your things together." He lifted the bolt from the door. "Lock it behind me."

Keeping his eyes open for trouble, Pace raced for the barn. Within minutes he had the horses hitched to Mercy's buggy. She was wearing her bonnet and a frown when she opened the door. For a second he thought she would argue. Instead, she lifted her wide golden eyes to him. "Will you at least kiss me goodbye?"

Her pleading look sent his heart pounding against his chest. "I hate having to send you away. But it's best." He cupped her face in his rough hands and kissed her firmly on the lips. "Take care of yourself, and be careful," he said. "And don't come back until I come for you." He picked up her satchel and the baby's basket. After helping her into the high seat, he made sure Josh was safe.

"I'll miss you, Pace."

He nodded, and slapped the rump of her horse to get the animal moving. He couldn't take a chance on letting Morrow and his cohorts see her.

As the dust from the buggy settled, he glanced toward the woods. They were there. Watching from the distance. But Mercy was safe, and he vowed to protect her with his very life.

After all, the heart he'd thought long dead went with her.

Twenty-two

He missed her like the devil.

Pace couldn't wait to reach town and see his wife. His chest fluttered at the thought of the woman who'd invaded his home and his life. He also couldn't wait to get rid of the three drifters who'd sent her away.

The three rode ahead of him, taking their time reaching town. Trailing behind, he knew it was dangerous to let his mind drift, but so far none of the men had hinted of anything ominous or threatening. Still, he didn't trust them any more than he could toss his stallion across a ravine. Eating a little dust was a cheap price to pay for caution.

Last night, he hadn't taken any chances. He'd made sure they were camped near the river, then he'd entered the cabin, bolted the door, and promptly slipped out the window. He couldn't bear to sleep in Mercy's bed without her. Since she'd taken over his home, her presence permeated the entire place. Besides, if he slept on the hill above the house, he could watch for an ambush. When he'd awoken, he'd found Morrow and his cohorts where he'd left them the night before.

They'd asked about work on some of the ranches or in town. To get them off his land and out of his life, Pace offered to ride with them into Pleasant Valley. Then they would be Jennings's problem.

And he would take his wife back home.

As they neared a grove of trees about a mile and a half from town, Morrow reined in his horse, turned, and waited until Pace was abreast of him.

"Reckon this is as far as you go with us, Lansing," the man said. His mouth quirked into a grin that would freeze boiling water at twenty paces.

Pace had seen that look before—seconds before Morrow had murdered a fellow prisoner. Too late, Pace dropped his hand to his holster. The other two men flanked him, and he felt the barrel of a gun in his side. He could have kicked himself for his carelessness. They meant to kill him, plain and simple.

"Just stay calm, and we won't kill you. Yet." Morrow grabbed Pace's gun and shoved it in his belt. "Now dismount and back away, very carefully. Watch your step, and maybe you'll see your woman and the kid again."

Chills raced over Pace. He didn't mind dying; he minded not seeing Mercy and watching Josh grow up. "I don't have money, or anything you want." He jumped to the ground, letting Dancer's reins drop. Surrounded as he was, he couldn't run, or get away. With three guns on him, he had no choice but to do as they said. He watched for an opening.

"Move away from the horse," Morrow ordered.

Pace braced himself for the shots. His only regret was that he hadn't told Mercy how much he valued her. In that last moment of his life, he realized that he loved her. And she would never know.

If they expected him to cry or beg, they would be disappointed. He stared at the men. Too bad the last thing he would see in this world were the ugly faces of three murderers. Morrow took Pace's gun in his hand. The snake was going to kill Pace with his own gun.

Not taking his eyes off his enemy, Pace watched as Morrow lifted the gun over his head. The blow glanced off his temple, and Pace slumped sideways. As the next blow came, he remembered how Billy had struck his head on the boardwalk and died. Lights exploded in his head. The pain doubled him over. This was fitting punishment for his crime. As darkness flooded his brain, he thought about Mercy. She would never know how he felt. Another pain shot through his head, and the darkness was complete.

"Josh doesn't seem very happy to be here with his old grandpa." Ezra sipped his coffee and studied Mercy across the table.

She forced a smile while bouncing Joshua on her knee. "It isn't you, Papa. He's always fussy like this whenever we're away from Pace." Mercy didn't add that she was every bit as upset at the separation.

"I have to admit I was a little surprised to see you yesterday. Did something happen? Did you and Pace have a disagreement?"

"No, Papa. Nothing happened." Nothing bad anyway. Her relationship with Pace was so new and fragile, she didn't want to share it even with her father. "Pace isn't anything like his reputation. He's been kind and gentle with me and the baby."

Her father studied her for a moment longer before he set his cup back on the table. "I can't say I haven't missed you. Even Miss LaRose and her girls asked about you at the Bible study on Monday."

She lifted her gaze, trying to find something behind her father's innocent remark. "How was the study?" she asked to draw him out.

"Very inspiring. You've done a fine job teaching the basics of the Word to the young ladies. They're quite intelligent and knowledgeable."

She laughed softly. "You see, I told you they weren't so bad."

He brushed his fingers through his graying hair. "I

never thought they were wicked. Though I can't condone their occupation, we both know that even Mary Magdalene was forgiven."

Mercy wondered exactly what her father felt for Miss LaRose. And if he could be as forgiving of a fallen woman today as he was of a woman who lived two thousand years ago. She certainly hoped so. Any fool could see how much they cared for each other. If only he could think of her as a prosperous businesswoman, like any shop owner or dressmaker. She just happened to operate a different business. Then he could accept her as the good, kindhearted woman Mercy knew.

"Well, I like them. Nobody in town has been kinder to me, especially since my marriage to Pace."

"Everything just took us by surprise. Certainly your sisters didn't mean to be unkind. They simply wanted the best for you. After all, Prudy did have a dinner for all of us last night. And she said she was sorry that Pace wasn't able to attend."

How could her father be so fooled? Didn't the man see anything? Prudy and Clifford knew that Pace had remained at the ranch when they extended the invitation. Mercy tried to refuse. She didn't want to see Clifford, or go anywhere near his home. But her father had practically dragged her from the house. Tim and Charity were invited, and she couldn't refuse without making a scene. Prudy claimed she wanted to do something nice for Mercy. Clifford made a show of offering a toast to Mercy and Pace—a wish for a long and happy life. Everybody smiled and added their congratulations. The duplicity nearly made her sick.

She hoped that Pace came to fetch her soon.

"Yes, it was very kind of them."

Ezra reached into his pocket for his tobacco pouch. "Looks like I'm all out of my favorite blend. Tim ordered some for me, I wonder if it's in?"

Eager to get out and do something useful, Mercy stood. "I'll go and check on it, Papa. The walk will do both me and Josh good."

"And you'd better pick up that Borden's milk you came to fetch."

She'd forgotten that she'd used the baby's milk as a reason for the unexpected trip into town. "Yes, I'll have Tim send it over here."

"Leave little Josh here. I'll look after him until you return. Besides, you need a few minutes alone."

His kindness touched her heart. She kissed him on the forehead. "Thank you, Papa. I would like to talk to Charity without having to worry about a squalling baby."

A few minutes later, she passed the bank and approached the mercantile. She wished she'd taken the other side of the street, or come in through the back alley. Anything to avoid Clifford, who stood on the boardwalk in front of the bank.

He flashed a secretive grin as she approached. Always the gentleman on the surface, he tipped his hat and nodded politely. "Good morning, dear sister-in-law." He puffed on a fat, stinking cigar. "Lovely day, isn't it." He blew out a puff of gray smoke, lowering his gaze to her bosom in an insolent glance that left her angry and shaken. He wasn't the least bit sorry for what had happened, and his look said that if they were alone, he would try the same again.

Too stunned by his veiled insult to care who was watching, she shoved past him and approached the mercantile. Behind her, she heard Clifford greet Mrs. Fullenwider and several other ladies, his voice so smooth you'd think he was spinning silk. Too angry to face her other brother-in-law, she sank to the bench in front of the store to gain her composure.

She was so mad, even the sky turned red. The nerve of that skunk. After the outrageous way he'd treated her, he needed his comeuppance. If she'd even hinted to Pace, her husband would have wiped the grin off that banker's slimy face with his fist. She frowned. Both she and Clifford knew she would do no such thing.

From the corner of her eye she watched three horsemen stop at the other side of the bank. Her heart skipped a beat. For just a brief instant she thought the one on the black horse was Pace. She shoved her eyeglasses up on her nose and looked again. At that moment a wagon pulled up in front of the mercantile, blocking a clear view. The horse looked like Dancer, Pace's horse, but she knew it couldn't be Pace. He would never go near the bank. He hated Clifford and avoided her brother-in-law at any cost.

"Mercy." She turned to face Charity in the doorway of the mercantile. "Come on in and keep me company."

After a quick glance over her shoulder, she followed her sister into the store. Two of the men had disappeared, leaving the shorter man holding the horses' reins. The trio were vaguely familiar, reminding her of the riders Pace wanted to protect her from.

Charity tugged her by the arm. "I have some fresh lemonade in the back. Let's sit and talk. Timmy is napping, and I finally have a few minutes to myself."

Mercy followed her sister. For the first time since she'd gotten involved with Pace, her sister was eager for her company. Maybe her family was finally accepting her marital status.

"I could use a cool drink."

"I thought so. Your face is red. Either you're very warm, or mad as heck."

There was no way she could share her problem with Charity. Yet she wondered if Clifford had at some time made improper overtures to her sister. Probably not. Charity would have told Tim, and there would have been trouble. No, Clifford had picked on Mercy because he had no respect for her and he knew she would keep the secret.

Because he thought Pace didn't care enough to defend her.

"I rushed over here to see if Tim had gotten Papa's pipe tobacco. It was warmer than I'd thought.," She fanned her overheated face with her handkerchief, hoping Charity accepted the explanation.

She nodded to the men playing checkers. Did they ever go home? she wondered. Every day that she'd worked at the store, the pair had hovered over the board, ignoring the customers, and not spending a penny.

Charity handed Mercy a tall glass of lemonade. The ice cooled her hand, and helped calm her temper. She settled on a rocker beside her sister.

The store was quiet that morning, but Mercy knew that later business would pick up. "I rather miss working here," she said. "It was nice getting to know our neighbors and hearing the latest gossip." Mercy was well aware that the latest gossip was about her and Pace.

"Well, I've certainly missed you. Tim expects me to be here every day cutting piece goods, filling orders, and even keeping records of the accounts." The rocker squeaked on the rough floorboards. "You know I'm not good at ciphering."

Mercy had to smile. Her sister wanted nothing more than to stay in the prim little house her husband had built for her, and be a mother to her son. Yet Tim had other ideas. He wanted to show his father that he could run the mercantile successfully, and make as much money as possible. If that meant using his wife as a free clerk, he was more than willing to do so. He'd been forced to hire Mercy when Charity became pregnant and had the baby. It didn't take long until he'd come to depend on Mercy's experience and skill in running the business. As long as the profits continued to rise each year, he didn't object to paying her salary. Now, instead of hiring another clerk, he was again urging Charity to perform the duties.

"Why don't you get him to hire somebody else? I'm sure there are men and women who could use the extra money from working for Tim."

Charity snorted and lowered her voice. "You know Tim. He's getting as greedy as his father. Papa Fullenwider already owns half the town, and Clifford owns the other half. Tim is jealous and wants his share. I wish you would leave that old Pace Lansing, and come back to town."

It all came down to what everybody else wanted. Neither of her sisters cared about Mercy's needs. "That isn't going to happen. I'm going back to the ranch as soon as Pace comes into town. That should be any time now." Mercy stood and set her empty glass on a shelf. "Papa is waiting for his tobacco. You can put it on his account."

Her hand on Mercy's arm, Charity looked at her with wide-eyed concern. "Mercy, he's treating you all right, isn't he?" she whispered. "I mean he doesn't hurt you or force his affections on you, does he?"

"Force?" Mercy bit back a laugh. Wouldn't her sister be shocked to know that it had been Mercy who'd all but forced Pace into her bed. "Of course not. Pace isn't at all like that. He's gentle, and kind, and—" Her words were cut off by the sound of gunshots.

Her heart in her throat, she raced to the window. People were scattering, and diving for cover. At that moment, Clifford slammed through the doorway. His coat was open, and his face red.

"Get the sheriff. Lansing just robbed the bank."

"No," Mercy screamed. "Not Pace."

Clifford grabbed her by the arm. "Get me a gun. It was Lansing and two other men. They made off with a sack full of money."

Heedless of the danger, Mercy darted onto the porch in front of the store. She watched the riders dash toward the end of town, the black horse galloping ahead of the other two. Sheriff Jennings appeared on the boardwalk, just as the riders passed the jail. Mercy watched horrified as he took aim with a rifle and fired. One of the riders tumbled from the saddle and fell onto the dusty street.

She recognized the men. They *were* the ones who'd come to the ranch yesterday—the reason Pace had sent her away. Fear clutched at Mercy's chest. She grabbed the upright post that held the overhang to keep from crumbling to the ground. Clifford was at her side, a gun in his hand. Tim appeared from the rear storeroom carrying a rifle.

"Let's go after them," Clifford snorted. "If Lansing isn't dead, we'll catch him and string him up this time." He glared at Mercy. "You won't stop us again."

"No, it wasn't Pace. He wouldn't steal anything." Her stomach heaved and she pressed her hand to her mouth to keep from throwing up. Pace wasn't a robber. It had to be a mistake.

Clifford stepped into the street and shot her a hateful glance. "I know Lansing when I see him. And everybody knows his horse. You even saw it. You can't deny seeing him."

Men ran into the street, mounting their horses. Sheriff Jennings had leaped onto his horse and was following the robbers out of town. "When they catch those men, you'll see it wasn't Pace."

Mercy prayed as she'd never prayed before that she was right. That Pace wasn't involved, and most of all that they wouldn't kill her husband.

Twenty-three

Pace fought the darkness. He battled against the oppression blacker than any cave or depth to which he'd sank. Had he died and gone to hell? Was this what death was like? This all-consuming darkness and pain?

His head pounded as if he'd been run over by a thousand stampeding bulls. He reached out and gathered a fistful of dirt. If he was dead, then the hereafter was as dusty as Kansas. It took all his strength to open his eyes. He touched his head and his hand came away sticky. Struggling to focus, he recognized the red stain as blood. His blood.

Overcome by pain, he sank back to the ground. He heard the pounding hooves of the herd that had crushed him. They were coming back to finish him off. The noise came closer, and he rolled to his knees in a vain effort to escape. Fighting nausea, he managed to crawl a few feet. Stars and fireworks flashed in his head, and he closed his eyes against the bright sunlight.

A gunshot exploded, and he dropped back to the dirt. This time he wasn't going to make it. Then he heard two more shots, yet the only pain was the one in his head. Something hit his hand and he grabbed for it. Cold metal settled in his palm.

"Take it, Lansing," came a voice from high above him. "It belongs to you." Devil's laughter echoed in the quiet air. The rattle of spurs and heavy footsteps receded, followed by more hoofbeats.

When he managed to open his eyes, he saw two of everything. The trees were swaying, and he felt as if he'd been caught up in a cyclone and slammed back to earth. He looked at the object in his hand—his gun. Sparks of memories flashed across his brain. He remembered thinking about Mercy and Josh. That was the instant before everything went black. He shook his head, unable to remember how he'd gotten caught in the stampede.

He tried to focus his eyes. A figure lay a few feet from him—a man, facedown in the dirt, with blood oozing from holes in his back. Pace managed to stumble forward. It didn't take a doctor to know the man was dead. He rolled the dead man over, and tried to place the face staring up at him with unseeing eyes.

Again he slumped to his knees. Then he remembered. The dead man was one of the drifters who'd been with Morrow. One of the two who'd surrounded him when Morrow had aimed to bash his head in.

Blinking to clear his vision, he glanced around. He was in a grove of trees not far from the road. Dancer stood a few yards away, his coat shiny with sweat as if he'd been ridden hard.

As he shoved to his feet, he heard more hooves, and men shouting. "He's over here."

Although he couldn't make out anything but wavy shadows, Pace waved the gun in the direction of the voice. The figures came closer, and one voice stood out louder than the others.

"Drop it, Lansing. And don't make any quick moves."

His head pounded as if somebody had taken a nine-pound hammer to it. Everything was confused. He wiped his hand across his face to see clearly. A rough hand shoved against his shoulder, forcing him to his knees. Somebody snatched the gun from his limp fingers.

"Let's string him up right here. This tree is as good as any other." The voices from his nightmares pressed from all sides. Lord, he prayed, let me wake up in bed with my wife, or asleep under the stars.

He squinted and saw the bodies surrounding him. "Leave him be," the most forceful voice shouted. He spotted the silver star and recognized Sheriff Jennings. "He'll stand trial, and this time he won't get away."

"What for?" the words came out from a throat dry as the western wind. "What did I do?"

When the rope slipped over his arms, anchoring them to his side, he panicked. Struggling to get free, he bumped against the body beside him. Every inch of his mind and body rebelled against being tied up, of being locked away, of losing his freedom. But there were too many of them. Within seconds he was trussed as neatly as a calf being led to slaughter.

"As if you don't know," came a raspy voice. "You robbed the bank and murdered your partner."

"No," he screamed. More pain exploded in his head. This time he welcomed the darkness.

Mercy paced the boardwalk in front of the jail, waiting for Jennings to return. For the past half hour, she'd kept a vigil, hoping, praying that the sheriff would return with the bandits. She knew that Pace would never rob a bank. But it looked as if she was the only person in town who professed his innocence.

As soon as word had spread, her father had come to her side. He'd left Joshua with his housekeeper, and he'd divided his time between encouraging Mercy and placating Clifford.

Her brother-in-law had loudly proclaimed that in spite of the bandanna covering the lower half of his face, Pace was one of the robbers. Clifford recognized him by his long black hair, and height. He'd even found the hat Pace had dropped during the robbery. Now Mercy held it tight in her fists, certain it was only a duplicate of the one her husband wore. Besides the hat as evidence, several people had recognized Dancer, Pace's big black stallion.

In spite of the evidence mounting against her husband, she fully expected the sheriff to ride back into town with the real culprit in tow. Then everybody would know that Pace wasn't the robber. Except for her father, none of the other townspeople wanted anything to do with Mercy. She stood alone, not wanting or needing their censure or sympathy. Her own sisters had kept their distance, commiserating with Clifford. Of course, the customers who'd lost money were angry enough to stone her right there on the street.

"Here they come," came the cry from a horseman who raced through town.

The posse followed slowly, led by Sheriff Jennings. He stopped at the hitching post in front of the jail. The waiting crowd converged on them. Mercy shoved her way to the front. Jennings led a large black stallion by the reins, a man tossed over the saddle, head down, and feet and hands tied under the animal's belly.

Her heart stopped beating, and she sagged against her father, who'd appeared at her side. "Pace," she whispered, recognizing her husband's prone body. Blood dripped from a wound on his head matting his black hair. He was as still as death.

Chills raced over her. Varied emotions blasted across her mind. Dead. Not Pace. Not the husband she loved. He was dead and he didn't even know she loved him.

Ezra caught her as her legs gave way. He hugged her tight to his chest. The town had branded her husband a bank robber, and killed him.

"Is he dead?" Clifford had reached the sheriff and pulled Pace's face up by the hair.

Anger gave her strength. Mercy grabbed her brother-in-law's arm and jerked him away. "Leave him alone. Papa will take care of him."

"Nobody's gonna do anything, Miss Mercy." Jennings dismounted and cut through the ropes that tied Pace to the horse. "He ain't dead. Not yet anyway. I'll see that he gets a fair trial and we'll let the judge decide his fate."

Not willing to believe him, she touched the pulse in her husband's neck. He was alive, but his breathing was slow and labored. "Get him down from there. He's hurt."

"Yeah, he tried to resist arrest. I had to knock him out to get him back to town."

Her heart twisted at the sight of her injured husband. The man she loved was trussed up like a calf at branding time. He'd been branded a thief and a murderer. But at least he was alive.

"Here's the man he killed," the deputy said, leading another horse. "Reckon they had an argument over the money."

Clifford puffed out his chest like a rooster. "Did you recover the bag with the money?"

"No, there wasn't a bag anywhere around. When we found Lansing, he was on the ground. Looked like they had a fight before Lansing killed this fellow."

Mercy wanted to scream her husband's innocence. Pace wouldn't have done it. He was a good man. She brushed her fingers along his face. "Pace, please wake up. Tell them you didn't do it."

He lifted glazed eyes to her. He blinked as if trying to focus. "Mercy," he said. At least he was alive and halfway alert. "Go away. Go home."

"Move aside, ma'am," Jennings ordered. He shoved Pace from the horse, and he landed prone on the street in the dust and manure. Jennings and his deputy each grabbed one arm and dragged Pace into the jail.

The crowd followed like vultures after a fresh carcass.

Mercy pushed past them and through the doorway. Nobody was going to keep her from seeing her husband.

"Everybody out," ordered Jennings.

"No," Mercy shouted. "I have to see my husband."

Clifford, too, pushed into the jail, followed by Ezra.

"Jennings, my daughter has a right to see her husband. She has to get him a good lawyer." Her father wrapped his arm across her shoulder.

"Okay, she can stay. You, too, Blakely. I want to get an official statement from you so I can wire a judge." He waved his arms. "The rest of you get out."

Mercy bit her lips to keep from crying. They untied Pace's hands, then thrust him into a barred cell. When they slammed the door and set the lock, she thought she would swoon. He would die if they locked him away again. And she would die if they took him from her and Joshua.

"Can't you see he's hurt? We have to get the doctor." Shaking off the deputy who tried to stop her, she moved to the cell. She pressed her face to the bars. Pace was sitting on the cold, bare floor, his head cupped in his hands. He looked up and met her gaze.

"Go away. Get out of here," he said between his teeth.

"No. I want to know what happened. Why did they arrest you?"

"Ask Jennings." He turned his back to her and mopped his face on his sleeve.

She turned to the sheriff, fury giving her courage. "Let me in there with him. He has a cut on his head, and we don't know what other injuries."

"Can't do that, ma'am. If you send for Doc, I'll let him look at Lansing. Until then, he's my prisoner, and I'll decide who sees him." The sheriff took her by the arm and gently removed her from the door of the cell.

Angrily, she shook off his hand. This whole thing was a nightmare that showed no sign of ending. "At least tell me why you arrested my husband. Why do you think he robbed the bank and killed that man?"

"Mercy." Her father draped his arm across her shoulder and helped her to a chair. "You look like you're going to swoon. Sit down." Ezra turned to face the sheriff. Wrapping his dignity around him like a cloak, he faced Jennings. "My daughter deserves to know the truth about what happened."

The sheriff propped his hip on the edge of the desk and hovered over Mercy. "Ma'am, it's plain as the nose on your face. Lansing robbed the bank with those other two. We shot one of them on his way out of town. Lansing made a couple of mistakes. He left his hat, and everybody recognized that stallion of his." Jennings glanced at Clifford, who nodded in agreement.

"I'm really sorry about this, Mercy," Clifford said. "I'll swear on a stack of Bibles that it was Lansing." Her brother-in-law's false sympathy made her even madder. He was thoroughly enjoying Pace's problems.

"You didn't see his face. You can't be sure it was Pace."

"When the posse caught up with them, we found Lansing leaning over the dead man with his gun in his hand. His gun had been fired, and his horse had been ridden hard. The evidence is indisputable. He killed his partner and we arrested him."

Her heart sank to her feet. Her mind went numb, and she felt as if she'd been slugged in the stomach. "That can't be true."

"It is, ma'am. Looks like Lansing's done it this time."

She glanced toward the cell. Pace hadn't moved, but his gaze met hers across the room. Anger, confusion, and hate glittered in the dark depths of his eyes. In the past few weeks, the forlorn look had lessened in his face, but now behind bars he looked like a man on the precipice of hell with one foot over the edge. Indeed he was.

"Take your daughter home, Reverend. I don't need a

hysterical woman around here." Jennings pulled out a plug of tobacco and shoved it into his jaw.

"I'm not going anywhere until I talk to my husband." Mercy pushed to her feet.

"Get her out of here, Preacher. I don't want to see nobody," Pace said in a voice of woe.

His words cut like a knife to her soul. He needed her now more than ever, yet his pride kept him from admitting it. Well, pride be damned. He was her husband and she needed him, too.

Her world in shambles, she ignored the men in the jail and approached the locked cell. It didn't matter what anybody said, she had to know the truth. And only Pace knew the truth.

He was standing, his hands clutching the bars. Dried blood was caked in his thick eyebrows which were pulled into a straight line. His clothes were filthy and torn. Dark stubble shadowed his jaw. But it was the desolation in his eyes that tore at her insides. Before he could move, she covered his hands with hers. He didn't pull back, but she felt the tension that radiated from him like bristles on a porcupine.

"I said to go home. I don't want you here."

She lowered her voice so only he could hear. "I won't go. I want to help you."

His eyes grew harder than coal and darker than midnight. "You can't help me. I doubt if they'll even wait for the judge this time. The town is primed for a necktie party. And I'm the guest of honor."

"Don't say that." She brushed her fingers across the back of his hands. "It has to be a mistake."

"You made it when you married me."

Her heart breaking into a thousand pieces, she forced down the bile that rose in her throat. She had to be strong. Pace needed her. She met his gaze without blinking. "Listen to me. I know you didn't rob the bank or kill that man.

I think I recognized him. Wasn't he one of the men who came to the ranch yesterday?"

"Yeah. He was with Morrow."

"Where is Morrow now? He could tell them you didn't do it."

If such a thing was possible, his eyes grew even bleaker. "Morrow wouldn't help his mother out of a mud puddle."

She ignored his sarcasm. "Are you hurt?"

"I've got a headache the size of Texas. But I'll live. For a little while anyway."

"Jennings had no business striking you." She reached out a hand and brushed the dirty hair from the cut on his temple. "Tell me what happened."

Pace caught her wrist and entwined his fingers with hers. "Said they were going into town to look for work. I wanted to make sure they kept going. So I decided to ride into town with them."

He squeezed his eyes shut as if struggling with the memory. "When we got to that grove, I must have let down my guard. They pulled their guns on me. Next thing I knew I woke up on the ground with my head pounding. I picked up my gun, and then Jennings and his posse were there arresting me."

"I knew you didn't rob the bank. We'll have to explain it to Jennings."

"No. They won't believe me or you. Your brother-in-law smells blood. He won't let the sheriff listen to either of us." He shifted his gaze to the men watching them. "I want you to do something for me."

"Anything. I'll hire the best lawyer. We'll convince the jury that you didn't do it."

"No. I want you to sell the land. You should get a good price for it. Take the money and leave Kansas with Joshua. I don't want him growing up knowing that his father was a bandit and killer."

The breath caught in her throat. "I won't leave you. You're innocent. I'll find a way to prove it."

"Woman, can't you listen to reason? I said to leave." He tightened his grip on her hands. "Start over. You'll get enough money from the land to travel, to go wherever you choose. Live your dream. Take back your father's name. I won't have you and Josh suffer on my account."

"I'll do whatever I have to."

He pulled back his hands, and shot her an angry glance. "Jennings, get her out of here."

"Pace, I love you. I have to help you." The tears she'd tried so hard to quell trailed down her cheek. "I need you."

"You can't love a murderer. Get out. Go back to your father's house and take care of the baby." He turned his back on her and sank to the hard cot. "Don't bother me again."

She clutched the bars and let the tears flow. "I won't give up on you. You're my husband, and I love you."

" 'Til death do us part. That shouldn't be much longer."

Gentle hands touched her shoulders. "I'll take you home, Mercy." Her father's soft voice was her undoing.

"Yes, Papa. Let's go."

Head held high, Mercy allowed her father to lead her from the dim jail and into the bright afternoon sunlight. She looked neither to the left nor the right, although she knew that half the town was watching her. Her face was damp with tears.

Pace may have given up, but Mercy hadn't. She would clear him in spite of himself.

And she knew just where to go for help.

"Do you believe he did it?"

Lily LaRose glanced over her shoulder at Cora, who watched from the window with her. Not taking her eyes from the scene unfolding on the street in front of the sheriff's office, she shook her head. "No. Pace Lansing may have his faults, but he isn't a thief. A crime like this would hurt Mercy and the baby, and from what I've seen, he's more than careful of her feelings."

"That's what I thought," Cora said. "He loves her too much to ever do something that abhorrent."

Word of the bank robbery had spread fast, and Pace had been named as the bandit from the first. The Ruby Slipper had emptied immediately and even the bartender had gone outside to watch the excitement.

"She's going to need our help. I'm sure her self-righteous sisters won't want to comfort her, or offer assistance with the baby." Cora let the curtain drop.

"At least she has her father." Lily's heart tightened as Ezra guided Mercy through the hostile crowd. "A man like the reverend will always support and protect his own." Feelings she'd never expressed aloud flooded Lily. She'd seen the minister's strength and kindness from the beginning. He'd never turned up his nose at the "fallen women," or criticized her openly. He was a man who would love fiercely, as evidenced by the way he'd stood beside his daughter. No wonder Lily loved him.

Cora placed a gentle hand on Lily's shoulder. "I was on my way to the mercantile when the men ran from the bank. I got a good look at the one they said was Pace. Something about him wasn't right. When he tried to mount the horse, the stallion balked and he slapped the horse hard across the rump with the reins. Pace wouldn't do that."

With Mercy out of sight, Lily stepped away from the window. "I wish we could help them. But Clifford Blakely is out for blood. He won't stop until Pace is hanging from the gallows."

"Humph! I don't trust that banker any more than a ripe polecat. I wouldn't be surprised if he wasn't lying just to get even with Pace."

Lily stared at her friend. Although Blakely had been one of Florrie's best customers, she didn't like the way he snubbed the very women he bedded. And that last time, when he'd hit her and left bruises, she'd ordered him out and barred him from ever coming back. "You might be right. But how could we prove it?"

Cora shrugged. "I don't know. But we can help Mercy get through this."

"Yes. Get some food together, and we'll go over to the parsonage. Right now that young woman needs to see a friendly face. And we can at least care for the baby while she tries to help her husband."

Twenty-four

Whether Pace liked it or not, whether Sheriff Jennings like it or not, Mercy was going to take care of her husband.

The crowds still lingered on the boardwalk and in the streets, as she made her way back to the jail. Daylight was almost gone, and lamps and candles glowed in the windows of the homes and businesses still open. Of course the bars were doing a landslide business. The men were anxious to see what was going to happen to Pace.

In times of trouble one knew who one's true friends were, Mercy thought. And although her sisters had avoided her, Miss LaRose and Cora had come to offer condolences. Not only that, but they'd brought supper and Cora offered to care for Joshua while Mercy went on her errand.

When she'd returned to the house that afternoon, the baby was in a fury. The housekeeper had become so distraught, she'd promptly quit her job and demanded her wages. It took a while to calm Joshua, but at least it kept Mercy's mind off Pace and the horrible situation. Lily and Cora had been God-sent, showing kindness where the church members and deacons had shown ill-will.

As she reached the street in front of the jail, the throng parted like the Red Sea before Moses. A deputy armed with a shotgun guarded the doorway.

Not at all intimidated by the rough-looking man, she

stared him in the eye. "Please let me pass. I have supper for my husband."

The deputy spit a wad of brown tobacco juice on the ground. "Sorry, ma'am. Nobody gets in. Sheriff's orders."

She knew it wasn't going to be easy, but she was bound and determined to make sure Pace wasn't beaten or injured any further. "Sheriff," she shouted loud enough to wake the dead. "Tell this man to let me pass."

Murmurs ran through the crowd that pressed closer. Jennings stuck his head through the door. "What do you want, Miss Mercy? Nobody is going to see the prisoner."

"I brought his supper and enough for you and your deputy."

That caught their attention. Home cooking was a heap of a sight better than what they could get at the café or prepare themselves. "What else you got in that basket?" Jennings asked.

"Food, and a change of clothes. You can check to make sure I haven't hidden any weapons." Boldly, she shoved her way past the two big men and entered the room. Immediately her gaze shifted to the cell and Pace, lying in the shadows on the bunk. Her heart twisted painfully. Seeing him like this was almost more than she could bear. But she had to muster all her strength to right this horrible wrong.

She set the basket on the desk stained with coffee rings and scarred with other unknown marks. With Jennings hovering over her, she removed three heaping plates, a whole pie, and jar of cold milk. He shoved her hands aside and pulled out the new shirt and denim trousers she'd purchased from the mercantile the day before as a surprise for Pace.

"As you can see, I've only brought a spoon for him, and nothing ominous is hidden in the clothes."

"I suppose it's all right." Jennings turned toward the cell, where Pace hadn't moved. "Lansing, your wife brought supper. Reckon it could be your last meal."

The deputy snickered as he reached for a plate. Anger seared through Mercy. She wasn't going to stand by and let the mob lynch her husband. "You said you'd sent for a judge. Surely he hasn't arrived."

"I'm expecting him in about three days."

"Meanwhile, I intend to see that my husband is clean and fed." She moved toward the cell, the plate in one hand, the clothes in the other. "Will you kindly fetch a bucket of water so he can wash up?"

The deputy slanted a glance at Jennings. "I ain't no maid," the man argued.

Jennings waved his arms. "Do it, then you can eat."

While Jennings held the shotgun on Pace, the deputy unlocked the cell and set a bucket of cold water just inside the door. He took the towel, clothes, and food from Mercy and placed them on the floor. Then, he hurriedly slammed the door shut. The loud metal clank echoed through the jail like a death knell.

Jennings signaled the man to move aside, leaving Mercy staring at her husband through the bars. So far, he hadn't moved, or uttered a sound. Except for the shifting of his eyes, he appeared to be dead. His gaze locked with hers. A thousand emotions bombarded her. Pain, fear, anxiety, desolation, it was all there, as real as the bars that separated them.

"Pace," she whispered. "Are you all right? Did they hurt you?"

From the corner of his eyes he slanted a glance at his wife. "I told you to stay away." He forced the words from his broken spirit. For two days and nights he'd tasted heaven; now he stood at the edge of hell watching the flames leap higher.

"I can't. I love you, and I want to help you."

Pain slashed through him at her confession. No matter that he loved her more than life itself, he didn't want her to love him. She deserved better. He had no choice but to make her hate him. "Even God can't help me now."

"I've brought your supper and clean clothes."

"So I can go to the gallows well fed and well dressed?"

She clutched the bars and pressed her face through the opening. Any fool could see what this was costing her. She'd been the one person in the world to believe in him. The woman who'd given him back his life, the hope that he'd lost. But it was all useless, it was all hopeless. Just when he needed it most, he'd given up.

"That won't happen. I won't let it. I'll find Morrow and make him tell the truth."

Fear raced through him. "Stay away from him, you hear? That man is dangerous."

"But I want to help."

"There's only one way you can help." He swung his feet to the floor and sat up. "Do what I told you, Mercy. Sell the land and get the hell away from this place. Start a new life for yourself and Josh. Who knows, you may find a man worthy of you."

"You're the man I love. I won't give up."

"Mercy . . ." The words *I love you, too* nearly escaped his lips. But knowing how he felt would only hurt her further when he was gone. Better to let her think he didn't care than to have her suffer on his account. "Go home."

Her shoulders sagging in defeat, she turned and walked slowly out the door. He prayed she wouldn't do anything foolish, like confronting Morrow. Not that he was anywhere within a hundred miles of Pleasant Valley. If the drifter had robbed the bank, he would have taken the money and hightailed it out of Kansas. He'd committed the perfect crime. Morrow was free, while Pace was going to pay with his life.

Despair wrapped a tight rope around his heart. He'd never been afraid of death. He'd been closer in his twenty-five years than most men in eighty. What he hated most was that he would leave Mercy and Josh. And that she would be forced to watch him die in disgrace.

He wanted to bang his head against the stone walls in sheer frustration. Being locked up was as close to hell as a man could get. But the next time he walked into the sunshine would be to his trial, then to his execution. Mercy could scream his innocence from the rooftops and nobody would believe her. They sure as heck wouldn't believe him. And he had too much pride to beg or scream. So he stood by silently and watched his heart and soul walk away.

Time was running out for Pace. Mercy had to do something. Standing in her father's kitchen the next day and stirring a pot of stew wasn't doing anybody any good. Joshua was asleep, and her father was in the parlor reading his Bible. She knew he was staying near the house because of her.

Earlier that morning, both her sisters had come to pay their respect. Prudy had enough compassion not to criticize or mention Clifford. Mercy appreciated their concern, but there was nothing they could do.

Mercy considered her options. Perhaps she should sell the land and use the money for Pace's defense. But she knew there wasn't time to contact a lawyer from St. Louis or Kansas City. Pace would be cold in his grave before a lawyer arrived.

If only she could find Morrow. More and more she was convinced that her husband had been framed for a crime he didn't commit.

Needing to keep busy, she'd even put a cake into the oven. Chocolate, Pace's favorite. Tears dimmed her eyes. She would be sure to bring him a big piece with his supper that night.

Seeing him behind bars, his freedom stripped from him, hurt worse then anything she'd ever experienced. She didn't know how she was going to survive if he went away to prison . . . or worse. That she refused to even think about.

The heat from the oven and the cookstove was stifling in the early afternoon. She opened the top buttons of her white shirtwaist to cool her heated skin. Perspiration mingled with tears on her face. If only she could do something.

Determined to be strong for her husband, she lifted her skirt and wiped her face on the hem. A breeze from the doorway cooled her limbs under the single thin petticoat. Too late she heard a noise on the porch. A shadow slanted across the kitchen floor.

"That's a fine turn of an ankle, dear sister."

Quickly dropping her skirt, she looked up to find Clifford's lecherous glance staring at her. "What are you doing here?" she whispered, not wanting to disturb her father.

His gaze dropped to the open neckline and her sweat-dampened chest. "I want to help you."

She turned away and hurriedly fastened the buttons clear up to her chin. She'd rather melt away with the heat than let him see an inch of her flesh. "How can you help me?"

He moved closer, until he'd backed her against the table. "I know a good lawyer in Kansas City. An old friend from college. With the right persuasion, I could convince him to come and help you." He lifted a hand and brushed the back of his knuckles across her cheek.

"Why would you want to help Pace? You hate him." She slapped his hand away and moved so that a chair separated them.

"True. But he has something I want, something you can give me in exchange for my help. Besides, if you play your cards right, I might not be able to identify Lansing as the bank robber. He might get prison time, but he won't hang."

By the lust in his eyes, she knew full well what he wanted. If it would save Pace, she would gladly sacrifice her virtue as well as her life. "What do you want?" she asked, needing to hear it from his mouth.

Clifford glanced around, making sure they wouldn't be seen or heard. Satisfied that her father was out of earshot, he reached out and snatched her wrist. Tugging her closer, he met her angry gaze. "Do I have to spell it out for you? I want what you've been giving Lansing for months."

Her heart clenched, but she wasn't surprised. "You'll be unfaithful with your wife's sister?"

"Dear Sister, you must have misunderstood. All I want is for us to be friends, to share a few hours now and then. Of course I'll take good care of you."

"If you want a woman, why not go to the Ruby Slipper?" She tugged her arm, but he only tightened his grip.

"You still don't get it. Lawyers cost plenty, and that's where I come in.

In spite of the stifling heat, chills raced up her spine. "You'll give me the money for . . ." She still couldn't bear to say the words.

He laughed, a wicked, evil sound. "Even you aren't worth that much, dear Mercy. But those five thousand acres are. You can mortgage that land and have all the money you need."

She twisted her wrist free. "And of course, your bank will lend me the money at a high rate of interest."

"That's the least I can do for family." His sly grin made her sick to her stomach.

"You forget, it isn't my land. I can't sell it, or mortgage it."

Brushing a speck of dust from his expensive wool coat, he again dropped his gaze to the center of her chest. "If Lansing is hanged, it will all belong to you."

Her stomach knotted. She couldn't let that happen. "If I get him to agree, will you wire your attorney friend?"

"As long as you agree to my terms, I'll wire him this evening. That should get him here in time for the trial."

Defeated, she sagged against the table. "Draw up the papers, and I'll get Pace to sign them."

"I'll take your word that you'll keep your part of our bargain."

A lump formed in her throat. As repugnant as she found the thought of Clifford touching her, seeing Pace hang was worse. She barely managed to nod her acquiescence.

"Good. I'll have them ready this evening." He bowed from the waist as politely as any fine gentleman. Only her brother-in-law was no gentleman. After one slow appraisal of her, he started toward the door. His hand on the knob, he glanced over his shoulder. "I'll expect you to forget those ugly eyeglasses, and to wear your hair loose."

He'd barely stepped from the porch when Mercy's control crumbled. What had she done? She clutched her stomach and doubled over in pain. She'd sold herself as surely as the women at the saloons. At least they were honest about what they were doing. Mercy was going to betray her husband to save his life.

"You want me to sign what?" Pace jumped up from the bunk and grabbed the bars that separated him from his wife. "Give my land to Blakely?"

She backed up a step, as if he could get to her. "It's a mortgage, so we can hire a lawyer for your defense."

"My defense? I've got no defense." Every muscle in his body tensed. He was so angry he could have twisted the bars with his bare hands. "They think I'm guilty. Face it. There's nothing you can do about it."

Tears perched on the rims of her eyes and she set her jaw. He'd known she was stubborn, but this was totally out of the question. "A lawyer can help you. I don't want you to . . ." The words trailed off to a whisper.

"Hang, Mercy. I'm going to hang." His throat tightened. She covered his hands with hers. Touching her was heaven. Not being able to hold her was hell. "Pace, listen to reason. Your freedom is worth whatever the cost."

"No. That's final. I'd gladly sign if you wanted to sell the land and get out of Kansas. But I won't let you waste it on me."

The tears flowed like a river down her cheeks. "It won't be a waste. I need you. Joshua needs you." Then she said what he'd dreaded even thinking since he'd been thrown into the dirty cell. "I might even be carrying a baby of my own."

He groaned deep in his spirit. The last thing he wanted was to leave a child branded as the son or daughter of a murderer. "That's not likely," he said, although he knew it was possible.

"The judge will be here in a day or so. A lawyer is our only chance."

"Can't you understand, woman. It's useless."

"But—"

"Quit arguing, Mercy. Jennings isn't going to let you stay much longer." Reluctantly he freed his hand from hers and reached into his shirt pocket. "Take this. It's my will. I want you to have the ranch. It's all I have to give you. It should bring a pretty penny, enough for you to get started somewhere else."

"Pace, quit talking like that. I won't leave. This is my home. I know in my heart that it will all work out."

He wished he had her faith, but he'd lost that years ago. It wasn't fair to let her keep hoping. "Promise me one thing."

She didn't even bother wiping away her tears. "Anything."

"Promise you won't watch when they . . ." He swallowed the bitterness that threatened to choke him.

"Don't say it. Please. Think about Joshua and how much he misses his papa. You'll be freed. Have faith."

"Miss Mercy," Sheriff Jennings called. "You'd best be

on your way. I'm already breaking the rules by letting you in here."

Bending her head, she kissed the top of his hand. "I love you. I'll be back tomorrow."

It took all his will not to reach out and anchor her to the spot. His hand tingled from her kiss. His body ached for her. Memories of her were all that kept him sane during the long, bitter nights in the cell. Memories he would carry to his grave.

Twenty-five

Tears blinding her, Mercy nearly bowled over the man standing in front of the bank. Her throat was so tight, she could barely utter an apology. He caught her arms and steadied her on her feet.

"Sorry," she grunted.

Through blurry eyes, she thought she was seeing things. A chill raced over her. The man was tall—as tall as Pace, and his dark hair touched the shoulders of his shirt. For a brief second, her mind played a cruel trick. She started to call out her husband's name. Then she blinked and realized she was wrong.

It wasn't Pace, it was Morrow. She'd gotten a good look at his harsh features the day he'd come to the ranch. In a strange way, he did resemble Pace. But this man's dark eyes were hard and cold, cruel and full of hate. Without a word of his own, he hurried on his way.

She bit her lip to keep from crying out, to keep from running for the sheriff. This was the man she'd thought never to find. And he was here in town, as big as life and bold as a shiny new penny.

Unable to help herself, she turned and followed the direction he'd taken. When he disappeared down the alley, she didn't know in which direction he'd gone. What was he doing here? He had the money from the bank robbery; surely he wouldn't hang around where he could be caught.

It was too strange for Mercy. She needed help in figuring it out.

On leaden feet, she walked slowly toward the Ruby Slipper. Of all the people she knew, Lily was the only one who would listen to her and not try to give advice. Or condemn her for marrying Pace. A lady couldn't walk boldly up the front entrance of the saloon, so she slipped into the alley between the mercantile and the bank. As she neared the rear lane, she heard a commotion coming from the back door of the bank.

Afraid Clifford would spot her, she pressed against the wall hiding in the shadows. Loud whispers, the sound of men arguing shot a bolt of fear through her. She recognized Clifford's voice, but the other man was a stranger. Snatches of the quarrel reached her.

"Leave town . . ." Clifford's voice rose in an angry growl.

"Not yet . . . have some fun . . . long time . . . women." The disjointed words almost came together into a sentence.

Something about the man's tone caused her to shiver. His was a cruel voice, the voice of a man who would brook no argument. She held her breath, afraid of being caught eavesdropping.

"Enough money . . . no more." Clifford's voice faded, and a door slammed shut.

For long moments, Mercy didn't dare move or even breathe. Then she saw him—the man Clifford had been arguing with. Morrow, the same man Pace said committed the crimes that had him in jail. Her knees turned to jelly. What connection did the drifter have with the banker? If the man had robbed the bank, why didn't Clifford recognize him and turn him in to the sheriff? Unless . . .

Her mind revolted against the thought. Unless Clifford knew the truth and was willing to let Pace die for a crime he didn't commit. It was hard to believe her sister had married a man that evil.

The stranger paused for a second and glanced around. Mercy pressed her back against the wall, making herself flat as a shadow. The pungent odor of smoke wafted toward her. She recognized the smell of the special cigars Clifford ordered from Cuba. After a second, he continued in the direction of the Ruby Slipper, the jingle of his spurs growing dim as he moved away.

She waited and waited for what seemed like forever. Finally willing to take a chance, she eased away from the wall. In a strange way, it all made sense. Clifford hated Pace. He'd made it clear that he wanted the land, and he wanted Mercy only because she belonged to his enemy. But to falsely accuse a man of murder was beyond her wildest imagination.

Now that she knew the truth, she had to prove it. Nobody would believe her over a respected banker. She turned in the direction of the Ruby Slipper. If anybody could help her, it was Lily and the girls.

At the rear entrance to the saloon, she raced up the steep stairs as fast as her legs would carry her. With the windows and doors open to catch a summer breeze, the loud music and voices drowned out her weak knock on the door. She hesitated only a second before she tried the knob and shoved open the door. The noise was even louder in here, sounds of merriment when her own heart was breaking.

Lily's door was partially open, and she slipped inside. "Miss LaRose," she called softly. "Are you here? Cora?" No answer. The only sounds were the male voices and tinkling piano from downstairs.

Of course, this being a busy night, the lady must be in the saloon tending to her business. Mercy passed the rooms where she knew Rosie and Florrie entertained their "guests." Cautiously, she moved down the hallway to the stairs that led to the main room. All the times she'd been

in the building during the day, she never dared venture
this close to the activity that went on among the customers.

More and more she was feeling like a thief or spy, skulk-
ing in corners and hiding in shadows. But she would do
that and more to save Pace. Hidden in a tiny alcove at the
head of the stairs, she studied the activity downstairs.
Surely she would spot Lily in the pink she always wore.

Her gaze shifted from one end of the large room to the
other. Thick smoke made her eyes water. At several tables,
men were playing cards; at others they were simply drink-
ing and talking. Rosie was wandering among the tables,
catching an eye here, and slapping away a hand there. Her
laughter rose above the din. Still there was no sign of Lily.

Letting her gaze once again sweep the room, she spied
a tall man with his elbow resting on the long, shiny bar.
He signaled for the bartender, who set a full bottle and
small glass in front of him. Her heart beat faster. It was
him. Morrow. She recognized the black hat, and the dark
hair that touched his shoulders. He shoved back his battered jacket, and his gun gleamed in the dim lights. His
gaze seemed to be following Rosie around the room. He
had his drink, and he wanted a woman. It was as clear as
the crooked nose on his face. Mercy fisted her hands until
the nails bit into her palms. If she'd had a gun, she would
have shot him right where he stood.

But that wouldn't do Pace any good. She would just hang
beside him. She had to get the man to confess, to admit
that he, not Pace, had committed the murder and robbery.
But how?

As Rosie passed him, he snatched the woman's arm. He
slid his arm around her waist and whispered into her ear.
She giggled, and whispered something back. He released
her and returned to his drink. He wanted a woman. Mercy
was a woman. All she had to do was get him alone and
make him tell the truth.

After all the time she'd spent mending the gowns, she

knew just where to find one that would fit her. Before she
could think things through, and let common sense stop
her, Mercy rushed into Rosie's room and tore open her
wardrobe. The gold gown hung there, ready and waiting.
Quickly, she stripped down to her drawers, and slipped on
the dress. She tugged the top up over her full breasts, and
when she noticed the lace from her drawers showing from
the slit in the side, she removed them too. Feeling decadent and naked, she bit her lip against her own shame.

She studied her image in the mirror. Shame or not, she
would waltz naked on a table to save Pace's life. Next to
go were her eyeglasses. She'd just pulled the pins from her
hair, when the door flung open.

"Rosie, can I borrow . . ." Florrie's voice trailed off.
"Who are . . . Miss Mercy? What are you doing?"

Caught like a mouse in a trap, she felt her stomach drop.
"Florrie, you've got to help me. There's a man down there,
he's the one who robbed the bank and killed that man,
not Pace. I've got to get him to confess." Her words gushed
out like water from a waterfall.

The woman stood dumbfounded, her mouth agape.
"What are you going to do?"

"Help me fix my hair and put on that cheek and lip
color. I can't have anybody recognize me."

"You want to go downstairs and be one of us?" She sank
on the bed. "Oh, no. Miss Lily will have my hide if I let
you do that."

Mercy grabbed the woman's arms. "You've got to help
me. They could get up a lynch mob tonight and hang my
husband. I won't let that happen. If I can get that man up
here, I can make him tell the truth." Mercy's heart was
beating so fast, she was afraid it would run away with her.

"Let me do it. I'll get him up here for you, and then
you can make him talk."

"I have to do this myself. The man is dangerous, and I

can handle him." Her hands were shaking so badly, she could hardly get the brush through her hair.

Florrie snatched the brush from her fingers. In a few deft movements, skillful hands twisted Mercy's hair onto the top of her head, leaving a few strands trailing down to her chin, and along her neck. "I shouldn't be doing this, Miss Mercy. Something tells me that you could get into a heap of trouble."

"It's a chance I have to take. I won't let them hang my husband for a crime he didn't commit." She glanced at herself in the mirror and, like that other time, hardly recognized the woman staring back at her. "I hope nobody recognizes me." Her knees trembled, and she gripped the edge of the bureau to keep from sagging to the floor.

The other woman pulled open a drawer and, after rummaging around for a second, pulled out a tiny mask with only small slits for eyes. "We wear these sometimes when the men want us to pretend, oh, never mind why. Nobody will recognize you, and I'll tell them you're a new girl Miss Lily is trying out."

Grateful for the idea, Mercy tied the tiny ribbon around her head. She looked like a different person, and she felt like she was on the outside looking on at a stranger.

"One more thing," Florrie said as she moved toward the door. "Slip this into the pocket, just in case you need it." She handed Mercy a tiny gun. "It's small, but it can be deadly."

"I don't want to shoot him." The gun felt like a ton in her palm. She tried to hand it back.

Florrie shook her head. "Better to be safe than sorry."

Mercy slipped the weapon into the deep pocket in the side of the skirt. It hit her leg, and for some reason, the cold metal was rather reassuring. "It's now or never," she said on a sigh. "I'd better get down there before he attaches to Rosie." She headed for the door before she had a chance to fully think things through.

In spite of the worried look on her face, Florrie shrugged. "I'll warn her about you."

The woman wasn't one tenth as worried as Mercy. Her stomach was doing an Irish jig in time to her heart pounding like a big bass drum. If this didn't work, she didn't even want to think about the consequences. "Here goes," she whispered, thinking about Pace locked in jail to give her courage.

She descended the stairway with Florrie at the side. Rosie was the first one to spot them. Her eyes narrowed, and her mouth pulled into an angry line as if to ask why a stranger was wearing her favorite gown. For a second, Mercy was afraid the woman would make a scene and snatch it from her. Florrie hurried her steps and stopped Rosie with a hand to her arm. After a quick whisper, Rosie raised her brows in wonder and stared at Mercy.

When Mercy reached them, Florrie raised her voice slightly. "Rosie, this here is . . . Violet. She wants to come to work for Miss Lily."

"Violet?" she muttered. Then dropping her voice to a whisper, Rosie added, "Miss Lily is going to kill you. And us, too."

Mercy forced a feminine laugh that turned several male heads. More than a few stood and grinned back at her. She whispered for Rosie's ears only. "The man by the bar, the one with the long black hair. He's the one."

Thankfully, Rosie didn't glance over her shoulder. "Be careful. He looks like a mean one."

"Are you gals gonna confab all night? You got some eager men out here," a customer shouted. "I'll take that new gal. Come over here, darlin'."

Lifting her gaze in the direction of the familiar voice, Mercy spotted her sister's father-in-law, Mayor Fullenwider, raising his glass to her. Even without her eyeglasses, she recognized the man as well as several other men from town.

Clutching the stair rail to keep from running back up-

stairs, she moved slowly the rest of the way to the floor. A
chill raced up her body when her bare leg slithered from
the opening in her dress. A thousand thoughts of hell and
perdition assailed her. She was a Jezebel, bound and determined to break every commandment her father had
ever taught. Remembering Pace's predicament, she set her
feet on the floor, and smiled at the men who tugged at
her and offered to buy her a drink.

Her knees were shaking so badly, it was a wonder she
even made it as far as the first table. There she was pulled
onto the lap of the man who'd offered a rope to hang
Pace. He whispered something that he would never even
mention to his wife, and asked how much it would cost
for a little of her time.

Too shocked to respond, Mercy jumped out of his grip
and shoved against his shoulder. His chair tipped over, and
the other men at the table laughed as he tried to right
himself. Mercy was afraid she'd bitten off more than she
could chew. Rosie and Florrie helped the hapless man up,
and laughingly told him watch out for Violet.

Mercy managed to make it to the bar where Morrow
clutched the whiskey bottle in one hand. She chanced a
glance at him, and found him studying her with his dark,
cruel gaze. Swallowing down her trepidation, she sauntered in his direction. Not wanting to appear too eager,
she paused near a table and glanced at the men playing
cards.

She ignored a few lewd suggestions and slowly approached her target. His gaze touched her breasts and
dropped to her leg. Mercy felt as if she'd been dunked in
a bucket of manure. It took all her strength to remain in
one spot, and smile up at him. She told herself that this
was the man who'd framed her husband. The man who
wanted to see Pace hanged. And she would gladly sacrifice
her life for the man she loved.

"Drink?" he asked, offering the bottle.

She shook her head. "I'm better without it," she whispered around a lump as big as a hen's egg in her throat.

From the corner of her eye, she spotted a flurry of pink lace. Oh, no. A half hour ago, she'd eagerly sought Miss Lily's advice. Now the lady was shoving her way through the crowds, confusion in her blue eyes. Mercy had to stop Lily before she ruined everything.

Florrie reached the lady an instant before Mercy and whispered in Lily's ear. She raised her voice. "Miss Lily, Violet's doing real good."

Lily's reaction was much like Rosie's. "Violet?" Almost in the same breath, she continued. "I told you to wait until I returned. You'll have to learn to take instructions if you're going to work at the Ruby Slipper."

Morrow stepped closer. "Is there a problem with this pretty little lady?"

Fingering a loose blond curl, Lily moved closer to the man. "None that I can see, sugar. But I'm not sure I can trust her with my customers yet. Rosie, come over here. This gentleman is interested in a lady."

"I want this one." Morrow draped a heavy arm across Mercy's shoulder. His touch sent shivers of repulsion over her. She fought against any outward show of her inner horror.

Lily nodded, and attached her hand to Mercy's arm. "You can have her, but I need to talk to her for a second." She winked at the man. "Special instructions for a special customer."

When they reached a door beneath the stairs, Lily turned her ire on Mercy. "What are you doing? I just came from your father's house where he's trying to get Joshua to sleep."

Mercy cringed against the anger coming from her friend. "That man is the one who robbed the bank. See how he resembles Pace. I think Clifford is in on it, too. I can't let them hang my husband for something he didn't do."

Lily glanced back toward the bar. "I can't let you go through with this. It's dangerous. You have no idea what a man like that can do to a woman."

"Please, Miss Lily. I've got to help Pace."

The jingle of spurs stopped all conversation. Morrow had followed them. She only prayed he hadn't heard what they'd said.

"I'm getting a mite lonely out here. What say I take both of you gals?"

With a flutter of feminine laughter, Lily flashed her brightest smile. "You got enough money for two of us, big boy?"

"Honey," he said, "I ain't been a boy since I was ten." He reached into his pocket and pulled out a roll of money. He peeled off a couple of bills and pressed them into Lily's hand. "I can get plenty more where those came from."

She studied the bills while Mercy watched. From all the time she'd spent in the upper rooms, she realized what Lily had seen. One of the bills had an R in the corner, and the other an F. Rosie and Florrie. To keep track of their earnings, Lily marked the money as each girl turned it in. Morrow must have gotten the money from Clifford at the bank.

"I'll tell you what I'll do. Since you're a new customer, and this is Violet's first night, I'll give you a fine bottle of my special whiskey. And I'll even let you have two girls for the price of one." She flashed him a wicked smile. "Which ones do you want?"

"I'll start with this one, and later, maybe the redhead."

Mercy shivered. She'd wanted to do this alone, but maybe she wasn't quite up to it. Lily was right, she had no idea how to handle a man like Morrow.

Lily ran her hand along his thick throat. "Have you ever heard of a *ménage à trois?*"

"Is that one of those French whores?"

"That's you and two ladies."

In spite of herself, a flush raced over Mercy's face. Maybe she could use some help after all. "I'm sure you'll like it," she managed to say.

"Good. Rosie," Lily called. "Get a bottle of our finest whiskey for this special customer." She removed her hand. "But you'll have to drink it down here. I don't allow hard liquor in the rooms. Makes such a mess."

Mercy hoped that the offer of free whiskey would loosen the man's tongue. She didn't think she could go through with taking him upstairs.

Fear battled with fury as Lily and Cora rushed from the rear of the Ruby Slipper. Mercy Lansing was getting herself in hotter water than she could even imagine. The few things she'd told Lily made complete sense, and even Cora agreed. Lily knew it wouldn't do any good to argue with the woman. Mercy's mind was made up. She intended to prove her husband's innocence, come hell or high water. And it seemed that was exactly where she was headed.

Only one person could help, and he was locked away tighter than an old maid's virginity. If this was the robber, let Pace take care of him.

Going strictly on instinct, Lily had only the most rudimentary of plans. What she was doing was wrong; it could get her and Cora thrown right into jail beside Pace. But it was the only way.

Thankfully, the boardwalk was empty, the spectators having gone home for supper or seeking other recreation. The Ruby Slipper had more customers than usual for a midweek night. They were all looking for action. Looked like they were about to get plenty.

The deputy was guarding the door with a shotgun in his hand when they approached. He stood when Lily stepped into the dim light. "Evening, Miss LaRose," he said. The man looked bleary eyed and half asleep.

"Rogers, I thought that maybe you could use a little refreshment." She reached into the basket on Cora's arm and fished out a full bottle of whiskey.

His eyes grew wide, and he all but snatched it from her fingers.

"Mind if we go in and speak to the sheriff?"

The man stepped away and shoved open the door. "Company, Jennings," he called. Cora remained at the door, closing it after the deputy.

Jennings jumped from his chair. "Miss LaRose, what can I do for you? Trouble over at the Ruby Slipper?"

Using all the feminine skills she'd developed over the years, Lily moved toward the man. He'd been interested in her for years, and that look told her his feelings hadn't changed. "No, I just wanted to see you. I've missed you the past few days."

He puffed out his chest like a bantam rooster. "Got to stay close to the jailhouse now that I've got me a notorious prisoner."

She sat on the edge of his desk and lifted her skirt just enough to show a bit of ankle. When he gaze drifted, she offered a little more flesh. "These silk stocking just won't stay up," she complained. With both hands, she started at her ankle and worked her fingers to her knee. So intent on watching her, Jennings didn't see Cora move behind him. He didn't know a thing until she brought the cast iron skillet down and his face fell to his desk.

"One down, one to go," Cora whispered. She moved to the side of the doorway.

"Rogers," Lily called. "Can you come in for a second?"

Instantly, the man was in the doorway. He took one step across the threshold, when Cora crowned him with her skillet. The man crumbled to the floor like a scarecrow with only straw for stuffing. Quickly they closed the door and dragged him into the room.

The commotion brought Pace to the bars. "What's going on?"

Lily produced the keys from the sheriff's pocket. "We're breaking you out of jail."

Mercy had never seen a man drink so much so fast. And

Twenty-six

Mercy had never seen a man drink so much so fast. And
the more he drank, the more his hands wandered. Thanks
to Rosie, those hands managed to stray to her more than
to Mercy.

When the bottle was empty, Morrow decided it was time
to go upstairs and get on with what he really wanted. If
Mercy blushed any redder, she would surely explode. The
eyes of half the customers in the Ruby Slipper were locked
on her. The other half were too drunk to care.

An arm around each woman, Morrow headed toward
the stairs that led to the private rooms upstairs. For the
first time since she'd known them, Mercy had a real idea
of what went on in those rooms, and what the girls had
to contend with in their customers. If the other men were
half as disgusting as Morrow, the girls deserved a lot more
credit than censure. It wasn't their fault they were forced
to earn their living this way. The men paying for their
services should be the ones to be criticized and con-
demned.

At the top of the stairs, Rosie led the way to her room.
Mercy checked to make sure the little gun was in her
pocket. She would use it on Morrow if need be to get him
to tell the truth. No matter how much they prodded and
talked about the excitement in town, the man hadn't mentioned a word about the robbery.

Rosie shoved open the door to her room and stood aside so Mercy and Morrow could enter. Mercy swallowed the lump in her throat. The bed waited in the middle of the room, and Morrow headed directly for it.

He fell across the bed, his dirty boots leaving mud on the clean quilt. His hard eyes shifted from one woman to the other. Mercy felt her skin crawl and goose bumps broke out all over her.

"Come here, there's plenty of me for both of you."

Mercy moved closer, but remained beyond his reach. "I like a man with a big"—she took a deep breath—"bank roll." Her face heated, and she was afraid he would know what she was up to. If only she could pull this off, she swore to be the best friend Rosie ever had.

Rosie sent her a warning glance. "It takes a lot of money for ladies like us."

An ugly laugh echoed in the room. "Ladies, I've got a big bank roll and something else even bigger. Enough for both of you."

"You rob a bank or something?" Mercy closed her fingers on the little gun. "I mean where else would you get so much money?"

Before she could move, the man snaked out a hand and grabbed her arm. She tumbled on top of him, landing prone across his body. "For a whore, you sure are curious about that money."

The enlarged ridge in his trousers pressed against her stomach. Nausea rose up in her throat. She prayed for strength to keep up the charade. "I want to get away from here, and I need a man, a real man to help me. But it takes money, lots of money."

"If you're real good, I might take you with me when I leave." He ran his hands up and down her back, cupping her buttocks with both hands.

She tried to roll off him, but he squeezed tighter. "Do you have enough money?"

"You might say that I robbed a bank, or a banker, for a fact. I'll get more money tomorrow, and anytime I want. That fool of a banker will pay, all right."

Mercy struggled against his grip. She glanced at Rosie for help. The other woman crept onto the bed, snuggled at his side, and rudely shoved Mercy off his chest. She promptly took Mercy's place.

Still lying on the bed, Mercy had to learn the truth. "I like a man who takes chances. Somebody robbed the bank yesterday. Was it you?" She bit her lip. How could she blurt it out like that? Surely, he wasn't stupid enough to tell the truth.

He reached out a hand and caught her jaw between hard fingers. "You sure are nosy. They got a fellow in jail for that. But I got the money." He laughed and pressed his lips to hers. Mercy kept her mouth locked shut, and fought to keep from throwing up.

Rosie reached over and pressed her hand against the lump in his trousers. "I don't like being ignored," she said.

The man released Mercy. "You ain't gonna tell on me, are you, little lady? Between me and that banker, we got Lansing right where we want him."

A chill raced over Mercy. She rolled away and pulled out the gun. Standing beside the bed, she pointed the barrel at Morrow's head. "You robbed the bank and you killed that other man, too."

His gaze narrowed on the gun. His angry grin showed tobacco-stained teeth. "I most surely did, but you ain't gonna tell nobody. That little pea shooter don't scare me."

Hands trembling, she tightened her finger on the trigger. "You'll tell the sheriff. I won't let Pace hang because of you."

"What do you care about Lansing?"

Rosie leaped from the bed and backed toward the door, her eyes wide with fear. "Mercy, be careful."

Mercy tore off the mask. "I'm his wife, and I won't let you get away with this."

He laughed, as if he found her feeble attempts funny. In one quick movement that caught her off guard, he grabbed her wrist. He twisted, but she refused to let the gun go. She fell back across the bed, and struggled against his greater strength. One hand on her wrist, he brought his other hand to her throat and squeezed. Unless she pulled the trigger, he would kill her. If she died, so would Pace, and Joshua would be left alone.

She pulled the trigger and fired into the air. For a tiny gun, the sound was deafening. Morrow jerked and loosened his grip. Then Mercy could breathe again.

Pace heard the shot the second he bolted through the rear doorway above the Ruby Slipper. All the way from the jail he prayed that Mercy wouldn't be harmed—that she had enough sense to remain in the saloon where she would be safe.

A fear worse than anything he'd ever experienced tore at his insides. If anything happened to his woman, he would kill Morrow with his bare hands. Lily had filled him in on what Mercy had in mind. The fool woman didn't have the good sense God gave a fence post.

Rosie stood in the hallway, her hand covering her mouth. He was too late. Without even seeing her, he knew that Mercy was inside that room with Morrow. His heart was racing, and he only wished his feet could keep up.

The woman pointed into the doorway and stepped aside. Pace darted past her. In a split second, he took it all in. The bed, the man, and the woman. Morrow was lying on top of her, his face red with anger.

With a growl more animal than human, Pace lunged toward the man. He pulled Morrow by the collar and flipped him off the woman. The man landed in a heap on the floor. Mercy remained on the bed, looking like a trapped rabbit. Her brown eyes were wide with terror, and red marks marred her throat and hands. The gold gown was pulled high on her legs, and her breasts were nearly bare.

"Mercy," he groaned, reaching for her.

"Pace, watch out."

From the corner of his eye, he saw the gun Morrow had pulled from his holster. If it meant his own life, he wasn't going to let Mercy get hurt. Spinning on his heel, he kicked the gun away, and fell on Morrow. This time he wasn't about to let Morrow get the upper hand. He owed the man—not only for what he'd done to him, but for laying so much as one finger on his woman.

He pounded Morrow in the face, his knuckles aching from the blows. Morrow stumbled back against the bureau, and came back at Pace. They exchanged blow after blow, equally matched in size and strength. Morrow rolled Pace to the floor, and straddled his middle. "I should have killed you instead of Buck," he muttered.

Fueled by anger and driven by revenge, Pace threw off the man. He ignored the noise and voices behind him. Only one thing mattered—paying back the man who had the nerve to try to hurt the woman Pace loved.

Heaving like a horse that had been run too hard, Pace caught Morrow by the front of his shirt and rammed his fist into the man's face. Blood spewed from the man's nose, trickling down his chin. Pace felt the bruises on his own jaw, and knew that within minutes his eyes would be swollen shut. But it was worth the pain to see Morrow suffer for his crimes.

"Pace, stop." It was Mercy's voice that broke through the haze that numbed his brain. "He confessed that he's the one who robbed the bank and killed that man."

He pulled back his fist and stopped. He'd wanted to kill.

He wasn't any better than Morrow. With a shake of his head, he dropped his fist and released the man.

Mercy's hands circled his arm, tugging him to his feet. "He's unconscious. Let the sheriff handle it."

As he stood, she flung herself into his arms. "I was so afraid for you," he said, nuzzling his lip into her hair. On the way from the jail, he'd thought he would never hold her again, inhale her sweet perfume, kiss her soft skin. She slipped her arms around his waist and pressed her face into his chest. Sweat poured from his face, and mixed with the blood that trickled from the split in his lip. None of that mattered, not even the pain in his face. The only thing that mattered was Mercy.

"How did you get here? How did you know?" she asked, her breathing as labored as his.

"Lily. She told me." He glanced at the lady trying to hold back the press of men eager to see the excitement. Looked like everybody in the bar had climbed the stairs and was in the hallway.

Mercy kissed his chest, his neck, his jaw. "Did the sheriff release you?"

"No." The angry voice rose above the din of the crowd. Heavy hands gripped his arms, pulling him away from Mercy. He'd been expecting Jennings from the second he slipped out the door and into the dark alley. Jennings twisted Pace's arms behind his back and secured his wrists with manacles. "You won't escape this time."

"You're all wrong, Sheriff," Mercy pleaded, tugging at Jennings's arms. "Morrow robbed the bank and killed that man. He confessed, he told me so."

"She's right," Rosie said. "I heard him."

Jennings stared at the man on the floor just beginning to stir. "Hold him, Rogers," he ordered. "I'll straighten this whole mess out one way or the other. Let's get both of them to the jail."

Mercy wasn't about to stand by and watch her husband

be snatched from her again. By that time others had jammed into the small room—Lily, Florrie, her father. Even her sisters and brothers-in-law were there staring at her. Doing the only thing she could think of, she reached for the gun Pace had kicked from the outlaw's hand. Shakily, she pointed the weapon at the lawmen.

"We'll straighten it out now. Pace didn't do anything. Morrow is the killer."

Pace stumbled against the sheriff. "Mercy, put it down. Somebody might get hurt."

"I don't care," she said, with more bravado than she felt. "He isn't taking you back to that jail."

"Mercy, give it to me." It was her father's hand that reached out. "I'll see that Pace is treated fairly."

Surrounded by faces from her family and trembling so badly, she was afraid of shooting Pace by accident, so she handed the weapon over to her father.

At that moment, Lily stepped into the melee. "Let's go into my suite and get this whole mess straightened out."

The sheriff glared at her. "You're in mighty big trouble, lady, helping a criminal escape."

Planting her hands on her hips, she glared back at the lawman. "I'd do it again if it meant keeping an innocent man from hanging."

Mercy looked up and spied Clifford at the back of the crowd. His face was pasty white, and he looked like he was going to be sick. He was to blame for all of the trouble that beset her husband. She itched to get her fingers around his scrawny neck.

"Okay, take him and we'll hear everybody's side." While Jennings shoved Pace down the hall, the deputy, assisted by Ezra, tugged Morrow behind them. The man started to twist out of their grips, but he was too weak from the liquor and the beating to escape.

Jennings shoved Pace to the small settee, and Mercy followed, settling beside her husband. After all the emotion that showed on his face only minutes ago, Pace had put on that stoic, blank expression he'd worn in the jail. Mercy touched a gentle finger to the bruises that marred his cheek and jaw.

"It will be all right, Pace. Didn't I promise you?"

He struggled with the manacles that held him captive. "Woman, when are you going to listen to reason? You could have been killed tonight, or worse."

Tears hovered at the brink of her eyes. "I did it for you."

"I didn't ask you to risk your life for me. I'm not worth spit."

She resisted socking him in his stubborn jaw, but it was already red and swollen from the fight. "You're my husband. That makes you worth your weight in gold." She pulled her gaze from him and watched the room begin to fill.

When her father and the deputy shoved the outlaw into a chair, Ezra approached Mercy and Pace. "That was quite a licking you gave that fellow, son. Reckon he'll be willing to tell the truth."

Mercy looked up at her father. "Papa, how did you know?"

"Cora fetched me. She said you might need some help. She has the baby, and she wants you to know that he's just fine and dandy."

In all the excitement, Mercy hadn't even considered the child she loved. Of course, Cora would take good care of the baby.

Prudy and Charity, dragging their husbands by the hands, shoved their way through the crowd and approached the settee. "Mercy, when are you going to learn to quit embarrassing us like this?" Charity scolded.

Setting her hands on her hips, Prudy glared at Mercy. "Just look at you. You look like a . . . a saloon woman. Please cover yourself."

With a tilt of her chin, Mercy leaned forward, showing

even more of her cleavage. "That's exactly what I intended, sister. Before you criticize me, you'd better have a little talk with your husband."

Pace shot a startled glance at Mercy. She hadn't meant to let that cat out of the bag, but Clifford's self-righteousness was more than she could bear. Again her husband struggled with the bonds that held him. For once, Mercy was grateful the sheriff had taken that precaution. Pace would have attacked Clifford and wound up in even deeper hot water.

The sheriff was trying to quiet the noisy crowd, when Mayor Fullenwider made his way into the center of the room. His gaze swept over Mercy, and his face reddened like a ripe tomato. Until that moment, he hadn't recognized Mercy as the woman he'd taken on his lap and boldly propositioned. He turned to the sheriff. "What's going on here? I heard the commotion all the way over to my office behind the hardware."

Jennings approached. "Mayor, we've got quite a situation here. Lansing escaped and beat up this man. Miss Mercy and Rosie say that he's the one who robbed the bank and killed that fellow. I don't know who to believe."

Mercy stood and shrugged into the wrapper Lily offered her. "Ask him yourself. He showed us the money he got from the bank. A few days ago when he came out to the ranch, he didn't have a pauper's dime to his name. Today he's rolling in money."

His face blanched as white as new fallen snow, Clifford spoke up for the first time. "Could be I made a mistake. Can't you see how much this fellow looks like Lansing? And he was riding that black stallion. I made a mistake. He's the one who robbed the bank. I'll bet you'll find the money in his pocket that came from my bank."

Morrow tried to rise, but was restrained by the sheriff and his deputy. "You cheating . . ." He let out a string of curses that left Mercy and her sisters cringing. "You set the whole thing up to blame Lansing. I ain't gonna take the blame for you."

"Who are you going to believe, a respected banker and member of our town council, or this criminal? He just got out of prison, and he's the one who killed his partner so he wouldn't have to share the money." Clifford slipped behind Prudy and set his hands on her shoulder.

What a stinking, lying coward, hiding behind a woman's skirts. Mercy would believe a bandit like Morrow over a cheat like Clifford.

"What you got to say, Lansing?" the Mayor asked.

"I didn't rob the bank, and I didn't kill that man. That's all I know."

Mercy bit her tongue to keep from revealing all she knew about her esteemed brother-in-law and his nasty schemes. If the whole truth came out, the people who'd be most hurt were her sister and the family.

"Guess I don't have any choice but to let Lansing go and to arrest this fellow." Jennings pulled a small key from his pocket and unlocked the shackles that bound Pace. Mercy wished she had a key that would unlock her husband's heart. "All of you had better be ready to testify when the judge gets here tomorrow." The sheriff shot a hard glance at Pace. "Take your missus home, Lansing, but be in my office tomorrow. The judge might want your statement."

Pace flexed his wrists and fingers in front of him. His eyes softened when he looked at Mercy. "I'll take care of you when we get home."

Although she wasn't sure what he meant, she was glad that he'd mentioned going home. "Yes, sir," she said, a tiny smile in her heart.

Jennings snapped the manacles on Morrow, who looked at Clifford with murder in his gaze. Only then did Mercy realize the danger she'd been in, of what she'd risked. But she would gladly do it again to save the man she loved.

The sheriff ushered his prisoner from the room. An embarrassed mayor followed. Lily shooed the rest of the onlookers out. Clifford glanced at Mercy, pleading with his eyes for her silence. Then he and Prudy followed behind Charity and Tim.

When Lily shut the door, only Mercy and Pace remained with Ezra and Lily. "This has been quite an evening," Lily said, sinking onto the chaise lounge.

Ezra followed, and sat at Lily's feet. His hand reached out and clutched hers, as if he wasn't even aware of what he'd done. "Mercy, you nearly gave your old father a heart attack. Thanks to Lily, it looks like everything will work out just fine."

Lily gazed at Ezra with so much love, it was a wonder her dense father couldn't feel it. "I did what needed to be done. That's all I've ever wanted to do."

"I owe you more than I can repay, ma'am," Pace said. "You risked a lot to save me."

"Mercy said you weren't guilty, and I believed her. Besides, I couldn't let Ezra's son-in-law hang. It would sully his good name."

With a soft laugh, Ezra lifted her fingers to his lips. "Lily, you're one incredible woman. I think you and I need to have a little talk. Let's go where we can be alone."

Lily's blue eyes grew wide. "Why Ezra, I didn't think you noticed."

Getting to his feet, Ezra puffed out his chest like a strutting rooster. "I'm not that old that I don't appreciate a beautiful woman. Come along, I think my daughter and her husband need to be alone."

On their way out of the room, Lily linked her arm with Ezra's. "Do you think this town could use a school for young ladies?"

Ezra laughed, a happy sound of a man on the brink of love. "My dear, that sounds like a splendid idea. Shall we discuss the project?"

Seconds later, Mercy stared ahead at the silent room. She was certain her father would be happy with Lily, but what about her own happiness? Beside her, Pace hadn't moved, nor spoken.

"Pace, please don't be angry with me. I only wanted to help."

He caught her arms and turned her to face him. "Woman, don't you realize the danger you were in? Not only would Morrow have raped you, he could have easily strangled you, or you could have shot yourself with that gun." One gentle finger touched the red marks left on her throat from the outlaw's hands. "I would have been forced to kill him, and I'd have gladly hung."

The tears she'd tried to stop finally burst forth like a dam that gave way in a river. "I love you, and I'll do it again and again for you. I need you, and I want to be your wife for a long time." He pulled her against his shoulder and she sobbed into his shirt. "Can't you learn to love me just a little?"

Pace dropped kiss after kiss on her hair, down to her ear, and finally he cupped her face in his big hands. He brushed the tears from her cheeks with his thumbs. "You ninny, don't you know how much I love you? I didn't want you to know, so you wouldn't grieve for me. It took a knock over the head to realize that you mean everything to me. The worst thing about being in jail was being separated from you. I only hope I can make you as happy as you've made me in the last few days."

She wrapped her arms around his neck, seeing the love shining in his eyes. He bent his head and met her lips. The kiss was long and hard, filled with all the love and passion she'd dreamed of. Her heart was beating so fast, she was certain he felt it. His hands stroked her back, and gently brushed across her shoulders.

When he finally lifted his gaze and met hers, he smiled like a young boy who'd just discovered what kissing a girl was like. "You're so beautiful, Mercy, any man would be proud to have you as a wife. The men in this town must be blind. But I'm grateful to them that they saved you for me."

Her heart bursting with love, she tugged him to his feet. "I suppose I'd better go find my clothes so we can go home."

He studied her for a moment, his eyes dark with emotion. "You cut quite a figure in that fancy gown, but I think you're even more beautiful in that blue calico, with the baby in your arms."

"Are you interested in having more babies?"

His smile turned her legs to jelly. "As many as you want. If you keep wearing that silk nightgown, I might never get any work done."

She brushed her hand along his stubbled jaw. "Oh, no, you won't get out of work that easily. We're partners, remember, and we have a ranch to run."

"And I owe my wife a trip to Philadelphia."

"The only trip I want is back to our homestead. You've already made all my dreams come true."

He kissed her on the tip of her nose. "Love, that's only the beginning."

Epilogue

Philadelphia, Summer 1876

"Hurry, Pace, we don't want to miss our train." Mercy adjusted her new hat at a jaunty angle over her dark hair.

Her husband sidled up behind her and wrapped his arms around her now slim waist. He pressed his hands to her flat stomach. "We have nearly two hours, love. I didn't think you'd be in such a hurry to leave your dream city."

She turned into his chest, and looped her arms over his broad shoulders. He was still the handsomest man she'd ever seen, and she'd seen plenty in their two weeks at the Centennial Exposition. In spite of his wearing a new black suit and white shirt, more than a few people thought him an Indian, and gathered around her husband when they should have been looking at the exhibits. His too-long black hair only added to the confusion. And she had to admit she was more than a little jealous. She couldn't wait to get him all to herself on their ranch.

"My dreams wait for me in Kansas. Do you think Joshua and Naomi missed us?" Neither their one-year-old son nor their three-month-old daughter had made a sound when they were put in the care of their grandparents.

He laughed. "With Cora, Lily, and your father to spoil them, they might never want to come home with us."

"I'm sure they have their hands full, what with trying

to get the school in operation, and now expecting a baby of their own." She rested her cheek against his stiff white shirt. "Who'd have thought all this a year ago?"

She felt the shiver that racked him at the memory. "I was scared to death they'd hang me, and I would never get to know our daughter or see her beautiful mother again."

So much had happened. Morrow had been sent back to prison, and nothing could be proved against Clifford. But he'd been made to pay. Prudy kept her husband on a tight leash, and thoroughly enjoyed spending his money. They'd returned from a trip to San Francisco the day she and Pace left home.

"The school is bound to be a success with all the little girls being born in Pleasant Valley. First Naomi, then Charity's little Adelaide. Cora won't make a prediction for Lily and Papa, but she hinted it might be twins."

Pace's laughter was muffled in her hair. "That old guy is going to show all of us up."

Indignant, she shoved out of his arms. "Papa is not old. You just hope you can keep up with him when you reach fifty."

He snuggled her closer, nearly tipping her hat from her head with his chin. "I can't keep up with him now."

"Did you notice the way that new railroad agent was looking at Cora at the station?"

"I saw the way she turned her nose up at him. But don't worry. With Lily and you advising her, the poor fellow doesn't stand a snowball's chance in Hades. Look what happened when those brothers rode into town and spotted Rosie and Florrie. The two fellows didn't know what hit them. Your papa had them hitched before their spit dried on the boardwalk."

With a giggle that said entirely too much, she shoved out of his embrace. As she shook her hips and eased away from him, he snagged the bow on her bustle and pulled her back against his chest. "Lady, you had me hog-tied and branded before I knew what hit me."

"Remember, Lansing, I saved your sorry hide a time or two."

"That's because you wanted me in your bed." He nuzzled the collar of her summer travel suit aside to reach the pulse that was pounding in her throat. "Speaking of beds, do you think we have time?" His gaze shifted to the big four poster.

She glanced at the watch pinned to her collar. Mentally, she calculated the minutes before they had to leave the boardinghouse, how long she took to dress, and how far they were to the railroad station. Oh, well, the trains were seldom on time.

"I'm not going to take off my hat."

He flung his new black Stetson hat toward the peg on the back of the door. "Love, that's the only thing you don't have to remove." With deft fingers, born of an urgent need, he helped her out of her clothes in record time. His suit followed, until they were lying naked in each other's arms.

She was certain she looked silly wearing only the little hat with the bird's feathers. But that didn't matter. She was with the man she loved, they were going home, and she never planned to leave Kansas again.

ABOUT THE AUTHOR

Jean Wilson lives with her family in Chalmette, Louisiana. She is currently working on her next Zebra historical romance, MY MARIAH, which will be published in November 1998. Jean's novella, PORTRAITS IN TIME, will appear in Zebra's time-travel collection TIMESWEPT SUMMER, which will be published in August 1998. Jean loves hearing from readers and you may write to her c/o Zebra Books, 850 3rd Avenue, New York, New York, 10022. Please include a self-addressed stamped envelope if you wish a response.